W9-BVQ-721

D0601327

THE USBORNE INTERNET-LINKED CHILDREN'S ENCYCLOPEDIA

Researched and written by
Felicity Brooks (Our World)
Fiona Chandler (History)
Phillip Clarke (Facts and Records)
Anna Claybourne (Science, How your Body Works)
Liz Dalby (Maps of the World)
Ben Denne (How Things Work, Our World, Animals)
Paul Dowswell (Animals, Space)
Rachel Firth (Science, How your Body Works)
Laura Howell (Animals and Plants)
Sarah Khan (How your Body Works)
Anna Milbourne (How Things Work)
Kirsteen Rogers (How People Live)
Caroline Young (How People Live)

Illustrated by David Hancock

Designed by Francesca Allen, Laura Hammonds, Nelupa Hussein, Stephanie Jones, Joanne Kirkby, Susie McCaffrey, Keith Newell, Susannah Owen, Ruth Russell, Karen Tomlins, Candice Whatmore and Helen Wood

Edited by Felicity Brooks, Anna Claybourne, Anna Milbourne, Kirsteen Rogers, Judy Tatchell
Art Director: Mary Cartwright
Cartography: European Map Graphics Ltd.
Digital manipulation: Roger Bolton, Keith Furnival, Fiona Johnson, Mike Olley, John Russell, Mike Wheatley
Picture research: Ruth King, Valerie Modd
Web site adviser: Lisa Watts
Consultant Cartographic Editor: Craig Asquith
Americanization editor: Carrie Seay
Indexer: Kamini Khanduri
Consultants:
Stuart Atkinson (Astronomy and Space)
John Davidson (Geography)
Liza Dibble (Farming)
Dr. Wendy Dossett (Religions)
H.M. Hignett (Ships and Boats)
Professor Michael Hitchcock (How People Live)
Sinclair MacLeod (Science)
Dr. David Martill (Dinosaurs)
Dr. Anne Millard (History)
Eileen O'Brien (Music)
Alison Porter (Technology)
Professor Michael Reiss (Science)
Dr. Margaret Rostron, Dr. John Rostron (Biology and Natural History)
Dr. Kristina Routh (Human Biology and Medicine)

Usborne Publishing is not responsible and does not accept liability for the availability or content of any Web site other than its own, or for any exposure to harmful, offensive, or inaccurate material which may appear on the Web. Usborne Publishing will have no liability for any damage or loss caused by viruses that may be downloaded as a result of browsing the sites it recommends. Usborne downloadable pictures are the copyright of Usborne Publishing Ltd. and may not be reproduced in prints or in electronic form for any commercial or profit-related purpose.

This edition first published in 2002 by Usborne Publishing Ltd.,
Usborne House, 83-85 Saffron Hill, London EC1N 8RT, England.

www.usborne.com

Copyright ©2002 Usborne Publishing Ltd. The name Usborne and the devices are Trade Marks of Usborne Publishing Ltd.
All rights reserved. No part of this publication may be reproduced, stored in a retrieval system, or transmitted in any form or by any means, electronic, mechanical, photocopying, recording or otherwise without the prior permission of the publisher. First published in America 2003. A.E.

Printed in Dubai.

THE USBORNE INTERNET-LINKED CHILDREN'S ENCYCLOPEDIA

Contents

7 OUR WORLD
8 Our planet
10 Day and night
12 The seasons
14 The weather
16 Storms and floods
18 Rocks and fossils
20 Earthquakes
22 Volcanoes
24 Following a river
26 Mountains
28 In the desert
30 Grasslands
32 In the rainforest
34 Seas and oceans
36 Waves
38 Currents
39 Tides
40 Coasts
42 Icy world
44 Caves and caverns
46 Useful Earth
48 World in danger
50 Getting warmer
52 Helping our planet

53 ANIMALS AND PLANTS
54 Living things
56 Cells
58 Animal world
60 Mammals
62 Baby mammals
64 Bird life
66 Bodies and beaks
68 Nests and chicks
70 Reptile life
72 Amphibians
74 Creepy-crawlies
76 Butterflies
78 Seashore life
80 Underwater life
82 Coral reefs
84 Sharks
86 Whales
88 Dolphins
90 Deep sea
92 Plant world
94 How plants grow
96 Trees and leaves
98 Fungi

99 HOW YOUR BODY WORKS
100 Your body
102 Bones and muscles
104 What happens to food?
106 Your brain and senses
108 Babies
110 Staying healthy
112 Doctors and medicine

113 HISTORY
114 Dinosaur world
116 The first people
118 The first farmers
120 Ancient Egypt
122 Ancient Greece
124 Ancient Rome
126 Viking raiders
128 Living in a castle
130 Inca cities
132 Ming China
134 Tudor England
136 Living in America
138 French finery
140 The American West
142 Victorian times
144 The First World War
146 The Second World War
148 The modern world

149 HOW PEOPLE LIVE
150 People around the world
152 Houses and homes
154 Cities and towns
156 How a country is run
158 Food and cooking

160 Clothes and fashion
162 Jobs and work
164 Farming
166 Going to school
168 Sports and games
170 Communicating
172 Art and painting
174 Acting and dancing
176 Music
178 Religions
180 Myths

181 SCIENCE
182 What is science?
184 What scientists do
186 Atoms and molecules
188 Solids, liquids and gases
190 How materials change
192 Energy
194 Forces
196 Hot and cold
198 Gravity
200 Floating
202 Friction
204 Magnets
206 Light and color
208 Sound
210 Electricity
212 Science words

213 HOW THINGS WORK
214 Clocks
216 Cameras
218 Movies
220 Televisions
222 Sound systems
224 Telephones
226 Computers
228 The Internet
230 Refrigerators
231 Microwave ovens
232 Toilets and faucets
234 Cars and motorcycles
236 Diggers
237 Tractors
238 Trains
240 Planes
242 Ships and boats
244 Submersibles and submarines

245 SPACE
246 Amazing space
248 Trips into space
250 A walk in space
252 Living in space
254 Satellites and space probes
256 Is anyone out there?
258 What's in our Solar System?
260 The Moon
262 The Sun
264 Mercury and Venus
266 Mars
268 Jupiter and Saturn
270 Uranus and Neptune
272 Pluto and beyond
274 Bits and pieces
276 Galaxies
278 Looking at the night sky
280 Space words

281 MAPS OF THE WORLD
282 About maps
284 Countries of the world
286 The world's environments
288 North America
290 South America
292 Asia
294 Africa
296 Europe
298 Oceania

300 Flags of the world
304 Earth facts and records
306 Space facts
308 Animal and plant records
310 Map index
312 General index
319 Acknowledgements

Using Internet links

There are lots of exciting places on the Internet where you can find out more about the different subjects in this book. The "Internet link" boxes in this book contain descriptions of websites that you can visit by clicking on links on the Usborne Quicklinks Website. Just go to **www.usborne-quicklinks.com** and enter the keyword "CE". Here are some things you can do on the websites described in this book:

- Follow a river from its source to the sea
- Search the deep sea for monsters
- Listen to songs from the First World War
- Build your own virtual roller coaster
- Take a tour of the Solar System

Usborne Quicklinks

At Usborne Quicklinks, you will also find pictures, quizzes and activity sheets that you can download and print out free of charge for use at home or school. All the pictures marked with a ★ in this book can be downloaded. They must not be copied or used for any commercial purpose. To find all these things, go to **www.usborne-quicklinks.com** and follow the simple instructions there.

Safety on the Internet

Here are a few simple rules to help keep you safe while you are online:

- Ask your parent's or guardian's permission before you connect to the Internet.
- Never give out information about yourself, such as your real name, address or telephone number.
- Never arrange to meet someone you started talking to on the Internet.
- If a site asks you to log in or register by typing your name or email address, ask permission from an adult first.
- If you receive an email from someone you don't know, tell an adult. Don't reply to it.

Site availability

The links in Usborne Quicklinks are regularly updated, but occasionally, you may get a message that a site is unavailable. This might be temporary, so try again later. If any of the sites close down, we will, if possible, replace them with alternatives. You will find an up-to-date list of sites at Usborne Quicklinks.

What you need

Most of the websites listed in this book can be accessed using a standard home computer and a web browser (the software that lets you look at information from the Internet). Some sites need extra programs (plug-ins) to play sound or show videos or animations. If you go to a site and do not have the necessary plug-in, a message will come up on the screen. There is usually a button on the site that you can click on to download the plug-in. Alternatively, go to Usborne Quicklinks and click on **Net Help**. There, you can find links to download plug-ins.

Notes for parents

The websites described in this book are regularly reviewed and the links in Usborne Quicklinks are updated. However, the content of a website may change at any time and Usborne Publishing is not responsible for the content on any website other than its own. We recommend that children are supervised while on the Internet, that they do not use Internet Chat Rooms, and that you use Internet filtering software to block unsuitable material. Please ensure that your children read and follow the safety guidelines printed on the left. For more information, see the **Net Help** area on the Usborne Quicklinks Website.

A COMPUTER IS NOT ESSENTIAL TO USE THIS BOOK

This book is a complete, superb, self-contained information book by itself.

Our world

Our planet

Our planet is called the Earth. It is the only planet where we know that plants, animals and people live.

The large areas of land are called continents. Each continent is divided into smaller areas called countries.

This is a house...

in a town...

in a country...

in a continent on planet Earth.

Planet Earth travels around the Sun. It takes one year to go all the way around.

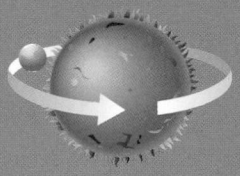

As it travels, the Earth spins around. It takes 24 hours to spin around once.

This is what you'd see if you went up in a spacecraft and looked at the Earth.

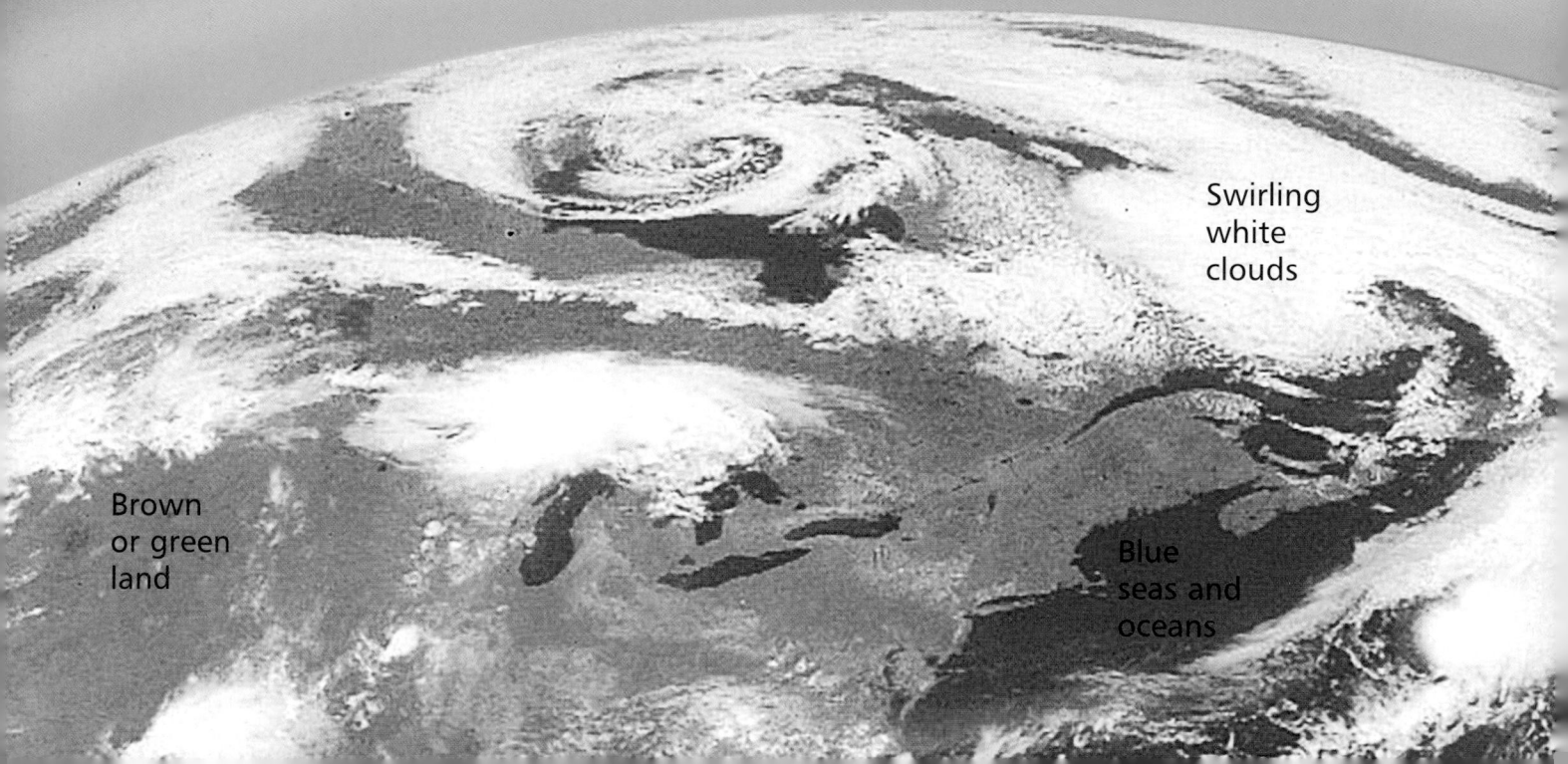

Internet links

Website 1 Watch a movie about the Earth's atmosphere, and try a quiz.

Website 2 Build your own virtual satellite.

For links to these websites, go to **www.usborne-quicklinks.com**

What's inside the Earth?

The Earth is made of rock and metal. If you could cut it open, you would see different layers inside. The picture on the right shows you what's inside the Earth.

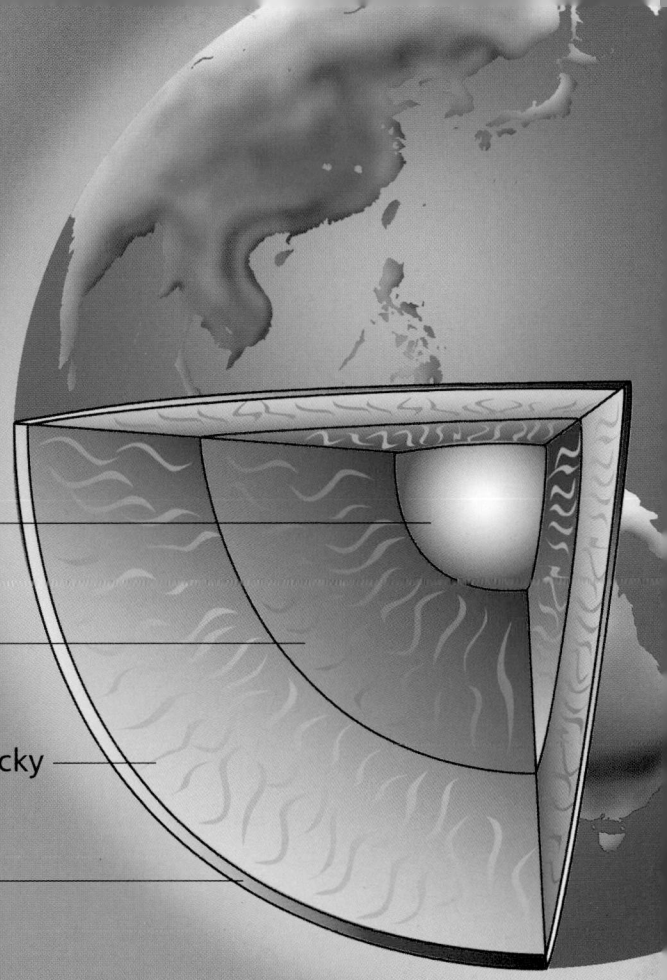

The atmosphere

The Earth is protected by an enormous blanket of gases, called the atmosphere. It stretches from the surface of the Earth over 560 miles into space. The sky you can see is part of the atmosphere.

The atmosphere helps to keep the Earth warm at night.

In the daytime, it helps to protect you from the Sun's heat and light.

The light, hazy blue on this photograph shows part of the Earth's atmosphere.

Day and night

When it is day for you, it is night for people on the other side of the world. When it is their day, it is your night.

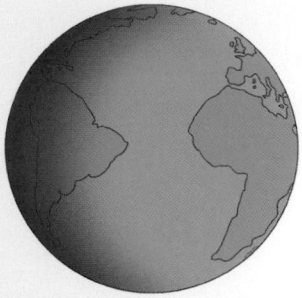

Sunrise

When your side of the Earth turns to face the Sun in the morning, the Sun is said to rise.

The Sun rising over a field

Sunset

When your side of the Earth turns away from the Sun in the evening, the Sun is setting.

The Sun setting over the sea

Turning Earth

Day changes to night, and night to day, because the Earth turns. As it turns, different parts face the Sun.

The part of the Earth with the USA on it is facing the Sun, so it's day in the USA.

A few hours later, the USA has turned away from the Sun, so it's night there now.

The Earth keeps turning all the time.

The Earth travels around the Sun this way.

After 24 hours, the Earth has turned all the way around, so now it's day again in the USA.

Moon in the way

The only time it is dark in the day is when the Moon blocks out the Sun. This is called a total eclipse of the Sun. A total eclipse doesn't happen very often and it only lasts a few minutes.

Internet link

For a link to a website where you can try a quiz, and watch a movie of an eclipse, go to **www.usborne-quicklinks.com**

This picture shows why an eclipse takes place.

The Sun, Moon and the Earth are all in a line.

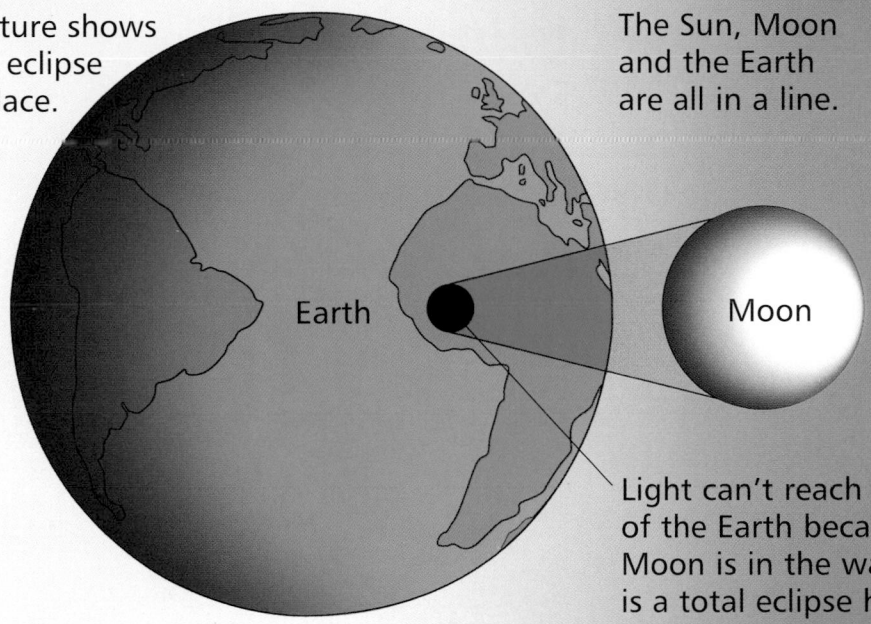

Sun

Light can't reach this part of the Earth because the Moon is in the way. There is a total eclipse here.

Make shadows

On a sunny day, you stop some sunlight from reaching the ground. This is what makes your shadow.

Try looking at your shadow on a sunny day. You will see that it always points away from the Sun. As the Sun rises higher in the sky in the morning, your shadow gets shorter. As the Sun sinks lower in the afternoon, your shadow gets longer.

Cloudy days

Even on a cloudy day the Sun is shining on your part of the Earth. You just can't see it because the clouds hide it.

Clouds like these may hide the Sun, but it is always there above them.

The seasons

In most places on Earth, the year is divided into four seasons. They are spring, summer, fall and winter.

Changing seasons

The weather changes from season to season. It is coldest in winter and hottest in summer. Many plants also change with the seasons. You can tell what season it is by looking at some kinds of trees.

North and south

The two halves of the Earth are called the northern and southern hemispheres. When countries in the southern hemisphere have their winter, countries in the northern hemisphere have their summer.

The picture on the right shows the Earth's two hemispheres. The imaginary line around the middle is called the equator.

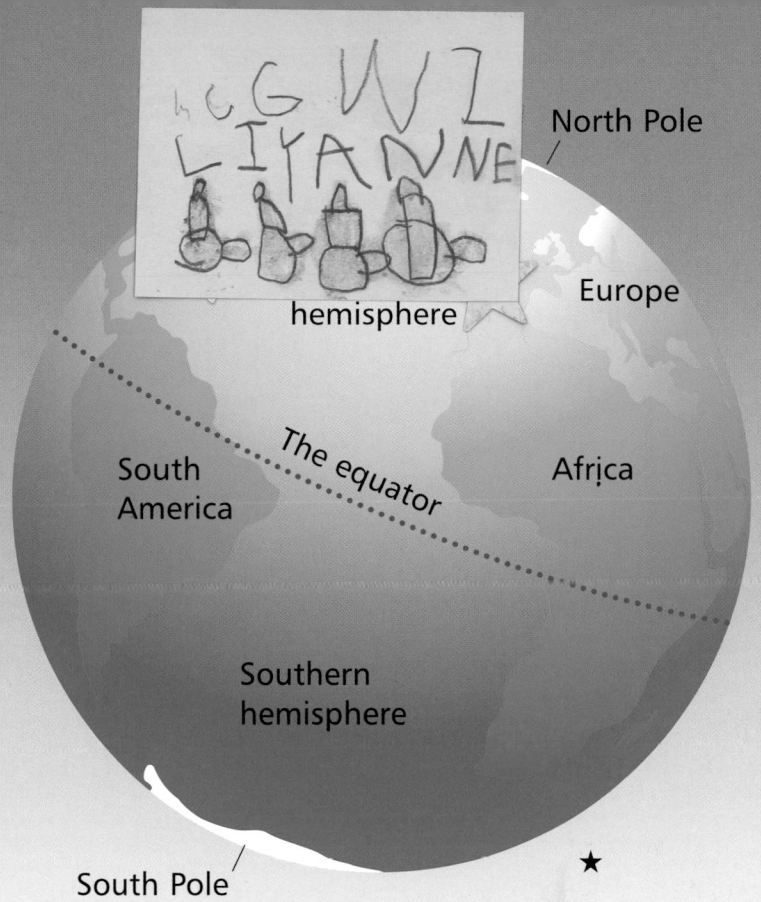

Internet link

For a link to a website where you can watch a cartoon and try a quiz about the seasons, go to **www.usborne-quicklinks.com**

What makes the seasons happen?

The Earth is tilted a little as it goes around the Sun. The hemisphere that is tilted toward the Sun gets more hot sunlight and it is summer there.

The hemisphere tilted away from the Sun has winter. Each year, first one half and then the other is closer to the Sun. This makes the seasons change.

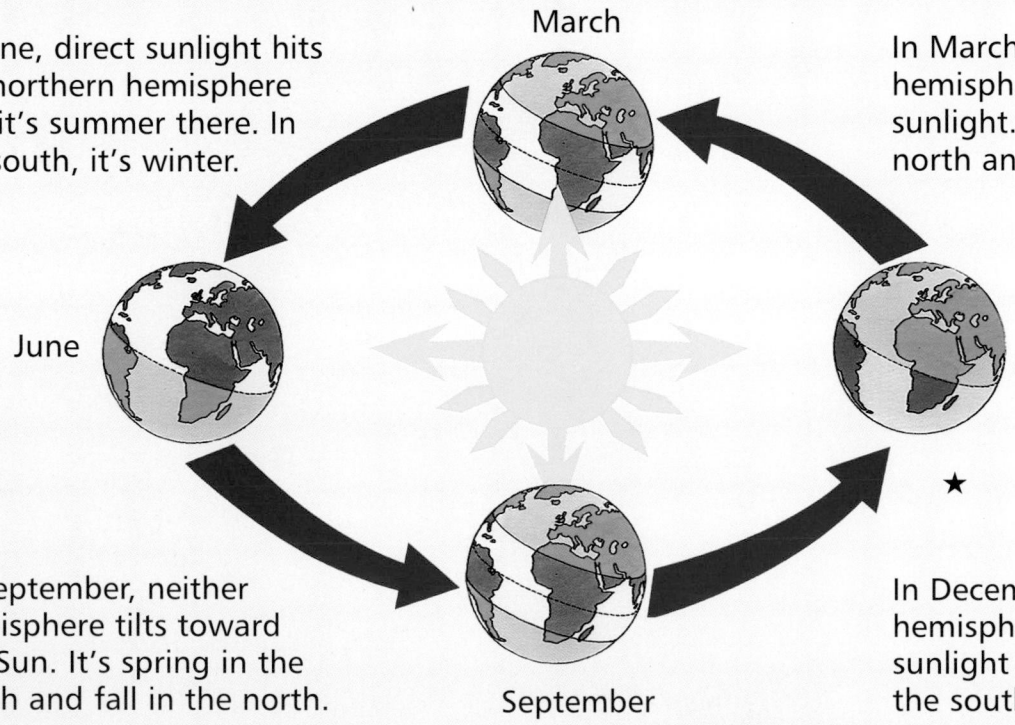

The weather

There are lots of different kinds of weather. It can be rainy, snowy, sunny or windy. The three main things that make the weather happen are the Sun, the air and water.

The Sun gives out heat.

The air moves to make wind.

Water makes rain and snow.

Rainy days

The amount of water in the world is always the same. Rain isn't new water. Follow the numbers to find out where rain comes from.

1. The Sun heats up the water in seas, lakes, rivers, and snow on mountain tops.

2. The water turns into water vapor, a gas which we can't see, and rises up into the sky.

3. Up in the sky, it's cooler and the water vapor turns back into tiny water droplets.

4. The water droplets bump into other droplets and join together to make clouds.

5. As more water is added, the droplets get bigger and heavier and fall back to the ground as rain.

6. The rain falls down to the ground where it flows back into seas, lakes and rivers.

Windy weather

When it's windy, it's because the air is moving around. You can't see the wind, but you can see it blowing leaves around and feel it on your face.

A gentle wind is called a breeze. It can help dry wet clothes.

Gales are much stronger winds. They can blow tiles off roofs.

Hurricanes are very strong winds that can do a lot of damage.

Rainbows

Sometimes it rains even though the Sun is shining. Raindrops split sunlight into different colors. When this happens you might see a rainbow. From the ground, it usually looks like an arch, but from an aircraft, it may be a circle.

Make a rainbow

You can make your own rainbow even when it's not raining, as long as the Sun is shining. You will need:

a plastic tray or bowl; a piece of paper; a mirror.

1. Put the tray of water in a sunny place, such as on a windowsill, or outside.

2. Stand the mirror in the tray so the Sun can shine through the water onto the mirror.

3. Hold the paper above the tray. Tilt the mirror until you see a rainbow on the paper.

Icy snowflakes

Snowflakes are made when it gets so cold that the water in a cloud freezes and turns into ice. Snowflakes all have six sides or points, but they form millions of different patterns.

Every snowflake has a different shape.

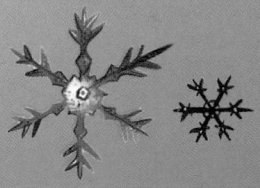

Internet link

For a link to a website where you can find out about different types of clouds and try a quiz, go to **www.usborne-quicklinks.com**

Storms and floods

In a big storm, the wind blows very hard. There's usually lots of rain or snow. There may be thunder and lightning too.

Types of storms

The pictures below show some of the things that can happen during different types of storms.

Lightning is a big spark of electricity in the sky. Thunder is the noise that the spark makes.

A tornado is a spinning funnel of wind. It whirls along sucking up anything in its path.

A hurricane is a huge storm with lots of wind and rain. It can destroy towns and forests.

The swirling clouds on this photograph of the Earth are a hurricane – a huge storm with lots of wind and rain.

Storms at sea

At sea, violent storms and huge waves can appear suddenly and cause terrible damage. Tornadoes, called waterspouts, sometimes pull sea water up into a spinning column. This sucks up anything in its path as it moves across the sea.

Giant sparks of electricity zigzag through the air during a lightning storm in Arizona, USA.

Floods

If a lot of rain falls in a short time, or if it rains for a long time, rivers get too full and spill onto the land. This causes floods, which cover land that is usually dry.

A flash flood is a sudden rush of water. It happens when a lot of rain falls in a short time.

Some floods happen when snow and ice melt. The soil is still frozen so water can't soak into it.

Huge waves can cause floods. They are made by storms, undersea volcanoes or earthquakes.

Monsoon floods

A monsoon is a wind that blows one way all summer and the other way all winter. In Asia, the monsoon in summer brings very heavy rain from the oceans.

Each year, homes and villages in southeast Asia are flooded by heavy monsoon rains. This photograph was taken in Vietnam.

Internet links

Website 1 Try experiments that show how storms happen.

Website 2 Discover more about floods and other disasters.

For links to these websites, go to **www.usborne-quicklinks.com**

Rocks and fossils

There are lots of kinds of rocks. Some are made by heat inside the Earth. Others are made from sand, mud and pieces of dead plants and animals.

This is a fossil of a sea animal called an ammonite.

Rocky layers

Sand, mud and pieces of plants and animals that sink and settle at the bottom of the sea are known as sediment.

Layers of sediment build up slowly. Over millions of years, the bottom layers get squeezed and stick together to become sedimentary rocks.

Fiery rocks

Sometimes, hot, sticky rock from inside the Earth breaks through the surface.

Hot, sticky rock pours out of a volcano. When it cools, it becomes hard. This kind of rock is known as igneous rock. Igneous means "fiery".

The Grand Canyon in Arizona, USA, is formed from layers of sedimentary rock.

This is a fossil of a sea animal called a trilobite.

This is the fossil of a sea creature called a sand dollar.

Fossils

Fossils are the stony remains of animals that lived millions of years ago. Most fossils are found in sedimentary rock.

Internet link

For a link to a website where you can find out how to look for fossils, go to **www.usborne-quicklinks.com**

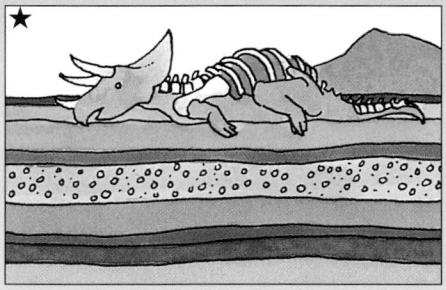

When an animal dies, its soft parts rot away leaving its bones. If they sink into mud, they get covered in sediment.

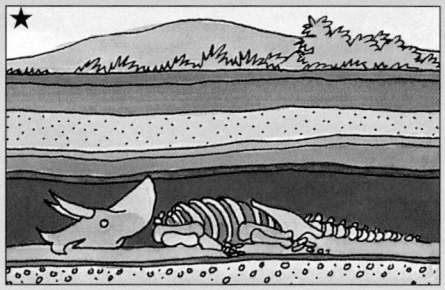

Over millions of years, the sediment layers slowly harden into rock. This keeps the shape of the animal's bones in it.

Millions of years later, people sometimes find fossil bones or shells inside rocks. They have to dig them up carefully.

The Colorado River made the Grand Canyon. It started to wear the rock away millions of years ago.

Earthquakes

An earthquake happens when huge rocks deep under the ground slip and push against each other. This makes the ground above shake.

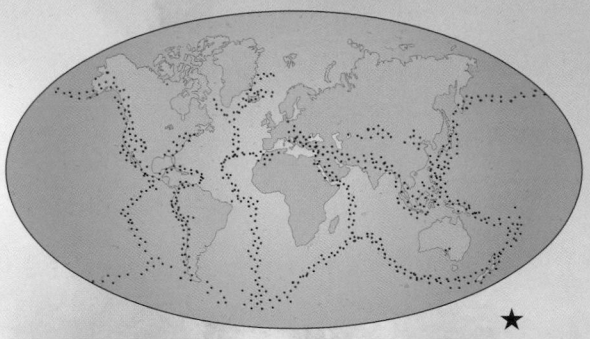

The red dots on this map show where earthquakes are most likely to happen.

Start of an earthquake

The place underground where an earthquake starts is called the focus. On the surface, the place right above the focus is the epicenter. The effects of an earthquake are strongest here.

Internet link

For a link to a website where you can watch animations of earthquakes, go to **www.usborne-quicklinks.com**

This house fell down in a big earthquake in California, USA, in 1994.

Earthquake effects

Most earthquakes are too weak to be felt by people, but some can cause great damage. The pictures below show some of the effects of an earthquake.

In a weak earthquake, hanging things, like birdcages, swing. Windows and dishes may start to rattle.

A stronger earthquake makes walls crack and pictures fall. Frightened people run outdoors.

In a very strong earthquake, buildings and trees fall down.

Staying safe

In countries where there are a lot of earthquakes, people are taught ways to stay safe. Children have earthquake-safety lessons at school.

Indoors, it is safest to shelter under a table.

Outdoors, you are safest in a big open space.

Earthquakes at sea

An earthquake that happens under the sea shakes the seabed. This sometimes creates huge waves, called tsunami (say "soonaamee").

In the deep ocean, tsunami are not dangerous and may pass under ships without anybody noticing. They only become enormous if they reach shallow water. Then they break and crash onto the land.

As the seabed moves, the sea above forms long, low waves.

If tsunami reach the coast, they are squeezed up into huge waves.

Earthquakes can cause huge waves, like this one. The biggest wave ever recorded was 37 yards high.

Volcanoes

A volcano erupts when hot, sticky rock from inside the Earth bursts through the surface. The hot rock, called lava, pours down the sides of the volcano and over the land.

This photograph shows a fountain of hot, sticky rock shooting out of a volcano.

Volcanic eruption

When a volcano erupts, lava comes out of a vent (opening) in the volcano's top or side. "Bombs" of rock may shoot up into the sky, and thick clouds of ash and gas may billow out. Sometimes a vent is in a hollow called a crater.

Lava is so hot it destroys everything it touches. The heat of the lava has set this wooden house on fire.

Volcano shapes

The lava cools and hardens into rock. Layers of lava and ash build up each time the volcano erupts, giving the volcano its shape. Some volcanoes are tall cones with steep sides and some are fairly flat with gentle slopes.

Many volcanoes are tall and steep. Their thick, sticky lava does not flow far before it hardens.

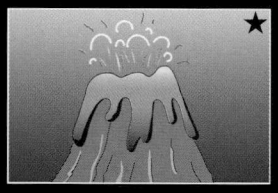

Some volcanoes are flatter. Their lava is runny. It spreads out quickly before it hardens.

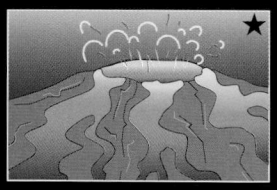

Sea volcanoes

There are lots of volcanoes under the sea. When one gets tall enough to appear above the waves, it makes an island.

This photograph shows clouds of steam and ash billowing from Surtsey, a volcanic island near Iceland.

A red-hot river of liquid rock is flowing down the side of this volcano.

Lava often moves quite slowly, so people usually have time to escape.

Alive, asleep or dead?

A volcano may be active (alive), dormant (asleep) or extinct (dead).

A volcano that erupts quite often is called an active volcano.

A dormant volcano hasn't erupted for a long time, but may erupt again in the future.

An extinct volcano hasn't erupted for at least a million years. Some towns are built on extinct volcanoes.

Internet link

For a link to a website where you can look at some amazing pictures of volcanoes, go to **www.usborne-quicklinks.com**

Following a river

A river starts high up in hills or mountains. The water comes from rain or melted snow.

It flows downhill until it reaches the sea. Follow this river to see how it changes.

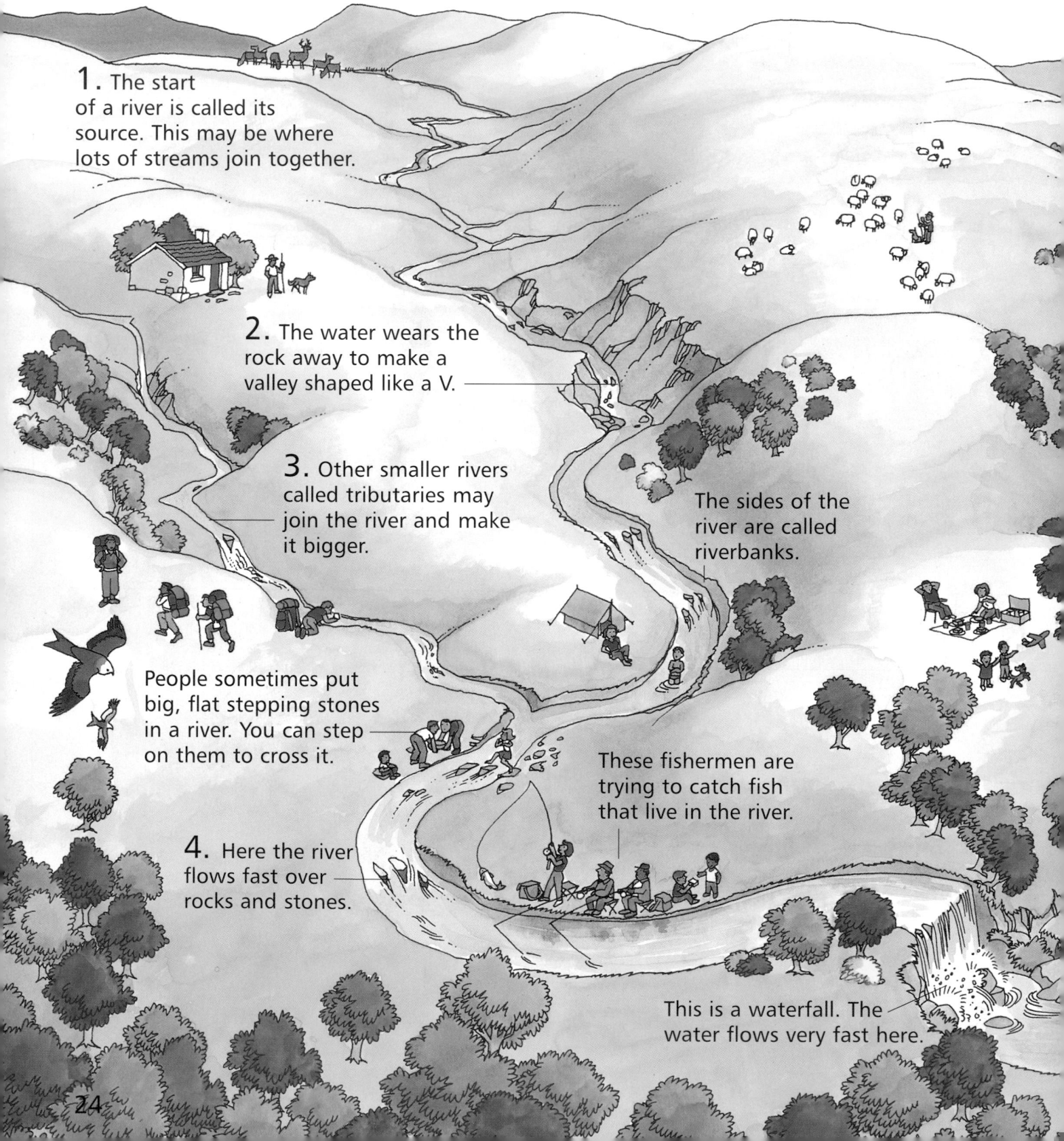

Waterfalls

A waterfall forms where a river flows from hard rock to soft rock. The water wears away the soft rock faster than the hard rock. This makes a big step.

This photograph shows water rushing over the Kanchan Waterfall in Cambodia.

9. The place where a river joins the sea is called the mouth of the river.

Lots of birds feed on the little animals that live in the sand.

Bank of sand

7. The river carries lots of sand and mud to the sea.

8. The river drops most of its sand and mud when it reaches the sea.

6. The river is deeper and wider on the outer edge of the bend.

5. Here the river starts to flow in big loops called meanders.

The arches on this stone bridge make it strong.

Internet link

For a link to a website where you can explore the parts of a river, go to **www.usborne-quicklinks.com**

Mountains

Mountains form over millions of years. Vast pieces of rock on the Earth's surface push against each other and force part of the land up into mountains.

Parts of a mountain

Some mountains have snow on their peak (top) all year around. The level where the snow ends is called the snowline.

Trees often grow on a mountain's lower slopes, but it's too cold for them to grow above a certain level. This is known as the treeline.

A group of mountains is known as a range. These mountains are part of a range called the Rocky Mountains in Canada.

This picture shows the parts of a mountain.

Glaciers

On the coldest parts of some mountains, snow builds up and turns into ice. Solid rivers of ice, called glaciers, move very slowly downhill.

Glaciers like this one carry stones and rocks downhill. As it warms up farther down the mountain, the glacier melts, forming streams.

Internet links

Website 1 See some stunning glacier photographs.

Website 2 Go on an interactive ski tour and find out what to do in an avalanche.

For links to these websites, go to **www.usborne-quicklinks.com**

Mountain life

Some plants and animals can live on mountains. They need to be able to survive in very cold temperatures and strong winds.

Mountain flowers such as purple saxifrage grow in short, round clumps.

Conifer trees have tough, narrow needles instead of broad leaves.

Golden eagles build their large nests on mountain rocks and ledges.

Mountain hares have thick fur which turns white in winter.

In the desert

Deserts are the driest places in the world. Sometimes it doesn't rain for many years. Most deserts are very hot in the day, but cool at night.

Internet link

For a link to a website where you can watch video clips of some desert animals, go to **www.usborne-quicklinks.com**

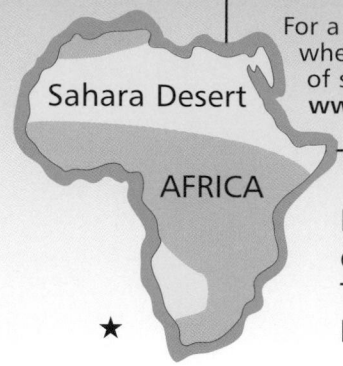

Deserts cover over a quarter of our planet. The biggest is the Sahara Desert in North Africa.

Desert homes have flat roofs, and small windows to keep out the sun.

Palm trees

An oasis is a place where there is water so plants can grow.

Camels can last a week without water.

Euphorbia plant

Antelopes

Most deserts are rocky and bare. Only parts of them are covered in sand.

Sandgrouse

Jerboas hop along like miniature kangaroos.

Desert plants

Many desert plants have long roots, and stems which can soak up water. Some, like the barrel cactus, can store water inside.

A barrel cactus swells with water when it rains.

A giant saguaro cactus may live for hundreds of years.

When the wind blows, the sand piles up into hills called sand dunes.

Lanner falcon

Desert people live in groups and move from place to place. They keep sheep, goats and camels.

Fennec foxes have huge ears which help them to lose body heat.

Saw scaled adders slither along with an S-shaped wiggle.

Grasslands

Plains, or grasslands, are big areas of land covered in grass. Bushes and some trees may grow there too. The picture below shows part of a grassland in Africa.

Grasslands, shown in orange on the map, cover about a quarter of the Earth's land.

Baobab trees can store water in their trunks.

Ostriches

Rhinos

Elephants

Thousands of insects called termites make these big mounds.

Baboons live in large groups called troops.

Lions live in groups called prides.

Weaver birds make complicated nests.

Acacia tree

Wildebeest

Tourists come in trucks and buses to see the animals.

Hyenas

Internet link

For a link to a website where you can read about some of the animals that live on grassy plains, go to **www.usborne-quicklinks.com**

Prairies and steppes

There are many names for grasslands around the world. Grasslands in Russia are known as steppes.

In North America, grasslands are called prairies. Most prairies are now used as farmland. Wheat grows well there.

Huge fields of wheat stretch across the grasslands of North America.

In the rainforest

Thick, green rainforests grow in hot, wet places near the equator. It is warm all year there and it rains nearly every day. Rainforests are home to thousands of different plants and animals.

Internet link

For a link to a website where you can find out more about rainforests, go to **www.usborne-quicklinks.com**

Amazon River

The biggest rainforest is the Amazon Rainforest in South America. The Amazon River runs through it.

Rainforest trees grow very tall.

Spider monkeys

Jaguar

Hummingbird

Morpho butterfly

Lichen

Arrow-poison frog

Orchids

Plants on trees

Many rainforest plants grow on the branches of trees. This is because there is more light up there than on the ground.

Seas and oceans

More than two-thirds of the Earth is covered with salty water. This makes the planet look blue from space.

The water is divided into five large areas called oceans. In some places these are divided into smaller areas called seas.

Watery world

It is like a different world under the oceans. There are deep valleys, huge mountains, forests of seaweed and many amazing sea animals.

Internet link

For a link to a website where you can find out fascinating facts about the oceans, go to **www.usborne-quicklinks.com**

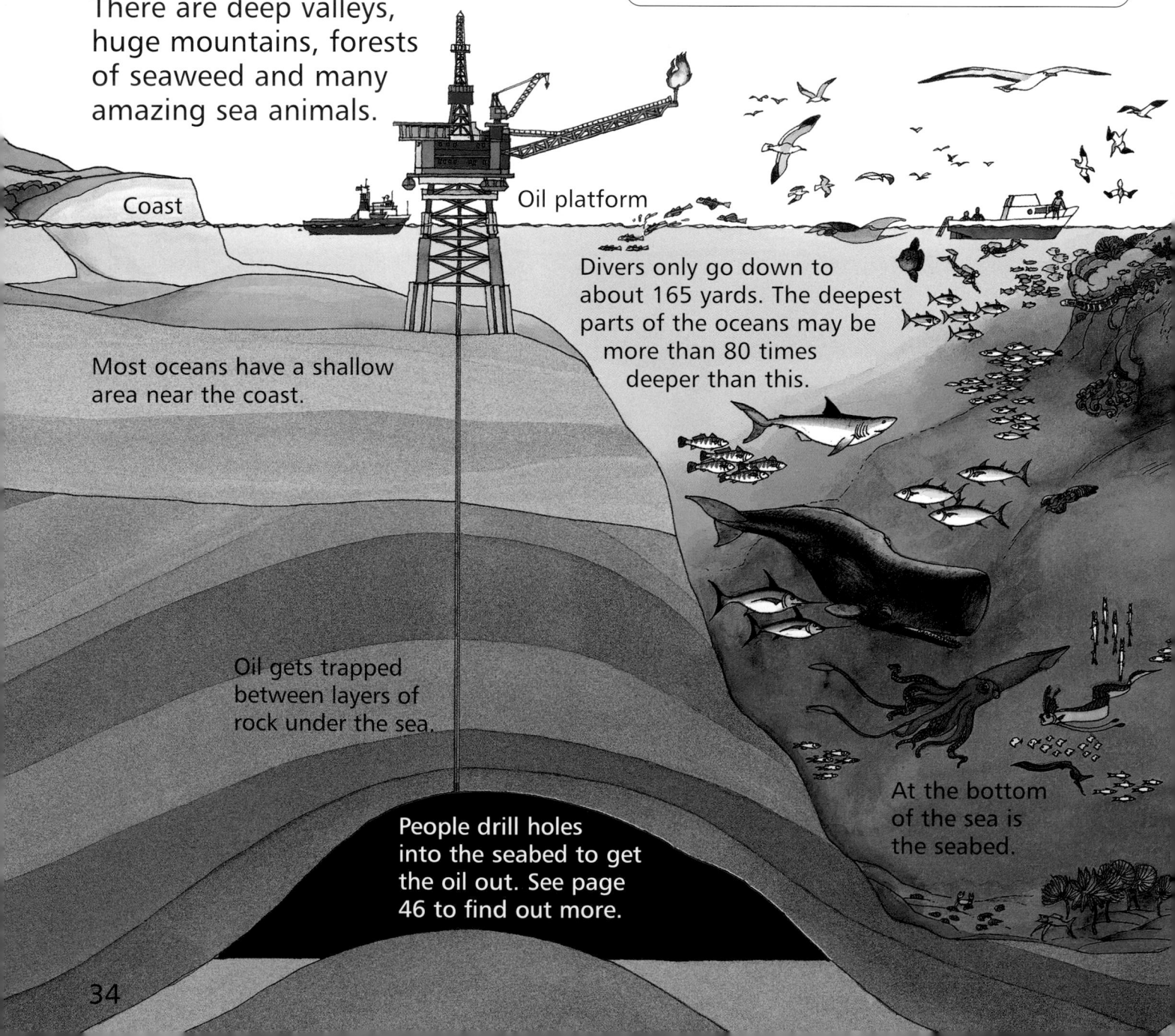

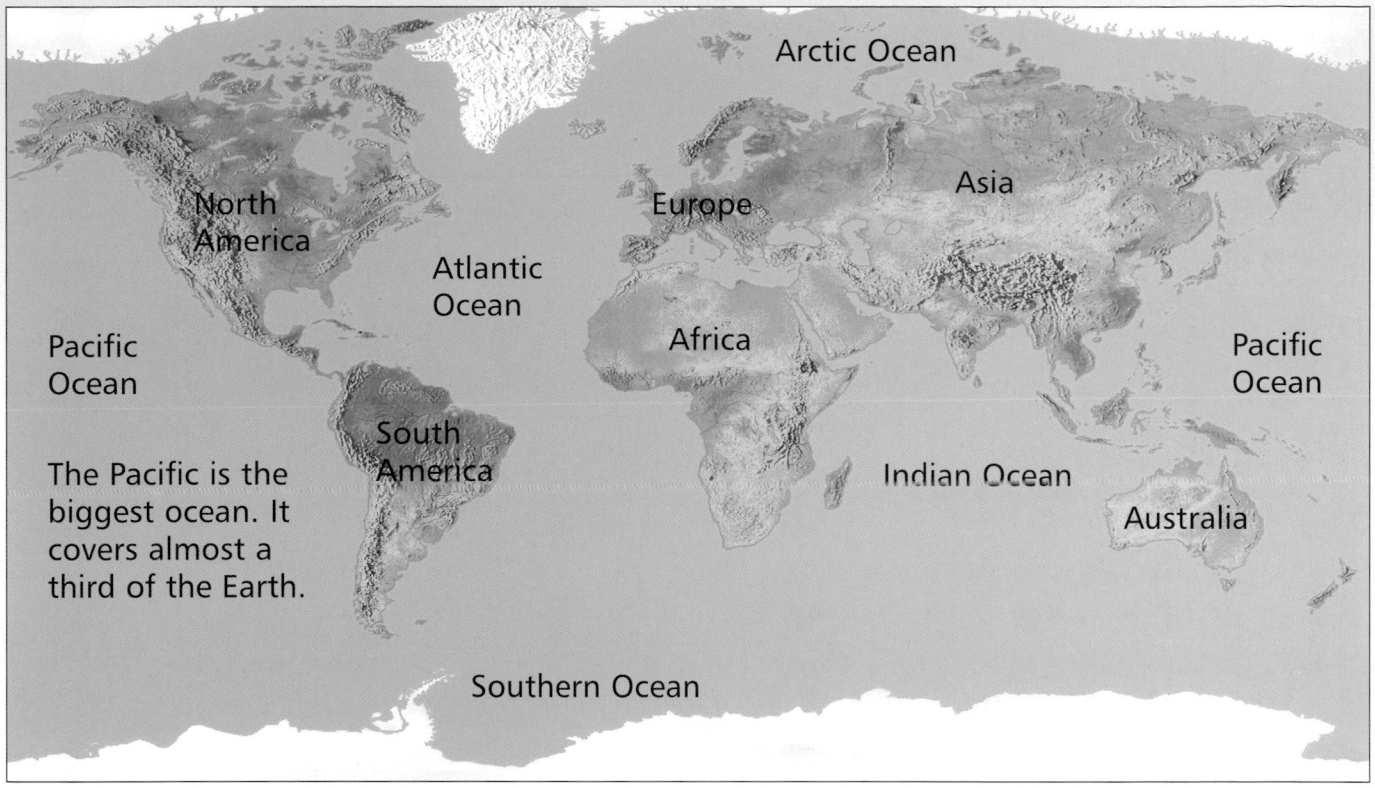

The Pacific is the biggest ocean. It covers almost a third of the Earth.

This map shows the five different oceans. Remember that the world is round, so the two parts of the Pacific Ocean join up.

Darkest depths

The deepest place in any ocean is the Mariana Trench in the Pacific. If you dropped a 2lb rock into the water there, it would take over an hour to reach the seabed.

Some islands are the tops of enormous undersea mountains.

Undersea volcanoes throw out boiling melted rock called lava.

The 88-floor Petronas Towers in Malaysia are among the world's tallest buildings. Even 28 of them stood one on top of the other in the Mariana Trench wouldn't quite reach the water's surface.

The bottoms of deep trenches are completely dark, but some animals live down there.

Waves

Waves are made far out at sea by the wind. They sometimes travel enormous distances across the oceans before finally crashing onto the seashore.

This picture shows what the different parts of a wave are called.

Making waves

Wind blowing across the sea makes ripples on the water. If the wind continues to blow, the ripples will get bigger and bigger, until they turn into waves.

When the wind blows across the tops of waves it creates foam on them and makes them grow.

Breaking waves

The shape of a wave is affected by the depth of the sea. This makes waves change shape as they get closer to the coast.

Internet link

For a link to a website where you can see a short movie about waves, go to **www.usborne-quicklinks.com**

As a wave gets closer to land, the water gets shallower. The bottom part of the wave starts to drag on the seabed and slows down.

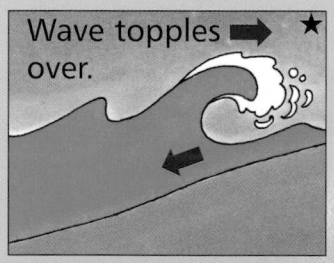

The top of the wave now moves faster than the bottom. This makes the top of the wave fall forward and topple over. This is called breaking.

Underwater energy

Waves are a kind of energy, moving through the water. Although the wave moves through the water, the water actually stays in the same place.

If you watch a wave, it looks as if the water moves along, but it doesn't.

When a wave passes under something such as a seagull, it just lifts it up.

When the wave has passed, the seagull is still in the same place as it was before.

Monster waves

The size of a wave depends on how strongly the wind is blowing and the distance it has covered. During storms at sea, strong winds create huge, powerful waves, which are big enough to sink a ship.

In some places, waves can be over 13 yards high. That's higher than a two-floor house.

Currents

Currents are like big rivers which flow through the oceans. Different currents flow at different speeds. Some only move seven miles a day. Others move up to 100 miles a day.

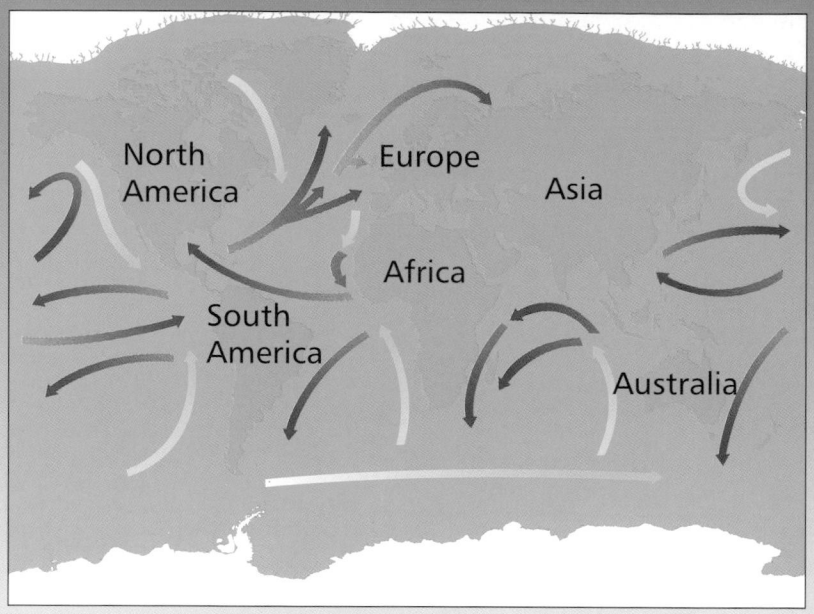

The map above shows the world's main currents.

Warm current Cold current

Carried by currents

Plant seeds are sometimes carried a very long way by a current. The new plant can grow a long distance away from its parent.

Internet link

For a link to a website where you can find out the names of all the different currents, go to **www.usborne-quicklinks.com**

Plant seeds, such as this coconut, fall into the sea. The current carries them away.

The seed sometimes travels for a long distance before reaching land.

Waves carry the seed onto another shore, where it may put down roots and grow.

Tides

The height of the sea is called sea level. The sea level in most places is constantly changing through the day as the sea moves up and down the beach. This movement is called the tide.

Tides sometimes come in very fast and trap people on beaches.

Tidelines

When the water reaches its highest point on a beach, it leaves behind a line of things from the sea. Then it starts to move back down the beach again. This line is called a tideline.

Seagulls search the tideline, eating pieces of food they find.

There is often lots of seaweed left behind when the tide goes out.

The bones of cuttlefish, called cuttlebones, are often washed up on beaches by the tide.

This is a dogfish egg case. It is called a mermaid's purse.

Coasts

Coasts are the places where the land meets the sea. Coasts are always changing shape as waves and the wind wear them away.

Making beaches

Beaches form on low, flat parts of the coast. Waves grind down big rocks and cliffs into smaller stones and pebbles, and finally into sand. Sand often also contains tiny pieces of broken seashells.

Internet links

For a link to a website where you can learn how and why sand from beaches all over the world is so different, go to **www.usborne-quicklinks.com** You can also browse a picture gallery of magnified sand grains and find out what singing sand is.

Changing coasts

Some parts of a coast are made of harder rock than others. These parts are worn away more slowly by the sea, and form a headland.

Sorting the stones

The smallest stones on a beach are always the ones nearest to the sea. This is because of breaking waves. As waves crash onto a beach, they slowly sort the stones into different sizes. Here is how it happens:

As waves break, they throw pebbles and stones onto the beach.

As the water flows back to sea, it carries little pebbles back with it.

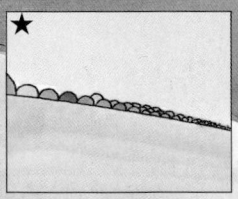

The bigger stones and pebbles are left farther up the beach.

Icy world

The places near the top and bottom of the Earth are called polar regions. They are very cold. Huge areas of land and sea are covered in ice and snow.

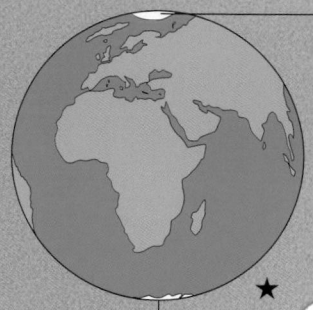

The area around the North Pole is called the Arctic.

The area around the South Pole is called the Antarctic.

Polar ice

The ice in the polar regions forms flat sheets and glaciers, and covers high mountains. In the summer, some of the ice melts, but in the winter it freezes solid again.

Many penguins live in the Antarctic. They have a thick layer of feathers and fat to keep out the cold.

What is an iceberg?

Icebergs are huge chunks of ice floating in the water. The small top part, or tip, floats above the water. The rest is hidden below. The pictures on the right show how an iceberg forms.

A sheet of ice moves over the land to the sea.

At the sea, the ice moves out over the water.

A piece of ice breaks off. This is an iceberg.

Life near the poles

Not many people live in the Arctic, compared with most other areas of the world. No one lives in the Antarctic all the time, but scientists go there to study its animals, weather and land. Tourists go to both places to climb, ski, and see the wildlife.

Internet link

For a link to a website where you can take a virtual tour of the Antarctic, go to **www.usborne-quicklinks.com**

Surviving the cold

Animals that live in the polar regions have to survive in very cold weather. They must keep warm and find food in icy conditions.

Polar bears make long journeys over the Arctic snow and ice in search of seals, birds, fish and plants to eat.

Antarctic icefish have special liquid in their blood to stop it from freezing.

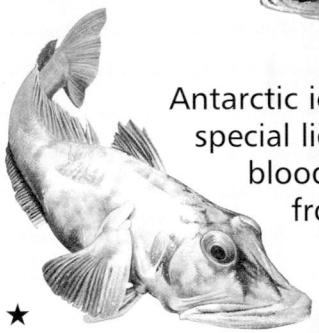

Walruses live in the Arctic. A layer of fatty blubber under their skins keeps them warm.

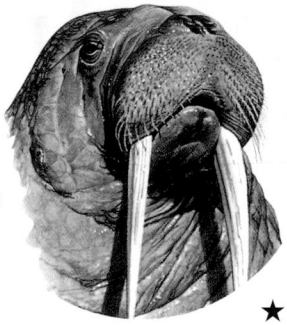

Weddell seals hunt for food under the Antarctic ice. They make breathing holes in the ice.

Caves and caverns

A cave or cavern is like an underground room with walls made of rock. Some caves are just below the surface. Others are very deep underground.

Caves like this one form slowly over many thousands of years.

How caves are made

Each time it rains, the rainwater seeps through cracks in the rock.

Over a long, long time, the water dissolves the rock and wears it away.

When the level of the water drops, empty caves and passages are left.

This man is one of a group of French cavers who climbed down into this cave in Hunan, China, to explore it.

Internet link

For a link to a website where you can find out about different kinds of caves, go to **www.usborne-quicklinks.com**

Rocky shapes

Some caves are full of strange, rocky shapes. These are made by water which has trickled through the rock and dissolved some of it. When the water drips, it leaves behind some of the dissolved rock. This builds up very slowly to make the rocky shapes.

Cavers

Cavers are people who explore caves for fun, or to find out more about them. Cavers often squeeze through narrow passages or wade through deep water to reach a cave. They have special clothes and equipment to keep them safe and help them explore the caves.

Bears, bats and bison

Brown bears and black bears sleep inside caves through the winter.

Many kinds of bats spend the winter in caves. They fly out in the spring.

Cave painting of a bison

A long time ago, people lived in caves. They made pictures on the walls. These pictures help to tell us what life was like then.

Useful Earth

We depend on the Earth to survive. It gives us food, water, air and all we need for building and making things.

It also gives us the fuel we need for cooking, heating and making machines and engines go.

Sand is used to make glass.

We eat many kinds of plants. Some are made into material, such as cotton, for clothes. Others are made into medicines.

Coal and oil

Coal is made from rotted trees and plants from millions of years ago. Oil began as tiny, dead sea animals. Coal and oil are taken from under the ground and used as fuels, but they are also used to make lots of other things.

Coal can be used to make paint, plastic, perfume, soap and the "lead" in pencils.

Oil and natural gas come from under the ground or under the seabed. People drill for them from rigs.

Oil can be used to make dishwashing liquid, plastic, gasoline, and dye to color material.

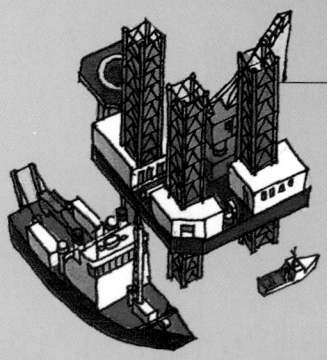

Oil rig

Wood from trees can be made into many things, such as furniture and paper.

Animals give us leather and wool as well as milk, meat and eggs.

Metal, coal, stone, clay and other useful things are dug out of the ground in places called quarries or mines.

Fishing boats catch fish from the sea.

Non-stop power

Oil, gas and coal may one day run out. There are many other ways of making power. They use things that will not run out, such as wind, water and sunshine.

Internet link

For a link to a website where you can click on different parts of a house to find out how energy can be saved there, go to **www.usborne-quicklinks.com**

These are wind turbines. The turning blades drive machines to make electricity.

Solar panels can soak up heat from the Sun and use it to make water hot.

Like the wind, flowing water can also drive turbines to make electricity.

World in danger

There are many things that we do to our world which put animals, plants and people in danger.

Smoke and fumes from factories and cars pollute the air.

Rainforest damage

Every year, huge areas of rainforests are cut down or burned. This is done for the wood, and to make space for farms. It destroys the homes of the animals that live there.

These rainforest trees are being burned to make space for farming.

Pollution

Litter, smoke from factories and cars, and oil spilled from ships at sea are all kinds of pollution. Pollution harms animals and people and the places where they live.

Litter looks horrible and can be dangerous for wildlife.

Chemicals from factories and farms can get into the water and soil.

Oil which spills from ships can harm sea animals.

Internet link

For a link to a website where you can learn more about wildlife and issues that affect our planet, go to **www.usborne-quicklinks.com**

Animals in danger

Some animals are endangered – there are only a few of them left and they could easily die out. This is because we have hunted them or destroyed the places where they live.

Rhinos are killed for their horns. This one has had its horns cut off so hunters will leave it alone.

Golden lion tamarins became endangered when rainforests were cut down.

Some types of leopards are endangered because people hunt them for their skins.

Fishing dangers

When fishermen catch too many fish of the same kind, the number of fish starts to go down. This is called overfishing. If this doesn't stop soon, some kinds of fish will die out completely. Fishing can also endanger ocean life in other ways.

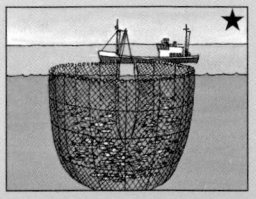

Purse seine nets are like big bags. They are used to catch tuna fish, but dolphins often get caught in the nets by mistake.

Trawl nets drag along the seabed to catch fish. They also pull up plants, and so destroy the homes of many sea creatures.

Getting warmer

Temperatures around the world are slowly rising. This is called global warming. There may be several reasons for it.

Scientists think that it may be caused by certain gases, known as greenhouse gases, in the Earth's atmosphere.

Greenhouse gases

Greenhouse gases trap heat around the Earth, making it warm enough for life to exist. But some things that people do make more greenhouse gases. These trap more heat, so the Earth gets warmer.

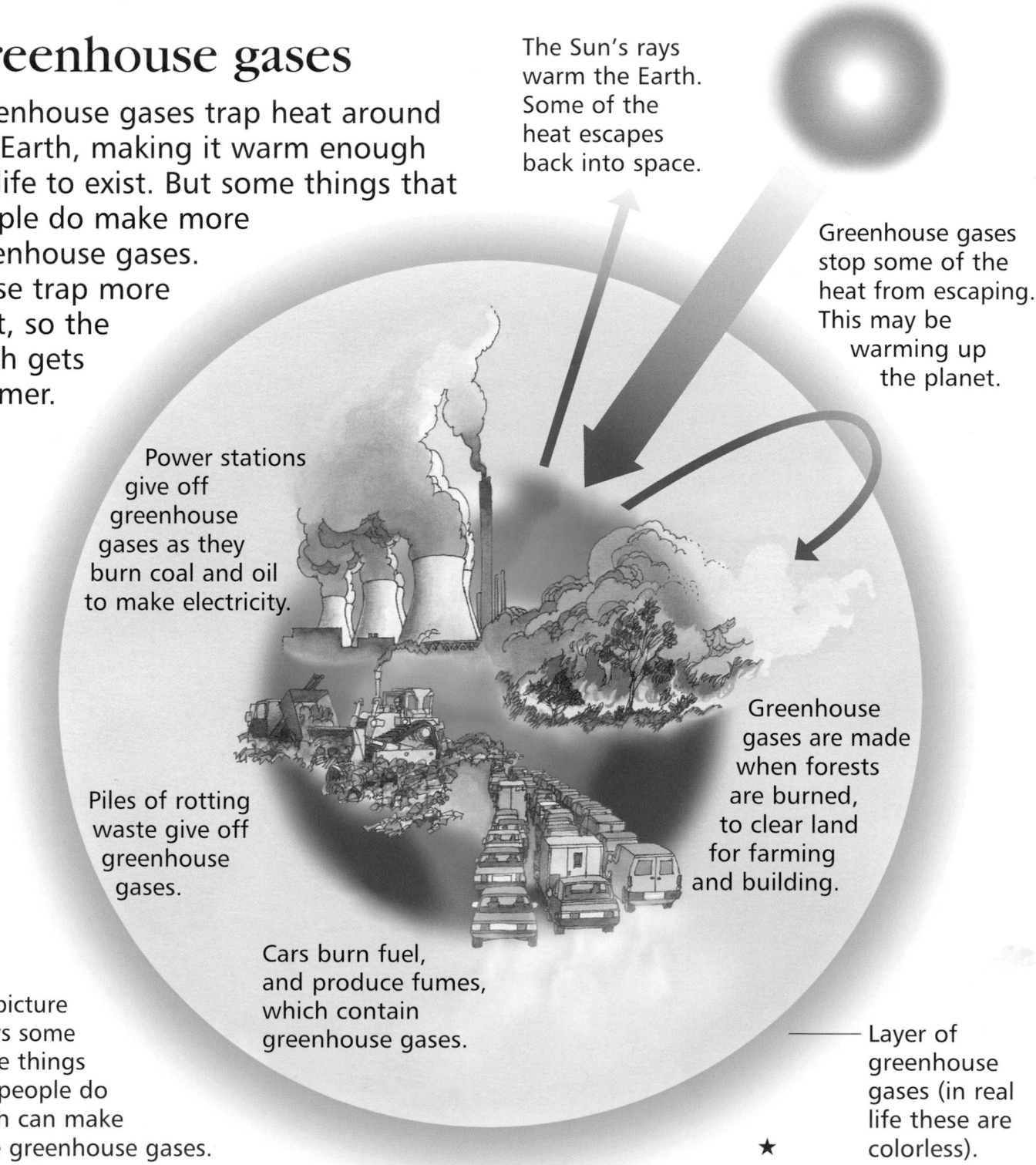

This picture shows some of the things that people do which can make more greenhouse gases.

★

Melting ice

As the atmosphere warms up, the ice in the Arctic and the Antarctic slowly starts to melt. The water goes back into the oceans, making the sea level rise.

The air gets warmer.

Ice melts into the sea.

The sea level rises.

Rising seas

If all the ice in the world melted, it would cause a worldwide disaster. The sea level everywhere would rise by more than 66 yards.

We can help to stop this by finding ways to make energy without burning fuels such as coal and oil (see page 47).

This picture shows what would happen to a town by the sea if the sea level rose by 66 yards.

Many islands in the sea would be flooded if all the ice in the world melted.

Internet link

For a link to a website where you can play games and learn about global warming, go to **www.usborne-quicklinks.com**

As ice melts at the poles, huge chunks of it fall into the sea.

Helping our planet

Look out for this recycling symbol on cans, bottles or boxes.

Everyone can do things to help our planet. Governments can make laws, for example, that control pollution and the way that areas of open land are used. There are many ways in which you can help, too.

How can you help?

Internet link

For a link to a website where you can find ways to help the planet, go to **www.usborne-quicklinks.com**

Take used cans, bottles and paper to a recyling center. The metal, glass, plastic and paper can be made into new things.

Save electricity by using low-energy light bulbs and switching off the light when you go out of a room.

Walk or cycle short distances, and go on longer journeys by bus or train. This helps to reduce pollution from cars.

Put up a bird table in your yard, and plant shrubs that give birds and other creatures food and shelter.

Some African governments are helping endangered animals, such as chimpanzees, by setting aside land where they can live safe from hunters.

Animals and plants

Living things

There are millions of living things on planet Earth. These include plants, animals and people. All living things share certain features.

Living things need a gas called oxygen. A fish gets oxygen from the water it takes in through its mouth.

Air and food

To stay alive, most living things need a gas called oxygen. They also need food. Plants make their own food using energy from the Sun. Animals get energy by eating plants or other animals.

A buttercup plant uses energy from sunlight to grow.

The snail gets its energy from eating the buttercup.

A thrush eats the snail, and gains its energy.

New life and growth

Living things can make new living things. These live on after their parents have died. Animals make babies, and plants produce new plants. As they get older, most living things grow and change.

These baby penguins look like small versions of their parents.

Some animals give birth to live babies. Penguins, like other birds, lay eggs with the babies inside.

Internet link

For a link to a website where you can find animal facts, nature games and stories, go to **www.usborne-quicklinks.com**

Moving

All living things can move. Most animals can move from one place to another. Plants can only move parts of themselves, and they usually move too slowly for you to see.

Some animals, such as this cheetah, can move at very high speeds.

Waste

Plants and animals produce stuff inside them that they don't need. They all have ways of getting rid of the waste.

Dung beetles eat the solid waste (dung) of other animals.

Sensitivity

Living things are sensitive to changes in the world around them, such as changes of light or heat. Animals usually react to these changes more quickly than plants.

A sunflower slowly turns so the flower always faces the Sun.

Fly

Venus flytrap

When a fly touches sensitive hairs on the leaves of a Venus flytrap, the leaves snap shut and trap the fly.

Cells

All living things are made up of tiny units called cells. Most cells are much too small to see. Scientists have to look at them through microscopes.

Internet link

For a link to a website where you can find cell pictures, activities and quizzes, go to **www.usborne-quicklinks.com**

This picture shows human fat seen through a microscope. The pink blobs are cells.

What is a cell?

A cell is a tiny structure with its own protective skin. Inside, a cell has even smaller parts called organelles. In many living things, such as humans, millions of cells stick together to make up body tissues such as skin, muscle and bone.

Plant or animal?

Animal cells have a skin called a cell membrane. Inside, the parts of the cell float in a watery gel. Plant cells have a cell membrane and a tough cell wall that gives them a fixed shape.

Both plant and animal cells have a nucleus, which controls the cell.

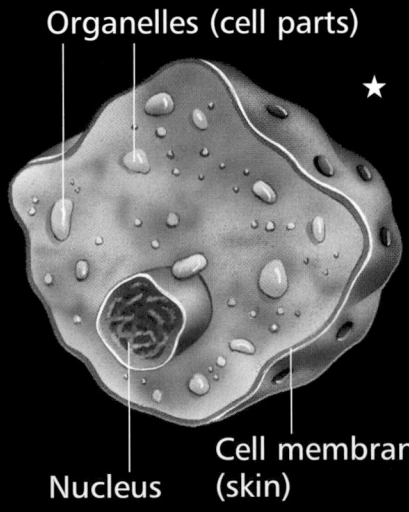

This picture shows an animal cell, cut in half so you can see inside it.

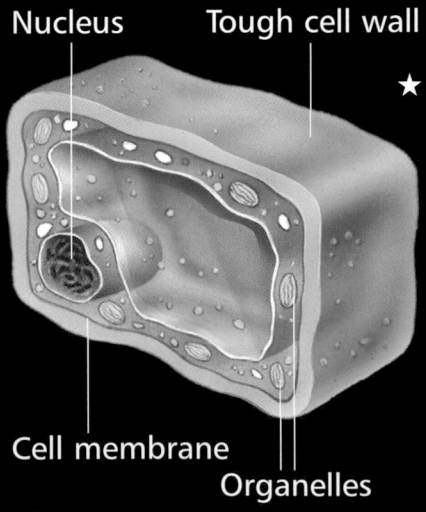

This picture shows a plant cell, cut in half so you can see inside it.

Single-celled creatures

Some very small living things have only one cell. There are single-celled animals called amoebas, and single-celled plants called algae.

Bacteria also have only one cell each. They are not plants or animals, but belong in a group of their own.

Bacteria are all around us. Most are harmless, but some, like these salmonella bacteria, can make you sick.

Bacteria are extremely tiny. This photograph was taken using a very powerful microscope.

Looking at cells

Microscopes make things look bigger. When microscopes were invented, over 300 years ago, scientists could begin to look very closely at living things, and cells were discovered.

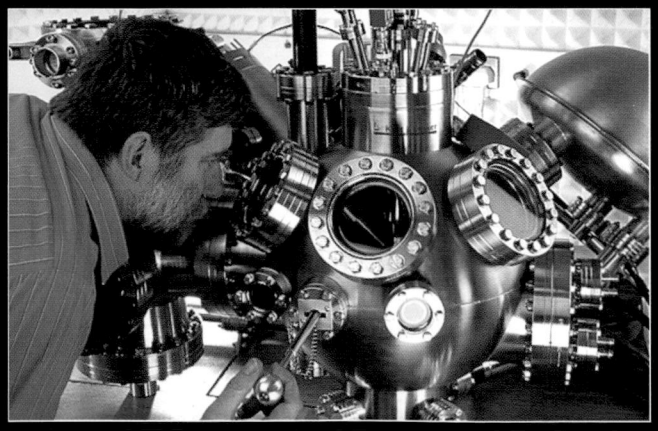

Today, powerful electron microscopes like this one help scientists to look deep inside cells.

Animal world

There are millions of different animals, from tiny bugs to huge whales. Here are some of the different types of animals you can find out about in this book.

This Arctic tern's shape helps it to fly.

Mammals

Mammals feed their babies milk. Almost all have hair or fur, and most are lively and curious. From polar bears to camels, mammals can be found all over the world.

Like all baby mammals, this lion cub is taken care of by its mother.

Birds

Birds are the only animals that have feathers. They all have wings, but not all of them can fly. Some are powerful runners or swimmers. All birds lay eggs, and take care of their babies.

Reptiles

Reptiles have dry, scaly skin and almost all lay eggs. You can find reptiles in most countries, especially in the warmer parts of the world.

This reptile is a type of African lizard called an agama. It has tough, dry skin, and spikes along its back.

Amphibians

Amphibians are animals with soft, damp skin. They can breathe on land or in water. An amphibian needs to keep its body moist to stay alive, even if it lives on land.

Frogs are amphibians. They are excellent swimmers and can breathe underwater.

Creepy-crawlies

The world is teeming with creepy-crawlies such as insects, spiders, centipedes and snails. The most common creepy-crawlies are insects. They all have six legs, and most have wings. There are nearly two million different types of insects.

Like most insects, this wasp can fly.

Water life

Many different animals live in water – from fish to mammals such as dolphins and seals, and creatures such as jellyfish and lobsters. Some animals are even able to live in the deepest ocean.

Sea anemones and fish are just two of the many types of animals that live in water.

Internet link

For a link to a website where you can find out lots about different kinds of animals, go to **www.usborne-quicklinks.com**

Mammals

The animals on these two pages look different, but they are all mammals. There are more than four thousand different kinds of mammals, including you – humans are mammals, too.

Chimpanzees live in the forests of Africa.

Keeping warm

A mammal's body makes its own warmth and it can keep its temperature the same whether the day is hot or cold. This is called being warm-blooded.

The fur on this chimp helps to keep its body warm when the weather is cold.

Food for baby

All mammal mothers feed their babies milk. They make the milk in glands, called mammary glands, on their chests or bellies. Milk is a rich food but it is easy for a baby to swallow.

This baby deer is sucking milk from nipples on its mother's belly.

Flying mammal

Bats are the only mammals that can fly. Their wings are made of flaps of skin, which stretch over the bones of their arms and fingers.

Fruit bat

Here you can see how a bat uses its arm as a wing. Long fingers support the wing skin.

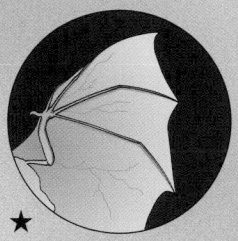

★

Internet link

For a link to a website with lots of facts about mammals, go to **www.usborne-quicklinks.com**

Swimmers

Some mammals, such as whales, live in the sea. Like all mammals, they breathe air, so they come to the surface regularly.

Humpback whale

Whales are the biggest animals in the world.

Egg layers

A few mammals lay eggs, rather than give birth. One is the duck-billed platypus. It lays its eggs in a nest in a riverbank burrow.

★

Duck-billed platypus

Baby mammals

Most newborn baby mammals are helpless and need a lot of care. Animals that can hide their young in a safe place, such as a nest, often have several babies. Animals that cannot do this usually have only one or two so they can guard them carefully.

Giraffe baby

Giraffes usually have only one baby at a time. A baby giraffe is an easy target for a lion. If an enemy comes near, the mother can kick it with her powerful legs.

Many babies

Mice have many babies at a time – eight is quite usual. The babies are born in a nest which keeps them warm. Many young are still caught by hunters such as owls and cats.

This giraffe mother licks her baby to clean it, so its scent does not attract an enemy.

Baby mice stay with their mother for less than a month.

Learning to hunt

Polar bear cubs spend two to three years with their mother, learning how to survive. The mother teaches them how to hunt. They leave her when they are old enough to hunt alone.

Baby polar bears stay close to their mother.

Pouch home

Marsupial mammals, like kangaroos, carry their babies in a built-in pouch. The baby feeds on milk from a nipple in the pouch. It also goes into the pouch if it is frightened or tired.

A baby kangaroo can travel this way until it is a year old.

Internet link

For a link to a website where you can watch videos of baby animals, go to **www.usborne-quicklinks.com**

Long childhood

Elephants take care of their babies for longer than any other animals except humans. A young elephant stays with its mother for up to ten years.

This baby elephant is learning to use its trunk to drink and bathe.

Bird life

Birds are the only animals that have feathers. Not all birds fly, but those that can't are usually superb swimmers or runners.

Fit for flying

Many birds are excellent fliers. Most of their bones are hollow, so they are light. Strong chest muscles power birds' wings. The sleek shape of their bodies helps them move quickly through the air.

A goose coming in to land lowers its feet, and spreads out its wings to slow down.

Body shapes

Birds have different body shapes. A goose's sturdy, muscular body is ideal for making long flights to warmer countries in winter. A kingfisher's arrow-like body lets it dart in and out of the water as it hunts.

A kingfisher uses its long, sharp beak to spear fish.

★

Internet link

For a link to a website where you can see pictures and facts about feathers, go to **www.usborne-quicklinks.com**

Types of feathers

Birds have three different kinds of feathers. Fluffy feathers, called down, keep them warm. Short, sturdy body feathers keep them dry. Long flight feathers help them take off, fly and land.

You can see this eagle's flight feathers on its wings.

Long flights

Birds are the greatest travelers in the animal world. Half of all types fly long distances to places where there is lots of food or where they can have babies. This is called migration.

In winter, these geese fly from Canada to Mexico in search of food.

This baby bird has a down coat to keep it warm in its cliff top nest.

Feather growth

Baby birds are covered in down feathers. They grow body and flight feathers when they are older. All feathers get dirty and untidy. Birds clean and smooth them down with their beaks to keep them working properly.

This heron is cleaning its feathers.

Bodies and beaks

The shape of a bird's body and beak help it to find and eat the kind of food it likes. You can see here that there are huge differences in body and beak shapes.

Sea life

Puffins live by the sea and hunt fish. Their stubby, muscular bodies and short wings help them swim well underwater. They can fly, but they are much clumsier in the air than in the sea.

Wings and claws

This bald eagle's huge wings let it glide effortlessly over water as it searches for fish. Its sharp claws hold fish tightly as it returns to its nest to feed.

★

This bald eagle has sharp claws for grasping fish.

This is a puffin. Its webbed feet help it paddle in the sea.

Beak shapes

Birds use their beaks as tools to help them find food. This toucan's long beak lets it reach for fruit among dense forest branches.

The toucan's jagged beak helps it to grip fruit firmly.

Diggers

Like many river and seashore birds, the scarlet ibis has a long, thin beak. It uses it to poke around for small shrimp and worms at the muddy edges of rivers.

Scarlet ibis

Spears and nets

Many birds eat other animals. Some are fierce hunters that can kill animals as big as a monkey. Here are three flesh-eating birds that use their beaks in different ways.

★

A heron uses its dagger-like beak to spear fish.

★

A vulture's hooked beak lets it tear meat from a dead animal.

★

A pelican uses its sack-shaped beak like a fishing net.

Internet link

For a link to a website with lots of information about birds' beaks and feet, go to **www.usborne-quicklinks.com**

Nests and chicks

Once she has laid her eggs, a female bird needs to sit on them to keep them warm. If the eggs get too cold, the babies inside will die.

A safe spot

Most birds build nests to protect the mother and her eggs from enemies. Nests also make a safe place for the babies when they hatch.

Internet link

For a link to a website where you can see images from a bluebird's nest box, go to **www.usborne-quicklinks.com**

Types of nests

Each type of bird has its own way of building a nest. Many are cup-shaped, and made of mud, hair, feathers and twigs.

A swallow's nest is made of mud and stuck to a wall.

A tailor bird sews big leaves together with plant parts.

A long-tailed tit makes a nest of moss, lichen and cobwebs.

This Eurasian tit's nest is made of twigs and reeds.

Breaking out

Birds sit on their eggs for two weeks or more. (Bigger birds sit for longer.) When the baby is ready to hatch, it chips its way out of the egg. Most bird babies need a lot of looking after.

This baby moorhen is chipping its way out of its egg.

A hoopoe feeding a hungry chick

Hungry babies

Baby birds are always hungry, and need a constant supply of food. An adult hoopoe, for example, must make hundreds of journeys to and from its nest every day. It brings insects and grubs for its chicks.

Protecting the family

Swans build large waterside nests from plant stalks. Their babies (called cygnets) stay with them for around four months. The parents protect their young and take them to feeding places. When the cygnets leave, they live alone until they find a mate.

This mother swan and her cygnets are gathered around their nest.

Reptile life

What makes a reptile a reptile? It has scaly skin, it lays eggs and it is "cold-blooded". This means its body does not make heat and is as warm or as cold as the air around it. Lizards, snakes, turtles and crocodiles are all reptiles.

This snake is a tree python. It hunts birds.

Snakes

All snakes are meat-eaters. Some eat insects and worms. Some can eat animals as big as a crocodile. You can find snakes all over the world, except in Antarctica.

Lizards

Most lizards are small, nimble creatures, although a few can grow to be as much as 10ft long. Like snakes, they can be found almost everywhere on Earth.

Internet link

For a link to a website with reptile facts, videos, pictures and games, go to **www.usborne-quicklinks.com**

Crocodiles

Crocodiles, and their close relatives, alligators, are fierce hunters. They can be found on riverbanks in hot countries. In the right conditions, crocodiles can live for over 100 years.

Nile crocodile

This calotes lizard lives in the forests of southern India.

Its long tail helps the calotes balance on thin branches.

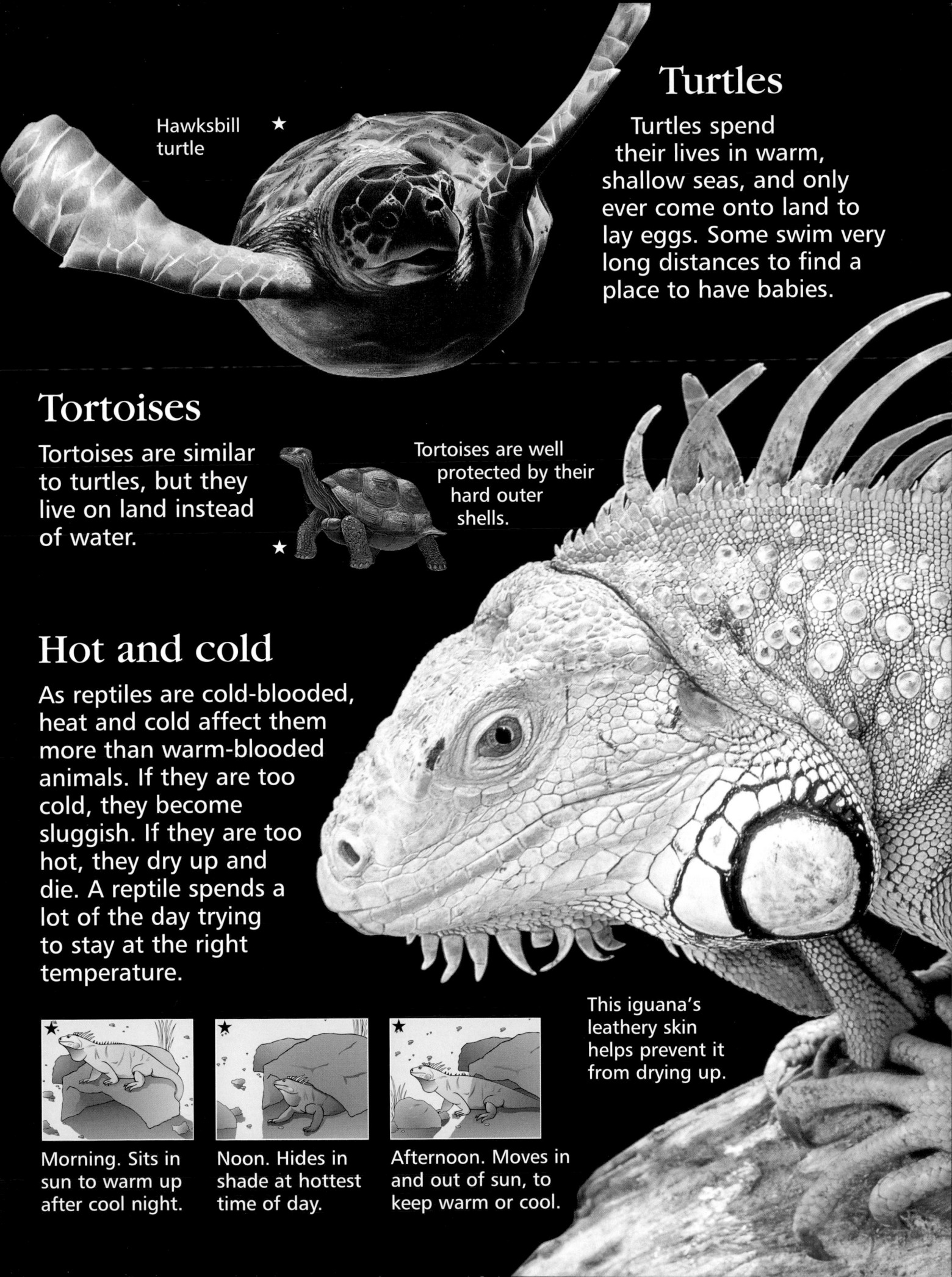

Hawksbill turtle ★

Turtles

Turtles spend their lives in warm, shallow seas, and only ever come onto land to lay eggs. Some swim very long distances to find a place to have babies.

Tortoises

Tortoises are similar to turtles, but they live on land instead of water.

Tortoises are well protected by their hard outer shells. ★

Hot and cold

As reptiles are cold-blooded, heat and cold affect them more than warm-blooded animals. If they are too cold, they become sluggish. If they are too hot, they dry up and die. A reptile spends a lot of the day trying to stay at the right temperature.

This iguana's leathery skin helps prevent it from drying up.

★ Morning. Sits in sun to warm up after cool night.

★ Noon. Hides in shade at hottest time of day.

★ Afternoon. Moves in and out of sun, to keep warm or cool.

Amphibians

Amphibians look a little like reptiles, but with soft, moist skin. They lay squishy eggs in water, where their young hatch and grow. Adults can live on land and in water. Frogs and toads are amphibians.

Slimy skin

Many amphibians have shiny, slimy skin. They need to keep their skin moist, even when they are on land. If their skin becomes too dry, they may die.

This tree frog lives in rainforest trees. Moisture in the air helps to keep its skin damp.

Getting air

Amphibians are clever breathers. They can take in air through their skin on land and underwater. Some have gills, like fish (see page 81). On land, many amphibians breathe through their mouths.

The frilly growths on this axolotl's head are gills. It uses them to breathe underwater.

Swimming

An amphibian's body has special features that let it walk or swim. Frogs, for instance, have webbed toes. They use these like flippers to push themselves through the water.

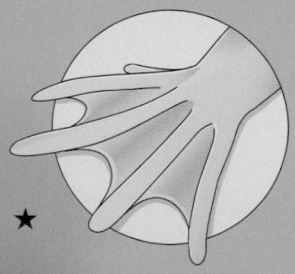

★ Webbed toes

Frogs and toads

Frogs have long, strong back legs. They use them to leap around on land, and swim in water. Many frogs have beautiful, bright skin. Toads have drier, warty skin.

Toad

Toads have shorter back legs than frogs. They waddle rather than hop.

Frog

Internet link

For a link to a website where you can find lots of weird and wonderful facts about frogs and toads, as well as games, jokes and pictures, go to **www.usborne-quicklinks.com**

Salamanders

A salamander has a long tail like a lizard. Most salamanders have foul-tasting skin which is brightly patterned. This warns their enemies not to try eating them because they will taste horrible.

The pattern on this salamander warns its enemies that it tastes bad.

Babies

Many frogs and toads lay lots of eggs at once. When they hatch, the babies live in water. They don't look like their parents at all. When they grow up, they move onto land.

These squishy blobs are frogs' eggs, called spawn. The babies, called tadpoles, hatch out of them.

After a few weeks the tadpoles start to grow legs. The back legs grow first, then the front legs.

Eventually, the tail shrinks away and the tadpole grows lungs. It can now breathe on land.

It takes about 16 weeks for a tadpole to become a frog. It still has a lot of growing to do.

Creepy-crawlies

The world is full of tiny creatures. Over four-fifths of all known types of animals are creepy-crawlies. Here you can see some of the different kinds found within this miniature world.

Types of insect

Although they look different, a bee and a dragonfly are both insects. They behave very differently though. For example, many bees live together in big groups, but dragonflies live alone.

The dragonfly (left) and bee (below) look very different, but they are both insects.

Southern hawker dragonfly

White-tailed bumblebee

Insect parts

All adult insects have six legs and three parts to their bodies – a head, a thorax, and an abdomen. Most insects have wings at some stage of their lives.

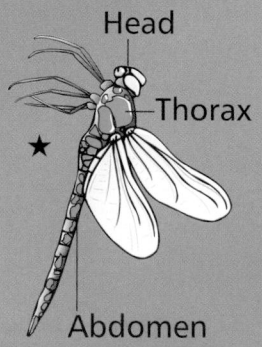

Spiders

Spiders are not insects. They are a type of animal known as an arachnid. Spiders have eight legs and two parts to their body. They never have wings. Many spiders spin webs to catch their food.

The golden orb weaver is one of Australia's biggest spiders. Females can be 2in long.

Lots of legs

Millipedes and centipedes have the most legs of any animal. Centipedes have up to 100 legs, while some millipedes have up to 700. Their bodies are divided into a series of segments. Like many creepy-crawlies, they have feelers called antennae on their heads.

Two rainforest millipedes

Internet link

For links to a website where you can take a closer look at insects, go to **www.usborne-quicklinks.com**

Slimy snails

Snails have a hard shell they can curl up in. This protects their bodies from enemies. Land snails, such as the one on the right, lurk in damp places, such as under leaves and stones. Some snails can live underwater.

A snail can pull its whole body into its shell if it is in danger.

This is a kind of snail called a grove snail. Like all snails, it slides along on its slimy belly.

Butterflies

Butterflies are among the most colorful types of insects. Most live for only a few weeks. They find a mate, lay eggs, then die.

Butterfly wings

Butterfly wings are covered in tiny colored, shiny scales. The shiny scales reflect light, which is why butterflies shimmer when they fly.

Butterflies visit plants to drink a liquid, called nectar, from flowers.

This butterfly is called a common blue. It has spread its wings to soak up the Sun's heat.

Open and shut

When a butterfly holds its wings open, it is gathering warmth from the Sun. This helps give it the energy to fly. When its wings are closed, it is resting. It faces the Sun, so its shadow is small and enemies are less likely to spot it.

Butterfly with wings open

Butterfly with wings closed

Internet link

For a link to a website where you can find many interesting butterfly facts, plus games and activities, go to **www.usborne-quicklinks.com**

Wing patterns

A butterfly's beautiful, patterned wings help other butterflies spot their own kind. Their wing patterns help butterflies in other ways, too.

The circles on a peacock butterfly's wings look like eyes. This frightens enemies.

A comma's ragged wings disguise it as a dead leaf when it is on the ground.

The African monarch is poisonous. Birds learn not to eat it.

An Arctic ringlet's dark wings help it soak up heat.

This mocker swallowtail is not poisonous, but birds think it is an African monarch and do not eat it.

The patterns on this tortoiseshell's wings help it attract a mate.

Making butterflies

A female butterfly lays her eggs on a plant. When an egg hatches, a caterpillar comes out and feeds on the plant. When the caterpillar is fully grown, it turns into a pupa, and then into a butterfly.

A caterpillar ready to turn into a pupa.

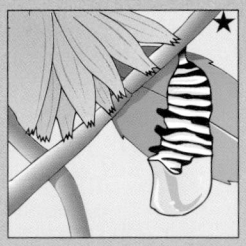

The pupa forms inside the body. It splits the skin.

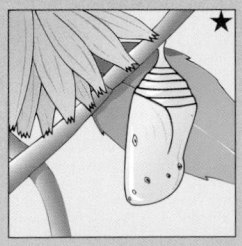

The pupa hardens. Inside, it is changing.

After two weeks a butterfly comes out.

The butterfly's body hardens and it flies off.

Seashore life

There are lots of things to spot on the seashore. Every day when the tide goes out, it leaves pools of water trapped among the rocks. Plants and animals make their homes in these pools.

Outside skeletons

A crab doesn't have a shell, but it has its skeleton on the outside. The skeleton is called a carapace. When the crab grows too big for its carapace, it wriggles out of it. Then its skin slowly hardens to make a new, bigger carapace.

Upside down

Barnacles cover the rocks along the seashore. They feed by sticking their legs out of the tops of their shells.

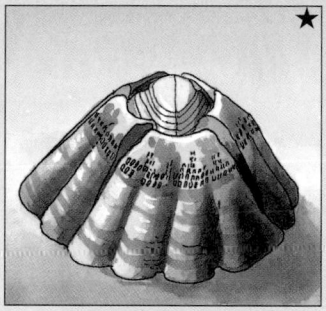

Tiny barnacles cling to the rocks in big groups. Their tough shells protect them from danger.

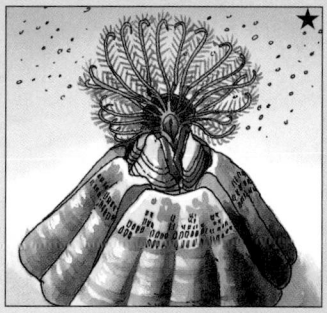

Barnacles open the tops of their shells to feed. Their legs stick out to pick up bits of food in the water.

Special air bubbles keep this seaweed floating near the surface of the water, where there is light.

Sea scorpions are fierce hunters. Their huge mouths can open very wide.

Internet link

For a link to a website where you can learn more about the seashore and print out pictures of seashore life, go to **www.usborne-quicklinks.com**

Starfish have five arms. If they lose an arm, another one grows in its place.

Hermit crab

Sea urchins have sharp spines on their shells to protect them.

Sea lemons scrape food off the rocks with their tongues.

Limpets

Strawberry anemones

Barnacles

Dog whelk

Underwater life

The oceans are full of living things. Some sea creatures are gentle and friendly, but others are fierce hunters.

Internet links

Website 1 Design your own fish.

Website 2 Fun facts about animals.

For links to these websites, go to **www.usborne-quicklinks.com**

Most types of shark are deadly hunters. They have sharp teeth for eating other animals.

Dolphins are one of the most intelligent and playful kinds of sea animal.

Coral reefs are beautiful underwater structures. Many different sea animals live on them.

Sea slugs collect other animals' poison and use it themselves against their enemies.

What are fish?

Fish are a group of animals that live in water. There are thousands of different kinds. They come in different shapes and sizes, but they all have gills and fins. Gills allow them to breathe underwater, and fins help them to move around.

Caudal fin

Most fish have flat tails, which they move from side to side to swim. Their strong tail muscles make swimming easy.

Fish use these top fins, called dorsal fins, to help keep their balance.

Slimy skin helps fish to move easily through water.

This flap, called the operculum, covers the fish's gills.

Fish use these fins, called pectoral fins, for turning.

This line, called the lateral line, helps fish to sense movement in the water.

Pelvic fins help fish to change direction quickly.

Breathing

Fish breathe by taking oxygen out of the water. Here's how they do it.

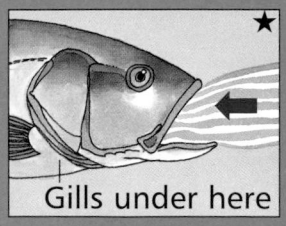

As a fish moves forward, it takes in water through its mouth. The water passes over its gills.

The fish's gills take oxygen from the water. The water then passes out under the fish's operculum.

Fish scales

Most fish are protected by a covering of tiny plates, called scales. These scales are waterproof, and help to protect the fish from pests and hunters.

Fish scales overlap each other, to make a protective cover.

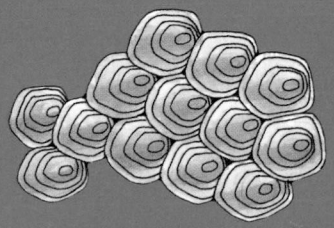

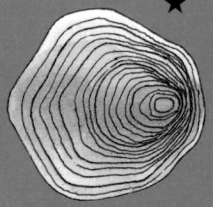

The rings on a fish's scales show how old the fish is. Some fish can live for up to 80 years.

Coral reefs

Corals live in warm, shallow seas. Although they look like plants, corals are really made of thousands of small animals. Large areas of coral are called coral reefs.

Angelfish live among corals. Their bright markings help them blend in with their background.

Internet link

For a link to a website where you can learn about lots of different kinds of corals, go to **www.usborne-quicklinks.com**

Coral animals

Coral animals, called polyps, are protected by hard skeletons. When they die, the skeletons remain and new polyps grow on top of them. Over time, a coral reef slowly forms.

There are four fish and an eel hiding in this coral reef. Can you spot them all?

Sea fan

Sponge

Sea urchin

Brittle star

Brain coral

Reef life

Coral reefs are full of nooks and crannies where animals can hide and make their homes. This means there are always lots of living things around them.

A coral meal

The animals in coral are well protected by their shells, but some fish, such as parrotfish, are able to eat them.

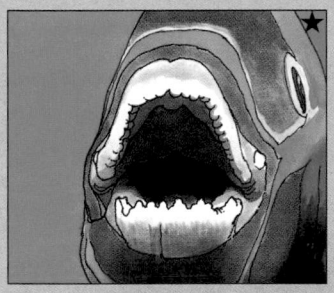

A parrotfish's teeth are all joined together to form a hard beak.

The parrotfish breaks off a chunk of coral, then uses its beak to crunch it up.

Giant clam

Feather star

Sea anemone

Sharks

Sharks are fish which live in oceans all over the world. There are more than 300 different kinds. Most are fierce hunters, with sharp teeth for catching and killing other animals.

Internet link

For a link to a website where you can find out about all kinds of sharks, including prehistoric ones, go to **www.usborne-quicklinks.com**

Whale sharks are not a danger to people. Divers can swim with them safely.

Great white shark

People killers?

Great white sharks like to surprise their prey from below and kill it with only one bite, to save energy. They sometimes attack swimmers, but scientists believe they do this by mistake, thinking that humans are other sea animals.

Great white sharks kill their prey by biting it. They can open their mouths very wide.

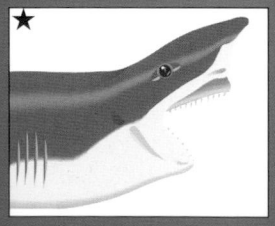

As their mouths open, their teeth point forward, helping them to take a bigger bite.

Whale sharks are the world's biggest fish. They can grow up to 40ft long.

Hammerhead sharks have eyes on each end of a long, flat head. This helps them to see all around as they swim.

Sharks swim by moving their tails from side to side.

Fin shapes

Sharks, like dolphins and whales, sometimes swim near the surface of the sea with their dorsal (back) fins sticking out of the water. Dorsal fins of different animals look different, as you can see below.

A common dolphin has a small, gently curved fin.

A great white shark's fin is sharp and triangular.

The fin of a killer whale can be as tall as a person.

Hundreds of teeth

Most sharks have at least three rows of teeth. As they lose the ones in front, teeth from the rows behind move forward to replace them.

A sand tiger shark's teeth point back so that fish it catches can't wiggle free.

Whales

Whales are the biggest animals in the world. They look like fish, but whales are actually mammals (read more about mammals on pages 60-61). Unlike most mammals though, whales do not have hair on their bodies.

This sperm whale is as heavy as six elephants. The heaviest animals on Earth are blue whales, which can weigh as much as 20 elephants.

Spout shapes

Mammals can't breathe underwater, so whales come to the ocean's surface to breathe. They breathe through holes called blowholes on top of their heads. When they breathe out, they shoot out sprays of water. This is called spouting.

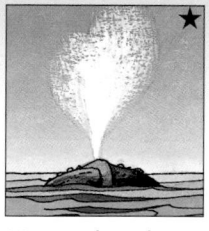

Humpback whale

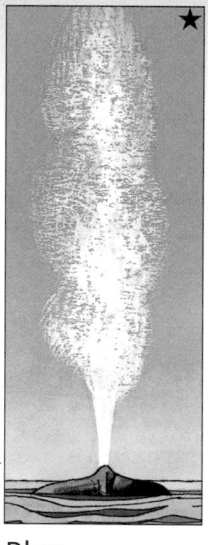

Blue whale

Right whale

Sperm whale

Minke whale

Different whales spout in different ways. By looking at the shape of a whale's spout, you can tell what kind of whale it is.

Sperm whales are the deepest diving whales, and can hold their breath for over an hour. They dive deep to catch giant squid to eat.

Internet link

For a link to a website where you can find out what whales sound like, go to **www.usborne-quicklinks.com**

Energetic whales

Even though they are huge, whales can be very energetic. Big whales, such as humpback whales, often throw themselves right out of the water. This is called breaching. Nobody knows exactly why they do it.

The whale on the right is breaching. It may be trying to knock the barnacles off its skin.

Whales often throw their tails in the air when they dive. This is called fluking, and helps them dive deep.

Dolphins

Dolphins are mammals that live in oceans all over the world. They often live in big groups. They are some of the most intelligent animals in the sea.

A group of dolphins is called a school. Some schools contain over a hundred dolphins.

Internet link

For a link to a website where you can find answers to all your questions about dolphins, go to **www.usborne-quicklinks.com**

Learning to breathe

Dolphins breathe air, so when a baby dolphin is born, its mother must quickly push it to the surface of the sea and teach it to breathe, or else it will drown. Sometimes, another dolphin helps her do this.

This dolphin has just had a baby. Now the baby must learn how to breathe.

The mother swims under her baby, and gently pushes it up.

The baby takes its first breath of air. Now it will know what to do.

Dolphins can swim at speeds of up to 25mph.

Fun and games

Dolphins are fast swimmers and amazing acrobats. Their speed helps them catch fish, but they also love to play and perform tricks. They can jump right out of the sea.

Spinner dolphins can jump up to 10ft out of the water, and spin around as many as seven times in the air.

These bottlenose dolphins are taking a look around. This is called spy hopping.

Using echoes

Dolphins find their way in the sea by making sounds which send back echoes. They can then tell what's around them by listening to the echoes. This is called sonar. Dolphins also use sonar to catch fish.

A dolphin makes a clicking sound which travels through the water.

When the sound hits some fish, it bounces back as an echo.

The dolphin can tell where the fish are by listening to the returning echo.

Deep sea

The deep sea is a very dark, cold place where some of the strangest creatures in the world live. There are no plants in the deep sea, so all the fish are hunters.

Hatchetfish have eyes on top of their heads so they can see fish which swim above them.

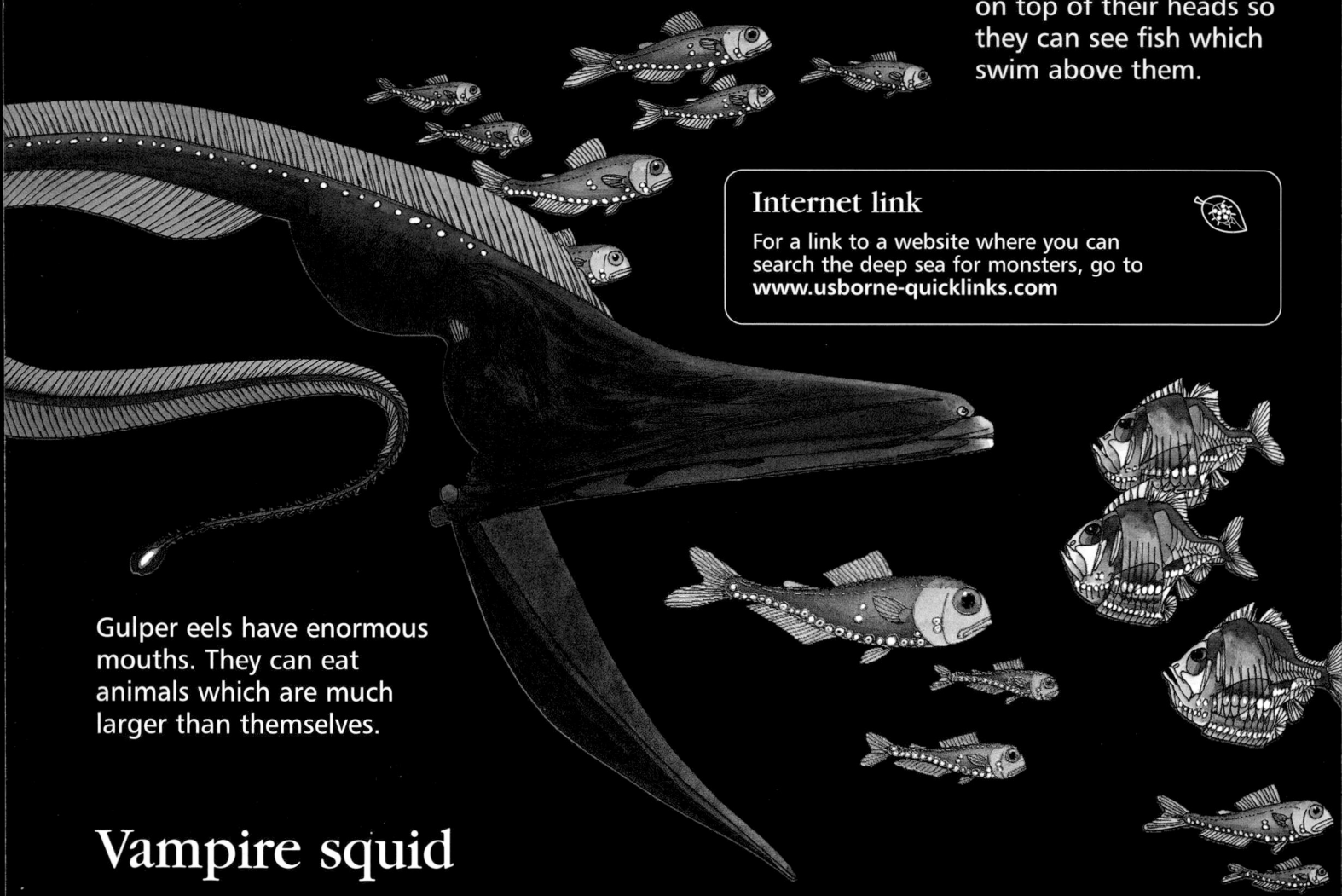

Gulper eels have enormous mouths. They can eat animals which are much larger than themselves.

Internet link

For a link to a website where you can search the deep sea for monsters, go to **www.usborne-quicklinks.com**

Vampire squid

Vampire squid live as deep as 3,000ft. Their big eyes help them see in the murky depths.

Vampire squid have a clever way of escaping from enemies. They can turn themselves inside out. The undersides of their tentacles are covered in sharp spikes, to stop other animals from eating them.

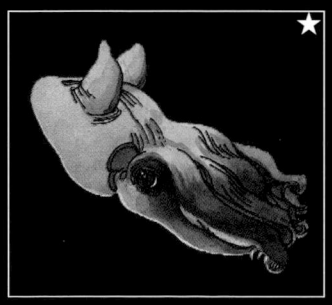

Vampire squid escape from enemies by putting their tentacles over their heads.

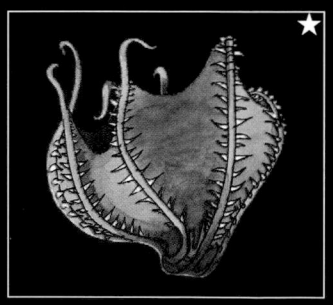

Their tentacles cover their bodies, making a spiky shield which protects them.

Seeing in the dark

Because it is so dark at the bottom of the oceans, some fish have ways of making light to help them see. Light also attracts other sea animals, so some hunters use it to catch food.

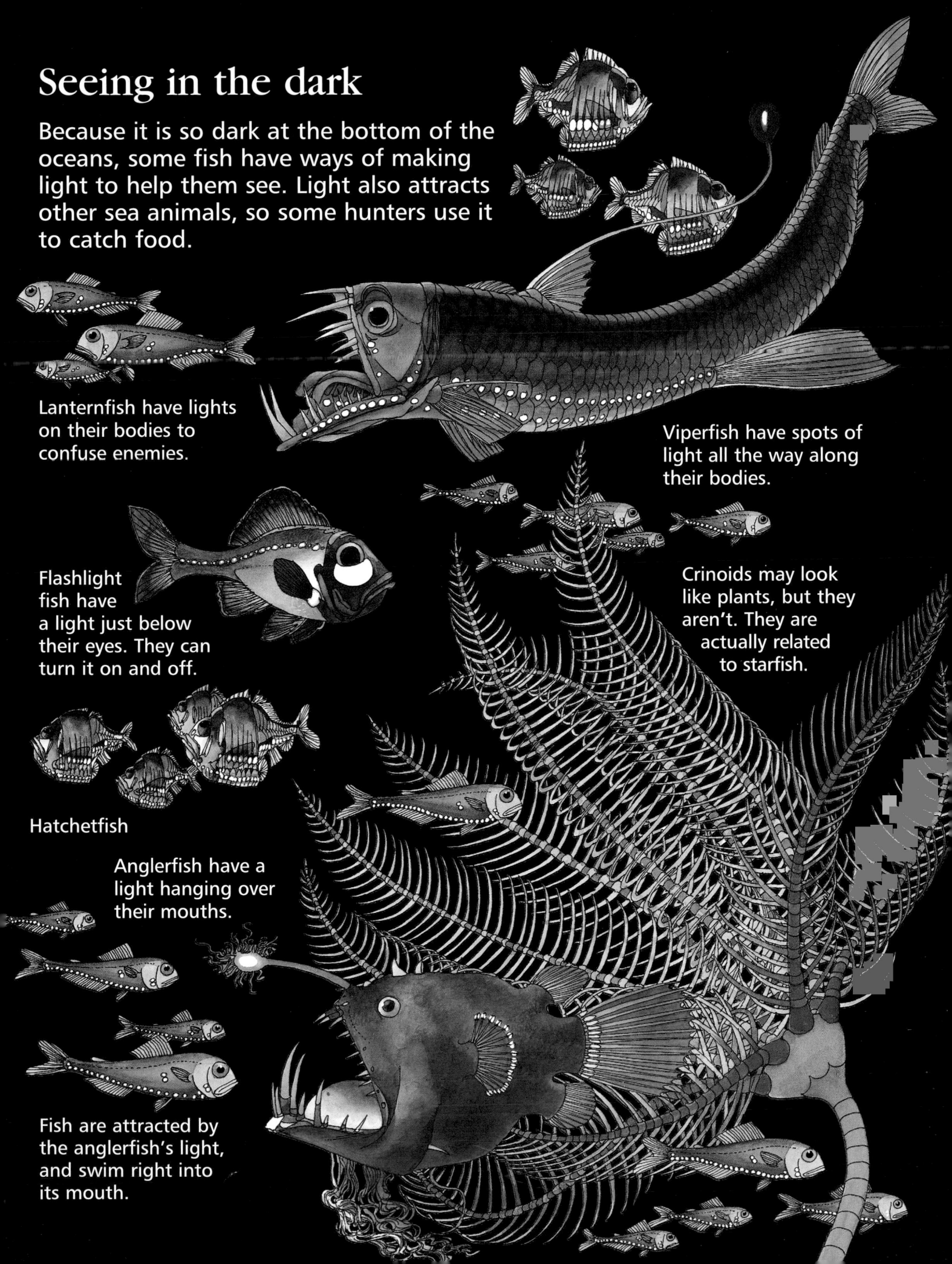

Plant world

Plants are different from animals in several ways. They can't move from place to place, and most can only react slowly to changes around them. Unlike animals, plants make their own food.

Plant groups

There are over 270 thousand different kinds of plants. They can be looked at in groups which are similar in some ways.

Ferns have stems, leaves and roots but no flowers.

Conifers have needle-shaped leaves and their seeds are made in cones.

Algae are simple plants with no stems, roots or leaves.

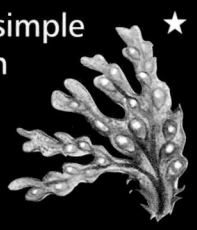

Flowering plants have roots, leaves and a stem. Their seeds develop from a flower.

Mosses have thin leaves but no proper roots. They grow near the ground in damp places.

Making food

Green plants use the Sun's energy to make food in their leaves. They turn water and minerals from the soil, and carbon dioxide gas from the air, into sugar. Sugar is food for plants. This process, called photosynthesis (say "foe-toe-sin-thuh-sis"), also makes oxygen.

Flowering plants

The largest group of plants are flowering plants. They include trees as well as flowers. Their main parts are the leaves, stem and roots.

Leaves have a green chemical inside which helps to make food. ★

The stem supports the plant. Water and food travel inside it.

Roots hold a plant upright and take in water and minerals.

Inside a flower

Flowers contain parts that can make seeds which will grow into new plants. To make the seeds, a yellow dust, called pollen, has to be carried from one flower to another. The wind and small animals do this job.

Pollen rubs off on a hummingbird's head as it feeds on nectar. ★

Internet link

For a link to a website where you can read about plant record breakers, go to **www.usborne-quicklinks.com**

Pollen sticks to a bee's body as it drinks nectar. This will rub off on the next flower it visits.

Many flowers have bright colors and a strong smell. These attract insects to the sweet liquid called nectar inside.

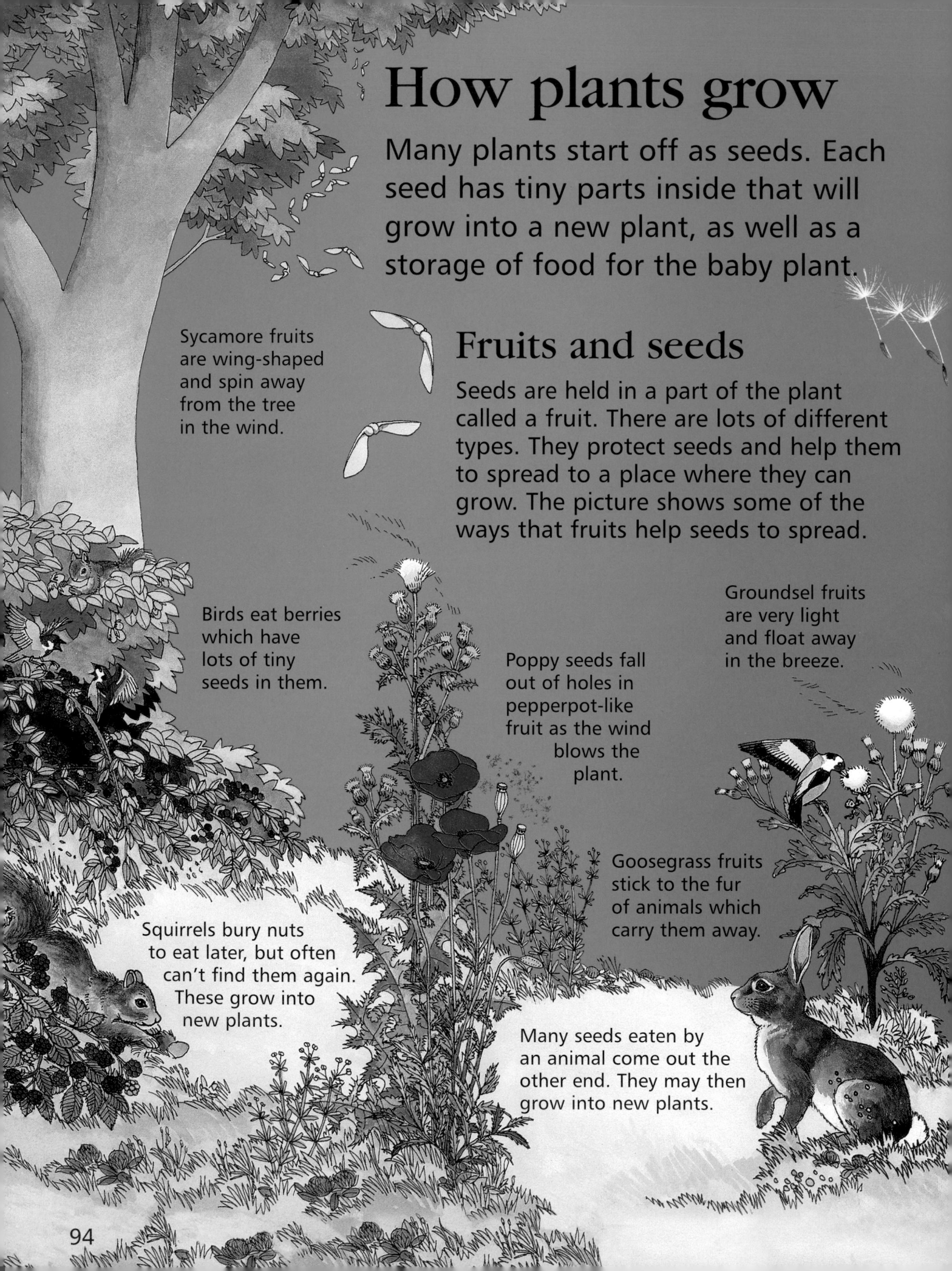

How plants grow

Many plants start off as seeds. Each seed has tiny parts inside that will grow into a new plant, as well as a storage of food for the baby plant.

Fruits and seeds

Seeds are held in a part of the plant called a fruit. There are lots of different types. They protect seeds and help them to spread to a place where they can grow. The picture shows some of the ways that fruits help seeds to spread.

Sycamore fruits are wing-shaped and spin away from the tree in the wind.

Birds eat berries which have lots of tiny seeds in them.

Poppy seeds fall out of holes in pepperpot-like fruit as the wind blows the plant.

Groundsel fruits are very light and float away in the breeze.

Goosegrass fruits stick to the fur of animals which carry them away.

Squirrels bury nuts to eat later, but often can't find them again. These grow into new plants.

Many seeds eaten by an animal come out the other end. They may then grow into new plants.

Starting to grow

To start growing, a seed needs water, warmth and oxygen. When it is warm enough, roots and a tiny shoot will push their way out. A plant at this stage is called a seedling.

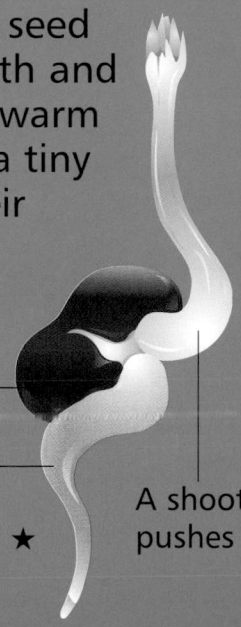

From seedling to plant

A seedling lives off the food stored in its seed until it grows leaves to make its own food. The plant grows and has flowers and seeds of its own. The seeds grow into new plants, and so on.

These dandelion fruits are being carried away by the wind.

Life and death

The changes that happen to a living thing during its life are called its life cycle. Different types of plants have life cycles of different lengths.

Snapdragons grow, flower, make seeds and die within one year.

Foxgloves live for many years, making seeds for new plants.

Internet link

For a link to a website where you can watch videos of seeds traveling to new places to grow, go to **www.usborne-quicklinks.com**

Grow a bean plant

You will need:
a glass jar; paper towels; dried kidney beans; a flowerpot; some compost.

1. Line a glass jar with damp paper towels. Put some dried kidney beans next to the glass.

2. After a few days, look for shoots growing up and little roots growing down.

3. To grow plants, put the seedlings in flowerpots of compost and water them.

Trees and leaves

A tree is a plant with a thick, woody stem called a trunk. Most trees can grow for hundreds of years. Some trees are small, but many are taller than a house.

Tree bark

As a tree grows, its outer layers become harder. When they die, they form a tough layer called bark. There are many different types.

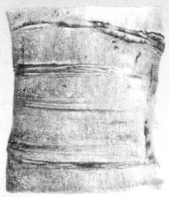

A beech tree has smooth, thin bark.

An English oak has cracked, ridged bark.

Cypress trees are evergreen, which means they don't lose their leaves all at once.

Getting bigger

Look at the rings in a tree stump. You can count these to find out the tree's age.

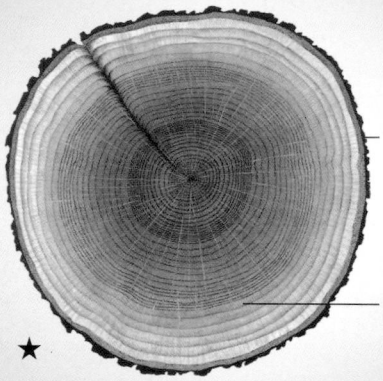

A tree grows from its middle out. One ring of new wood builds up each year, making the trunk thicker.

Tree roots

A tree uses its roots to take in water from the soil. They also act as an anchor. Tall trees, such as the cypress trees below, could not stay standing without their strong roots.

Looking at leaves

Leaves contain a green chemical which absorbs sunlight to help make food (see **Making food** on page 92). When leaves die, the green chemical fades away and they change color.

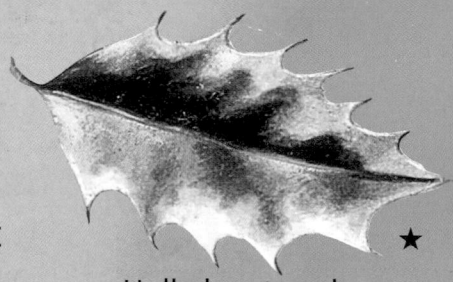

Holly has tough, spiky leaves.

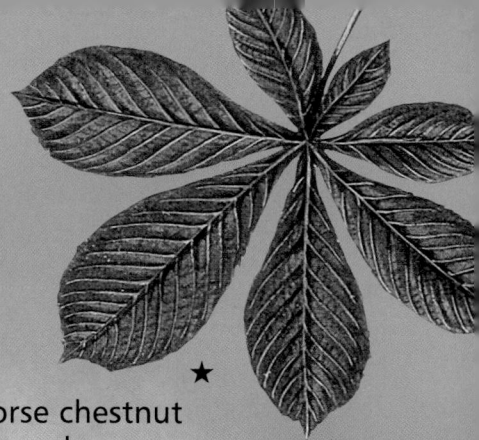

Horse chestnut leaves have seven separate parts, called leaflets.

Losing leaves

Many types of trees lose all their leaves every fall. They are called deciduous trees. Trees that don't lose their leaves all at once are called evergreens.

Atlas cedars have bunches of thin, sharp leaves.

Oak trees have soft leaves with a wavy edge.

Internet link

For a link to a website where you can find out more about trees, go to **www.usborne-quicklinks.com**

Green leaves turn beautiful shades of red and gold before they fall from the tree.

Seeds and fruits

All trees produce flowers, which grow into fruits. Fruits contain seeds which can grow into new trees.

This acorn is the fruit of an oak tree.

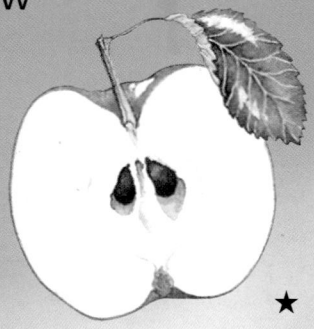

An apple has several seeds in its core.

Fungi

Fungi are not plants because they can't make their own food. Instead, they feed on living or once living things.

Types of fungi

Fungi come in thousands of different shapes and sizes.

Mushrooms and toadstools are fungi. You can eat some types but others are deadly poisonous.

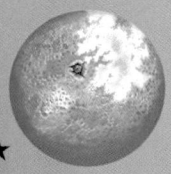

The green furry blobs you sometimes see on fruit or cheese are a type of fungus known as mold.

These inkcap toadstools are growing and feeding on an old, moss-covered log.

Spores

Fungi don't make seeds or pollen. Instead, they shed clouds of tiny specks, called spores. These are scattered all around by the wind, and grow into new fungi.

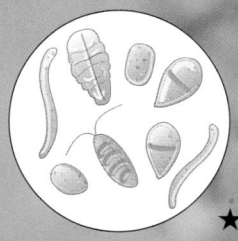

Fungus spores seen using a microscope

Useful fungi

Some types of fungi are very useful. A fungus called yeast is used to make bread and wine. Some medicines are made from fungi, too.

Internet link

For a link to a website where you can browse a gallery of fascinating fungi photographs, go to **www.usborne-quicklinks.com**

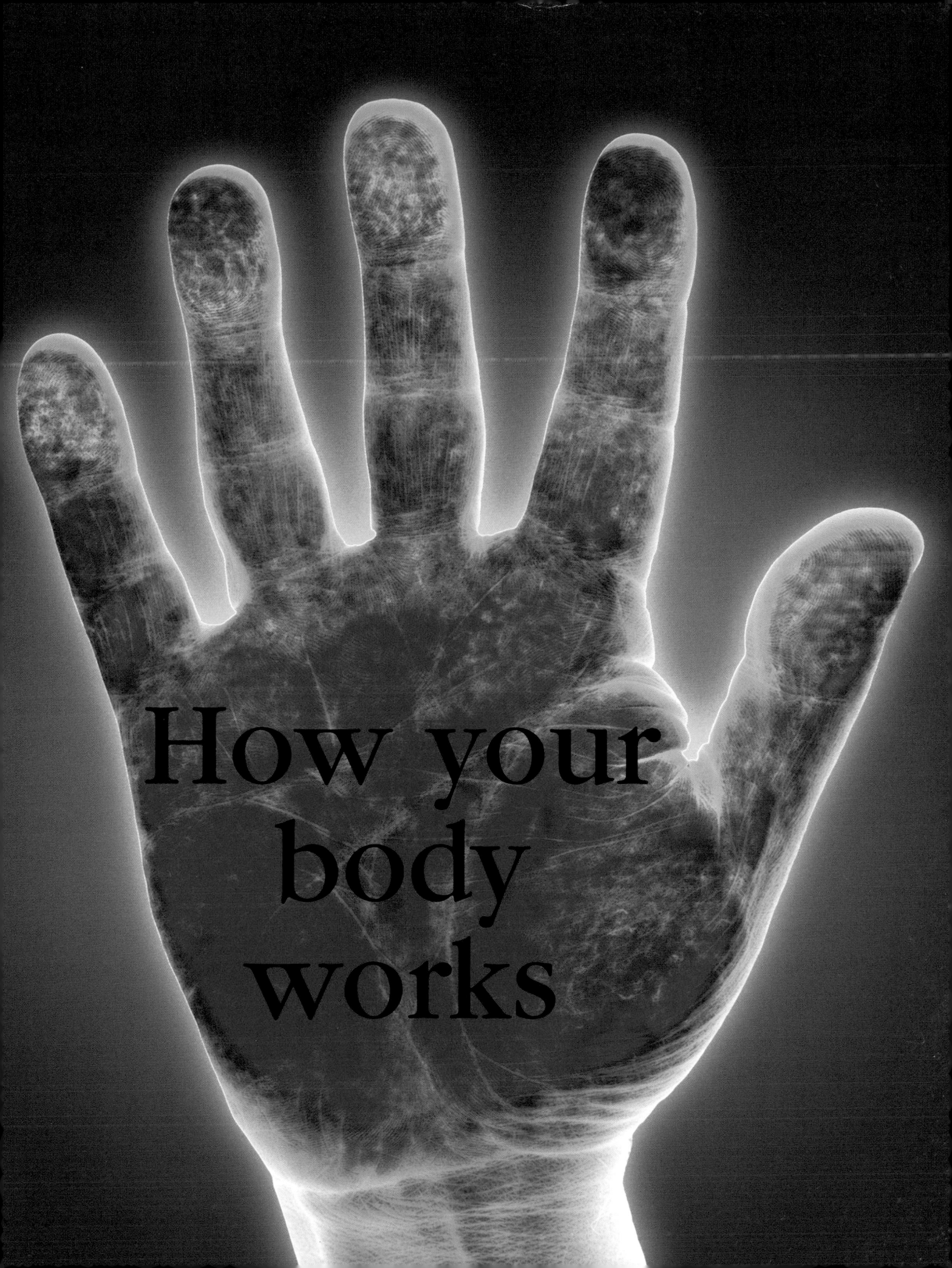

How your body works

Your body

Have you ever wondered what's inside you? Your body is made up of lots of separate parts. They all do different jobs to help you stay alive.

Organs

Organs are important body parts such as the heart, lungs, stomach and brain. Most of them are in the upper body and head. You can see some of the main organs in this picture.

Each organ has a special job to do. For example, your stomach holds the food you eat, and your lungs take air into your body.

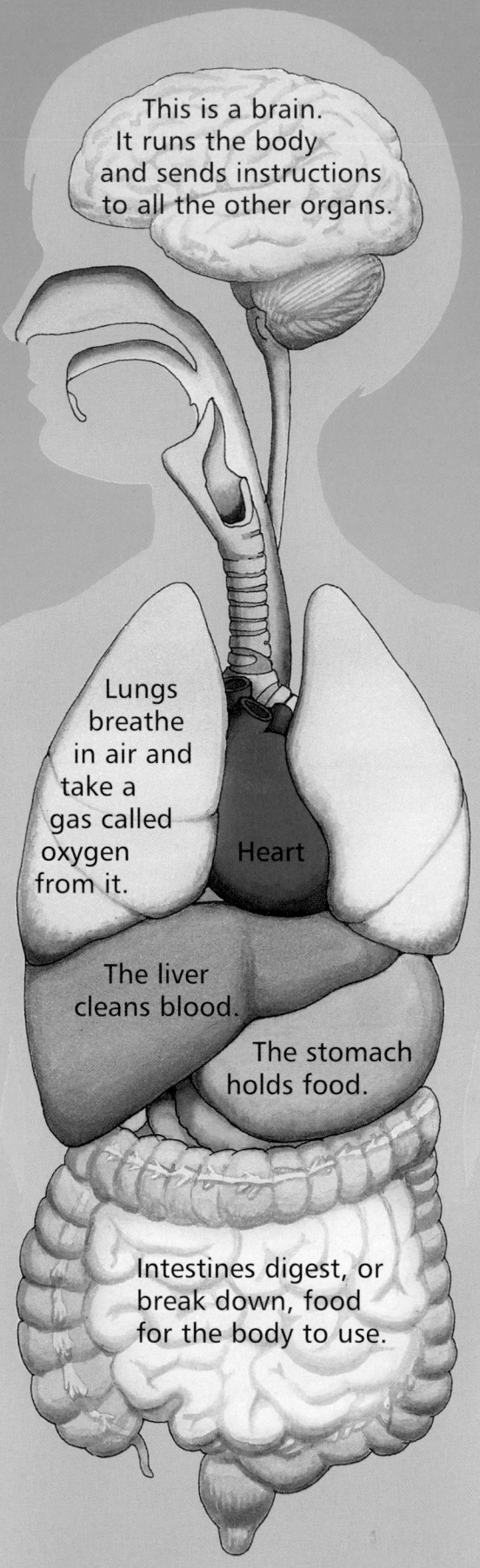

How much air do your lungs hold?

You will need: a plastic bottle with a lid; a bendy straw; a bowl of water

1. Fill the bottle with water and put the lid on. Hold it upside down in the bowl and take off the lid.

2. Push the straw into the neck of the bottle. Breathe in deeply, then blow gently into the straw until your lungs are empty.

All the air you breathe out will be trapped at the top of the bottle. This is how much air your lungs can hold.

Blood

As well as organs, a human body contains up to nine pints of blood. The heart pumps blood around the body along thousands of tubes called blood vessels. As it flows along, blood delivers oxygen and food to every part of the body.

Blood is made of cells (see page 56) floating in a liquid called plasma. This picture shows different types of blood cells.

Platelet (part of a blood cell)

White blood cell

Red blood cell

Feel your pulse

To feel your blood being pumped around your body, press two fingers on the inside of your wrist. The beating you feel is called your pulse.

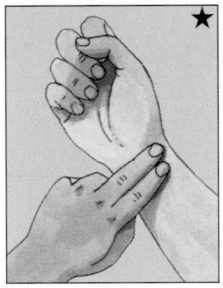

Internet link

For a link to a website where you can discover some amazing facts about your heart, and watch animations showing how blood flows around your body, go to **www.usborne-quicklinks.com**

Safe in your skin

Your skin gives your whole body a waterproof covering, and protects your insides from dirt and germs. Skin is made up of two main layers.

This close-up photograph shows the layers in human skin.

Hair

The top layer of skin is called the epidermis.

Underneath the epidermis is a thicker layer called the dermis.

Hair shaft

Hair root

Hair follicle

In some places, the epidermis reaches deep into the dermis and forms a hair follicle. A hair can grow out of each follicle.

Bones and muscles

Bones and muscles are your body's support system. They hold you up and let you move around. Without them, you'd be nothing but a helpless blob.

Your skeleton

Together, your bones make up your skeleton, which acts as a framework for your whole body. Bendable joints where bones meet let you move into different positions.

Bones protect your insides too. For example, rib bones in your chest stop the organs inside from getting squashed.

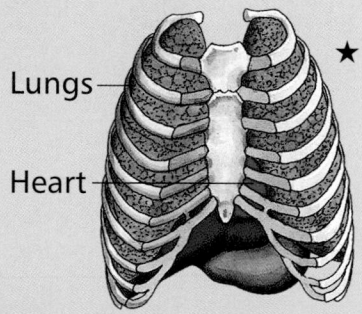

Soft skeletons

A baby's bones are partly made of a flexible material called cartilage. As the baby grows, most of the cartilage slowly turns into hard bone.

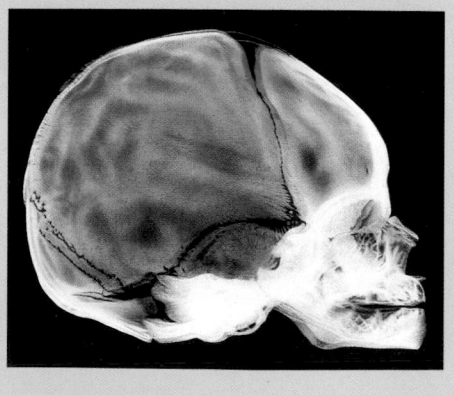

This is an X-ray picture of a newborn baby's skull. As the baby grows, the gaps in its skull close up and the skull hardens.

This shows an adult human skeleton with some of its main bones and joints named.

Skull
Jaw bone
Collar bone
Shoulder blade
Breast bone
Ribs
Vertebrae (back bones)
Elbow joint
Wrist bones
Pelvis
Hip joint
Finger bones
Coccyx (tail bone)
Femur (thigh bone)
Knee joint
Fibula
Patella (kneecap)
Tibia (shin bone)
Foot bones
Ankle joint

Muscles

The bones of your skeleton are moved by muscles. These help you move in all kinds of ways, from walking or swimming to playing the recorder or using a computer.

You also have other muscles (in your heart, for example) that work without you even thinking about them.

Internet link

For a link to a website where you can watch a short movie and try a quiz about muscles, go to **www.usborne-quicklinks.com**

There are over 600 muscles in the human body. This picture shows some of the main ones.

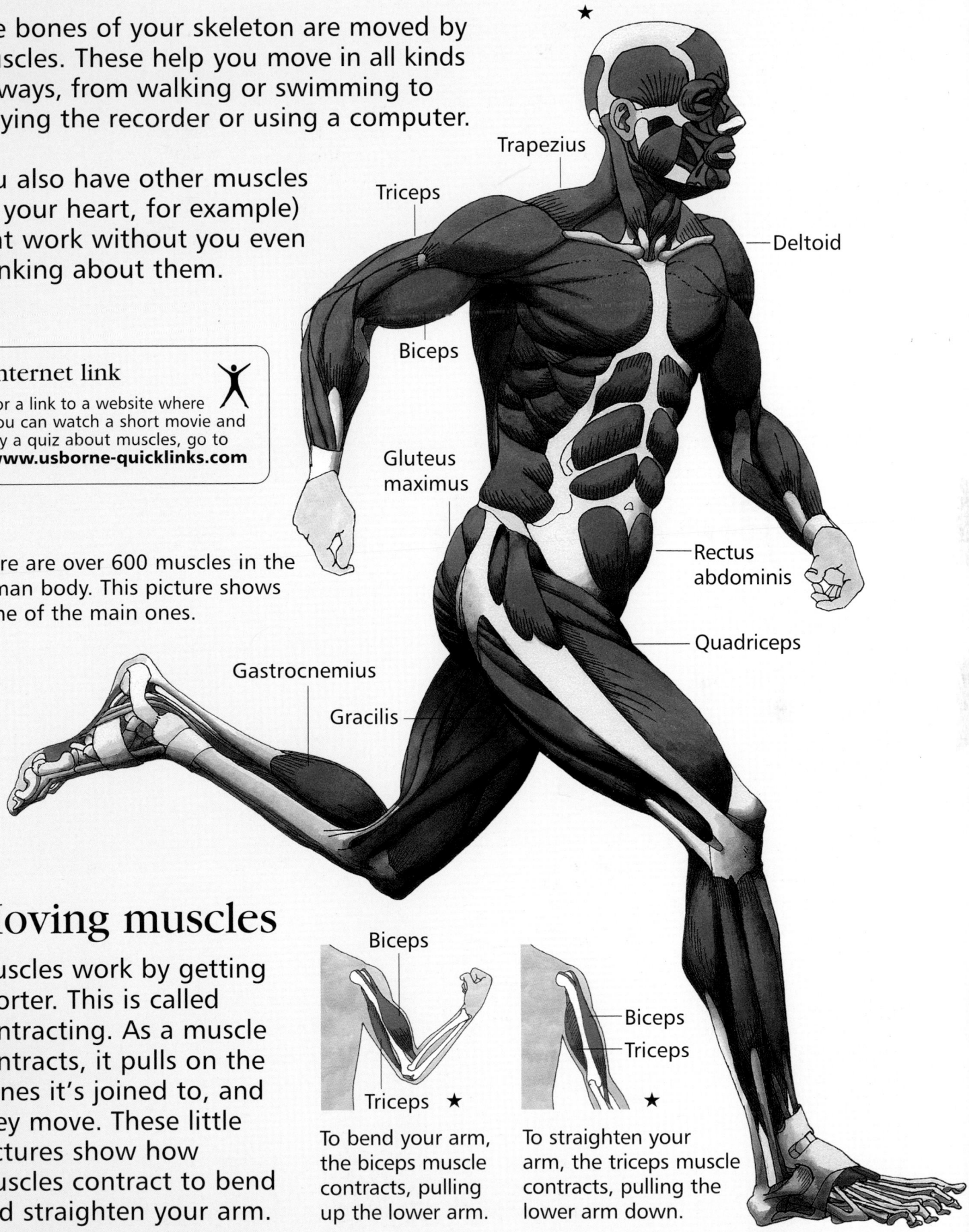

Moving muscles

Muscles work by getting shorter. This is called contracting. As a muscle contracts, it pulls on the bones it's joined to, and they move. These little pictures show how muscles contract to bend and straighten your arm.

To bend your arm, the biceps muscle contracts, pulling up the lower arm.

To straighten your arm, the triceps muscle contracts, pulling the lower arm down.

What happens to food?

The food you eat gives you the energy you need to live. But to get this energy, you have to turn food into chemicals in your body. This is called digestion.

Your food's journey

As food travels into and through your body, it gets turned into smaller and smaller pieces. Follow the steps on the big picture to find out how this happens.

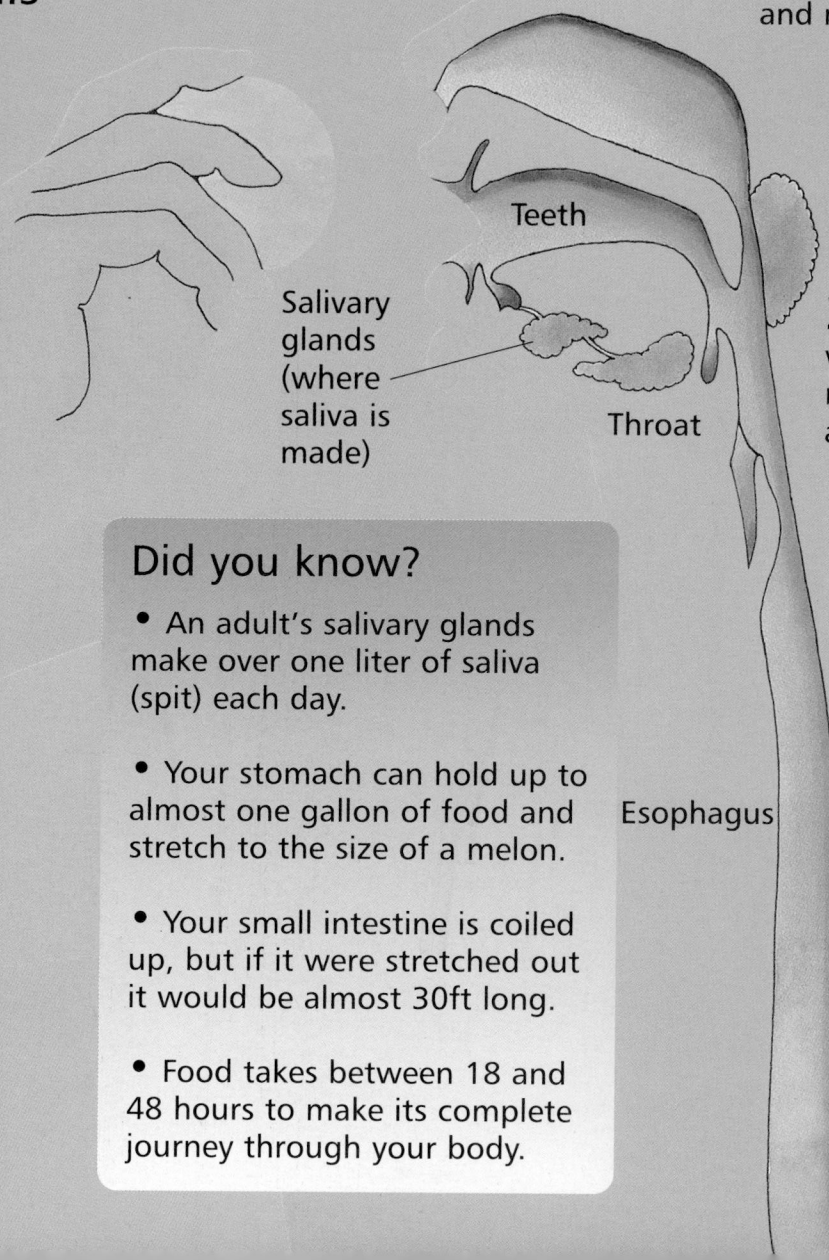

1. When you chew food, your teeth cut and mash it up.

2. Saliva (spit) mixes with the food, making it soft, mushy and easy to swallow.

3. When you swallow, food is forced down your throat into a tube called the esophagus.

4. Muscles in your esophagus squeeze the food down into your stomach.

Did you know?

- An adult's salivary glands make over one liter of saliva (spit) each day.
- Your stomach can hold up to almost one gallon of food and stretch to the size of a melon.
- Your small intestine is coiled up, but if it were stretched out it would be almost 30ft long.
- Food takes between 18 and 48 hours to make its complete journey through your body.

Internet link

For a link to a website where you can find out more amazing facts about your digestive system, go to **www.usborne-quicklinks.com**

Food for your cells

After food has been broken down into chemicals, it is carried all around your body in your blood. Some food is used to give your cells the energy they need to work – for example, to make muscles move. Some food is used to build new cells and repair injuries.

If you eat more food than you need, your body stores it as fat. This is why you get fatter if you eat a lot and don't exercise much.

Waste

Most food contains parts that can't be digested, such as seeds and fruit skin. They go into your large intestine and collect into lumps, which end up in the toilet.

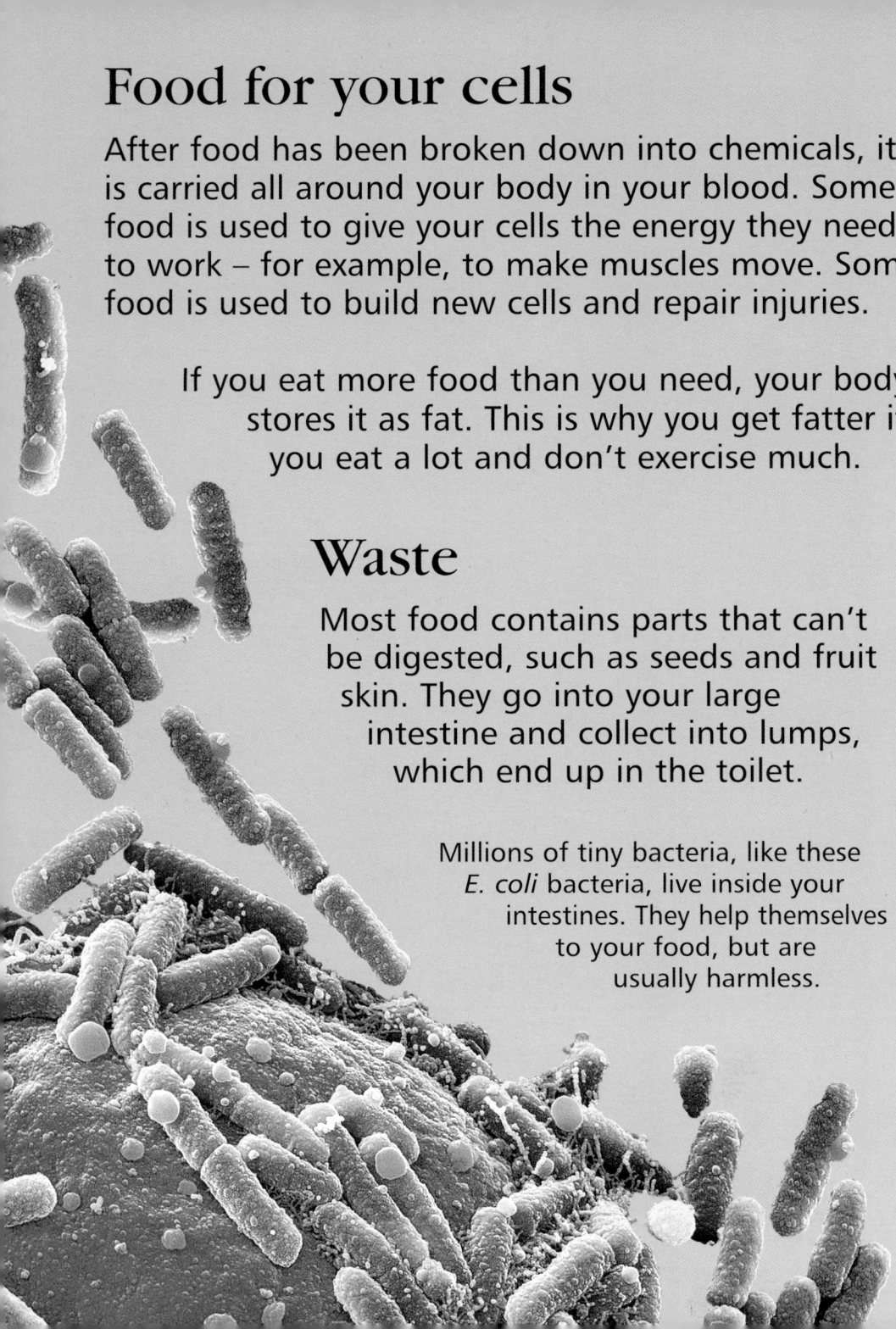

Millions of tiny bacteria, like these *E. coli* bacteria, live inside your intestines. They help themselves to your food, but are usually harmless.

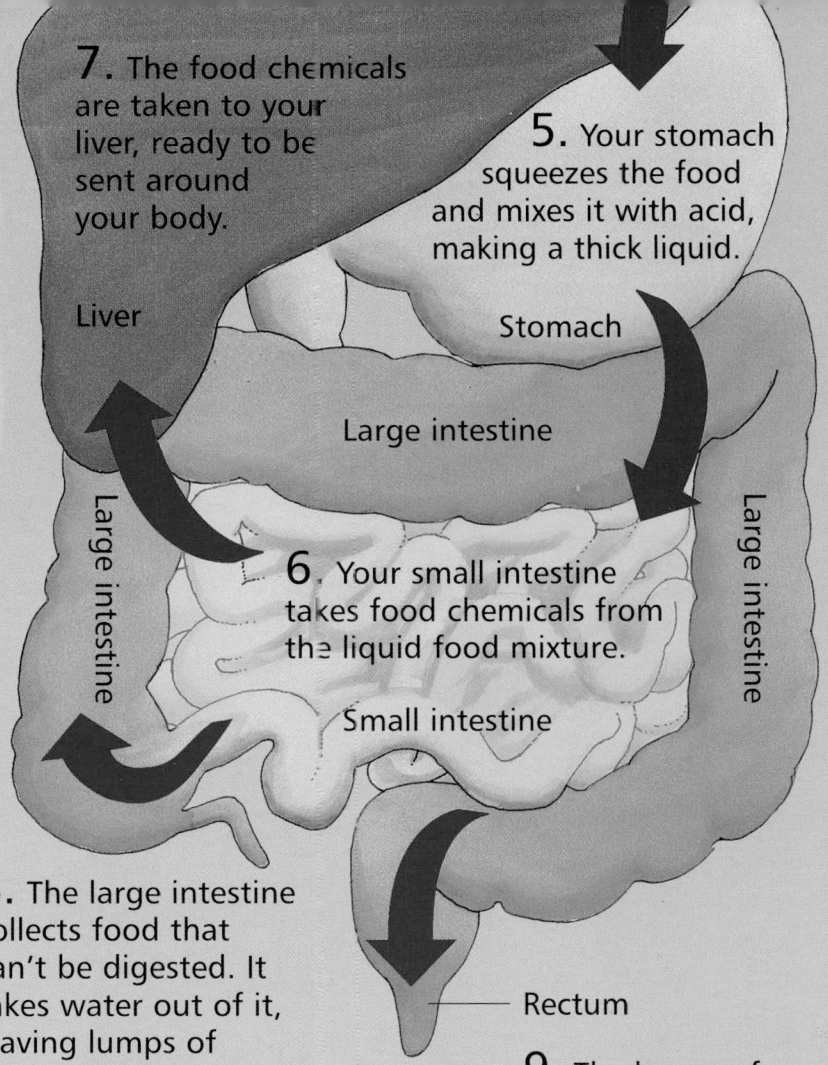

5. Your stomach squeezes the food and mixes it with acid, making a thick liquid.

6. Your small intestine takes food chemicals from the liquid food mixture.

7. The food chemicals are taken to your liver, ready to be sent around your body.

8. The large intestine collects food that can't be digested. It takes water out of it, leaving lumps of waste called feces.

9. The lumps of waste from your large intestine are squeezed out of your rectum when you go to the bathroom.

Your brain and senses

Your brain controls your body. Your five senses – sight, hearing, touch, taste and smell – tell your brain what's going on around you, so it can make decisions.

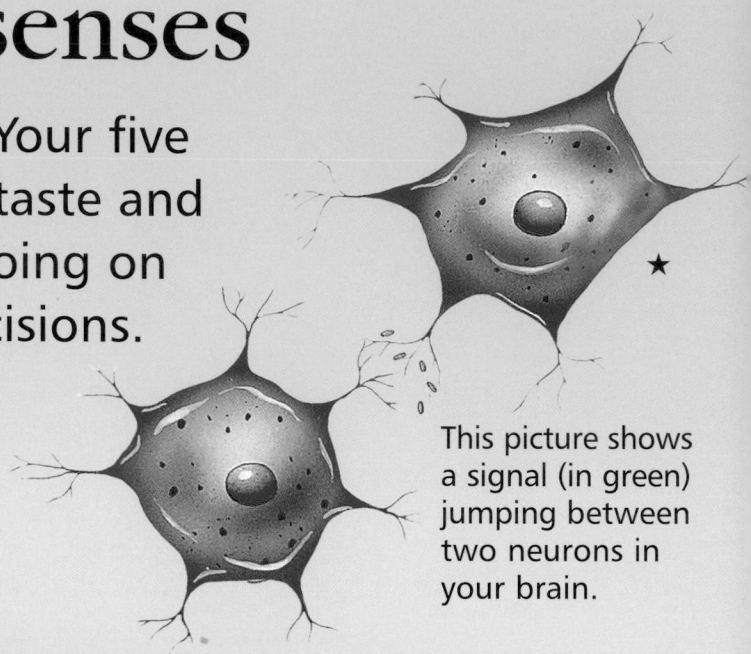

This picture shows a signal (in green) jumping between two neurons in your brain.

Brain bundle

Your brain is made of a big bundle of cells called neurons. When you think, your neurons are passing signals to each other. Neurons also link your brain to your sense organs and to other parts of your body.

This scan of a person's head shows the brain inside the skull.

The skull, shown here in blue, protects your brain.

The brain is this blue and yellow area. The yellow lines are folds in the brain's surface.

The brain stem links your brain to your spinal cord and so to the rest of your body.

Seeing things

You see things because light bounces off them and goes into your eyes. Your eyes collect the light patterns and turn them into signals your brain can understand.

1. Light bounces off an object.

2. The light enters your pupil, which is the black dot in the middle of your eye.

3. Patterns of light hit your retina, an area of light-sensitive cells on the inside of your eye.

4. The optic nerve (made of neurons) carries signals to your brain.

Internet link

For a link to a website where you can find some amazing facts about senses, go to **www.usborne-quicklinks.com**

How you hear

Sounds make tiny particles in the air vibrate (move to and fro). You hear when these vibrating particles hit your ears. The vibrations are turned into signals that are sent to your brain.

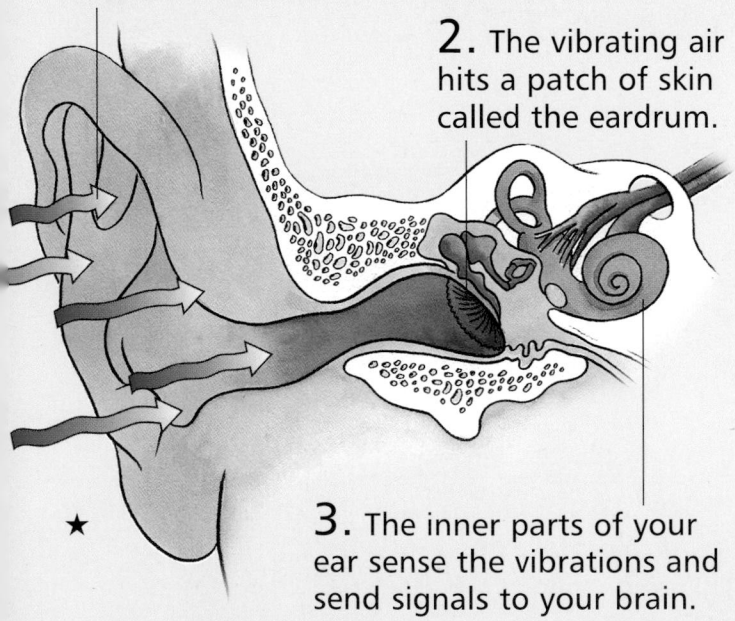

1. Sounds make vibrations travel through the air.

2. The vibrating air hits a patch of skin called the eardrum.

3. The inner parts of your ear sense the vibrations and send signals to your brain.

Taste and smell

Sensitive spots called taste buds on your tongue can detect a few simple tastes. Sensitive cells in your nose detect different smells, and also help you tell the difference between flavors.

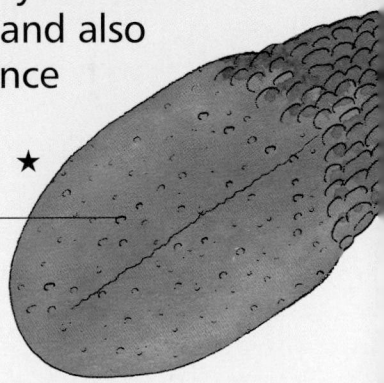

Tiny pink bumps on your tongue have taste buds in them. The bumps are easier to see after a drink of milk.

Touch

There are millions of sensitive nerve endings in your skin. They can feel heat, cold, pressure and pain.

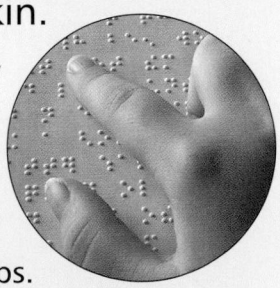

Some blind people use their fingers to read Braille writing, which is made up of tiny bumps.

Babies

Babies come from inside their mothers. After growing there for about nine months, they are big enough to live in the outside world.

This unborn baby has been growing inside its mother for eight weeks.

Making a baby

To make a baby you need a grown-up man and a grown-up woman. The woman has little eggs inside her body. The man makes tiny swimming cells called sperm inside his body.

The sperm swim into the woman's body. When one sperm joins up with an egg, a baby starts to grow.

Inside the mother

The baby grows inside the mother's womb. This is filled with a watery liquid which helps keep the baby safe. A tube joins the baby to its mother. It carries oxygen, food and drink from the mother's body to the baby.

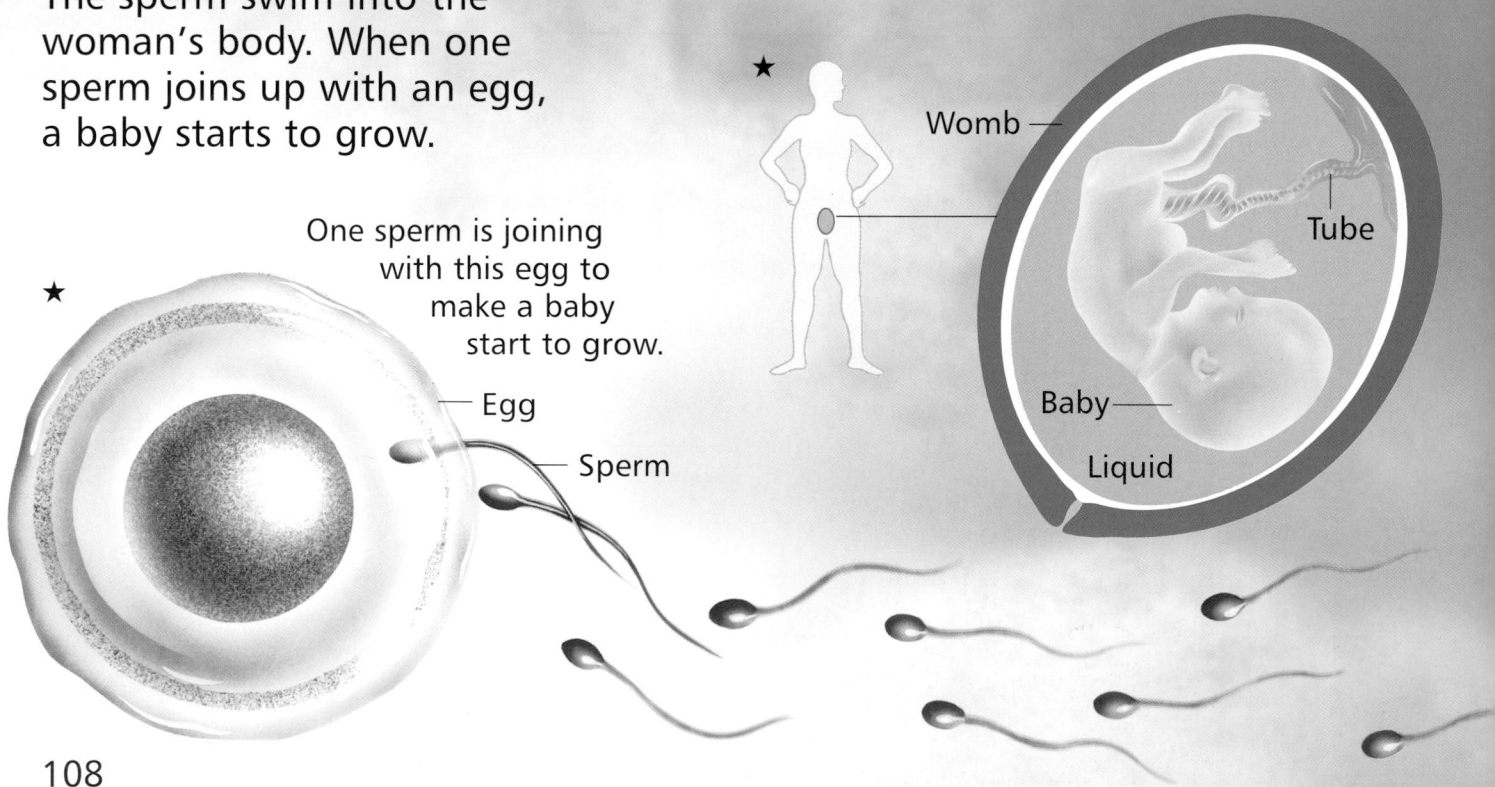

One sperm is joining with this egg to make a baby start to grow.

Growing and moving

After about four months, the baby has grown so much that it makes a bump in its mother's tummy. Sometimes, the mother can feel the baby kicking and wiggling inside her.

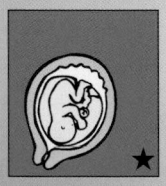

Unborn baby at four months

Unborn baby at six months

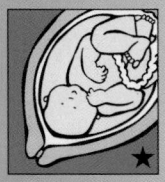

At nine months, the baby is ready to be born.

Internet link

For a link to a website where you can watch a short movie explaining where babies come from, then try a quiz, go to **www.usborne-quicklinks.com**

This baby boy is four days old.

Being born

When the baby is ready to be born, the mother's womb starts to squeeze. The baby comes out of an opening between the mother's legs. It can take many hours for the baby to be born. It makes the mother tired.

Like Mom or Dad?

The baby may look like its father, its mother, or a mixture of both. Who it looks like depends on its genes. These are instructions in the baby's cells that tell the body how to grow. A baby's genes come from the father's sperm and the mother's egg.

Each sperm has half the genes needed to make a baby. The rest of the genes come from the mother's egg.

Staying healthy

When your body isn't working properly, you might feel ill. There are lots of ways to take care of yourself and help your body stay healthy.

Eating well

You need to eat different types of food to stay healthy. The picture below is a guide to how much of each type of food you should eat every day.

Keeping clean

Keeping clean helps to stop harmful germs from building up on and in your body and making you ill. Washing your hands after using the restroom and before eating helps stop germs from spreading. Brushing your teeth helps get rid of the germs that make holes in your teeth.

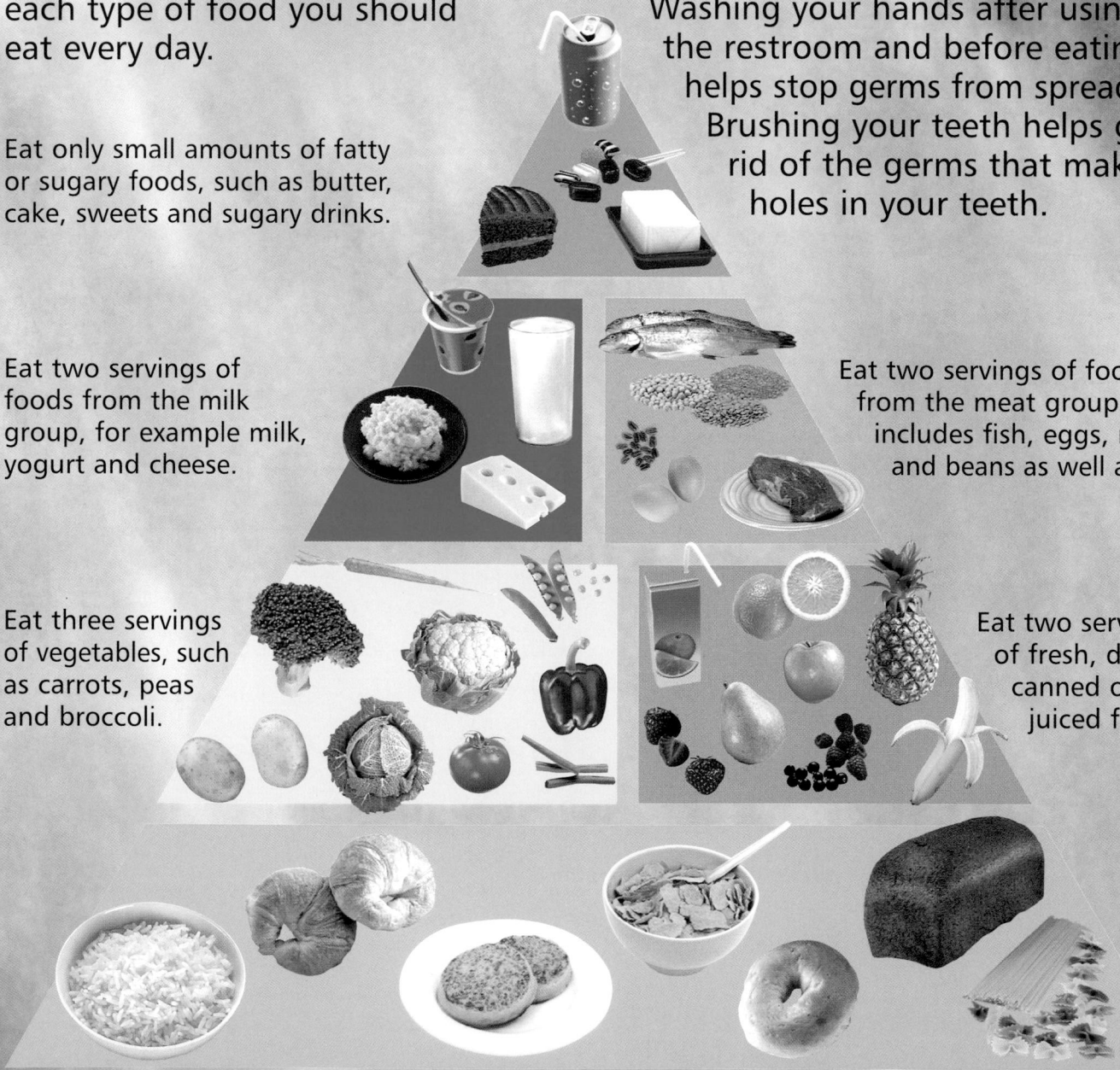

Eat only small amounts of fatty or sugary foods, such as butter, cake, sweets and sugary drinks.

Eat two servings of foods from the milk group, for example milk, yogurt and cheese.

Eat two servings of foods from the meat group. This includes fish, eggs, nuts and beans as well as meat.

Eat three servings of vegetables, such as carrots, peas and broccoli.

Eat two servings of fresh, dried, canned or juiced fruit.

Eat six servings from the grain group each day. This group includes bread, pasta, rice and cereals.

Keeping fit

Exercising is an important way of taking care of your body, and can be great fun too. Different types of exercise can help your body in different ways.

Jogging and skipping strengthen your heart and lungs, so you can be active for longer.

Canoeing and rowing make your muscles stronger so they work better without straining.

Gymnastics and dancing help you to bend and stretch more easily, and keep you from getting stiff.

Swimming is a good way to exercise and keep your body healthy.

Sleeping

It is very important to get enough sleep. While you are asleep, your body tissues have the chance to grow and repair themselves. Children need more sleep than adults because there is more growing to do.

Internet link

For a link to a website where you can find out how to stay healthy and safe, go to **www.usborne-quicklinks.com**

Doctors and medicine

When you are ill, you might visit a doctor. A doctor's job is to find out what is wrong and tell you what to do to feel better. Doctors also give people advice on how to stay healthy.

Finding out

The doctor asks how you are feeling and checks your body for signs of illness. You may need to have some tests done to find out what is wrong.

X-rays are used to take pictures of the bones inside your body. This picture shows a broken arm.

Making it better

The pictures below show several ways the doctor might help you get better. Sometimes she may just tell you to rest a lot or change what you eat.

You may have to take medicine, either by drinking it in a liquid or by taking some pills.

A doctor may put a needle into your body to give you medicine. This is an injection.

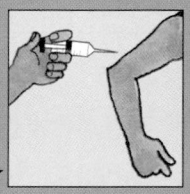

A broken bone may need a plaster cast. This holds the broken ends together so that the bone mends straight, not crooked.

Internet link

For a link to a website where you can find out what medicines are and how they work, go to **www.usborne-quicklinks.com**

History

Dinosaur world

There were animals on Earth long before there were any people. Different kinds of animals lived at different times. At one time, the biggest and fastest animals on Earth were the dinosaurs.

There were many kinds of dinosaurs. Here you can see one of the biggest and one of the smallest compared with a person.

★

What were dinosaurs?

Dinosaurs belonged to a group of animals called reptiles (see page 70). All reptiles have scaly skin. Birds also have some scaly skin, and experts think they are probably a kind of dinosaur too.

All dinosaurs lived on land. Some hunted other animals for food, but many of them ate plants. Most dinosaurs died out 65 million years ago, long before the first people appeared. Only the birds survived.

Internet link

For a link to a website where you can explore the world of the dinosaurs, go to **www.usborne-quicklinks.com**

Baby dinosaurs grew inside eggs laid by their mothers. These babies have just broken out of their eggs. This is called hatching.

Sea and sky

At the time of the dinosaurs, there were also lots of flying reptiles in the sky. They were called pterosaurs (say "terra-sors"). Other huge reptiles swam in the sea.

Diplodocus was a huge, plant-eating dinosaur. It was longer than two buses placed end to end.

This is Triceratops (say "try-ser-a-tops"). It had horns for fighting off attackers.

This sea reptile is called an ichthyosaur (say "ick-thee-oh-sor"). It was a powerful swimmer.

Pterosaurs had big, leathery wings. This is a pterosaur called Pteranodon (say "ter-ran-oh-don").

Tyrannosaurus rex was taller than an elephant.

This dinosaur had long, sharp teeth for tearing up meat.

This fierce dinosaur is called Tyrannosaurus rex (say "tie-ran-oh-saw-russ rex"). It was a meat-eater.

Claws for holding onto food

20,000 to 12,000 years ago

The first people

The first people lived by hunting animals, catching fish and gathering plants to eat. As the seasons changed, they moved around from place to place looking for food.

In the summer, people lived in tents that they made from branches and animal skins.

In the winter, when it was cold, they sometimes sheltered in caves.

Finding food

People spent a lot of time looking for food. They hunted deer, horses, bison and wild pigs for meat. They also ate whatever plants and small animals they could find.

These are some of the things that the first people ate.

Berries

Fish

Snails

Mushrooms

Dandelion leaves

Nuts

Crabs

Birds' eggs

Shellfish

Lizards

These animals were painted on the wall of a cave at Lascaux, in France. Can you guess what kinds of animals they are meant to be? (Answers on page 320.)

Cave paintings

Inside the deepest, darkest caves, people painted pictures of the animals they hunted. They may have thought that the pictures were magical and would help them with their hunting.

Internet link

For a link to a website where you can see lots more cave paintings, go to **www.usborne-quicklinks.com**

Stone tools

The first people used tools made from a kind of stone called flint. They used spears tipped with a sharp, flint point for hunting. They also made flint axes and knives for cutting up meat.

Later, people made arrows with flint tips like this.

The first farmers

Farming began when people learned how to plant seeds to grow food. They also tamed animals, such as sheep and cows. This meant that people could stay in one place, instead of moving around to find food.

This clay pot was made by early farmers in Turkey.

Growing food

Around 12,000 years ago, people in the Middle East began growing wheat and barley. They ground the grain into flour for making bread.

These are wheat plants. You can see the grains at the top of each stalk.

Making things

Farmers didn't need to spend all day looking for food, so they had time to learn new things. They made clay pots for storing and cooking food. They also learned how to make cloth by spinning and weaving wool.

This is part of a farming village in the Middle East. It has a wall around it to keep out wild animals.

This man is offering gifts to a statue of the village goddess.

New tools

The first farmers made tools from stone, bone and wood. Later, people learned how to make things from metal. The first metal tools were made of copper.

Ancient Egypt

The Ancient Egyptians were farmers who lived along the banks of the Nile. They used water from the river to help them grow food. The Egyptians were ruled by a powerful king called a pharaoh.

A gold mask from the tomb of the pharaoh Tutankhamun

Internet link

For a link to a website where you can explore inside the Great Pyramid, go to **www.usborne-quicklinks.com**

Pharaohs and pyramids

Some pharaohs were buried inside huge, stone pyramids on the edge of the desert. The pharaoh's body was placed in a secret room in the middle of the pyramid. There are still about 80 pyramids in Egypt, and each one took at least 20 years to build.

These are the pyramids at Giza. Three pharaohs and their wives were buried here.

A pharaoh called Menkaure was buried inside this pyramid.

This is the Great Pyramid. It is made up of over two million stone blocks.

Menkaure's three wives were buried in these smaller pyramids.

Mummies and coffins

The Egyptians tried to stop dead people's bodies from rotting away. They thought this would allow them to have another life after they died. They took out the person's insides, dried the body out and wrapped it in bandages. Bodies kept like this are called mummies.

The insides of the body were kept in jars like these.

Mummies were put inside painted wooden coffins like this one.

Picture writing

Egyptian writing was made up of lots of small pictures, or symbols, called hieroglyphs (say "hi-ro-gliffs"). There were over 700 different symbols. Here are just a few of them:

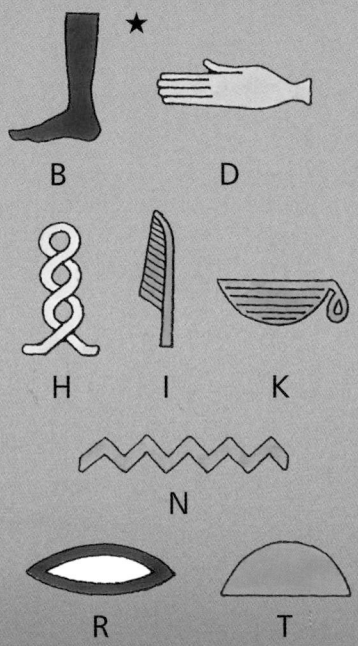

See if you can spot the symbols for "I", "N", "R" and "T" in this Egyptian painting.

Ancient Greece

In ancient times, Greece wasn't all one country like it is today. Instead, each city had its own rulers. The greatest of these cities was Athens, which was famous for its learning and plays.

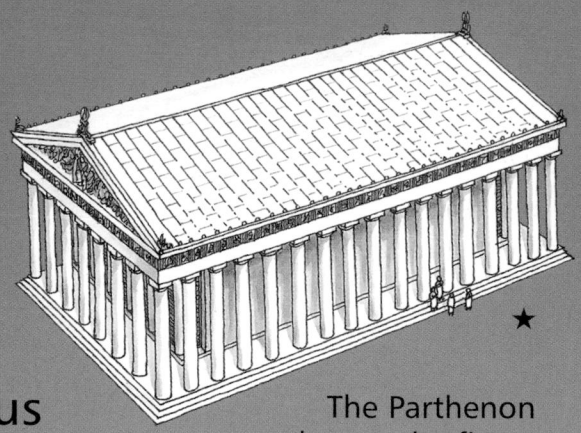

The Parthenon temple was the finest building in Athens.

Big buildings

In every city in Greece, people built huge, stone temples for their gods and goddesses. Greek temples usually had a triangular-shaped roof held up by rows of tall pillars.

These are the ruins of the Parthenon temple. It stands on a hill high above the city of Athens.

Spot the pillar

The Greeks used three types of pillars in their buildings. Can you spot which type they used for the Parthenon?

A Doric pillar

An Ionic pillar

A Corinthian pillar

The walls and pillars are made from a stone called marble.

This is how big people look compared with the Parthenon.

The first plays

The first great plays in the world were written by the Ancient Greeks. They believed that performing the plays would please their gods. People put the plays on at festivals which lasted several days. There was a prize for the best play.

★ Here you can see Greek actors putting on a play at a festival.

Musicians

Actors playing gods can fly through the air on this crane.

Scenery

Stage

The actors wear masks and costumes to show which parts they are playing.

These actors are called the chorus. They perform songs and dances to explain what is happening on the stage.

Internet link

For a link to a website where you can visit the Ancient Olympic Games and watch a Greek play, go to **www.usborne-quicklinks.com**

The Olympic Games

The Greeks loved athletics and they organized competitions all over the country. The most famous was the Olympic Games, which took place every four years at Olympia.

This Greek painting shows an athlete training for the long jump.

Ancient Rome

About 2,000 years ago, Rome was one of the biggest cities in the world. At that time, the Romans ruled all the lands around the Mediterranean Sea. These lands were called the Roman Empire.

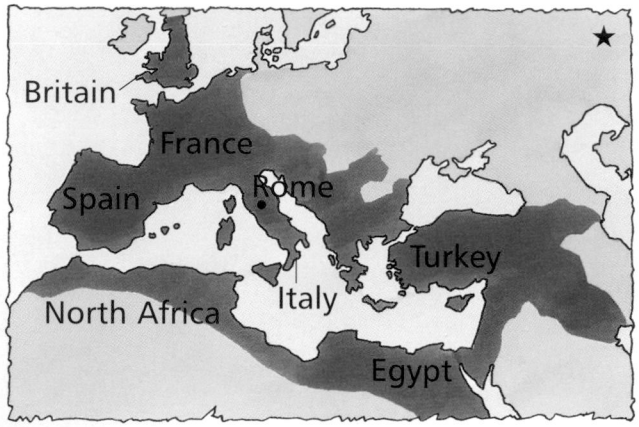

On this map, all the lands shown in red were once part of the Roman Empire.

Roman soldiers wore iron helmets and carried wooden shields.

The Roman army

The Romans had a huge army of well-trained soldiers. They used their army to fight for new lands and to protect the Empire from enemies. Most soldiers fought on foot using a spear, a sword and a dagger.

Roman soldiers built long, straight roads linking towns all over the Empire.

Internet link

For a link to a website with information, activities and fun facts about the Romans, go to **www.usborne-quicklinks.com**

Home comforts

In Rome, rich people lived in comfortable houses with large gardens. Some houses even had toilets, running water and a kind of central heating.

This is a Roman house. Parts of it have been cut away so you can see inside.

Bedroom

Study

Hall

Garden

Dining room

Kitchen

Pool (for catching rainwater)

The family has rented this room to a shopkeeper.

On the floors, there were pictures called mosaics. They were made from lots of small stones.

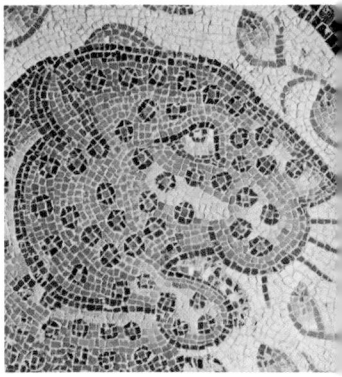

Roman pastimes

The Romans loved watching chariot races. These took place at a huge racetrack called a circus.

People also enjoyed watching gladiators fight each other. Gladiators often died in these brutal fights.

Most Romans went to the public baths every day to relax, exercise, meet friends – and to get themselves clean.

Viking raiders

The Vikings came from Norway, Sweden and Denmark. They were great sailors and traders, but they were also fierce warriors. They attacked and robbed villages all around the coasts of Europe.

This man is dressed as a Viking warrior.

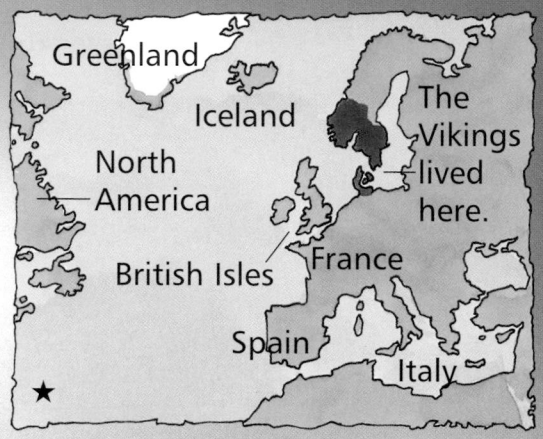

The Vikings sailed to all these places.

A Viking longship

Viking ships

The Vikings made their attacks in fast boats, called longships. The ships were strong enough to sail across rough seas. They weren't very deep, so they could also travel up shallow rivers.

This carved dragon's head is meant to scare enemies.

The Vikings in this ship are on their way to launch a raid.

There's a big oar at the back for steering the ship.

Viking homes

Viking chiefs lived in large homes called longhouses. Each longhouse had only one big room, where everyone ate, worked and slept. There weren't any windows, so it must have been very dark inside.

Internet link

For a link to a website where you can have fun spotting the things that don't belong in a Viking house, go to **www.usborne-quicklinks.com**

Viking crafts

The Vikings made beautiful brooches, arm rings and belt buckles from gold, silver and bronze. They also carved spoons and combs from pieces of animal bone and horn.

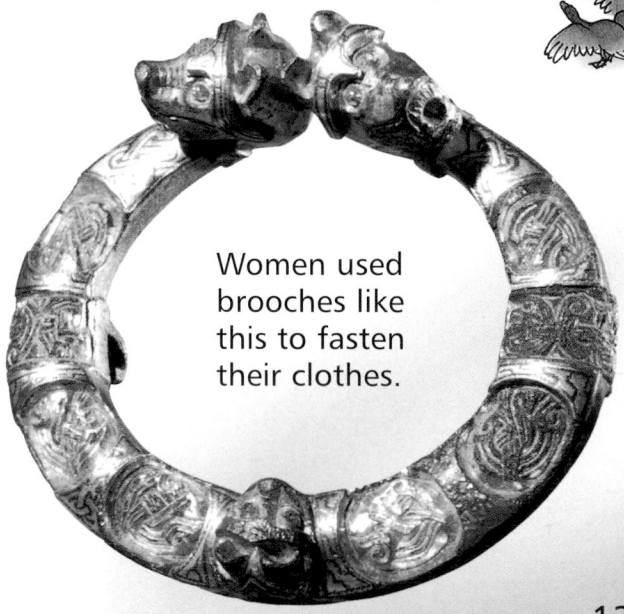

Women used brooches like this to fasten their clothes.

Living in a castle

In the Middle Ages (between 500 and 1,000 years ago) kings and lords in Europe often fought each other for land. They built castles with strong, stone walls to protect themselves from their enemies.

Inside a castle

A lord lived in a castle with his family and all his soldiers and servants. It must have been very cold inside, because the first castles had no glass in the windows.

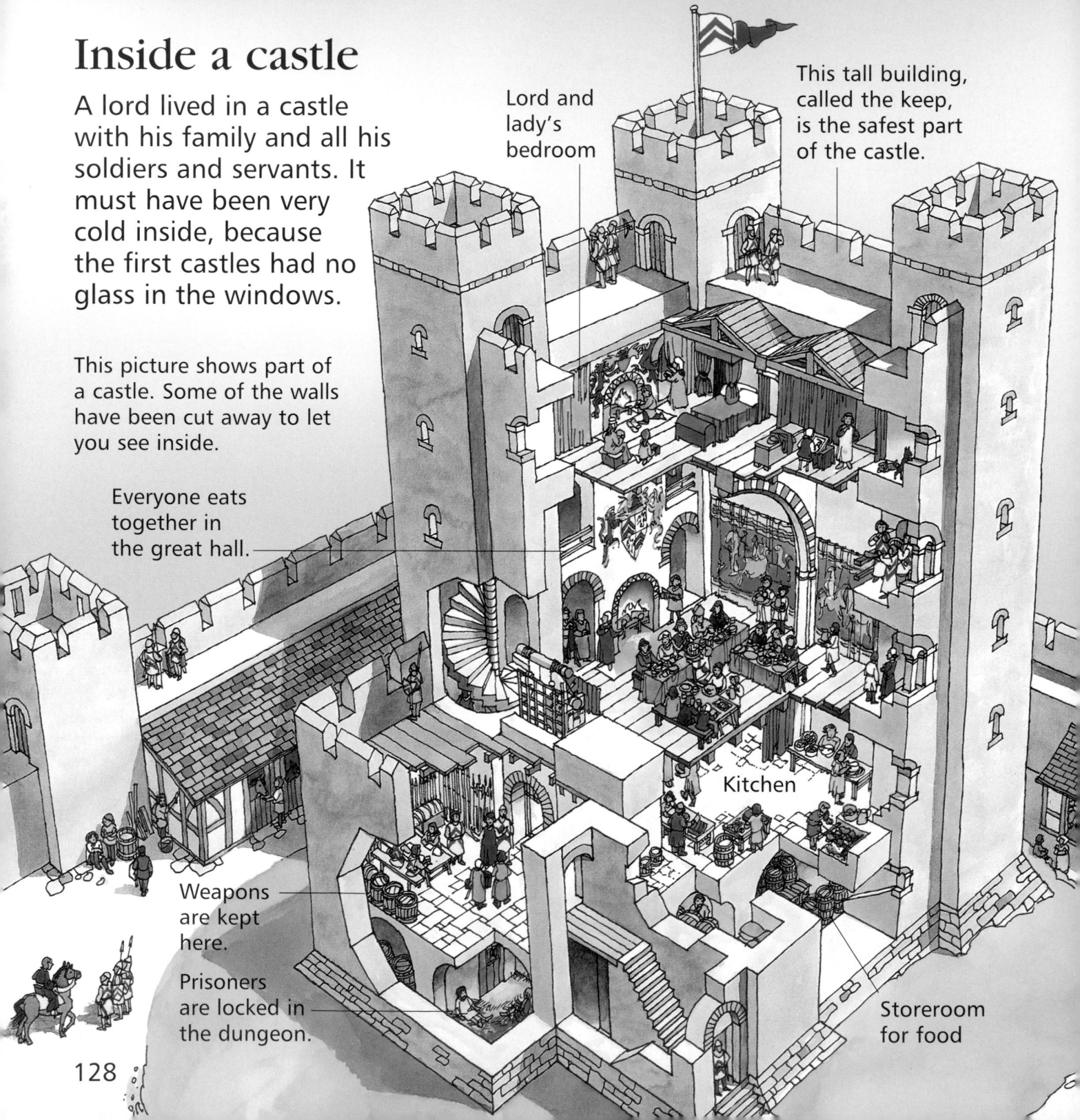

This picture shows part of a castle. Some of the walls have been cut away to let you see inside.

Noble knights

Knights were soldiers who fought on horseback. Only boys from noble families could train to be knights. A good knight had to be strong and brave. He also had to promise to fight only for his lord.

This picture from the Middle Ages shows two knights taking part in a contest called a joust.

Painted shield

Chainmail shirt made from lots of metal rings

This knight is being knocked off his horse.

This long spear is called a lance.

Internet link

For a link to a website where you can explore a castle and meet the people who lived there, go to **www.usborne-quicklinks.com**

Fun feasts

Feasts took place in the great hall of the castle. The guests ate lots of rich food, such as roast swan, spiced beef, squirrel stew and sugared mackerel. For dessert, there might be apple pie or honey cakes.

This wall keeps enemies out.

Guards look out for enemies.

A jester told jokes to make the guests laugh.

Musicians, called minstrels, played their instruments and sang.

These people are acting out an old Inca festival at the city of Cuzco, in Peru.

550 years ago

Inca cities

The Incas lived in the Andes mountains of South America. Most of them were farmers, but they were also great builders. They were ruled by an emperor called the Inca.

Cities of stone

The Incas built huge cities from massive blocks of stone. They used stone hammers to shape the blocks so they would fit together perfectly. Each city had temples, palaces, and observatories for watching the stars.

Machu Picchu is 7,700ft above sea level.

This is the ruined Inca city of Machu Picchu, high up in the Andes mountains.

On the road

The Incas built stone roads to link their cities together. Teams of runners used the roads to carry messages from city to city. The roads were also used by soldiers, traders, and farmers taking food to market.

Llamas were used for carrying heavy loads.

The Incas made bridges out of reeds, so people could get across valleys and rivers.

Food and drink

Inca farmers grew corn, potatoes, peppers, beans, tomatoes and squash. They kept guinea pigs for their meat. Women made a drink called chicha by spitting chewed fruit into warm water.

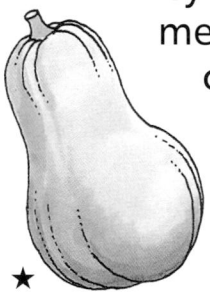

Squash

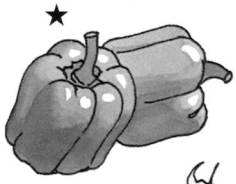

Peppers

Tomatoes

Beans

Corn

Farmers grew food on wide ledges, called terraces, that they dug into the mountainside.

Internet link

For a link to a website where you can explore the city of Machu Picchu, go to **www.usborne-quicklinks.com**

The Chinese invented gunpowder. They used it for making fireworks, as well as weapons.

500 years ago

Ming China

Around 500 years ago, China was ruled by a family of emperors called the Ming. The Ming emperors made Beijing their capital city. They lived there in a huge palace, called the Forbidden City.

The Forbidden City

The Forbidden City was made up of great halls, temples, courtyards and gardens. It was surrounded by a wall and a moat (a big ditch filled with water). Only the emperor's family and servants were allowed inside.

In this picture, you can see a royal procession outside the Hall of Supreme Harmony in the Forbidden City.

The buildings are made of wood and bricks glued together with steamed rice and egg whites.

The palace has 9,999 rooms and is as big as 74 soccer fields. It took a million workers 14 years to build.

Officials and soldiers

Made in China

In Ming times, the Chinese made many beautiful things. They are especially famous for making a kind of fine pottery, called porcelain. They also made a very expensive kind of cloth, called silk.

Porcelain jar

This wooden box is covered with a shiny varnish called lacquer.

This picture was painted on silk. It shows two Chinese officials.

Time for tea

The Chinese started growing tea about 1,700 years ago. At first, they used the leaves to make medicines. Later, tea became a very popular drink. The Chinese made their tea in teapots and drank it out of little bowls.

Chinese workers picking leaves from tea plants

Internet link

For a link to a website where you can look around the Forbidden City, go to **www.usborne-quicklinks.com**

The emperor rides in a coach pulled by elephants.

500 to 400 years ago

Tudor England

The Tudors were a family of kings and queens. They ruled England for over a hundred years and made the country rich and powerful.

These coins came from the wreck of a Tudor warship.

This is a painting of King Henry VIII. He divorced two of his wives and had two of them beheaded.

Henry VIII

Henry VIII became king when he was 17 years old. He married six times, but only had three children. Henry also had an argument with the Pope (the head of the Church in Europe) and set up his own English Church.

Internet link

For a link to a website where you can find out more about Henry and his wives, go to **www.usborne-quicklinks.com**

Explorers and pirates

In Tudor times, many explorers sailed to North and South America. They brought back new foods, such as potatoes. Some English explorers were pirates too. They stole treasure from Spanish ships on the coast of America.

Elizabeth I

Queen Elizabeth was the last and greatest of the Tudors. She ruled England for 45 years. During her reign, England fought off an attack by a group of Spanish ships, called the Spanish Armada.

This is a portrait of Elizabeth. She loved clothes and owned 260 different dresses.

Plays and playhouses

In Elizabeth's time, people loved going to see plays. In London, actors performed in playhouses such as the Globe. The most popular plays were written by William Shakespeare.

Here you can see actors performing a play at the Globe.

Living in America

In 1620, a group of English people, called the Pilgrims, went to settle in North America. The Pilgrims were very religious. They wanted to be free to worship God in a way they weren't allowed to in England.

The Pilgrims sailed to America on a ship called the *Mayflower*. This is a copy of their ship.

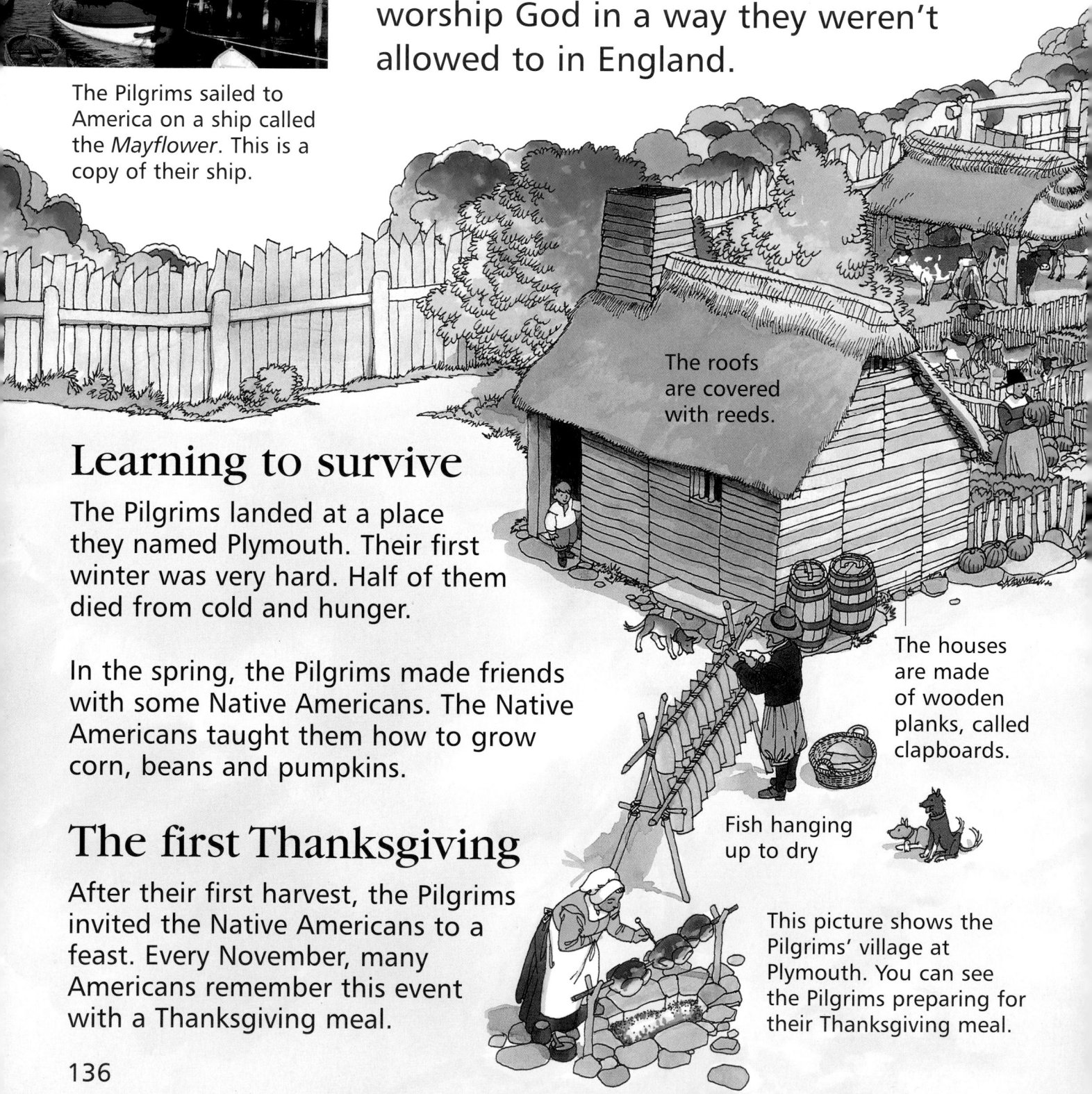

Learning to survive

The Pilgrims landed at a place they named Plymouth. Their first winter was very hard. Half of them died from cold and hunger.

In the spring, the Pilgrims made friends with some Native Americans. The Native Americans taught them how to grow corn, beans and pumpkins.

The first Thanksgiving

After their first harvest, the Pilgrims invited the Native Americans to a feast. Every November, many Americans remember this event with a Thanksgiving meal.

This picture shows the Pilgrims' village at Plymouth. You can see the Pilgrims preparing for their Thanksgiving meal.

Internet link

For a link to a website where you can explore the Pilgrims' village, go to **www.usborne-quicklinks.com**

A new country

More and more Europeans came to settle in North America. At first, all the settlers who lived on the east coast of America were ruled by Britain.

In 1783, the settlers won a war against the British and began ruling themselves. They called their new country the United States of America.

This is George Washington, the first President of the United States of America.

French finery

Around 350 years ago, the most powerful ruler in Europe was King Louis XIV of France. Louis became king when he was just five years old and he reigned for 72 years. He was fabulously rich and lived a life of luxury.

This is the Hall of Mirrors in the palace at Versailles. One of its walls is covered with 17 huge, arched mirrors.

The king's palace

Louis built a magnificent new palace at Versailles, near Paris. He filled it with priceless furniture, paintings and statues. Louis lived there with his family, his advisers, and over 1,500 servants. Lots of rich French nobles lived in the palace too.

Internet link

For a link to a website where you can look inside the palace of Versailles and explore the gardens, go to **www.usborne-quicklinks.com**

Inside the palace, there are 700 rooms and 67 staircases.

This is Louis XIV's palace at Versailles. It took 47 years to build.

The fountains used so much water they could only be turned on for three hours at a time.

French fashions

In the 1700s, rich nobles at Versailles wore the most fashionable clothes in Europe. Their clothes were made of the finest silk and were decorated with beautiful embroidery, jewels, lace and ribbons.

Here you can see what rich French nobles were wearing in the 1770s.

Lace cravat

Women had very tall hairstyles, up to 3ft high.

Silk breeches

Silk stockings

Men wore wigs made of human, horse or goat hair.

Some skirts were so wide that women had to go through doors sideways.

Rich and poor

In 1789, the poorer people of France rebelled against the rich. They killed the king, the queen and hundreds of nobles, and began ruling the country themselves. This was called the French Revolution.

The American West

At first, Europeans who settled in North America stayed near the east coast. Then, explorers found ways to the West. Later, families began to cross America looking for land to farm.

Most families started their journey in Missouri, in the United States. These are the routes they took to the West.

This is Chimney Rock, one of the landmarks on the Oregon Trail.

On the move

Families who went to live in the West were called pioneers. They made the long, hard journey in wagons pulled by oxen. Sometimes, they were attacked by Native Americans.

The pioneers have to cross mountains, rivers and deserts.

Here you can see some pioneers on their way to the West.

The wagons are covered with cloth stretched over wooden hoops.

Inside the wagons, there is plenty of food for the journey, as well as farm tools and furniture.

Going for gold

In 1848, gold was discovered in California, on the west coast. Thousands of people rushed there hoping to get rich. This was called the Gold Rush.

These men are looking for gold at the bottom of a stream.

★

Internet link

For a link to a website where you can see more landmarks along the Oregon Trail, go to **www.usborne-quicklinks.com**

Cowboys and cattle

The grassy plains of the West were good for farming cattle. Men called cowboys herded the cattle across the plains. They loaded them onto trains to be sold in the East.

This is what a cowboy wore.

★

Fighting for land

As farmers moved west, they took land away from the Native Americans who lived there. The Native Americans fought hard to keep their land, but they lost most of it in the end.

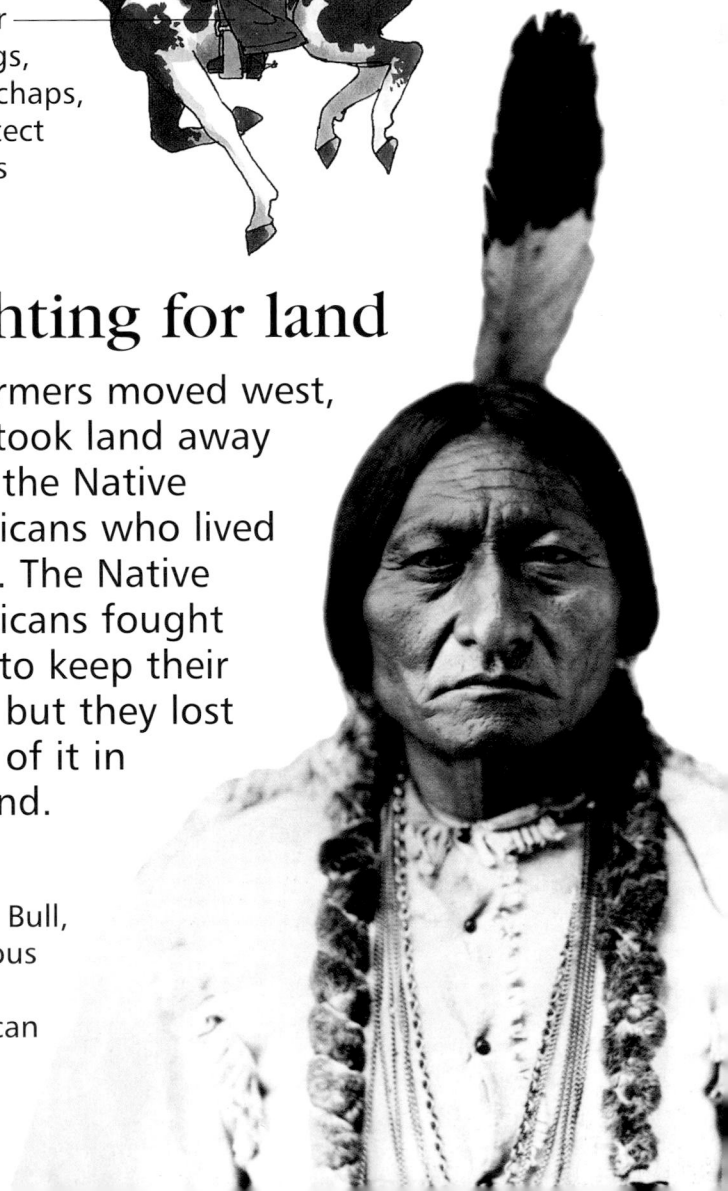

This is Sitting Bull, a famous Native American chief.

Victorian times

The time when Queen Victoria ruled Britain is called the Victorian period. By then, there were lots of factories in Britain. Towns grew bigger, as people moved there to work in the factories.

Steam trains like this carried passengers and goods cheaply from town to town.

Living in a town

Rich people owned grand houses at the edge of the town. Factory workers lived in rows of tiny houses, with no running water or inside toilets. The air was full of smoke from the factories, and the streets were filthy. People often got sick and died.

Internet link

For a link to a website where you can travel back in time and visit a Victorian house, go to **www.usborne-quicklinks.com**

Here you can see part of a Victorian town. Can you spot a policeman catching a thief in the street?

Up to 20 people live in each tiny house.

People burn coal to keep warm. Chimneys let out the smoke.

People work long hours in cloth factories like this one.

The streets are lit by gas lamps.

Victorian children

Boys from rich families went to school. Girls were usually taught at home.

Children from poor families had to work in coal mines and factories.

Homeless children were sent to live in a harsh place called a workhouse.

Victorian fashions

In the 1850s and 1860s, women wore dresses with very wide skirts. The skirts were held out by a circular frame called a crinoline. To make their waists look smaller, women wore a kind of tight underwear called a corset.

Victorian women's underwear looked like this.

Bonnet tied under the chin

This picture from a Victorian fashion magazine shows what women were wearing in 1859.

The First World War

The First World War began in 1914. On one side were Britain, France, Belgium and Russia, who were called the Allies. On the other side were Germany and Austria. Later, many other countries joined in too.

The poppies that grew on the battlefields became a symbol for remembering the war.

Internet link

For a link to a website where you can listen to songs from the First World War, go to **www.usborne-quicklinks.com**

In the trenches

A lot of the fighting happened in northern France. Soldiers on both sides dug rows of deep ditches, called trenches, to protect themselves from enemy bullets.

The soldiers lived in the trenches for weeks at a time. During a battle, they climbed out and charged at the enemy. Millions of men died in these terrible battles.

Here you can see some British soldiers in a trench.

The men rest in holes dug into the sides of the trench.

Wooden walkways, called duckboards, stop the soldiers from sinking into the mud.

Officers live in underground shelters, called dug-outs.

The men's feet are always wet and often get sore.

New weapons

Both sides tried new ways of fighting to win the war. The Germans were the first to use poison gas, while the British invented tanks.

German fighter plane

Both sides used planes to spy on enemy trenches and to shoot down enemy aircraft.

Tanks could run over barbed wire and machine guns, but they often broke down.

German submarines, called U-boats, attacked ships on their way to Britain and France.

Soldiers wore masks to protect them from poison gas.

German trench

A soldier called a sentry keeps watch.

Machine gun

Barbed wire

Sandbags

The trenches are full of rats, fleas and lice.

The war ends

In 1917, the United States of America joined the war on the side of the Allies and helped them to win. The war finally ended at 11 o'clock on November 11, 1918. It had killed over 16 million people.

On November 11 every year, many people around the world remember those who have died in wars.

The Second World War

The Second World War started in 1939, when Germany attacked Poland. Later, Japan attacked the United States. Lots of countries joined together to fight the Germans and the Japanese.

There wasn't much to eat during the war. This British poster is telling people to grow their own food.

In Britain, children from big cities were sent away to the countryside to keep them safe from the bombs.

The Blitz

In just a few months, the Germans took over most of western Europe. Then they began bombing cities in Britain. This was called the Blitz. The bombs wrecked buildings and killed thousands of people.

Later in the war, the British dropped bombs on German cities. These are the ruins of the city of Cologne.

Internet link

For a link to a website where you can find out what life was like for children in the Second World War, go to **www.usborne-quicklinks.com**

Pearl Harbor

In 1941, Japanese planes attacked Pearl Harbor, in Hawaii, killing over 2,000 Americans. The United States joined the war, and the fighting spread to the Far East and the Pacific Ocean.

American ships on fire in Pearl Harbor. Many ships and planes were damaged or destroyed.

American soldiers landing on an island in the Pacific Ocean

The Holocaust

The German leader Adolf Hitler wanted to kill all the Jewish people in Europe. During the war, he had six million Jews murdered. This terrible crime is called the Holocaust.

The war ends

Germany and Japan didn't have enough soldiers or weapons to win the war. The Germans were forced to stop fighting in May 1945.

These Russian soldiers are flying their country's flag in Berlin, the capital city of Germany.

In August, the Americans dropped two huge bombs on Japan. The Japanese finally gave up. The war was over, but it had killed more than 50 million people.

The bombs dropped on Japan were a new kind of bomb, called an atom bomb.

The modern world

On this page, you can read about some of the discoveries and inventions that have changed people's lives since the end of the Second World War.

1952 The first passenger jet began flying.

1957 The first nuclear power station began working in the United States.

1958 The microchip was invented. Microchips are an important part of computers.

1961 Yuri Gagarin was the first person to travel into space.

1962 Live TV pictures were sent from the United States to Europe for the first time.

1967 A doctor named Christiaan Barnard carried out the first heart transplant.

1969 Neil Armstrong was the first person to walk on the Moon.

1969 The jumbo jet flew for the first time.

1972 A game called Pong was the first computer game.

1975 The first home computers were sold in the United States.

1976 Concorde began flying. It was the first passenger plane to travel faster than the speed of sound.

1979 The first mobile phones, or cell phones, went on sale in Japan.

1981 The first PC, or personal computer, was made.

1981 The American space shuttle made its first flight.

1982 The first compact discs, or CDs, went on sale.

1982 A patient was given an artificial heart for the first time.

1989 The World Wide Web was invented. The Web allows people to get information from the Internet quickly and easily.

1990 A huge telescope, called the Hubble Space Telescope, was sent into space.

1994 The Channel Tunnel opened between Britain and France.

1997 A sheep called Dolly was the first large animal to be cloned. A cloned animal is an exact copy of another animal.

This is the space rocket that took Neil Armstrong to the Moon in July 1969.

How people live

People around the world

There are more than six billion people living in the world today. No two of us are the same, as nobody looks, thinks or feels exactly the same as anybody else.

Each of the 13.5 million people living in Shanghai, China, is different in the way he or she looks, thinks and feels.

What is a person?

Humans are probably the most intelligent creatures on Earth. We can make things, solve problems and create beautiful works of art. Most scientists believe that it took an extremely long time for us to develop into the amazing people we are today.

The way we look

Everyone looks different from everyone else in the world. For example, some people are taller or shorter than others, with darker or lighter skin or eyes of a particular shape. Even identical twins don't look exactly alike.

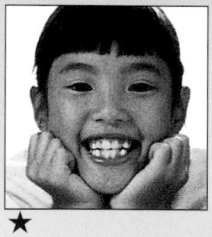

★

★

★

These children have different skin and hair colour and different shaped eyes, noses and mouths.

Internet link

For a link to a website where you can learn about the lives of four children around the world, go to **www.usborne-quicklinks.com**

What we think

People have many different beliefs about the world around them. These beliefs are often called a religion. You can find out more about the religions of the world on pages 178-179.

These Aboriginal boys from Australia are taking part in a ceremony to mark their change into adults. The patterns painted on their skin are believed to help them grow.

What we say

Today, there are at least five thousand languages. Some are used by only a few people. Others, such as Mandarin Chinese, are spoken by many millions.

Six month old babies could learn to speak any language.

What we do

People in each part of the world have their own ways of doing things. These are called traditions and customs. Along with beliefs, they affect how people behave, including what they wear, what they eat and how they celebrate important times in their lives.

For example, the way we greet other people varies from place to place.

In countries such as Germany, people usually shake hands when they meet.

French people often greet each other with several kisses on the cheeks.

In India, people put their hands together and bow their heads to greet each other.

Houses and homes

Homes have many uses. These include being places where we eat, sleep and keep our things. Any type of building, such as a house, a hut or a tent, can be someone's home.

Building homes

In some countries, builders make houses, often using wood, stone or bricks. In other places, people build their own homes. They use materials that are easy to find, such as wood, mud or grass.

These round homes in the Kalahari Desert in Botswana are built from woven sticks covered with mud. The roofs are made from grasses.

Beating the weather

Houses have to be built in a style that protects the people who live in them from the weather.

In hot countries, many houses have shutters to keep out the sun, so the house stays cool inside.

Snow settles on the sloping roof of this Swiss chalet and helps to keep the heat inside the house.

In places where floods often happen, many houses are built on stilts to keep them dry.

What's in a house?

A house has areas where you can sleep, prepare food, eat and relax. In some homes, everything is done in one room, but many houses have a different room for each activity. Most have a bathroom too.

Internet link

For a link to a website where you can be an architect and design your own home, go to **www.usborne-quicklinks.com**

Rain collects in the gutter and flows down the pipe into a drain.

Tiles on the roof keep out the rain.

The attic can be used for storing boxes and other things.

Wooden boards keep out the wind and rain.

Bedroom

Bathroom

The garage is for putting cars in.

Meals are prepared and cooked in the kitchen.

This is the living room where people relax.

These shutters can be closed when it is hot to keep out the sun.

On the move

Some people, who are known as nomads, don't live in one place all the time. They move from place to place, taking their homes with them. They might travel to find work, or to find food and water for their herds of animals.

This family from central Asia travels from one place to another, living in a tent called a yurt.

Cities and towns

A city is a big, busy town where many people live and work. About half of all the people in the world live in a town or city. Many cities have tall buildings because of the shortage of land.

Living together

People living in towns and cities need houses, schools, hospitals and stores. They also need places where they can enjoy themselves, such as parks and theatres. There must be work for people to do, too, so they can afford to live there.

In the middle of a city, there are often large and well-known stores as well as many smaller ones.

Cities have restaurants, museums and theatres where people can enjoy themselves.

As in many cities, these buildings in New York, USA have many floors on top of each other to use less land. Most cities have parks for people to enjoy. This is New York's Central Park.

City problems

Many people like living in a city. There is plenty to do, and stores and schools are nearby. But city life is not always easy. For example, it can sometimes be hard to find a job, or a home that you can afford to live in.

There are often too many cars in cities. They jam the roads and fill the air with fumes.

Sinking city

Around 19 million people live in Mexico City. So much water has been pumped from underground lakes beneath the city to provide for them that now the streets are sinking a little more each year.

Internet link

For a link to a website where you can look at photographs of cities around the world, including London in the UK and Barcelona in Spain, go to **www.usborne-quicklinks.com**

How a country is run

The way a country is run and the people who lead it are very important for the people who live there. The leaders decide what laws are made and how much money can be spent, for example on schools and roads.

Who's in charge?

The people who run a country are called the government. A government that people choose, or vote for, is called a democracy.

If one person or a group of people rules a country without giving anyone a choice, it is called an autocracy.

Bill Clinton was President of the USA from 1993-2001. The President is the head of the government.

In 1994, for the first time, all South African people were allowed to vote for their government. People lined up for hours waiting to vote.

Making a choice

In a democracy, people choose their government in an election.

On election day, adults cast a vote, by putting a mark or a number on a paper by the name of the person they want to support.

Without showing anyone who they voted for, they put their paper into a locked ballot box.

After an election, all the votes on the ballot papers are counted. The person with the most support wins.

Divided power

In 1783, the people of America decided to divide power three ways. America has an elected President. Americans in each state also vote for people to work with the President in Congress. Judges in the Supreme Court make sure their decisions are fair.

This is the White House in Washington, DC, where the US President makes decisions.

Nelson Mandela worked hard to bring democracy to South Africa. In 1994, he was elected President.

Ballot paper

Ballot box

At the top

In the past, many countries were ruled by kings, queens or emperors. When a ruler died, the power to rule was usually passed on to a son or daughter. Today, there are not many really powerful royal families.

This sceptre belongs to the British king or queen. It is a symbol of his or her power.

Internet link

For a link to a website where you can be the US President for a day, go to **www.usborne-quicklinks.com**

Food and cooking

The food people eat and the way they cook is very different around the world. Everyone needs food, but at least 800 million people in the world do not have enough.

A healthy diet can include brown bread, nuts and eggs, and plenty of fruit and vegetables.

Growing and buying

The main food of a country is called its staple food. Rice is the staple food of about half the world. Other staples include corn, wheat and potatoes. Some people grow their own staple foods. Others buy them in stores and markets, along with many other foods such as fruit and vegetables.

A vegetable market in Hong Kong, China

How people cook

Cooking food can make it taste better and keep longer. It helps kill germs that might make you ill too. Cooked food is also easier to digest (see page 104). There are many different ways of cooking.

This Indian woman is cooking meat in a clay oven called a tandoor.

In China, food is often cooked in round metal pans, called woks.

Internet link

For a link to a website where you can find out more about food and do some fun activities and puzzles, go to **www.usborne-quicklinks.com**

A famous Spanish dish is called paella. It is cooked in a shallow pan, sometimes over a wood fire.

Mealtime customs

There are many different ways of eating across the world. Some people kneel on the floor to eat, and some sit at high tables. Many people use their hands to eat, while others use chopsticks, or a knife and fork.

In China, even young children use wooden sticks, called chopsticks.

Feasts and festivals

When people celebrate, food is often a big part of the festival. It is important in several religions too. For example, during the holy month of Ramadan, Muslims eat nothing during the day until sunset. When Ramadan ends, they hold a feast to celebrate.

Clothes and fashion

People may have first worn clothes to protect them from the weather. Over time, clothes became a way of showing where you came from, what job you did and how rich you were. Today clothes can say a lot about you.

Women wearing traditional dresses in western Tibet

What is fashion?

A fashion is a style that is only popular for a short time, so fashions change all the time. Some of the clothes on sale in stores are based on styles first seen at big fashion shows in New York, Paris and Milan.

Internet link

For a link to a website where you can find out all about traditional Indian clothes, go to **www.usborne-quicklinks.com**

Following fashion

People who want to be fashionable wear the latest styles however unusual they may be. Things such as huge wigs and skirts, that were once very popular, often look strange to us now.

These Japanese girls have dyed their hair and wear bright clothes to look fashionable.

Traditional clothes

In some places, people still wear the style of clothes they have worn for centuries. They follow tradition rather than fashion. A country's traditional dress is called its national costume.

This young Masai woman is wearing traditional bead necklaces.

This Japanese woman wears a gown called a kimono.

This Moroccan water carrier is wearing a traditional hat.

This Indian woman wears a sari over a small top.

Clothes for climates

People usually wear clothes that suit their way of life. This means dressing for the climate where they live and for the work they do. Find out more about work clothes on page 162.

In cold climates people wear many layers of clothes. Air trapped between the layers keeps out the cold.

People who live in hot, damp places, such as rainforests, often wear very little. This helps to keep them cool.

In hot, dry, desert climates, people wear loose robes to shield them from the scorching sun.

Jobs and work

The main reason people work is to earn money for themselves and their families. Many people enjoy their work. For others, it means earning just enough to survive.

This boy has a part-time job before school each day. He delivers newspapers to people's homes.

Changing times

In the richer parts of the world, the way people work has changed through the ages.

For centuries, most people farmed a small piece of land.

About 200 years ago, people began working in factories.

Now many people work in an office, or at home, using a computer.

Working clothing

For some jobs, people have to wear special clothes. This may be a uniform that makes them easy to spot. It may be things such as hard hats and goggles that help protect them while they work.

A chef's hat stops hairs from dropping into the food while he is cooking. His apron protects his other clothes.

Motorcycle courier

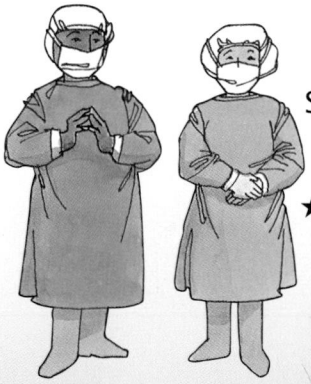

Surgeons

Welder

Can you guess why all these people wear special clothes?

Builder

Police officers

Teamwork

Many people work as part of a team. Each person in the team has a different job to do. This team of workers is building a brick house.

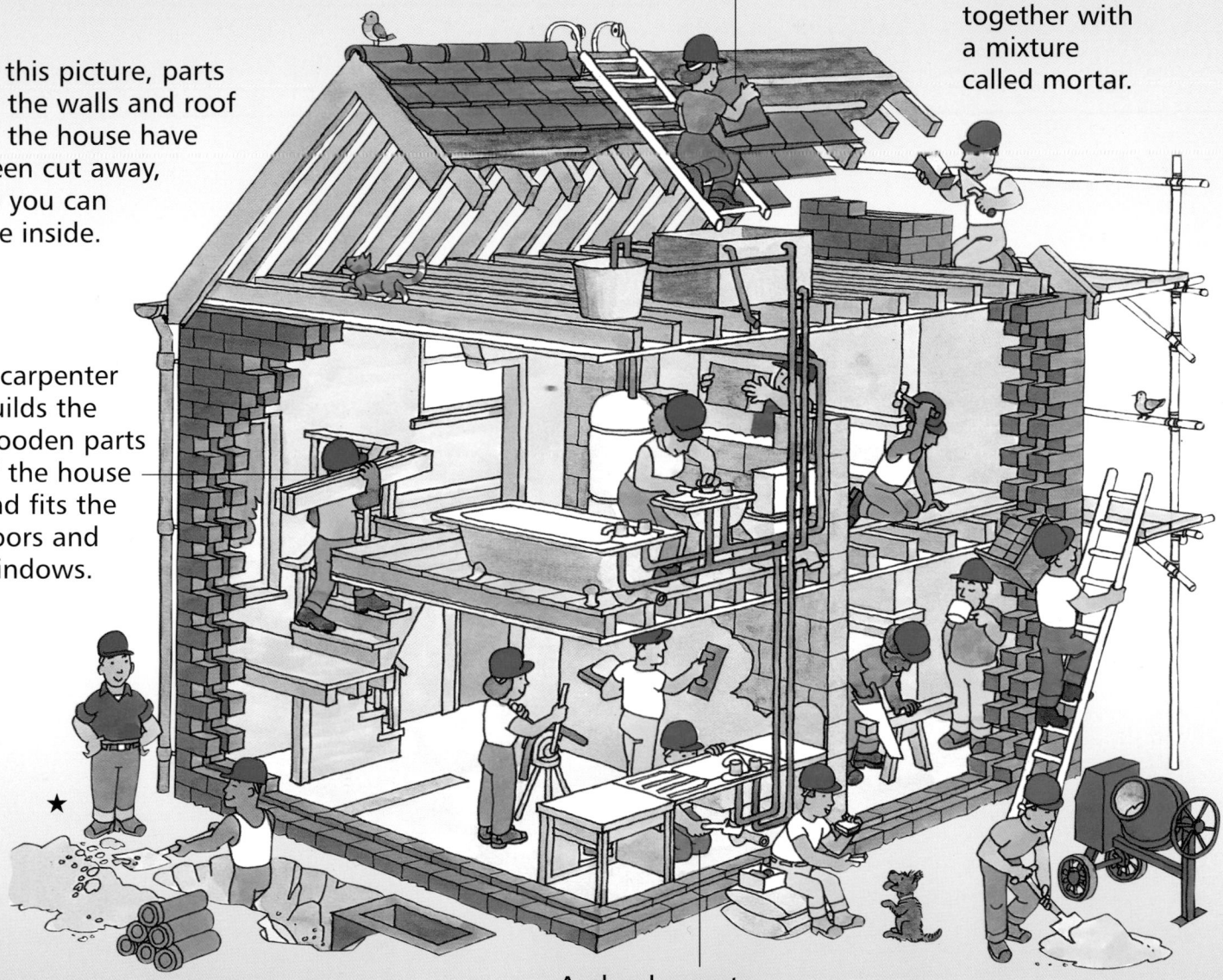

A roofer fixes the tiles to the roof.

Bricklayers stick the bricks together with a mixture called mortar.

In this picture, parts of the walls and roof of the house have been cut away, so you can see inside.

A carpenter builds the wooden parts of the house and fits the doors and windows.

These men are digging a hole to put pipes in. The pipes will bring clean water into the house and take dirty water away.

A plumber puts in the water pipes inside the house.

This man is mixing the mortar for the bricklayers.

Internet link

For a link to a website where you can click on different jobs to find out what people do, go to **www.usborne-quicklinks.com**

Children at work

In many countries, children start work at 16 or 18, after they have left school. In other places, children start work much younger. Over 350 million of the world's children do some kind of work.

Farming

Farmers grow crops and keep animals to feed people. Some farmers produce food just for their own family. Others sell their food to stores for other people to buy.

These farmers in Thailand are planting rice shoots by hand.

On big farms, machines help farmers to plant and gather, or harvest, crops.

This machine is called a combine harvester. It is cutting wheat.

A tractor is a very useful farm machine. This one is pulling a trailer to collect the wheat grains.

Growing crops

The type of crop a farmer can grow depends on the soil, the type of land and the weather in the place where he lives. Rice needs hot, wet weather. Wheat grows best in cooler, drier places.

Internet link

For a link to a website where you can find out how milk gets from a cow to your cereal, go to **www.usborne-quicklinks.com**

Keeping animals

Keeping animals is called livestock farming. Animals give us milk, wool, eggs and leather, as well as meat. Some farmers keep just one kind of animal.

Farmers keep sheep for meat, wool and milk.

Hens are kept for their eggs as well as their meat.

Goats are kept for their milk, meat and skin.

Cows give us milk, meat and leather. One cow can make over 3,000 gallons of milk each year.

Using chemicals

Some farmers need to produce as much food as they can in a short time. They use machines to spray crops with chemicals to help them grow and to kill pests and diseases.

These sunflowers are being sprayed with fertilizer to help them grow. Some people worry that these chemicals are bad for us.

Organic farming

Farming without chemicals is called organic farming. It is harder to produce lots of food this way, but many people think organic foods are healthier than other kinds.

Many farmers are now growing organic fruit and vegetables to sell in local markets.

Going to school

Children go to school to learn the things they need to know when they grow up. Only about half of the children in the world go to school.

The young girl on the left is helping to prepare palm fruit for her family to eat. She is from the Kpelle tribe in Liberia, Africa.

Skills to survive

In poorer countries, many children do not have time to go to school. They have to work to help their family survive. They do not learn to read or write, but are taught other skills they need, such as hunting and farming.

Kinds of schools

Schools and ways of learning can be very different around the world. Some schools do not have walls, chairs or even books.

These children in a mountain village in Nepal sit outside on the ground to learn.

This Australian boy lives far from a school. He learns at home, using the Internet.

These children at a school in the USA work at desks inside a classroom.

What can you learn?

All schools teach basic skills such as reading, writing and using numbers. As you get older, you can learn more and more different subjects. There are other things you can do at school too, such as playing sports or using a computer.

At some schools you can learn to play a musical instrument and join a band or orchestra.

Older children may do chemistry experiments in a school laboratory.

Computers are useful for many subjects. Computer skills are often called ICT (Information and Communication Technology) skills.

Some schools have team sports, such as softball, baseball or basketball.

Taking tests

In most schools, you have to take important tests called exams. These show how well you understand the things you have learned. You need to pass these tests if you want to go to college or a university.

Internet link

For a link to a website where you can visit different schools around the world, go to **www.usborne-quicklinks.com**

Sports and games

People play sports and games for fun, to keep fit, because they want to win, or as part of a festival. There are hundreds of sports. Many need fitness and skill.

Internet link

For a link to a website where you can find out all about the Olympic Games, ancient and modern, go to **www.usborne-quicklinks.com**

Playing together

Some games and sports, such as archery, are played by just one person. Others, such as baseball and hockey, are played in teams. In a team sport, everyone has to work together to succeed.

In a team game, such as ice hockey, each player has his own job to do. Here a goalkeeper tries to stop another player from scoring.

Useful sport

Sports and games can be very good for you. Playing a sport helps to keep you fit and healthy. Even computer games can teach you to think quickly and solve problems.

Playing a team sport, such as soccer, helps to keep you fit and can be fun.

The Olympic Games

The world's main sporting event is the Olympic Games. The first Games were held in the town of Olympia, in Ancient Greece. Athletes showed off their skills at many sports, such as running and wrestling. The Games are now held every four years, in different cities around the world.

The winners of the Ancient Olympics were given a garland of laurel leaves as a prize.

Today, Olympic winners get gold medals. Runners-up get silver and those in third place get bronze.

Sports for all

Anyone can enjoy sports. For instance, athletes with disabilities often have specially designed racing wheelchairs. The main sporting event for wheelchair athletes is the Paralympics.

These athletes are taking part in time trials to qualify for the Paralympics.

Communicating

There are many different ways of telling each other things. This is called communicating. We can use noises, such as sirens, or signs, such as flashing lights. The main ways we communicate are by talking, pictures and writing, though.

Some signs and symbols can be understood by people who speak different languages. Can you guess what these symbols mean?

Keeping in touch

Televisions, telephones and the Internet allow us to share information quickly and easily. People thousands of miles apart can get in touch in seconds by picking up the phone or sending an email or text message. TV allows us to find out what is happening all over the world.

:-)	Happy	I-O	Yawning
:-o	Wow!	:-D	Laughing
:-(	Sad	;-)	Winking

These symbols are called smileys or emoticons. You can add them to emails to show how you are feeling.

A Masai farmer in Kenya using his mobile phone

Writing it down

To record what they said, early people made marks that stood for words. This is how writing began. The first types of writing were rows of pictures. These then became letters, which stood for sounds.

In Ancient Egypt, men called scribes kept records.

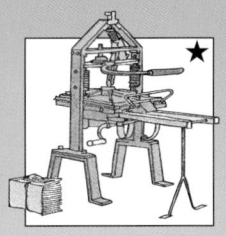

In Europe, the printing press was first used in about 1450.

Now most writing is done on computers.

Internet link

For a link to a website where you can find out how a book is made and learn how to make your own books, go to **www.usborne-quicklinks.com**

Spreading the word

Writing a book or newspaper is a way of sharing facts, news, ideas and stories with many people. Books were first printed in China over 1,000 years ago. In Europe, until about 550 years ago, the only way to make a book was to write it all out by hand.

A German man named Johannes Gutenberg invented the first printing press in Europe. This machine could print many copies of the same book. Now if a book is popular, millions of copies are made and people all around the world can read it.

This boy is choosing books to borrow from a library. Libraries hold thousands of books on different subjects.

Art and painting

Every work of art is different. Artists may try to create something which is beautiful, or shocking, or shows people how they feel. Whoever sees their work usually feels something, too; they may like it, or they may hate it.

What is art?

People often disagree about what is a work of art and what is not. Many artists say that anything at all can be art. In some cases a work of art can be hard for anyone but the artist to understand.

This painting is by a famous French artist named Paul Gauguin who died in 1903. It shows a mother and daughter in Tahiti and is called *When will you marry?*

Making art

Not every work of art is painted. Art can be made in many ways, using stone, clay, wood, metal or other things. Pieces of art which are not flat are often called sculptures.

You can see sculptures outside in cities. This sculpture by Henry Moore stands by the River Thames in London.

Different styles

There are many styles of art. Some artists work from real life and try to copy what they see. Others don't try to show real things. They use colors, lines and shapes instead.

Aboriginal art, from Australia, is usually painted on tree bark or rocks. It is used to tell stories. This shows a crocodile and a fish called a barramundi.

Traditional art

Some types of art are traditional. This means artists have worked in the same style for thousands of years. There are many kinds of traditional art around the world.

Is it art?

Artists are always trying out new ways of making art, but other people don't always accept them. Many people think photos and movies can be art. Some artists use computers to help them create art. Others use leaves, lights or even old cars.

Internet link

For a link to a website where you can go on an art safari and make your own art, go to **www.usborne-quicklinks.com**

A group of artists half-buried ten cars in a field in Texas, USA in 1974. They called their sculpture *Cadillac Ranch*. You can still see it there.

Acting and dancing

All over the world people act and dance to entertain each other. They might use acting and dancing to celebrate an event, tell a story, communicate a message or to show feelings.

These people are making a movie. The cameramen are filming the actors. Actors in movies may have to repeat a scene many times before it is right.

On the stage

A story which is acted out is called a play. A person who writes plays is known as a playwright. Some plays tell true stories, but others are made up. Plays performed in front of other people are "live", so each performance is a little different. Plays are often performed in theatres.

Movies

Movies are stories that are acted out and recorded on film, so we can watch the same performance over and over again. People can go to the theatre to watch movies, or see them at home on video or DVD.

These stage actors are performing in a famous comedy called *A Midsummer Night's Dream* by William Shakespeare.*

On stage, clothes, make-up, masks, scenery, lights and music may be used to create different feelings.

*See page 135.

Ways of dancing

There are many ways of dancing, and each one needs different skills. Some dances are fast, while others are slow and graceful. You can learn the steps and movements of a dance or make up your own. Most kinds of dancing are done with music.

Ballet dancing uses many carefully-planned movements. Some take years of training to do well.

Why do we dance?

We don't really know why people dance or how dancing began. It may have started as a way of celebrating something, worshipping gods or telling a story. Today, many people dance to keep fit or just for fun.

Dancers in Bali use every part of their body in their dance, including their eyes, face, neck and hands.

Internet link

For a link to a website where you can go on a journey through the history of ballet, go to **www.usborne-quicklinks.com**

Music

Music is a pattern of sounds put together to make a tune or rhythm. People have many different ideas about what music should sound like.

Musical sounds

You can make music just with your body by singing, clapping, whistling or humming. Musical instruments, such as the ones below, can help you make all kinds of other musical sounds. Here are some groups of instruments.

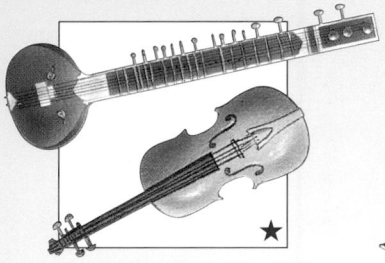

These are string instruments. You pluck their strings or stroke them with a bow.

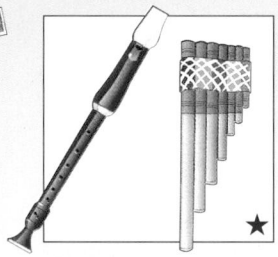

These are wood-wind instruments. You blow into them to make a sound.

Percussion instruments make sounds when you hit, shake or scrape or them.

These are brass instruments. You play them by buzzing your lips on the mouthpiece.

These boys are making music with cymbals, drums, horns, clapping and singing, during Bahag Bihu, an Indian spring festival.

Why make music?

Music can make us want to dance, sing, or even cry, and people often use it to show how they feel about something. It may be used to celebrate big events such as weddings, and in religious ceremonies.

In West African music, rhythms are usually more important than tunes. These Gambian women are dancing to the rhythm of a drum.

Types of music

There are two main types of music: classical and popular. Each type contains many musical styles and traditions.

Jazz is a style of popular music. It began early in the last century in New Orleans, USA. This jazz musician is playing a saxophone.

Internet link

For a link to a website where you can find out about instruments of the orchestra, go to **www.usborne-quicklinks.com**

Playing together

Some types of music can be performed by one person. Many types are played or sung by people in groups. A group of musicians playing together is often called a band.

A large group of musicians playing different instruments is called an orchestra.

Religions

A religion is a belief in something greater than any person. It may be a belief in one God, or in several gods.

For some people, religion is more to do with the way they live their life. There are many religions in the world.

Like many boys in Buddhist countries, this boy is spending time as a monk, learning about his religion.

Buddhism

Buddhism teaches people to think deeply about life and what is really important. This thinking is called meditation. Buddhism is based on the ideas of a south Asian prince who became known as the Buddha.

Christianity

People who follow Christianity are called Christians. They believe that God watches over them and wants them to be good. Christians believe that a man named Jesus was the Son of God. The Christian holy book is the *Bible*.

The birth of Jesus is called the Nativity. Christians celebrate this at Christmas.

Hinduism

Hinduism has many gods and beliefs. The main god is Brahman. Hindus believe that people have many lives, one after the other. This pattern only ends when the believer becomes close to Brahman.

The Hindu god Krishna is usually shown with blue skin. ★ Here he is playing his flute.

Islam

Followers of the religion of Islam are called Muslims. They obey the laws of God, who is called Allah. A man named Muhammad taught Allah's laws. These were written down in the Muslim holy book, the *Qur'an*.

This Muslim girl is praying to Allah.

Judaism

Followers of Judaism are called Jews. They worship God in a building called a synagogue. The Jewish holy day, or Shabbat, is from sunset on Friday to sunset on Saturday.

This boy is in a synagogue, reading from the Jewish holy writings. He is wearing a cap and shawl to show that he respects God.

Sikhism

A person who follows Sikhism is called a Sikh, which means "learner". Sikhs believe in one God, whom they worship in a building called a gurdwara. There, they listen to readings from the Sikh holy book, the *Guru Granth Sahib*.

This is a symbol of Sikhism. It is called the khanda. ★

Internet links

For links to websites where you can find out more about the religions described on these pages, go to **www.usborne-quicklinks.com**

Myths

Myths are stories filled with strange creatures, gods and goddesses and amazing happenings. They are often tales of good and evil.

Neptune was the Roman god of the sea. He could control the oceans.

Myths and gods

People may have made up myths to explain why puzzling things happened before science gave us the answers. For instance, the Romans believed that tidal waves and earthquakes happened when the sea-god Neptune was angry.

Myths and monsters

There are many incredible monsters described in the world's myths.

The yeti is an ape-like creature that lives on snowy mountains. People disagree whether the yeti is real or mythical. ★

Dragons appear in myths from many parts of the world. This dragon is from China.

Creation myths

Every country has its own myths, but they are often about the same things. For instance, there are many different creation myths explaining how the world began.

Internet link

For a link to a website where you can read myths and legends from around the world, go to **www.usborne-quicklinks.com**

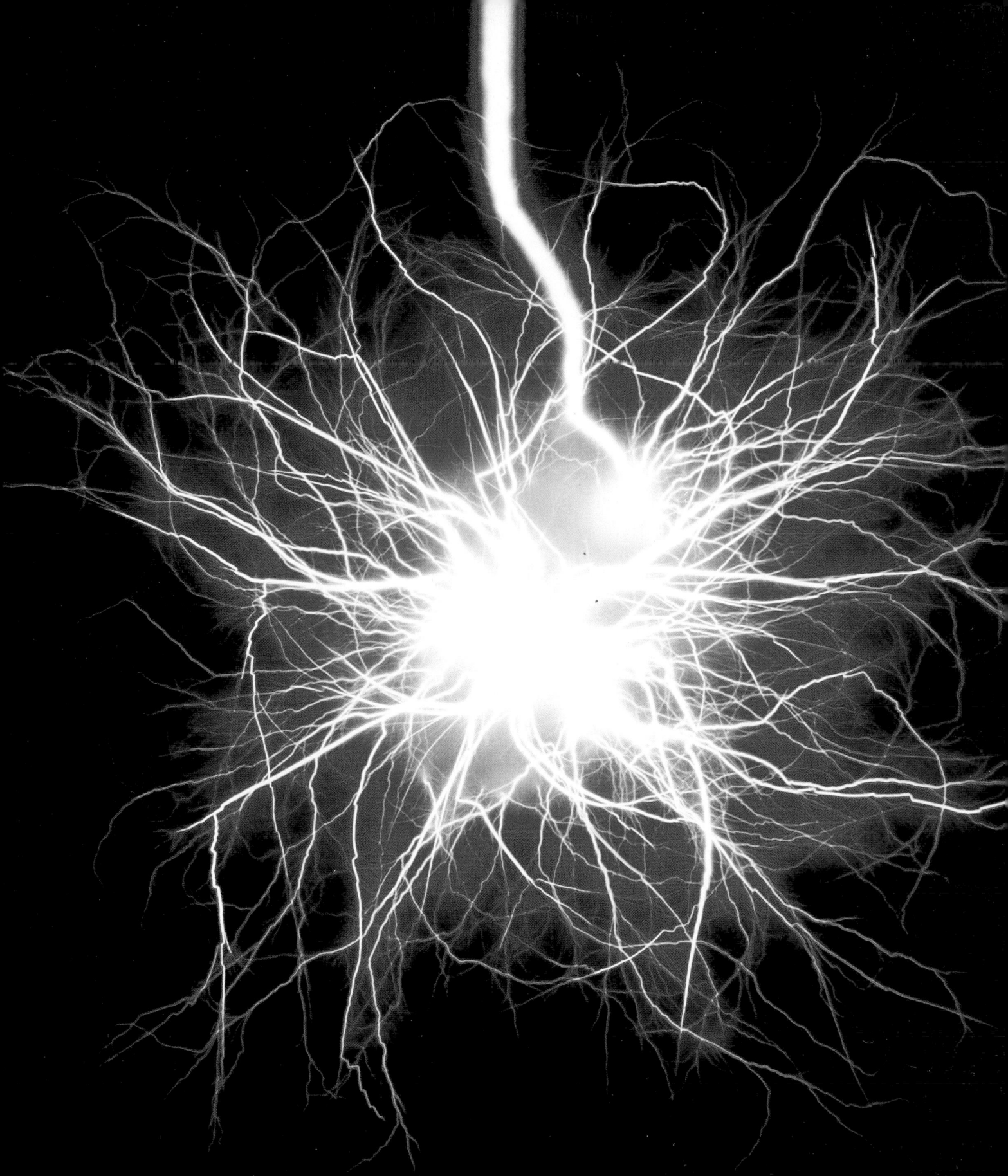

Science

What is science?

Science is what we know about the world around us. Why do volcanoes erupt? What is gravity? Is there life on other planets? How do our brains work? Science tries to answer all these questions and many more.

Scientists have found out why leaves turn red or brown in the fall.

Being a scientist

People who do science are called scientists. They study things by looking at them closely, asking questions, and doing experiments to find out how they work.

Scientists can use their scientific knowledge to help them invent things, like this cell phone.

Scientists who study animals, such as this macaw, are called zoologists.

Internet link

For a link to a website where you can find out about some of the useful things scientists have invented, go to **www.usborne-quicklinks.com**

Studies of macaws have shown that their bright feathers may help them to find a mate.

Scientists have found 17 different species (types) of macaws in the wild.

Branches of science

There are hundreds of different kinds, or branches, of science, and many different kinds of scientists. Here are just a few of them.

Biologists study living things.

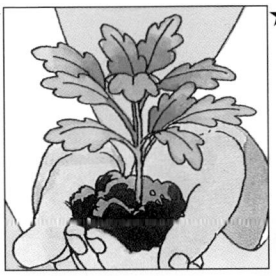

Botanists study just plants.

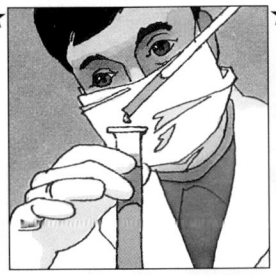

Chemists study chemicals.

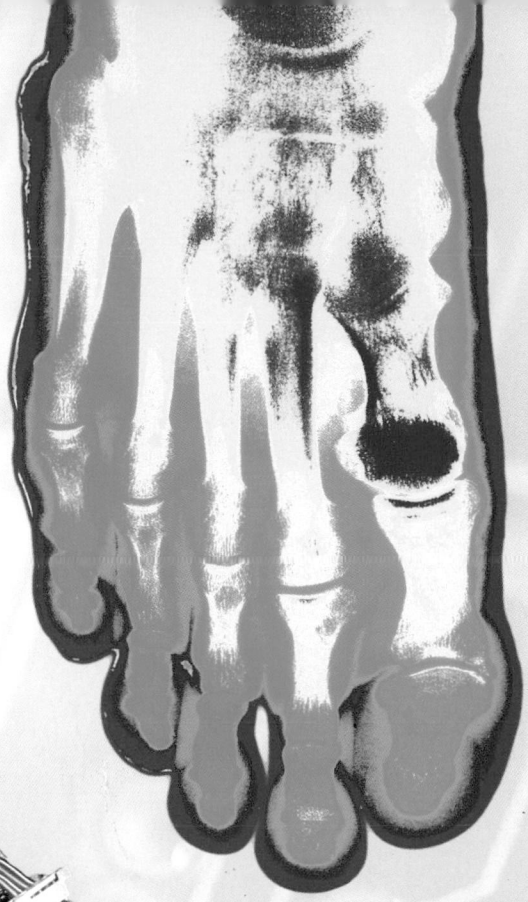

Medical scientists use X-ray machines to look inside people's bodies. The picture above is an X-ray photo of a foot. Can you see the bones?

Technology

Scientists can use their understanding of the world to design or invent new things. Without science, we wouldn't have many of the machines and medicines we have today. Using science in this way is called technology.

This is a machine called a robot. It can move around and make its own simple decisions.

Some types of robots can do dangerous jobs instead of humans.

What scientists do

To find out about things, scientists do experiments. These are tests that show how living things, objects or substances behave.

Internet link

For a link to a website where you'll find lots of fun science experiments to try out, go to **www.usborne-quicklinks.com**

Asking questions

Scientists use experiments to help them answer questions. For example, a scientist might ask, "does music make plants grow faster?"

As an experiment, she could take two groups of plants and play music to just one of them, to see which grew faster.

These pictures show a simple experiment on plants.

A scientist grows two similar groups of plants.

Music is played to only one of the groups.

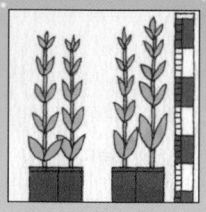

Later, the two groups can be compared.

Theories

Scientists think up theories that might explain how things work. For example, they might have a theory that penguins travel to a certain area because there is more food there. Then they do experiments to test their theories.

Scientists write down their results and repeat their experiments to make sure they work.

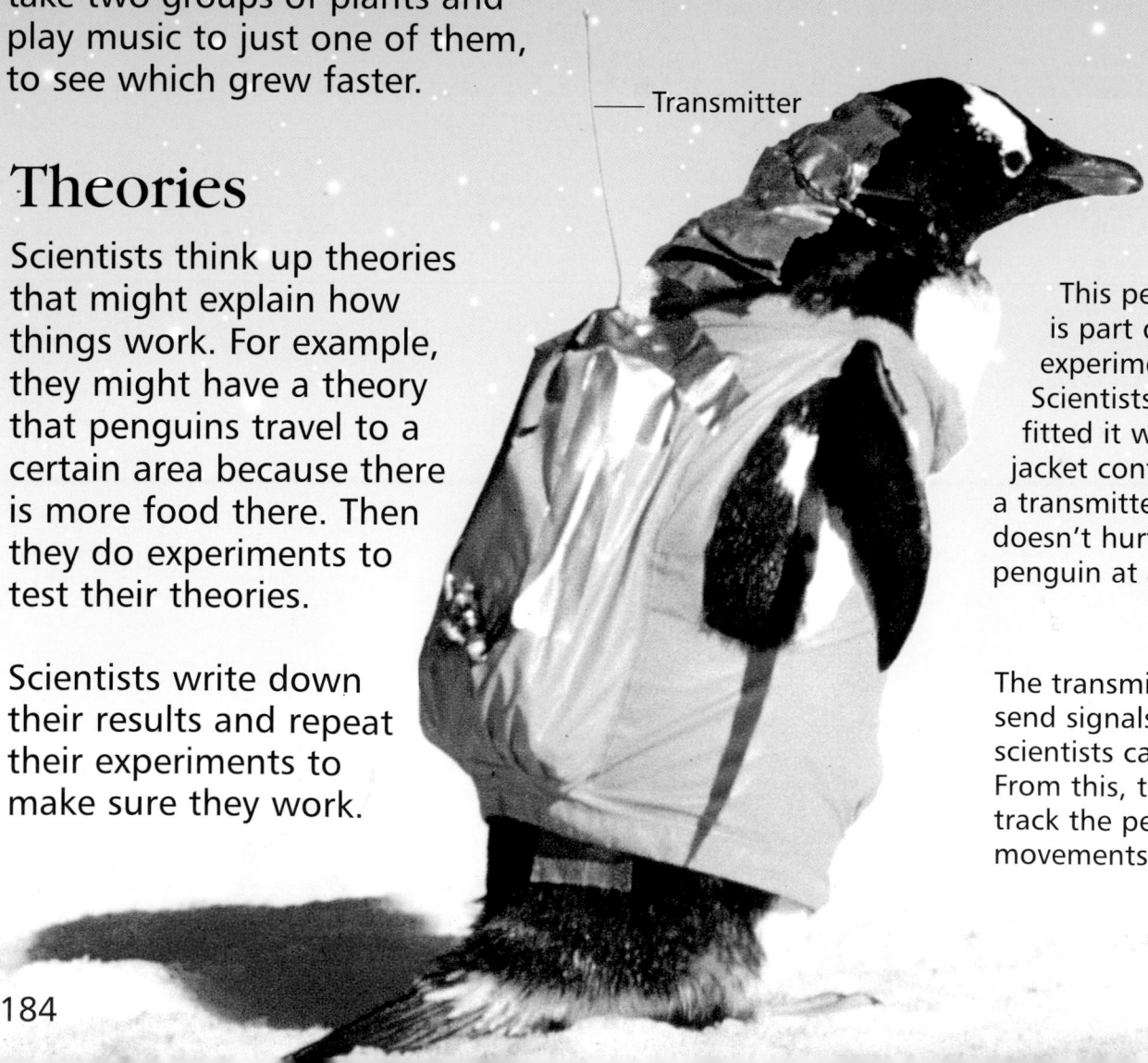

This penguin is part of an experiment. Scientists have fitted it with a jacket containing a transmitter. (It doesn't hurt the penguin at all.)

The transmitter will send signals that the scientists can collect. From this, they can track the penguin's movements.

Observing

Observing means watching and measuring things very carefully. It's an important part of being a scientist.

This is a comet. Comets are balls of ice and dust that zoom through space. By observing the path of a comet, astronomers can work out where it will go next.

Scientists often use tools to help them observe things. For example, astronomers (space scientists) use powerful telescopes to study planets, stars and galaxies.

Telescopes make far away things look closer. There is a huge telescope in this building that a team of astronomers uses to watch the night sky.

Do your own experiment

Find out if adding salt to water will make a difference to how things float in it. You will need:

2 half-full glasses of water; 2 fresh eggs; 10 heaped teaspoons of salt

1. Stir the salt into one glass of water until it has dissolved and is invisible.

2. Put an egg in each glass. Do both eggs float? Do they both behave the same way?

You can find out more about floating on pages 200-201.

Atoms and molecules

Scientists have found out that everything is made out of tiny particles called atoms. Atoms can join together in groups called molecules.

Internet link

For a link to a website with interactive experiments about atoms and molecules, go to **www.usborne-quicklinks.com**

What is an atom?

An atom is like a tiny ball. It has a center, or nucleus, and outer layers called shells. There are about 100 types of atoms.

Atoms are so tiny that you can't see them. A piece of paper, such as this page, is about a million atoms thick.

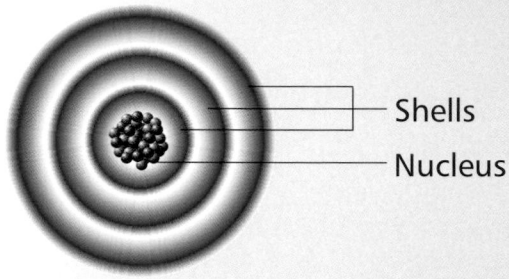

Atoms are made up of even smaller particles. You can see some of them in the nucleus of the atom above.

In atom diagrams, different colors are used to show different types of atoms.

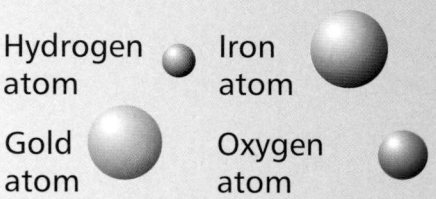

Making molecules

Atoms sometimes join together to make bigger units called molecules. This joining together is called bonding.

These pictures show two types of atoms bonding to make water molecules.

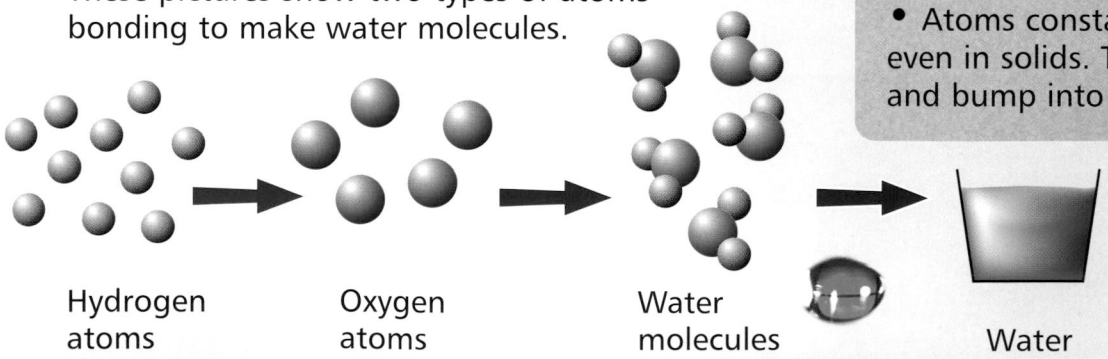

Water is made up of lots of water molecules.

Did you know?

- Most of an atom is empty space.
- Some types of atoms, such as francium, do not exist naturally. They can only be made by scientists in a science lab.
- Atoms constantly move around, even in solids. They jiggle, vibrate and bump into each other.

Materials

All the things around us – rocks, air, water, sand, glass, wood, plastic, and even our bodies – are made of atoms and molecules. Scientists call all these different types of stuff "materials".

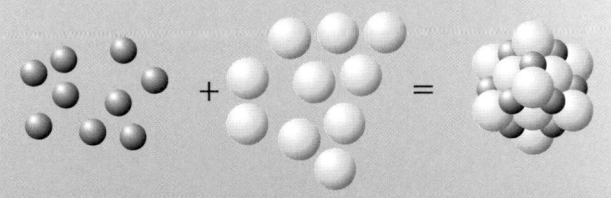

Sodium atoms | Chlorine atoms | Table salt molecules

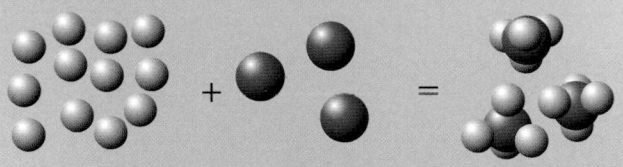

Hydrogen atoms | Carbon atoms | Methane gas molecules

Materials hunt

Can you find things made of these materials in your home or classroom?

★ Paper

★ China

★ Plastic

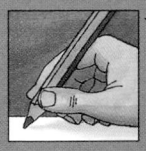
★ Wood

★ Glass

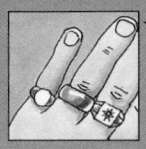
★ Metal

Chemists mix materials together in glass beakers and flasks like these.

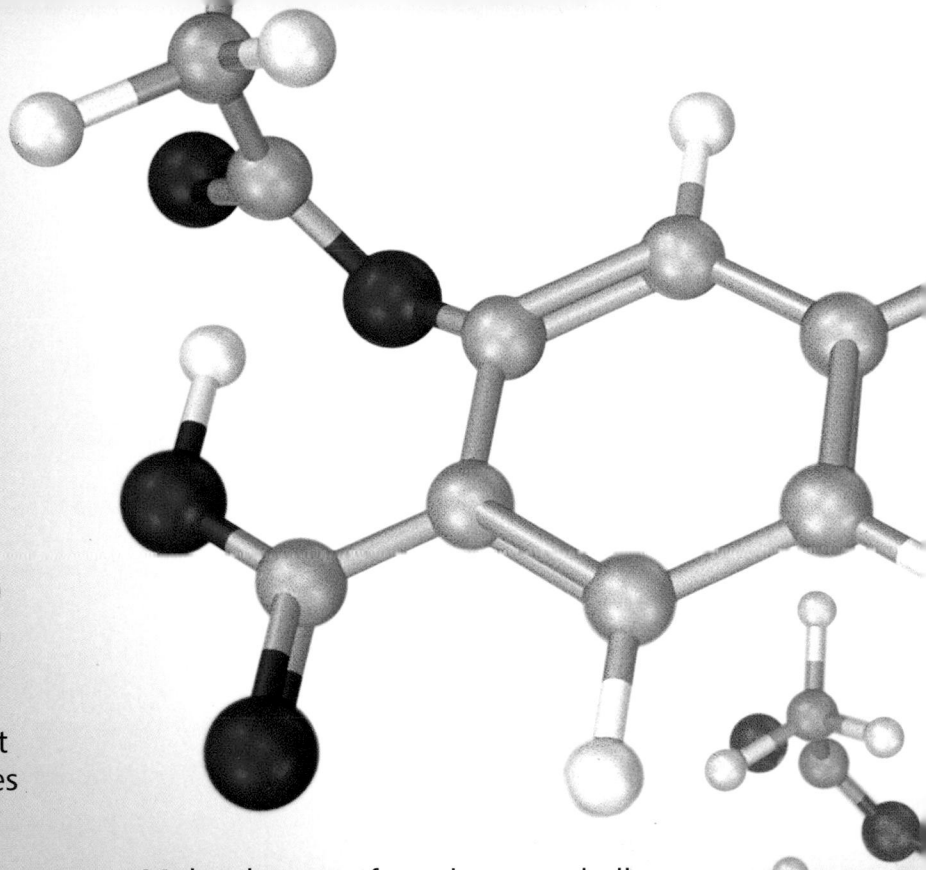

Molecules are often shown as balls (the atoms) and sticks (the bonds between them). This shows parts of two molecules of aspirin.

Chemistry

Different materials behave in different ways. For example, if you heat butter, it melts, but if you heat an egg, it gets harder. Salt dissolves quickly in water, but sand doesn't.

Scientists called chemists study how materials behave, change, and bond together. This kind of science is called chemistry.

Solids, liquids and gases

Most materials can exist in three different forms: solids, liquids and gases. In solids, molecules are packed together. In liquids and gases, they're more spread out.

Internet link

For a link to a website where you can find more examples of solids, liquids and gases, go to **www.usborne-quicklinks.com**

Gold is a solid.

Solids

The molecules in solids are firmly attached to each other and don't move around much. Because of this, most solids stay the same shape.

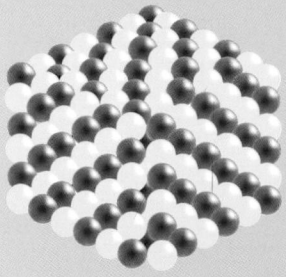

Molecules in solids are squashed tightly together.

Drinks are liquids. They flow into every part of a container.

Liquids

The molecules in liquids are not so squashed together. They can move around more and are not as firmly fixed to each other. This is why liquids can flow, splash and be poured.

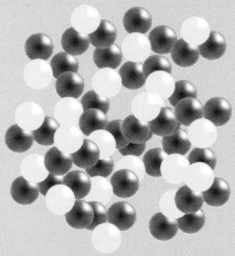

Molecules in liquids are not squashed together.

Gases

The molecules in gases are not attached to each other at all and move around all the time at high speeds. This means that gases quickly spread out to fill the space they are in. They have no shape of their own.

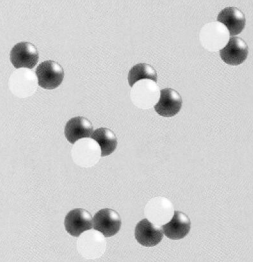

Gas molecules don't stick to each other at all.

Many gases are invisible. You can only see this gas because it is burning.

Make a gas

You can make carbon dioxide gas and blow up a balloon with it. You will need:

a narrow-necked jar; some baking soda; some vinegar; a balloon; a teaspoon

1. Fill a quarter of the jar with vinegar. Put the soda into the balloon, using the teaspoon.

2. Stretch the neck of the balloon over the top of the jar. Don't let any soda spill into the jar.

3. Quickly lift the balloon up to tip all of the soda into the jar. The vinegar will react with the soda, making bubbles.

When the vinegar and soda react (see page 191), they make carbon dioxide gas which fills the balloon, blowing it up a little.

Three forms

The same material can exist as a solid, a liquid or a gas. For example, water exists as a liquid, as solid ice, and as a gas called water vapor.

There is water vapor (water gas) in the air. As it cools, it forms clouds and may turn into rain.

Ice is frozen water. It is a solid.

Water in rivers and seas is a liquid.

How materials change

Materials can change all the time. They can grow, shrink and change between a solid, a liquid and a gas. They can also combine to make new materials.

Changing state

Materials can change between solid and liquid, or between liquid and gas. These changes are called changes of state. They often happen when materials heat up or cool down.

★ 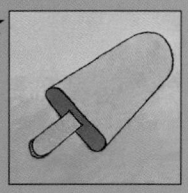

When juice gets very cold, it turns from a liquid to a solid. This is called freezing.

★ 

Wax turns from a solid into a liquid as a candle burns. This is called melting.

★ 

When you heat water, it turns from a liquid into a gas. This is called boiling.

★ 

When water vapor cools, it turns into a liquid – rain. This is called condensing.

Inside a freezer, it's cold enough for water to freeze into ice.

Getting bigger

Water expands (gets bigger) when it freezes. Most materials, however, shrink as they get colder and expand as they get hotter. For example, a thermometer* contains a liquid that expands as the temperature rises.

A thermometer contains liquid in a narrow tube. (In this photo, the liquid is black.) As the liquid warms up, it gets bigger and fills more of the tube.

Make water get bigger

Here's what you will need:

a plastic bottle (don't use a glass bottle); a piece of foil; a freezer

1. Fill the bottle to the top with water. Cover the top with the foil.

2. Stand the bottle upright in the freezer. Leave it there overnight.

3. The water pushes the foil upward as it freezes and gets bigger.

 *For more about thermometers, see page 197.

Mixing materials

Materials can be mixed together to make new materials. If you mix sand, cement, broken stones and water, you get concrete. Concrete is useful for building, because it is stronger than any of the ingredients by themselves.

Internet link

For a link to a website where you can find out how to make your own simple chemical reaction, go to **www.usborne-quicklinks.com**.

The Catedral Metropolitana in Brazil is made of 16 curved concrete columns.

Reactions

In a mixture, materials are combined but their molecules do not change. Sometimes, however, materials react with each other. This means that when they are mixed, their molecules change and they turn into different materials.

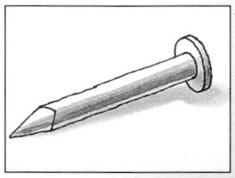

Rusting happens to iron when it is left out in the rain or in damp air.

Molecules of iron react with oxygen atoms and water molecules.

The reaction makes a new type of molecule called iron oxide, or rust.

These rocks formed in Mono Lake in California, USA because of a reaction between two different chemicals in the lake.

Energy

Energy is the power that makes things happen. You can't see it, but it's all around you, making all kinds of objects move and work.

All kinds of energy

Energy comes in many types, or "forms". For example, heat, light, electricity and sound are all forms of energy.

Electrical energy flows into lights and changes into heat and light energy.

Internet link

For a link to a website where you can find out all kinds of things about energy, go to **www.usborne-quicklinks.com**

People shouting and machines moving release a lot of sound energy.

The same energy

You can't destroy or make energy. This means the amount of energy in the Universe* is always the same. But one form of energy can change into another form.

Plants change light energy from the Sun into food energy.

 *For more about the Universe, see page 212.

Movement energy

Whenever something moves, it has energy. The energy of something that is moving is called kinetic energy.

To fly, these birds change energy stored in their bodies into kinetic energy.

At the top of the roller coaster, the car contains stored energy.

As the car goes down the hill, stored energy changes into kinetic energy.

These flags have kinetic energy as they flutter in the breeze.

These children have a lot of kinetic energy because they are running fast.

Stored energy

Potential energy is energy that is stored, ready to use. When it's used, it turns into another form of energy, such as kinetic energy or heat.

As the hammer is lifted up, it gains a store of potential energy.

Food turns into stored energy in our bodies. A candy apple will give this boy enough energy to walk for 20 minutes.

This boy's video camera uses electrical energy that's stored in a battery.

Forces

A force is a push or a pull that makes an object do something. For example, if you kick a ball, the force of your kick makes the ball move. Forces can also make things change their direction, speed and shape.

Direct forces

Some forces work by touching the object they are pushing or pulling on. These are called direct forces. Kicking a ball, lifting a pen or pulling your sock off are all examples of direct forces.

Pushing a sled is a direct force.

Pulling a sled uphill on a rope is a direct force.

From a distance

Some forces don't have to touch the things they work on. For example, gravity* pulls you down when you jump off a wall. A magnet pulls paperclips toward it. Scientists are still not sure how these distant forces work.

Forces can stop things too. This snowdrift has a force that has stopped this sled.

Gravity is a distant force. It is pulling the sleds downhill, but not touching them.

Internet link

For a link to a website where you can find out about the forces in toys, go to **www.usborne-quicklinks.com**

*For more about gravity, see pages 198-199.

Balanced forces

When something isn't moving, you might think that there are no forces working on it. In fact, there are, but they are balanced against each other, and cancel each other out.

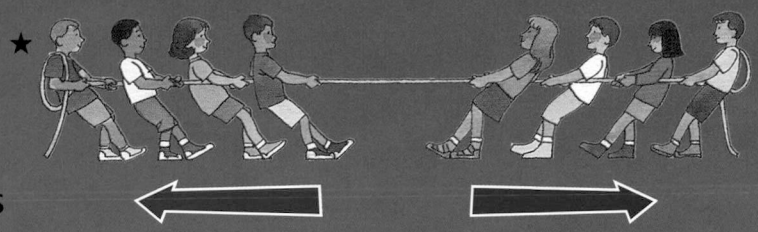

These two tug-of-war teams are not moving, because the forces they make are balanced. To win, one of the teams must use more force.

Using forces

We use forces all the time to move things, lift things and travel around. Machines help us to use forces to do things we can't do on our own. They turn our energy, or other forms of energy such as electricity, into the right kinds of force to do different jobs.

A digger turns electrical energy into a pulling force to scoop up a heavy load of soil.

Scissors are simple machines. Their sharp blades use the force of your fingers to cut things.

Hot and cold

Heat is a form of energy. Whenever you heat something up, you are giving it more energy.

Heating up

When many materials heat up, their molecules spread out. This makes them expand, or get bigger. When they cool down, they contract, or get smaller, again. As air heats up, it expands a lot, making it much lighter than cold air. This is why hot air balloons float.

The hot air inside these balloons is lighter than the air they float in. For more about floating, see pages 200-201.

Moving around

Heat moves from hotter to colder places. For example, hot food gets cold because its heat moves into the cooler air around it. You can't usually see heat, but it can be photographed with an infrared camera.

This picture was taken using an infrared camera. The red areas show where the buildings are giving out the most heat.

The Golden Gate Bridge in San Francisco, USA

Bridge gaps

Bridges often get slightly longer as they heat up in the sun. Large bridges have special joints with gaps in them, so that there's room for them to expand.

This is an expansion joint. Joints like these allow bridges to expand and contract. Without them, bridges could break and collapse.

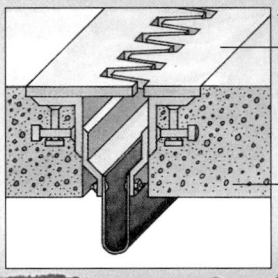

When a bridge expands in hot weather, these plates are pushed together.

Bridge

Expansion and contraction

You can do an experiment to see how air expands when it is heated and contracts when it cools down. This is what you will need:

a bowl; a bottle; a balloon

1. Ask an adult to hold the empty bottle under hot water for a minute. Stretch the balloon over its neck.

2. Half-fill the bowl with cold water and stand the bottle in it. The air cools and shrinks, pulling the balloon inside.

3. Empty the bowl and ask an adult to add hot water to it. The expanding warm air pushes the balloon out again.

Internet link

For a link to a website where you can watch a cartoon and play a game about heat, go to **www.usborne-quicklinks.com**

Measuring hotness

Temperature means how hot something is. It is measured in degrees Centigrade (°C) or degrees Fahrenheit (°F). Normal room temperature is about 20°C (68°F).

Temperature is measured using a thermometer. Can you see what the temperature is on this thermometer?

Gravity

When you jump up in the air, you drop back down again. This is because there's an invisible force pulling you down to the ground. This force is called gravity.

Mars

Pulling together

All objects have gravity and make a slight pull on other objects. With small objects, this force is too weak to have an effect. But huge objects like planets have enough gravity to pull other things toward them.

Mercury

In empty space, far away from stars, planets and moons, there is hardly any gravity. This is why astronauts float.

Gravity on other planets

The bigger an object is, the stronger its gravity is. Very big planets, like Jupiter, have much stronger gravity than Earth. Small planets and moons have weaker gravity than Earth.

Jupiter's gravity is more than twice as strong as Earth's. If you could visit Jupiter, you wouldn't be able to move because its gravity is so strong.

Jupiter

Jupiter's moon Io is quite small and its gravity is much weaker than the Earth's. You could jump many times higher on Io than you can on Earth.

This is Io, one of Jupiter's many moons.

The Sun

Venus

The Earth is in orbit around the Sun.

The Moon is in orbit around the Earth.

Testing gravity

Gravity pulls objects at the same speed, even if they have different weights. Try testing this yourself. You will need:

tissue paper; a coin; two identical boxes (such as camera film boxes or food containers with lids)

1. Carefully tear a piece of tissue paper the same size as the coin. It will be lighter than the coin.

2. Drop the paper and the coin from the same height. The paper falls more slowly because air gets in its way.

3. Now put the coin in one box and the paper in the other. Put the lids on and drop both boxes together.

4. The boxes have the same air resistance and land at the same time, even though they are different weights.

Internet link

For a link to a website where you can find out how much you would weigh on planets which have more or less gravity than Earth, go to **www.usborne-quicklinks.com**

In orbit

In space, large objects orbit, or travel around, each other. Planets orbit the Sun. Moons orbit planets. This happens because of gravity.

Gravity doesn't pull planets and moons right together, because they're moving too fast. This diagram shows how orbits work.

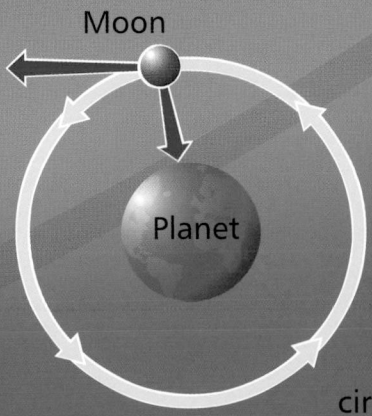

Moons move very fast. A moon is always trying to fly away from its planet in a straight line.

Meanwhile, the planet's gravity pulls the moon toward it. The two forces balance out and the moon circles around the planet.

Floating

If you throw a stone into a pond, it will sink to the bottom. But if you put a balloon in some water, it will float. Why do some things float and others sink?

Weight and size

Floating is all about density – how heavy something is for its size. For example, a cork is light for its size. A piece of iron the same size as a cork is much heavier, because iron is denser than cork. Objects that are denser than water sink in water. Objects that are less dense than water float in water.

Internet link

For a link to a website where you can find out how to make a raisin float and sink in a carbonated drink, go to **www.usborne-quicklinks.com**

These inflatable rings are light for their size and float well.

If you try to push an inflatable ring under water, you'll feel the water pushing back.

Upthrust

Things float because water pushes up on them more than they push down. This upward force is called upthrust. If an object is denser than water, the water cannot provide enough upthrust, so the object sinks.

Does it float?

Guess which things will float in water and then see if you were right. You will need:

a bowl of water; solid things, such as a cork, a candle, a coin, an apple, a raisin, a plastic toy, an eraser.

1. Make a chart to compare your guesses with what actually happens.

2. Try floating different objects and write down which of them really float.

Will it float?

	Guess	Actual
Cork	✓	
Coin	✓	
Candle	✗	
Apple	✗	

How do ships float?

Some ships are so huge, it seems amazing that they float – but they do. Even if a ship is made of heavy iron, it has a lot of air inside it. This makes the ship less dense than water, so it floats.

This big cruise ship is light for its size because it has lots of air inside it.

This floating red buoy is used to warn boats that this stretch of water is dangerous.

Floating in air

Floating in air is just like floating in water. Anything that is less dense than air will float in it. But because air is very light itself, not many other things are light enough to float in it.

People are almost the same density as water, and just barely float. Air-filled life belts can help people to float better.

These balloons are filled with a gas that's less dense than air. It makes them float.

Salty sea

Salty water is denser than pure water. This makes it easier for people to float in it. A lake in Israel called the Dead Sea has water that's so salty, it's very easy to float in.

This woman is floating in the very salty water of the Dead Sea.

Friction

Whenever an object tries to slide across a surface, it is slowed down by the two surfaces gripping each other. This force is called friction.

Internet link

For a link to a website where you can set the friction, speed and shape of a rollercoaster ride, go to **www.usborne-quicklinks.com**

The rough...

Friction slows things down because objects have rough surfaces. The rougher the surface, the more friction there is, and the more the object slows down.

This snowboarder can move very fast because there's not much friction between the smooth snow and the smooth snowboard.

...and the smooth

Very smooth surfaces don't have much friction and often feel slippery. If you are on a smooth surface, you can move fast without being slowed down very much.

Getting a grip

As well as slowing down moving things, friction helps things stay still. If it weren't for friction, we wouldn't be able to grip onto anything, or even stand up without slipping.

The soles of walking boots are molded into rough ridges. This makes lots of friction to keep the walker from slipping.

Hot friction

Wherever there is friction, there is heat. This is because as objects rub together, friction turns kinetic, or movement, energy into heat energy. There's more about energy on pages 192-193.

When a Space Shuttle comes back to Earth, it glows red hot because of friction between its surface and the air.

Coin warmer

To see how friction heats things up, try to warm up a metal coin using friction. You will need:

a coin; a pad of paper

1. Hold the coin flat on the paper with one finger on top of it, like this:

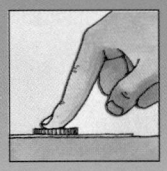

2. Press down and rub the coin very fast from side to side about 50 times.

The coin warms up because there is lots of friction between it and the paper. The friction turns the energy of the coin's movement into heat energy.

Streamlining

Even air and water cause friction when things move through them. Cars, planes and boats are built so that water or air can move past them in smooth lines to reduce friction. This is called streamlining.

Dolphins have streamlined bodies which help them to move fast in water.

Magnets

A magnet is a piece of metal that can pull some other types of metal toward it. Magnetism is a force. It happens because of the way atoms are arranged inside the metal.

Iron filings (tiny bits of iron) stick to the parts of this horseshoe-shaped magnet where its magnetic force is strongest.

Pushing and pulling

Magnetic forces are strongest at the two ends of a magnet. These ends are called the north pole and the south pole. If you try to put two magnets' poles together, they will either stick to each other or push each other away.

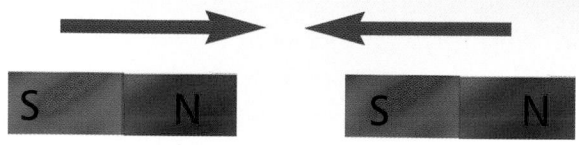

A north pole and a south pole always pull toward each other. This is called magnetic attraction.

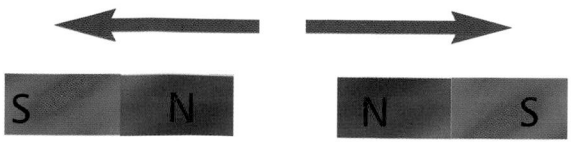

Two poles of the same type always push each other away. This is called magnetic repulsion.

Magnetic fields

The area of force around a magnet is called its magnetic field. Our planet is magnetic and has its own magnetic field. It pulls compass needles so that they always point north.

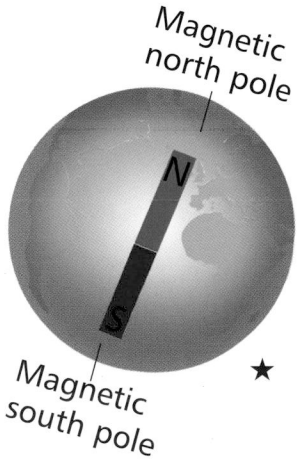

Like all magnets, the Earth has magnetic north and south poles. They are near the North Pole and South Pole you can see on a globe*.

*See page 13.

Magnets at work

You might use magnets to stick notes on your refrigerator. They are also used inside motors, DVD players and watches. Because magnets only attract some metals, such as iron, they are also used to separate materials from each other.

Which metals?

Try testing different metal things around your house with a magnet. You will need:

a magnet; metal objects, such as pins, coins, scissors or jewelry

Will it stick?

	Guess	Actual
Tin can	✓	
Coin	✓	
Bottle	✗	
Ball	✗	

1. Guess which objects the magnet will attract.

2. Now test them by seeing if the magnet sticks to them.

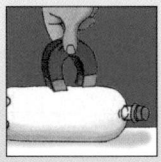

The objects the magnet sticks to probably contain some iron, steel or nickel.

This huge magnet is being used to separate different types of metal so that they can be reused.

"Maglev" trains use magnetic repulsion to make them float just above a rail. This allows them to move very smoothly.

Internet link

For a link to a website where you can find out how to make a magnet maze, go to **www.usborne-quicklinks.com**

Light and color

Light is a form of energy. Most of the light on our planet comes from the Sun. Light comes from other places too – electric lights, candle flames and even some types of animals.

Lines and shadows

Light always travels in straight lines. If light hits an object that's not see-through, it can only shine past it, not around it. This makes a shadow where the light can't reach.

★ Light shines in straight lines. Shadows happen because rays of light cannot bend around objects.

Light can turn a corner if it reflects (bounces) off a surface, such as a mirror.

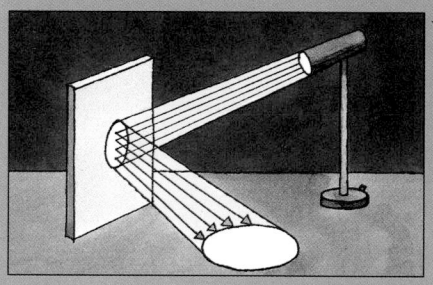

★ You can make light turn a corner. If you shine a lamp at a mirror, the light will bounce off it.

Glow worms can make light as bright as the display lights on a stereo.

The speed of light

When you flip on a light switch, light seems to fill the room instantly. This is because light travels very fast. It moves at 186,000 miles per second.

It takes eight minutes for light to travel from the Sun to the Earth.

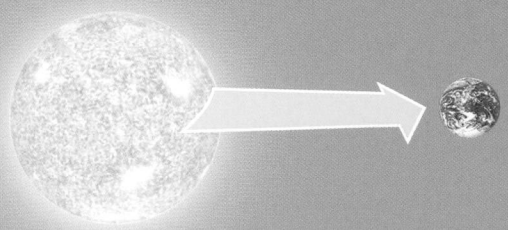

Internet link

For a link to a website where there are activities to help you to find out more about colors, go to **www.usborne-quicklinks.com**

Seeing light

We see things because our eyes are designed to collect and sense light (there's more about eyes on page 107). When we see an object, we're really seeing light reflecting off it.

We see the Moon because light from the Sun reflects off it.

A piece of shaped glass called a prism can split white light into all its colors.

White light shining into prism

Prism

Separate colors of light shining out of prism

Colors

Bright white light is made up of different colors of light mixed together.

We see colors because some objects only reflect one color of light. For example, a green leaf only reflects green light, so it looks green.

Sometimes raindrops act like mini-prisms. They split sunlight into lots of colors, making a rainbow.

Did you know?

- Most people can detect more than 10 million different shades of color.
- Some people are "colorblind". They can see some colors, but find it hard to tell the difference between red and green.
- Many animals see only in shades of gray, not in color.
- Scientists think it's impossible for anything in the Universe to travel faster than light.

Sound

Sound is a form of energy. It is made of vibrations (back-and-forth movements) that can move through air, solid things and liquids, but not through empty space.

Sound vibrations

When you hit a drum, speak or clap, molecules in the air vibrate. We hear sounds because the vibrations travel through air, or other substances, and hit our ears. (Read more about ears on page 107.)

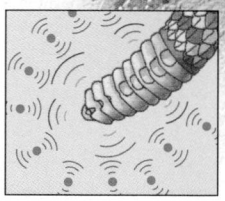

A rattlesnake can make a rattling sound with its tail to scare enemies. The movement of rings on its tail makes molecules in the air vibrate.

The loudest sounds, such as a rocket lift-off (180 decibels), will damage your ears.

Loud and soft

The volume (loudness) of a sound depends on how big the vibrations are. Volume is measured in units called decibels. This chart shows how loud different sounds are in decibels.

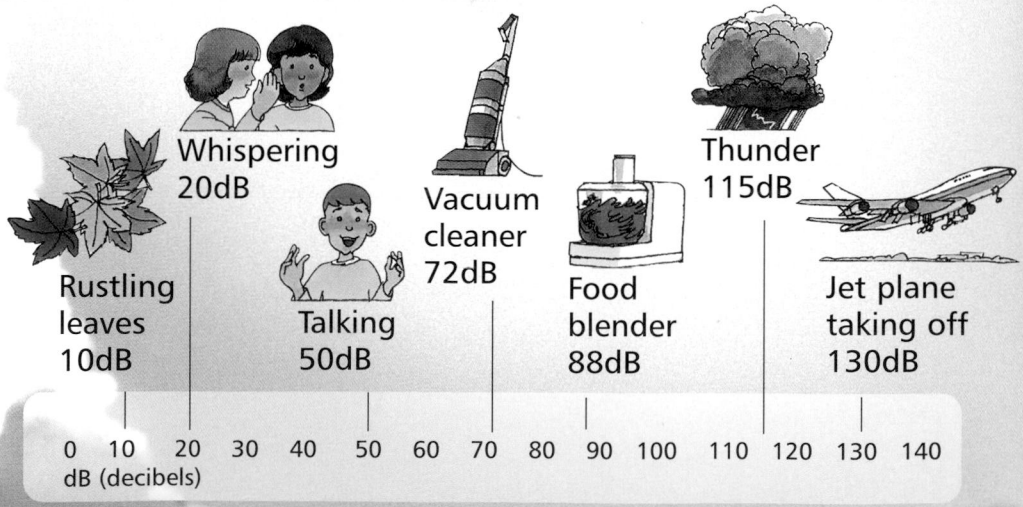

High and low

Fast sound vibrations make high sounds. Slower sound vibrations make lower sounds. The highness or lowness of a sound is called its pitch. Some animals can hear pitches we can't hear.

Internet link

For a link to a website where you can find out how to make a musical instrument and make your own sounds, go to **www.usborne-quicklinks.com**

This farmer's whistle makes a very high sound. Dogs can hear it, but people can't.

Elephants can make sounds so low that people can't hear them.

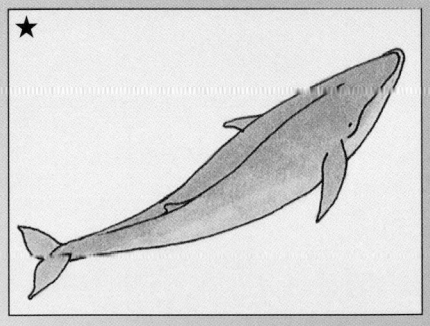

Scientists know that blue whales make the lowest, loudest sound of any animal.

Making music

Musical instruments have parts that vibrate to make sounds. When someone plays an instrument, they make different notes by changing the speed of the vibrations.

Feel sound vibrations

You can't normally feel sound vibrations in the air, but you can in this experiment. You will need:

a radio; a blown-up balloon

Turn the radio on and hold the balloon next to its speaker. The vibrations travel through the balloon and into your fingers.

On a violin, shorter strings vibrate faster and make higher-pitched notes. Violin players make the strings shorter or longer with their fingers.

Electricity

Electricity is a very useful form of energy. It can easily be changed into other forms of energy, such as light and heat. It makes lights, televisions and computers work. Most of the electricity we use comes from power stations.

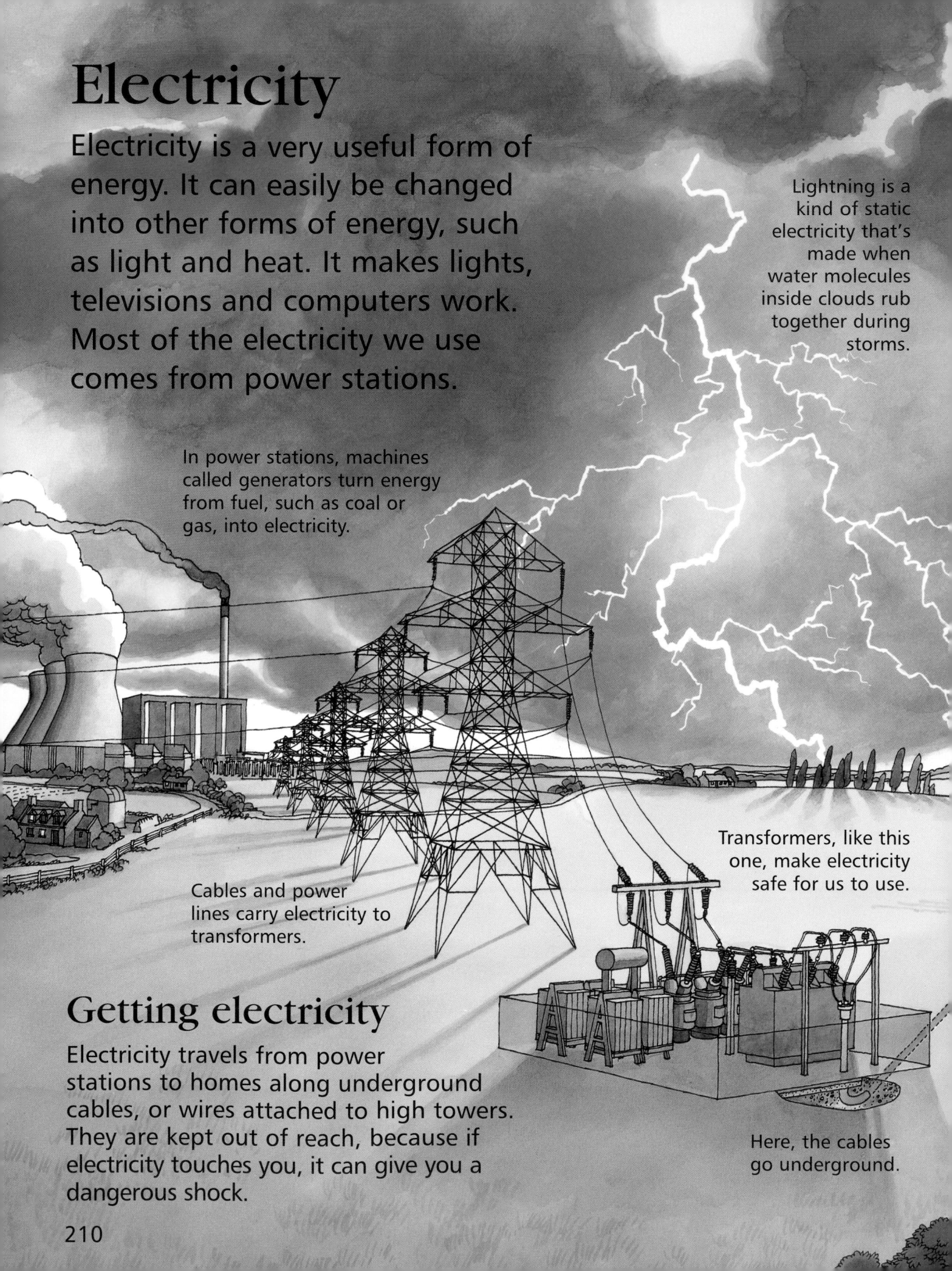

Getting electricity

Electricity travels from power stations to homes along underground cables, or wires attached to high towers. They are kept out of reach, because if electricity touches you, it can give you a dangerous shock.

Using electricity

When an appliance, such as a toaster, is plugged in, it is connected to the electricity supply. Electricity flows into it and gives it the energy to work. Plastic does not conduct, or carry, electricity well, so it is used to cover electrical appliances. This stops you from getting a shock.

Can you guess which of these uses the most electricity in one minute?

Answer: the hairdryer

Internet link

For a link to a website where you can find out how to make electricity from a lemon, go to **www.usborne-quicklinks.com**

Static electricity

Static electricity is a form of electricity that builds up in some substances when they are rubbed together. It can make objects stick to each other. Do you ever feel a small shock when you touch metal? This is caused by a small build-up of static in your body as you move around.

Make static electricity

You will need:

a balloon; a sweater

1. Blow up a balloon, and rub it up and down on a sweater a few times.

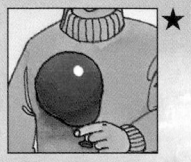

2. Gently put the balloon on the wall. Static electricity makes it stick there.

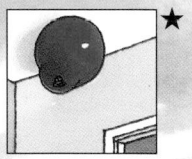

Transformer

The orange and yellow lines show the route the cables take underground.

Electricity flows from the underground cables into homes.

Science words

atom one of the very tiny units that everything is made of.

chemical reaction a change that sometimes happens when two materials are mixed together.

contract get smaller.

density how heavy a material is for its size.

electricity a form of energy which is used to make machines work.

energy the power that makes things work. Heat, light, movement and electricity are all forms of energy.

expand get bigger.

experiment a scientific test to find out about how something works.

force a push or a pull. Forces can make things move, stop, speed up, slow down or change shape.

friction a force that slows things down as they rub or slide against each other.

gravity a force that pulls objects toward other objects. (Usually smaller objects to larger objects.)

heat a form of energy which we can feel. It flows from warmer objects into cooler ones.

kinetic energy the kind of energy that something has when it moves.

light a form of energy that we can sense with our eyes.

magnet a piece of metal that pulls some types of metal toward it.

materials the different kinds of stuff all around us, such as water, metal, wood, glass and plastic.

molecules tiny particles made up of atoms. Everything is made of them.

nucleus the central, most important part of an atom.

observe look at something carefully.

particle a very small piece or part.

pitch how high or low a sound is.

poles the parts of a magnet where its pulling power is strongest.

potential energy energy that's stored up and ready to use.

robot a machine that can do a job in a similar way to a person.

science what we know about the Universe and how things work.

technology using science to invent machines and other useful things.

temperature how hot something is.

theory an idea about how something works or why it is the way it is.

Universe everything that exists in space.

upthrust a pushing force that makes things float.

How things work

Clocks

Most clocks have two or more hands that move around the clock face to show the time. But how does this happen?

Internet link

For a link to a website where you can learn about different kinds of clocks, go to **www.usborne-quicklinks.com**

What's the time?

To show the right time, the hands on a clock have to move at different speeds from each other. Each time the minute hand moves all the way around the clock face, the hour hand just moves to the next number.

In this picture, parts from the inside of a wind-up clock are all stretched out, so you can see them clearly.

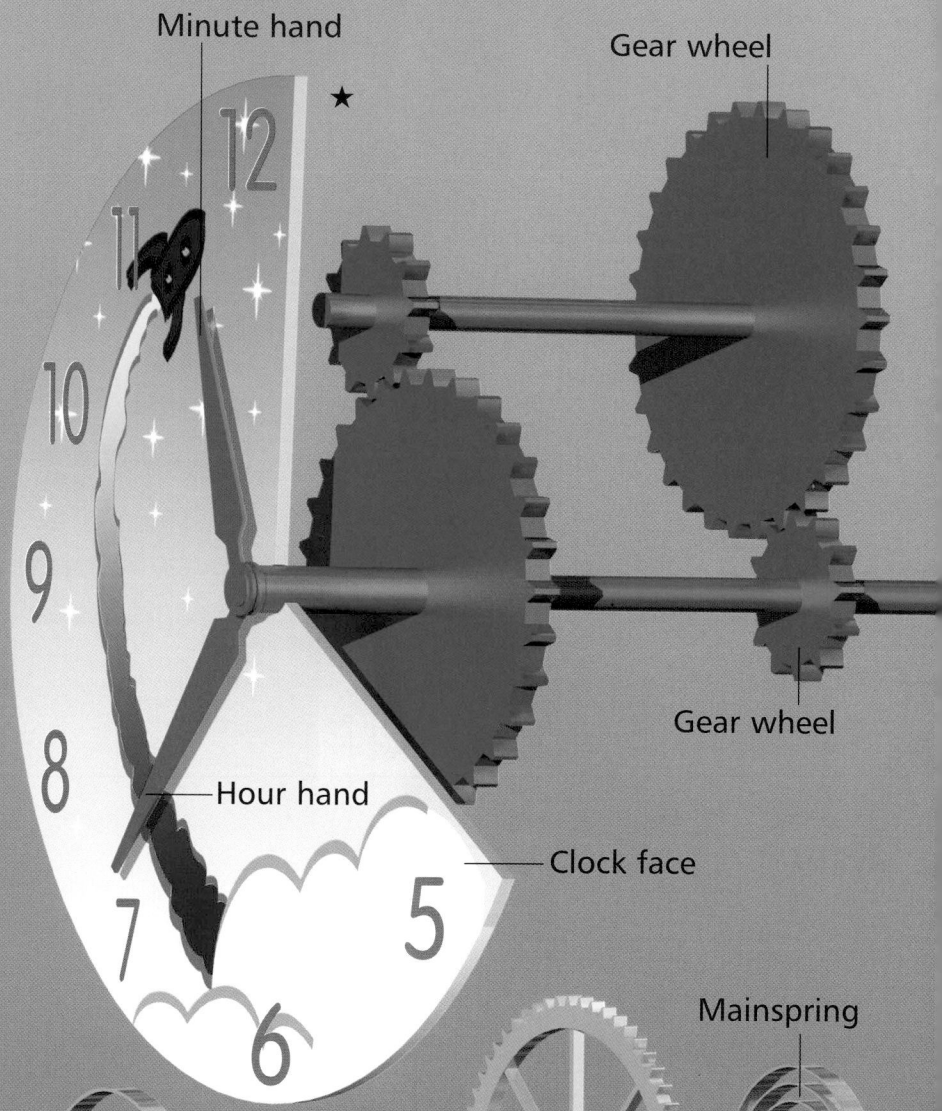

Spring power

A part called the mainspring makes a clock's hands move. This is a curled-up strip of metal that unwinds slowly.

When you turn a knob on the back of the clock, it winds the spring into a tight roll.

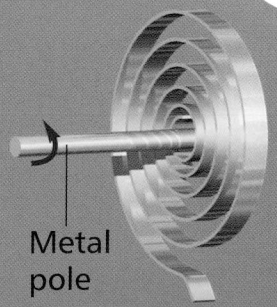

The spring starts to unwind. As it unwinds, it turns a metal pole attached to its middle.

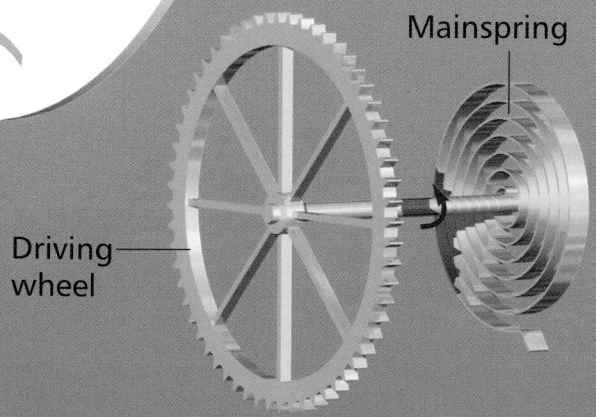

The pole is attached to a driving wheel. As it turns, it makes the driving wheel turn.

The lever and escape wheel

The mainspring would unwind all at once without a part called the lever. The lever moves back and forth at the same speed all the time. This controls how fast the mainspring unwinds, as shown here.

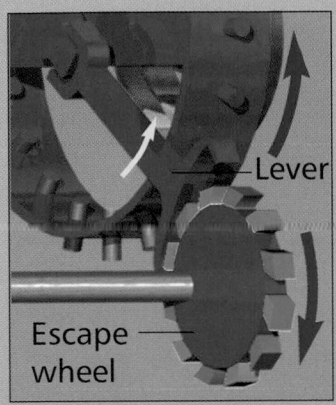

As the lever moves forward, it pushes the escape wheel forward one notch.

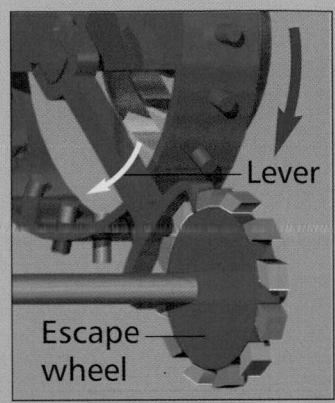

The lever moves back again, catching the next notch of the escape wheel.

The escape wheel is joined to the driving wheel. Each time the escape wheel moves forward one notch, it lets the driving wheel and mainspring move a little too.

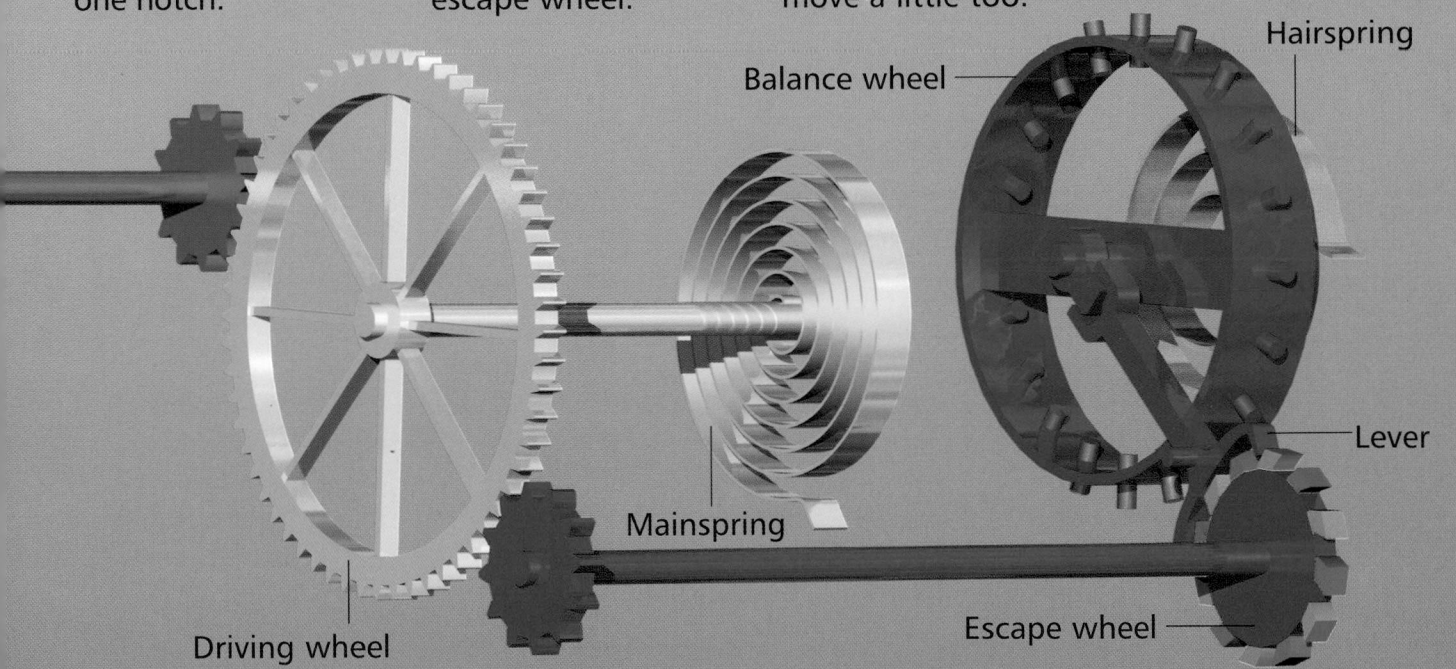

Gears and teeth

The driving wheel turns little wheels called gears, which make the hands move at different speeds. They are locked together by teeth, so as one moves, it moves the others. The fewer teeth a gear has, the faster it moves.

The small gear moves around faster than the big one, because it has fewer teeth.

Cameras

Cameras are small machines used for taking photos. Digital cameras have tiny computers in them that store the photos. Other cameras store them on film.

In the picture below, the back of this camera has been cut away, so you can see inside.

This glass lens lets light into the camera.

Using film

Photographic film comes in a roll that fits inside the back of a camera. It is made of a type of plastic that changes when light shines on it.

Part of this film case has been cut away, so you can see the film inside.

A length of film stretches across the inside of the camera behind the shutter (see below).

This is the viewfinder. You look through it to see your subject (what you're taking a picture of).

You push this button to take a photo.

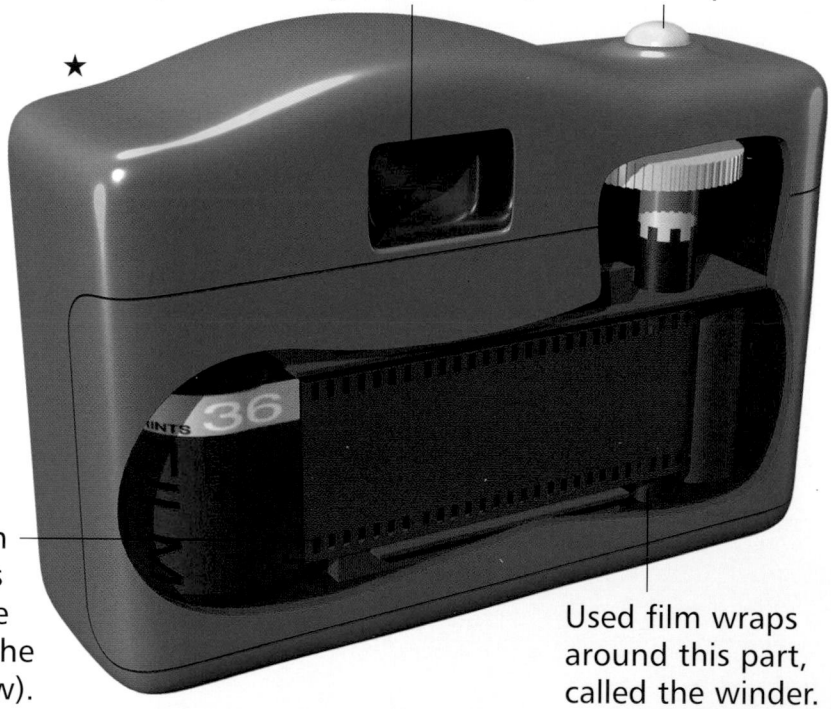

Used film wraps around this part, called the winder.

Taking pictures

When light shines on things it reflects, or bounces, off them. This allows you to see them.* A camera also uses light reflecting off things to take pictures.

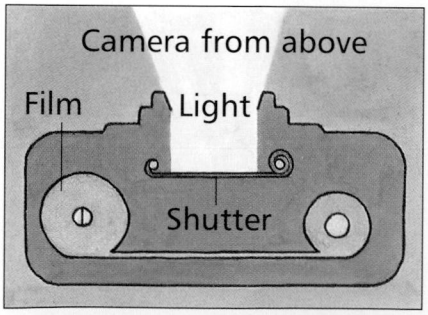

Inside the camera, a flap called the shutter usually covers the film. It stops any light from touching it.

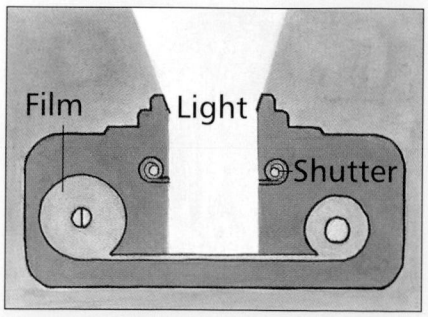

If you press the button, the shutter opens for a moment. Light comes through the lens, making a picture on the film.

 *Find out more on page 107.

From film to photo

Making film into photos is called developing. It is difficult to do, so most people send or take their film to a company to have it developed. There, a machine dips the film in chemicals to make small pictures called negatives. Then, it shines light through the negatives onto special paper to make the photographs.

On a negative, dark areas look light, and light areas look dark.

This photo is made from one of the negatives on the left. Can you see which one?

Internet link

For a link to a website where you can make your own camera, go to **www.usborne-quicklinks.com**

Digital cameras

Because a digital camera doesn't use film, its pictures don't need developing. Instead, they can be loaded onto a home computer so that you can see them on screen. Digital photos can also be printed out or sent to other computers by email.

Digital photos are made of tiny squares called pixels.

A digital camera

Movies

A movie is made from a long strip of photos, called frames, shown very quickly one after another. The long strip is called film. Movies are shown in theatres using a film projector.

Film

Reel

This glass lens projects the light (sends it outwards).

This is a film projector with parts cut away, so that you can see inside.

This bulb shines a bright light through each frame.

Reel

Showtime

A film projector has two big wheels, called reels. The reels turn, winding the film off the top reel and onto the bottom one. Each frame of the film passes in front of a bulb, which shines a bright light through it.

The pictures below are frames of a galloping horse.

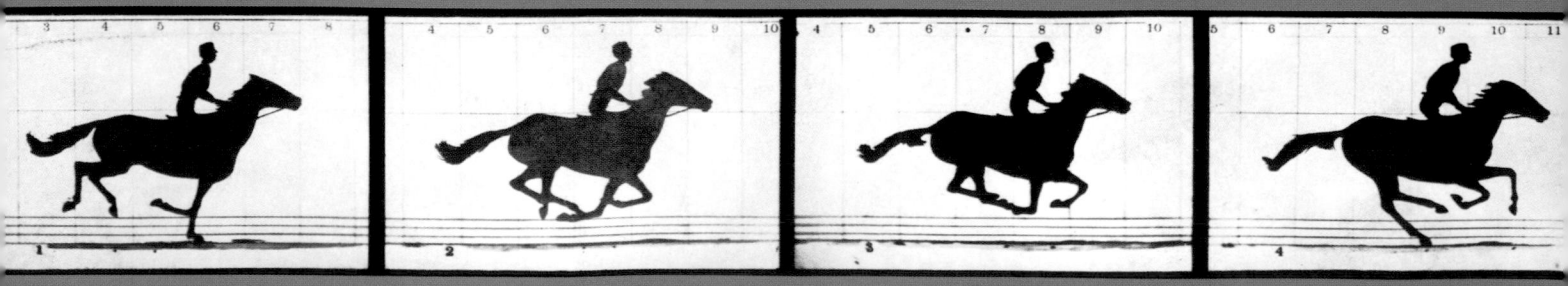

Moving pictures

Most projectors show 24 frames every second. This is much too fast for you to be able to see one frame changing to the next. This makes it look like one, moving picture.

When the light hits the screen on the far wall of the theatre, it makes a much bigger copy of the frame in the projector.

© Disney Enterprises, Inc./Pixar Animation Studios

Internet link

For a link to a website where you can learn how to make your own movie, go to **www.usborne-quicklinks.com**

Make your own flip book movie

A flip book works in the same way as a movie. Here's how to make a mini-movie of somebody jumping up and down:

1. Get a notebook and draw a stick person, like the one here, on the last page.

2. On the page before, draw another person, just starting to jump up in the air.

3. Keep doing this until you have pictures of the person jumping up and down.

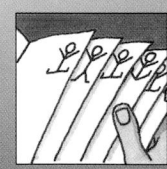

4. Flip through the pictures quickly. It will look like a film of the person jumping.

Televisions

Have you ever wondered where television programs come from and how they reach your screen? And if you could look inside a television set, what would you see?

These parts, called electron guns, fire electricity at the screen to make the picture.

Television screen

Electricity travels across this space, called the cathode ray tube and hits the back of the screen.

Parts of this television set have been cut away, so you can see inside.

Pictures

Televisions work like movies by showing lots of pictures quickly, one after another. Each picture on a television is made up of tiny lines.

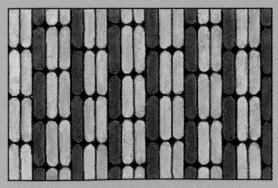

On the back of the screen is a thin layer of red, green and blue lines. They are too tiny to see.

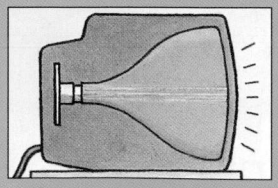

The electron guns fire electricity at the screen. When it hits the lines, it makes them glow.

The lines are so tiny that the colors seem to mix, making all the colors you see on the screen.

Getting the pictures

Television programs are made in television studios. Then they are turned into invisible signals called radio waves (see page 223) and sent into the air. Below, you can see how the radio waves get to your television.

Internet link

For a link to a website where you can learn more about how TV works, go to **www.usborne-quicklinks.com**

A television station sends radio waves out to a transmitter tower. They travel quickly through the air.

Transmitter towers pick up the radio waves and send them in all directions. This is called broadcasting.

Radio waves from a transmitter tower can travel a long way to reach lots of televisions.

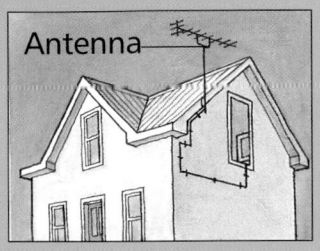

Antennae collect waves and pass them to televisions by a cable. Televisions turn them back into programs.

Satellite television

Some television signals come from spacecraft called satellites. Satellites orbit (travel around) the Earth. They can cover a much bigger area than transmitter towers.

Satellite televisions pick up radio waves from space using a kind of antenna called a satellite dish.

This satellite in space picks up radio waves and broadcasts them back to Earth.

A television station sends radio waves into space.

Sound systems

You can use sound systems for listening to music or the radio. They have lots of different parts.

Internet link

For a link to a website where you can watch a movie about sound, go to **www.usborne-quicklinks.com**

This shows a sound system, with parts cut away, so you can see inside.

This is one of the two speakers. The sound comes out of them.

CDs go on a tray, which slides in and out of the CD player.

The CD player

CDs have sound stored on them in code. Inside a CD player, a CD spins around very fast. A thin beam of light, called a laser beam, shines onto the CD and reads the code.

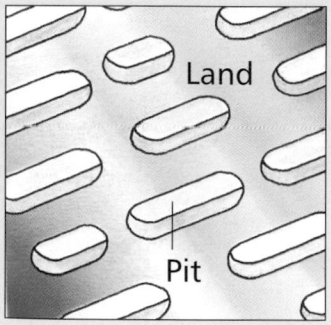

The coded sound is on the underside of a CD. The code is made of flat parts, called land, and dips, called pits.

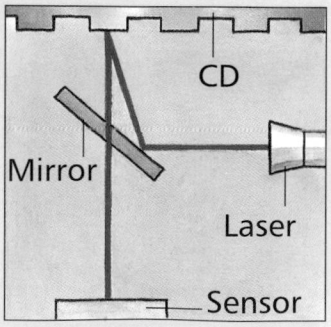

A laser beam reflects off a mirror onto the spinning CD. If it hits land it bounces off, and hits a sensor.

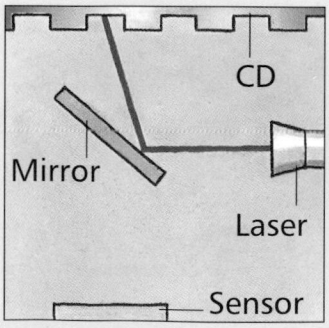

If the beam hits a pit, it doesn't bounce off. The sensor can tell from this that the beam has hit a pit.

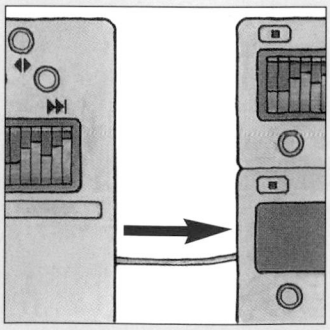

The CD player turns the sound information from the sensor into another code, which it sends to the amplifier.

The amplifier

The amplifier's job is to change the information it gets from the radio or CD player into an electrical signal. It sends this signal to the speakers.

The speakers

Most sounds are made by making air move quickly.* Parts inside a speaker shake to make the air around them move. This turns signals from the amplifier into sounds you can hear.

Radio waves

Radio stations make programs and send them into the air as radio waves. Radio waves are invisible signals that can carry information. Radios pick up the signals and play the programs.

*Find out more on pages 208-209.

Telephones

Telephones all over our planet are linked together. This means that people can talk to each other wherever they are in the world.

This is a telephone with some of its plastic case cut away, so you can see the electrical parts inside.

The part you listen to is called the speaker.

The plug fits into a socket in the wall. Wires in the wall give it power and link the phone to others.

The part you speak into is called the mouthpiece.

Sending signals

If you call a friend, your phone sends a signal to his or her phone. This only takes a few seconds, even if your friend lives a long way away.

1. To call a friend, you dial his number. This sends a signal out of your phone and down a wire.

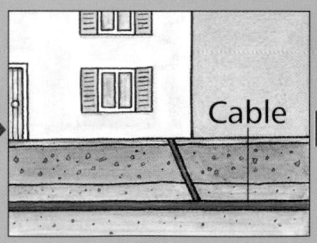

2. The wire carries the signal out of your home to a bigger wire, called a cable, under the ground.

3. The cable carries the signal to a telephone exchange. This is a building full of computers.

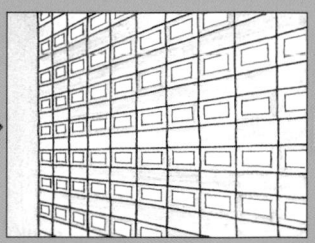

4. The computers at the exchange read the number you dialed. It tells them where to send the signal.

Mobile phones

Mobile phones send signals called radio waves (see page 223) to connect to other phones. The waves travel through the air, so mobiles can be used almost anywhere.

To make a call, a mobile phone sends out radio waves. The waves are picked up by the nearest transmitter tower.

There are transmitter towers all over the world. They are linked to exchanges (see step 3. on opposite page).

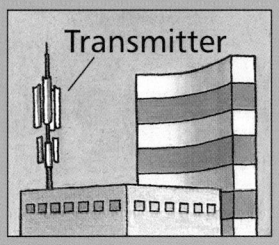

To make a mobile ring, an exchange sends out radio waves to lots of towers. The phone picks them up from the nearest one.

Internet link

For a link to a website where you can watch a movie about how phones work, go to **www.usborne-quicklinks.com**

The antenna sends and picks up phone signals.

This is the speaker.

This screen displays information, such as phone numbers.

This part, called a SIM card, contains information about the phone, such as its number.

This is the battery. It stores power to make the phone work.

Parts of this mobile phone have been cut away, so you can see inside.

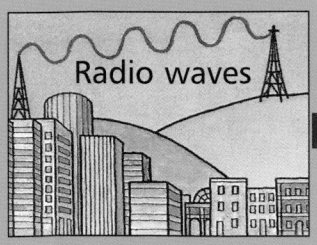

5. Some signals go along cables. Signals going a long way are sent as radio waves (see page 223).

6. The signal travels to the exchange nearest your friend's home. There are exchanges all over the world.

7. This exchange sends the signal to your friend's home. It travels to the phone and makes it ring.

8. Your friend picks up the phone. This connects the two phones, so you can talk to each other.

Computers

Computers can help people to do all kinds of things, from writing letters to flying space rockets. They can store information and do complex calculations very fast.

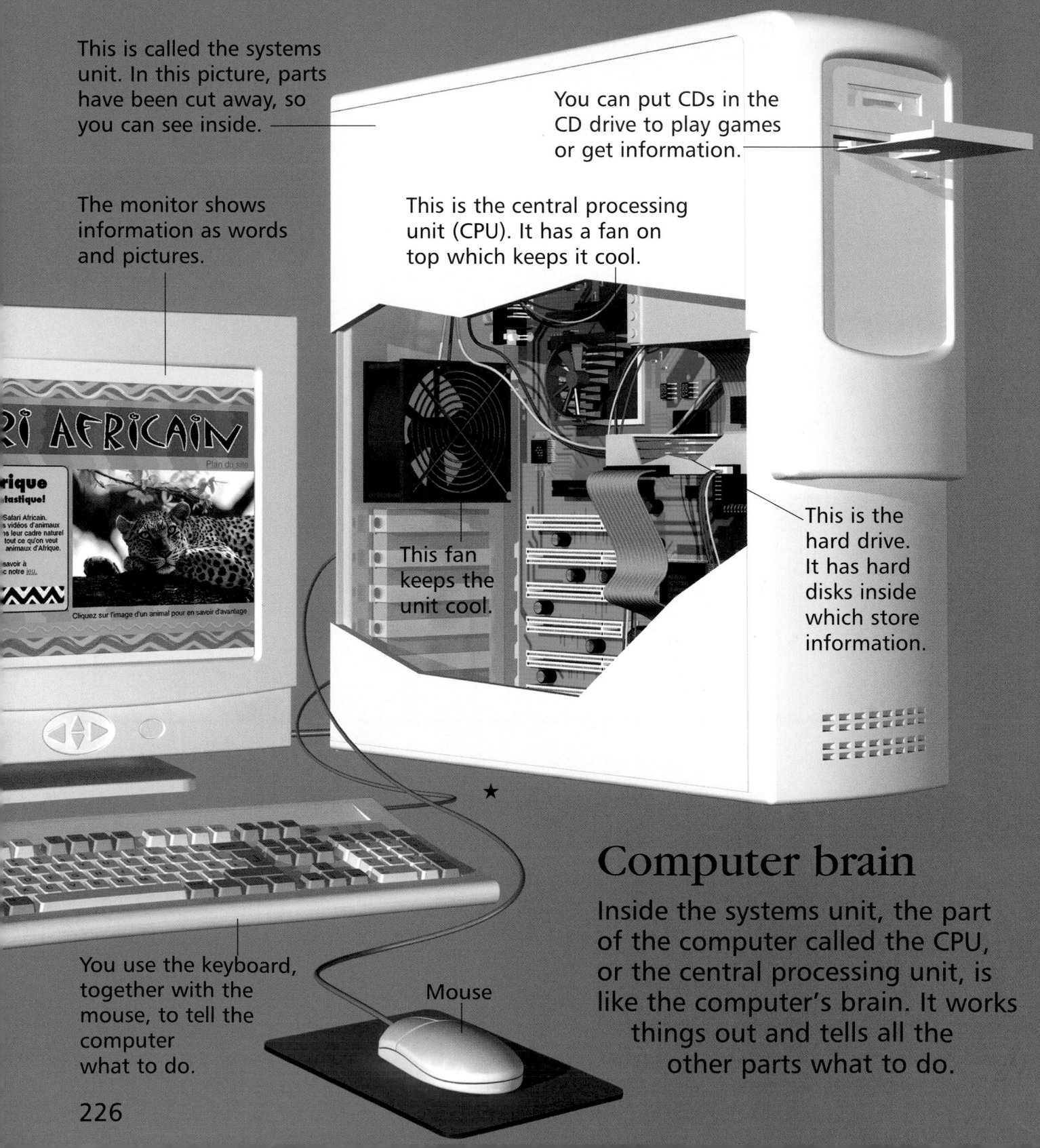

Computer brain

Inside the systems unit, the part of the computer called the CPU, or the central processing unit, is like the computer's brain. It works things out and tells all the other parts what to do.

Computer programs

Computers can't actually think for themselves. People have to write sets of instructions for them, called programs. These are stored inside the systems unit in the hard disks. The computer uses these instructions to carry out tasks.

Using a program called Microsoft® Paint, you can draw pictures using a computer.

Sending messages

The different parts of a computer are used for doing different tasks. To work, the computer sends messages between the different parts.

You press a key on the keyboard. This sends a message down a wire into the systems unit.

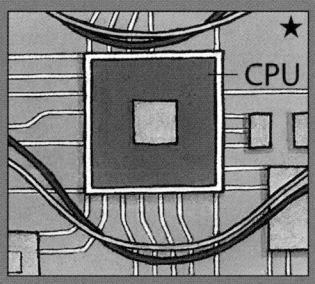

Inside the systems unit, a message is sent to the CPU. The CPU works out what to do.

A message is sent to the monitor. The screen shows you what the computer has done.

Useful robots

Robots have computers inside them that make them work a little like people or animals. They can be used in factories to make cars or other things. Scientists are now trying to create robots that can learn things by themselves, like people can.

This is a robot giraffe. It has little computers inside it which make it move very much like a real giraffe.

Internet link

For a link to a website where you can learn more about computers, and a website with movies of all kinds of robots, go to **www.usborne-quicklinks.com**

The Internet

Computers can be linked together to share information. A group of linked computers is called a network. The biggest network in the world is called the Internet.

Some computers send messages to satellites in space. Satellites send them to other computers.

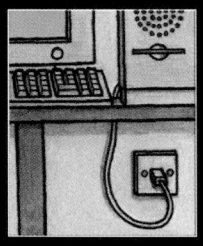

Computers can be attached to telephone lines. Information travels along these lines.

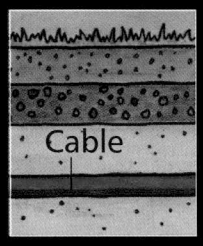

Some computers are connected by cables. Cables go under the ground or under the sea.

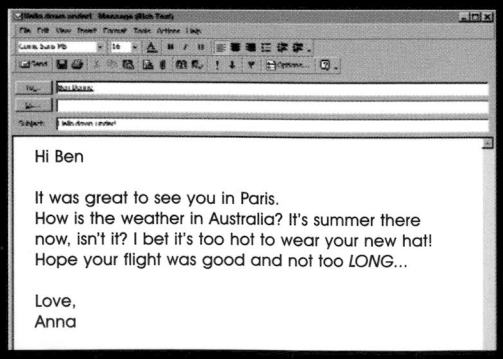

Hi Ben

It was great to see you in Paris.
How is the weather in Australia? It's summer there now, isn't it? I bet it's too hot to wear your new hat! Hope your flight was good and not too *LONG*...

Love,
Anna

An email message

Websites and email

Part of the Internet is called the World Wide Web. The Web is made up of websites, which are pages of information. Websites are stored on powerful computers called servers. Servers can also send messages called emails between computers.

Addresses

There are millions of websites on servers all over the world. To help you find the one you want, each site has its own Web address.

This is a website address.

http://www.usborne.com

"www" stands for World Wide Web.

Internet link

For a link to a website where you can do fun quizzes to learn about using the Internet, go to **www.usborne-quicklinks.com**

These are pages from websites.

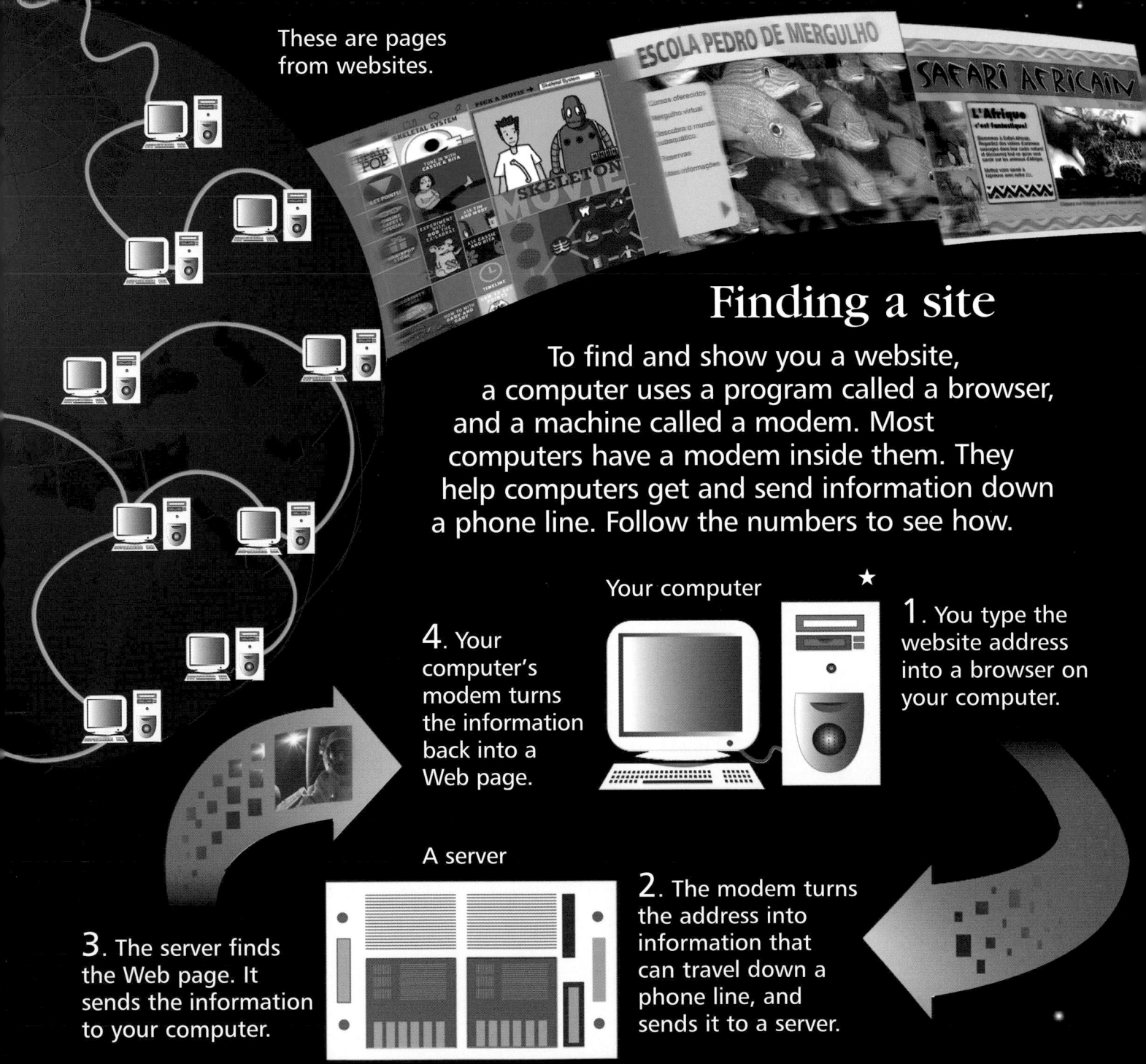

Finding a site

To find and show you a website, a computer uses a program called a browser, and a machine called a modem. Most computers have a modem inside them. They help computers get and send information down a phone line. Follow the numbers to see how.

1. You type the website address into a browser on your computer.

2. The modem turns the address into information that can travel down a phone line, and sends it to a server.

3. The server finds the Web page. It sends the information to your computer.

4. Your computer's modem turns the information back into a Web page.

Refrigerators

Food stays fresh longer if it is kept in a refrigerator. A refrigerator stays cool by pumping liquid refrigerant through pipes.

Keeping cool

When you get wet, your skin cools down as it dries. This is because the water turns into a gas, or evaporates. As liquid evaporates, it absorbs heat, and this is also what keeps a refrigerator cool. Follow the numbers on the big picture on the right to see how.

Red arrows show heat.

The light inside

The light inside a refrigerator comes on whenever you open the door. When you shut the door, it presses against a switch, turning the light off.

When the refrigerator door opens, the switch pops up and the light comes on.

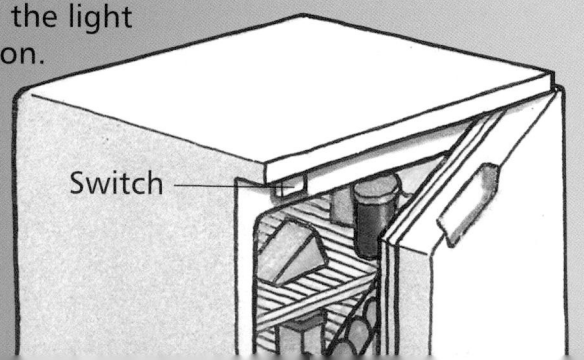

1. Refrigerant liquid is pumped into the evaporator coil. It starts to evaporate.

Evaporator coil

2. As it evaporates, the refrigerant absorbs heat from the food and air in the refrigerator.

Condenser coil

3. Refrigerant gas goes into the condenser where it turns back into liquid, or condenses. It lets off heat into the air outside.

Pump

This is a refrigerator with parts cut away so you can see how it works. ★

Microwave ovens

A microwave oven can heat up food much more quickly than a normal oven can. To do this, it uses invisible waves called microwaves.

Internet link

For a link to a website where you can watch a movie about how refrigerators work, go to **www.usborne-quicklinks.com**

Hot and cold

Everything in the world is made up of very tiny parts called atoms.* They are much too small to see, but when something gets hot, it's because the atoms in it are moving quickly.

When something is cold, the atoms in it move slowly.

In something hot, the atoms move more quickly.

Bouncing waves

A microwave is a kind of radio wave (see page 223). Microwaves can travel through the air and through water, too. Food contains water, so microwaves can travel through it. When they do this, they make all the atoms move around more quickly. This heats the food up.

Microwaves are invisible but the red arrows show how they travel.

Magnetron – this makes the microwaves.

Part of this microwave oven has been cut away, so that you can see inside.

This plate turns around so the microwaves go into all parts of the food.

Microwaves bounce off the oven's metal walls.

*Find out more on pages 186-187.

Toilets and faucets

The water you use in your home probably comes from a place called a reservoir. Linked-up water pipes carry it to toilets, faucets and showers around the house. This is called plumbing.

Reservoirs are enormous man-made lakes. Water is stored in them until it is needed.

1. A main service pipe brings water into a house.

Water tank

2. The water is stored in a tank. Two pipes come out of it.

Toilet

Sink

Shower

3. One pipe goes to this tank, called a cylinder, which heats the water.

4. Dirty water leaves through pipes called drainpipes.

Main service pipe

Drainpipe

Down the drain

Dirty water and waste from toilets flows through underground pipes to places called sewage stations. At a sewage station, all the dirt and waste is removed, so that the water can be used again.

The picture on the right shows a sewage station from the air. The dark circles are enormous tanks of dirty water.

Around the bend

Water for flushing a toilet is stored in a tank called a cistern. Here's what happens when you flush:

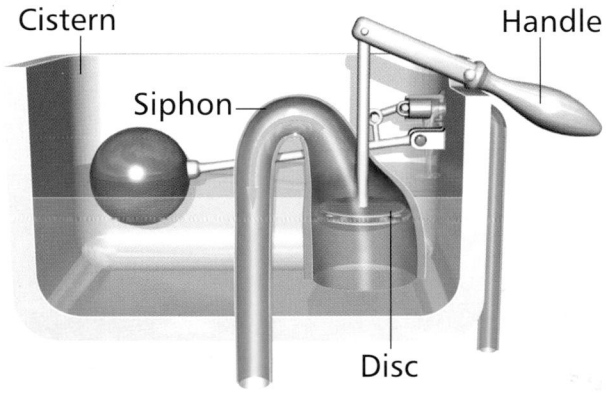

When you push the handle, the disc lifts up. This pushes water over the top of the siphon. As the water falls, it sucks the rest of the water with it.

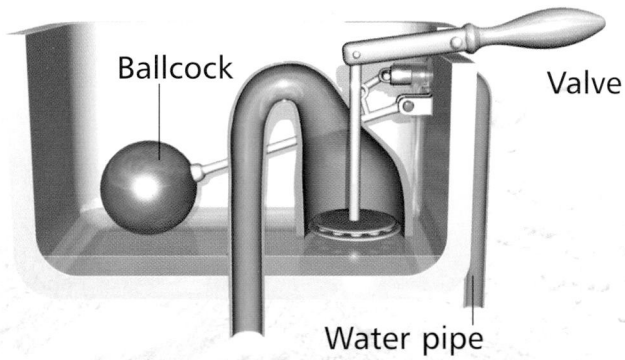

As the cistern empties, the disc drops, and a float, called a ballcock, drops too. This pulls a valve out of the pipe so more water flows into the cistern.

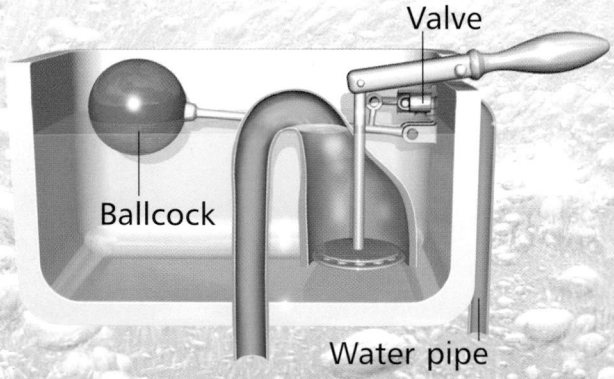

As the cistern fills again, the ballcock rises. When it is full, the ballcock pushes the valve back into the pipe. This stops any more water from getting in.

Internet link

For a link to a website where you can read about the history of toilets, go to **www.usborne-quicklinks.com**

When you flush a toilet, the water carries the waste around the bend and down the drain.

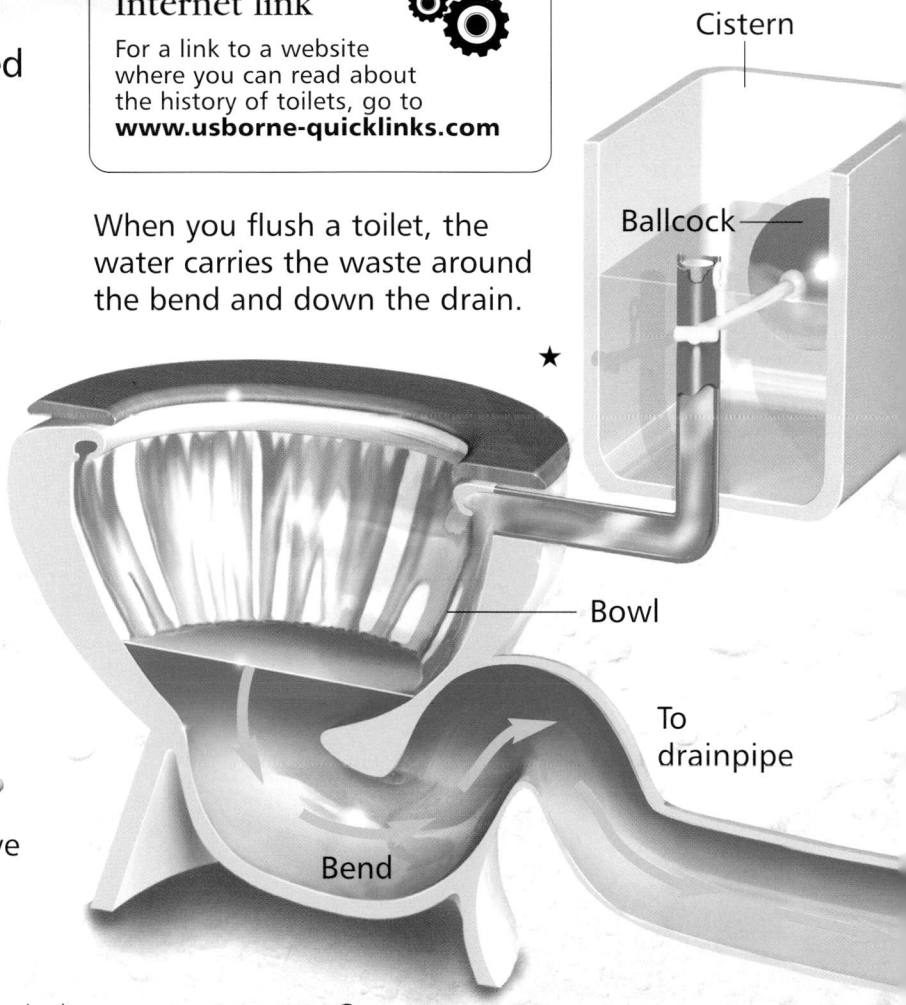

Turning a faucet

Inside a faucet, there is a long screw with a disc, called a washer, on the end. When you turn the faucet handle, it turns the screw. This moves the washer up to turn the faucet on, or down to turn it off.

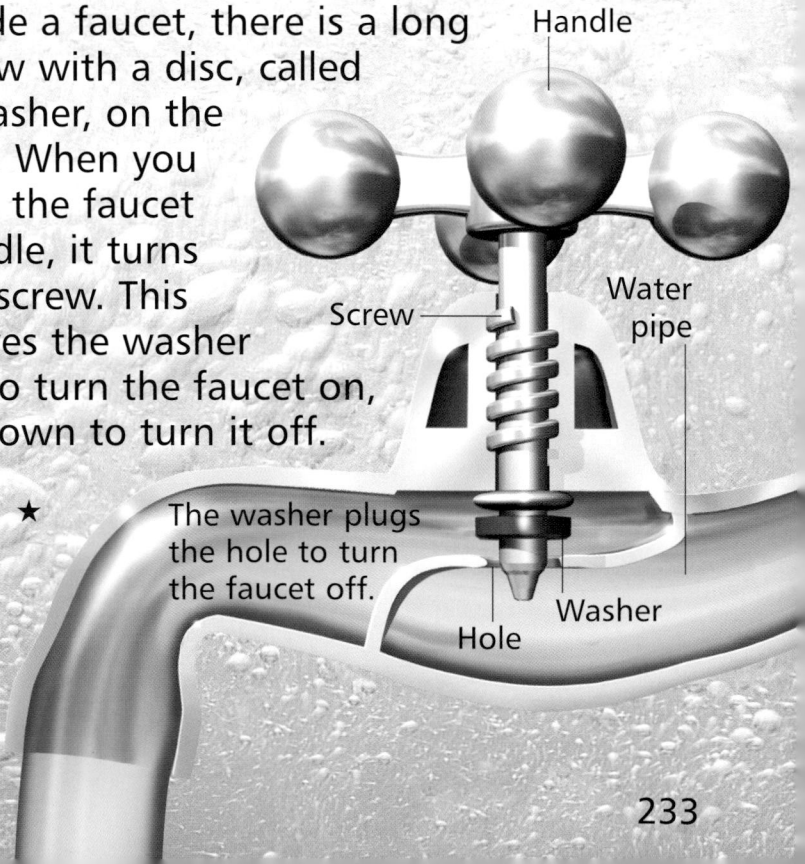

The washer plugs the hole to turn the faucet off.

Cars and motorcycles

Cars and other vehicles, such as trucks, vans and motorcycles, have engines in them to make them go. They need fuel to make the engines work.

This is the engine.

There are four of these cylinders inside this engine. Each cylinder has a piston inside it.

Spark plug

MINI COOPER S

This type of car is called a MINI COOPER S. Parts of it have been cut away, so you can see inside.

★

The wheel is cut away here to show the brakes.

How does the engine work?

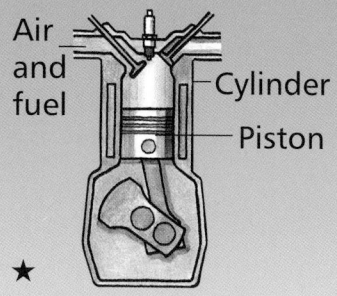

★

A piston inside the cylinder moves down, sucking air and fuel into the cylinder.

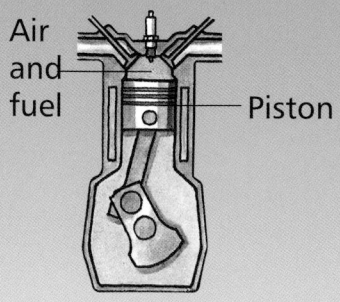

The piston then moves up again. This squashes the air and the fuel together.

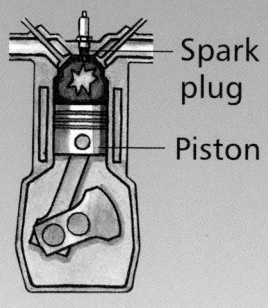

The spark plug lights the fuel. It burns with a bang, pushing the piston down.

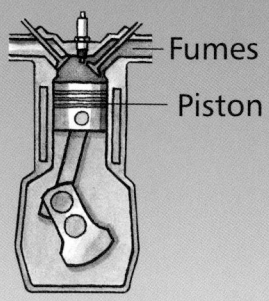

There are fumes left. The piston moves up, pushing them out of the cylinder.

Internet link

For a link to a website where you can find out more about how a car engine works, go to **www.usborne-quicklinks.com**

An exhaust pipe takes fumes away from the engine.

Fuel tank

Exhaust pipe

How the wheels turn

The pistons in an engine are connected to a pole called the crankshaft. As they go up and down, they turn the crankshaft, which makes the driveshafts turn. The driveshafts make the front wheels go around.

The whole car is pulled along by the front wheels.

Piston

Driveshaft

Crankshaft

Motorcycles

Motorcycles work in a similar way to cars. They have smaller engines than cars, but can accelerate (speed up) much quicker. A driver twists the handles on a motorcycle to accelerate.

Disc brakes

Cars and motorcycles have kinds of brakes called disc brakes to make them slow down or stop.

When you press a car's brake pedal, a liquid called brake fluid is pushed down a pipe to the brake pads.

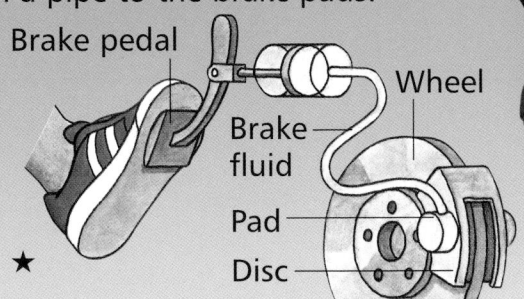

The pads push on the discs. The discs grip the wheels which stops them from turning.

A rider makes the bike lean all the way over to go around bends.

Diggers

A digger, or excavator, is a machine for digging large holes. The kind of digger you can see here is called a backhoe excavator. It uses a metal bucket, called a backhoe, to dig into the ground.

Internet link

For a link to a website where you can learn more about how diggers work, go to **www.usborne-quicklinks.com**

These parts move the digger's arm.

These hinges allow the arm to move.

The digger's body can spin around.

This is the digger's arm.

When it's muddy, these crawler tracks help the digger to grip.

Teeth

The backhoe's metal teeth cut into the earth, helping it to dig.

Moving the arm

A digger's arm moves using metal discs, called pistons, inside oil-filled tubes, called cylinders. These are attached to different parts of the arm by metal rods. The driver can move the pistons up and down in the cylinders, making parts of the arm move. Here's how the driver moves the backhoe:

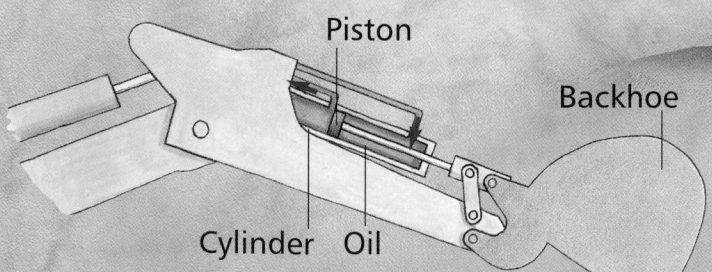

The driver pulls a lever. Oil pumps into the bottom and out of the top of a cylinder. This pushes the piston up, pulling the backhoe up.

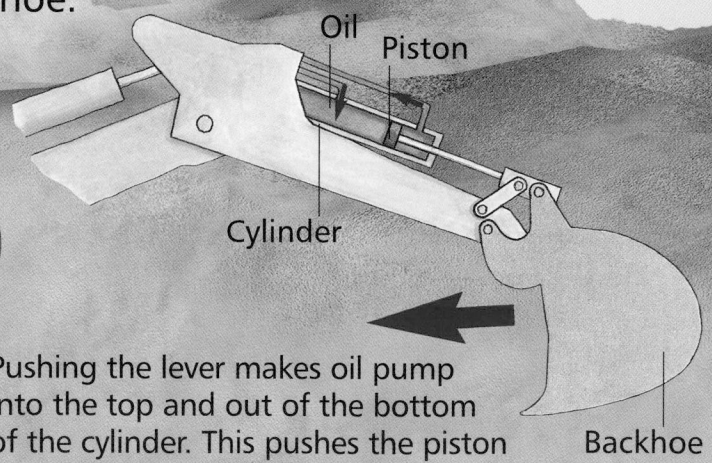

Pushing the lever makes oil pump into the top and out of the bottom of the cylinder. This pushes the piston down, which pushes the backhoe down.

Tractors

Tractors' big engines are extremely powerful. This makes them useful for lifting and pulling heavy things.

This shows a tractor with part of the front cut away, so you can see inside.

The part where the driver sits is called the cab.

Large wheels with tough tires help tractors to keep their grip in mud.

Tractors move slowly, so their engines don't use much fuel.

Tools can be attached to these metal links at the back of a tractor.

This is the PTO (power take-off). It is connected to the tractor's engine.

Power tools

At the back of a tractor there's a metal pole called a power take-off, or PTO. Tools connected to the PTO get power from the tractor's engine. Below are two of the tools that a farmer can attach to a tractor to do different jobs.

A post driver bangs fence posts into the ground. The farmer moves it to where he wants to put a post.

When the farmer presses a button, a big weight rises and falls, hammering the post into the ground.

A hay baler collects up dried grass, called hay. Tubes inside it spin, rolling the hay into a cylinder called a bale.

When the baler is full, it opens, and the new bale rolls out. The hay can be used for feeding farm animals.

Trains

Trains move along specially built tracks to take people and things from one place to another. They often travel huge distances: the longest train track in the world is over 5,500 miles long.

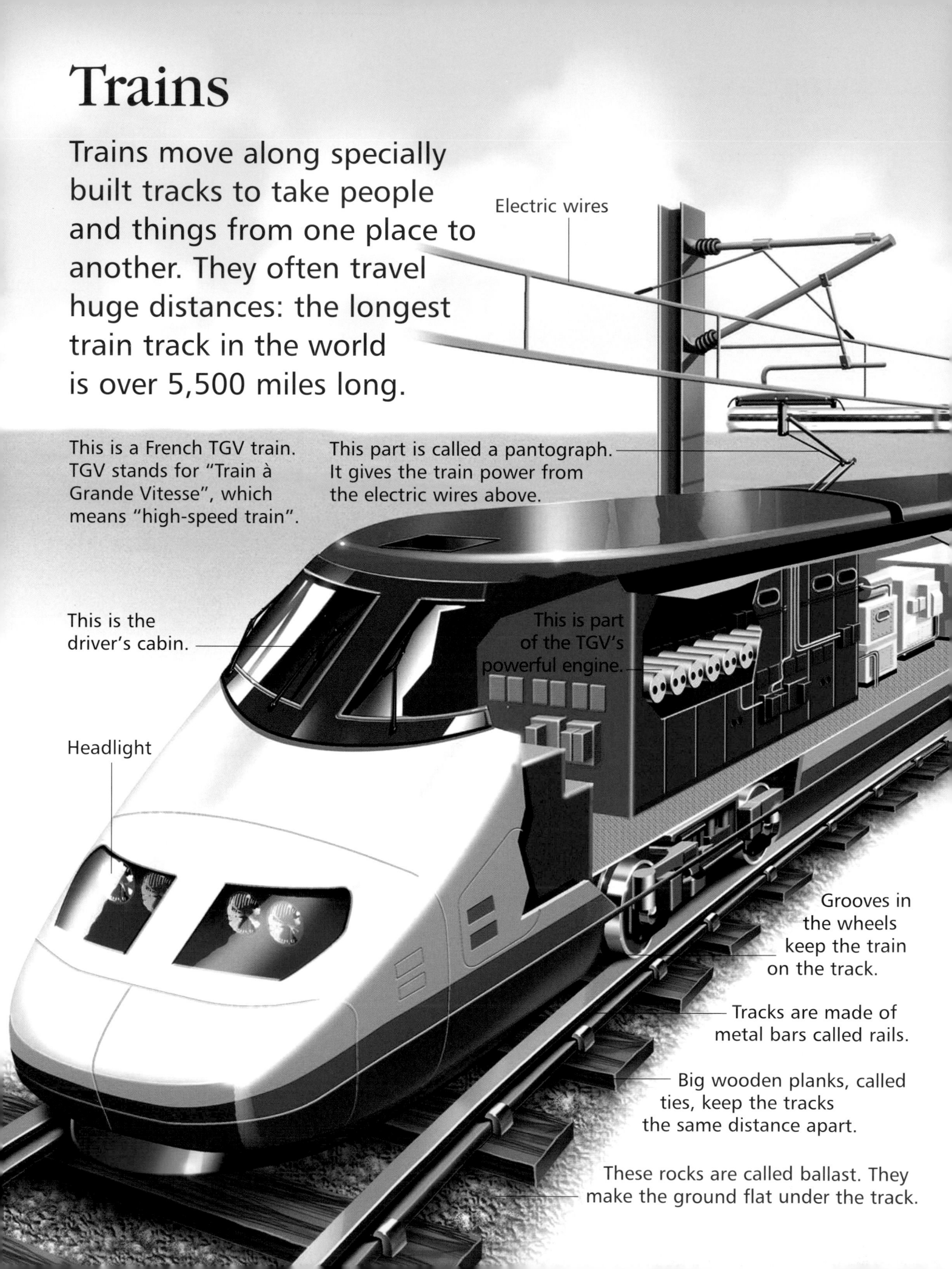

Getting faster

Scientists are always looking for ways to make faster trains. This train, called a maglev, doesn't even touch the rail. It uses magnets to push it through the air.

Magnets on the sides of the train push it along very quickly.

Magnets on the bottom of the train pull it toward the rail.

A Japanese Bullet Train can travel at more than 180mph.

The sections of a train are called cars.

Most TGV cars have seats for up to 60 passengers.

In the driver's seat

The train driver sits in a cabin, called the control cabin, at the front of the train. The picture below shows the controls inside the cabin of a TGV train.

Internet link

For a link to a website where you can hear old-fashioned steam train noises, go to **www.usborne-quicklinks.com**

This button stops the train very quickly in an emergency.

This lever controls the speed of the train.

This shows how fast the train is going.

The driver can talk to the controller on this radio.

★

Planes

Flying in a plane is the fastest way you can travel. Planes are able to fly because they have powerful engines and specially shaped wings.

Internet link

For a link to a website where you can learn how to make paper planes, go to **www.usborne-quicklinks.com**

Take-off

A plane's wings are more curved on the top than on the bottom. This shape is called an airfoil. Follow the numbers below to see how it helps a plane to take off and fly.

The tip of this plane's wing shows the airfoil shape.

Engine

★

These arrows show how the air flows.

1. The plane's powerful engines make it go forward very quickly. Air rushes past the wings.

2. Because of the airfoil shape, air flows faster over the tops of the wings than underneath them.

3. The air under the wing pushes up more than the air on top of it pushes down. This lifts the plane up.

Make a wing

See how air flowing fast over one side of a piece of paper makes it lift, like a plane's wing. You will need:

a piece of thin paper, 2in x 6in

1. Hold the short side of the paper to your lips, letting it hang down.

2. Blow across the top of the paper. It will lift up into the air.

Concorde planes have very pointed noses. This shape lets the air flow past smoothly so that Concorde can fly at supersonic speed (faster than the speed of sound).

These arrows show how the air flows.

Steering the plane

Planes have parts on their wings and tails that can move. To make the plane go in different directions, the pilot uses the controls to move these parts.

Rudder

Aileron

Elevator

Elevator

To make the plane climb, the pilot tilts the elevators up. Air pushes on them, making the tail go down and the nose go up.

To turn the plane, the pilot turns the rudder, and tilts one aileron up and one down.

To make the plane dive, the pilot tilts the elevators down. Air pushes on them, making the tail go up and the nose go down.

Flight control

The pilot controls the plane from the cockpit at the front. Inside the cockpit, the control panel of a small plane looks like this.

This dial shows how high in the sky the plane is flying.

This dial shows the direction in which the plane is flying.

The pilot moves these controls to steer the plane.

Ships and boats

Ships and boats are often used for carrying people or heavy things around the world. Big boats are called ships. Some, like this cruise ship, can hold up to two thousand passengers.

In this picture of a cruise ship some parts have been cut away, so you can see inside.

Funnel

Lifeboats like this can be used in emergencies.

The back of a ship is called its stern.

Four propellers push the ship forward.

Four engines power the propellers.

Internet link

For a link to a website where you can find out more about how boats float, go to **www.usborne-quicklinks.com**

How do boats float?

If you could put an enormous lump of metal that weighed the same as a boat into the sea, it would sink. A boat can float because it is hollow, and because of its special shape. You can find more about how things float on pages 200-201.

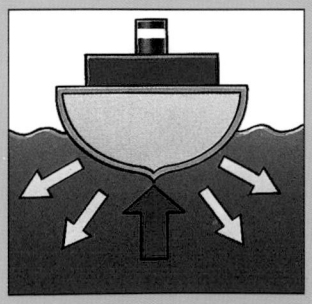

When a boat is in water, it pushes downwards. The water pushes back, which makes the boat float. This is called upthrust (see page 200).

Make your own boat

Try this to see how a boat's shape makes it float. You will need:

a large bowl of water; a lump of modeling clay

1. Take the clay and roll it into a ball. Put it in the bowl of water. It will sink.

2. Cup the clay in one hand. Use your thumb to make it into a boat shape.

3. Put the clay in the water again. This time its shape will help it to float.

The radar mast is used for communication, and to check for other ships in the area.

The front of a ship is called its bow.

Theatre

The body of a ship is called its hull.

The bottom of a ship is called its keel. It keeps the ship steady in the water.

Moving forward

Boats need power to move through the water. Here are some of the different ways they can get it.

Some boats have engines attached to propellers. The propellers spin around and push the boat forward.

Rowboats have oars with flat ends. The rower pulls the oars through the water. This pushes the boat along.

A sailboat, or yacht, has tall sails. The wind blows against them and pushes the boat through the water.

Submersibles and submarines

Submarines are machines that people can use to travel underwater. Small submarines, called submersibles, are used for exploring the oceans. Below is a submersible called Deep Flight.

This picture shows the Deep Flight submersible in use.

These flaps on the wings can tilt to move Deep Flight up and down in the water.

Deep Flight gets its power from ten batteries (five along each side).

This part is see-through, so the pilot can look around.

These bottles are filled with air for the pilot to breathe.

Propeller

DEEP FLIGHT

Engines, called thrusters, turn the propellers. They push the submersible forward as they spin.

The pilot guides the submersible using these hand controls.

Powerful lights help the pilot to find his way in the dark sea.

Going down

Deep Flight uses its wings to go up and down, but big submarines rise and sink in a different way.

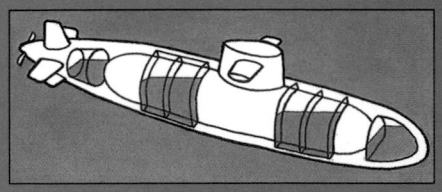

To dive down, tanks inside a submarine fill with water. This makes it heavy, so it sinks.

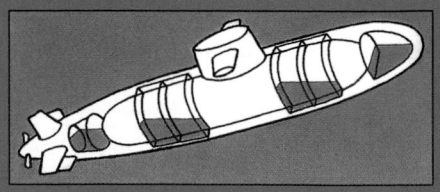

To come up, the water is pumped out. This makes the submarine lighter, so it rises.

Space

Amazing space

Space is full of amazing sights. Some you can see with your own eyes, or with a telescope or binoculars. Here are some of the things you can find out about in this part of the book.

Spacecraft

Rockets have been going into space for the last 40 years. They have taken people as far as the Moon. Spacecraft without people in them have visited distant planets such as Uranus and Neptune.

This American rocket is taking three people to the Moon.

Astronauts

People who travel into space are called astronauts. They have to train for many years before their trip.

This astronaut wears a space suit to "walk" in space. ★

Stars

A star is a blazing ball of very hot gas. The Sun is a star.

Below you can see new stars being made from clouds of dust.

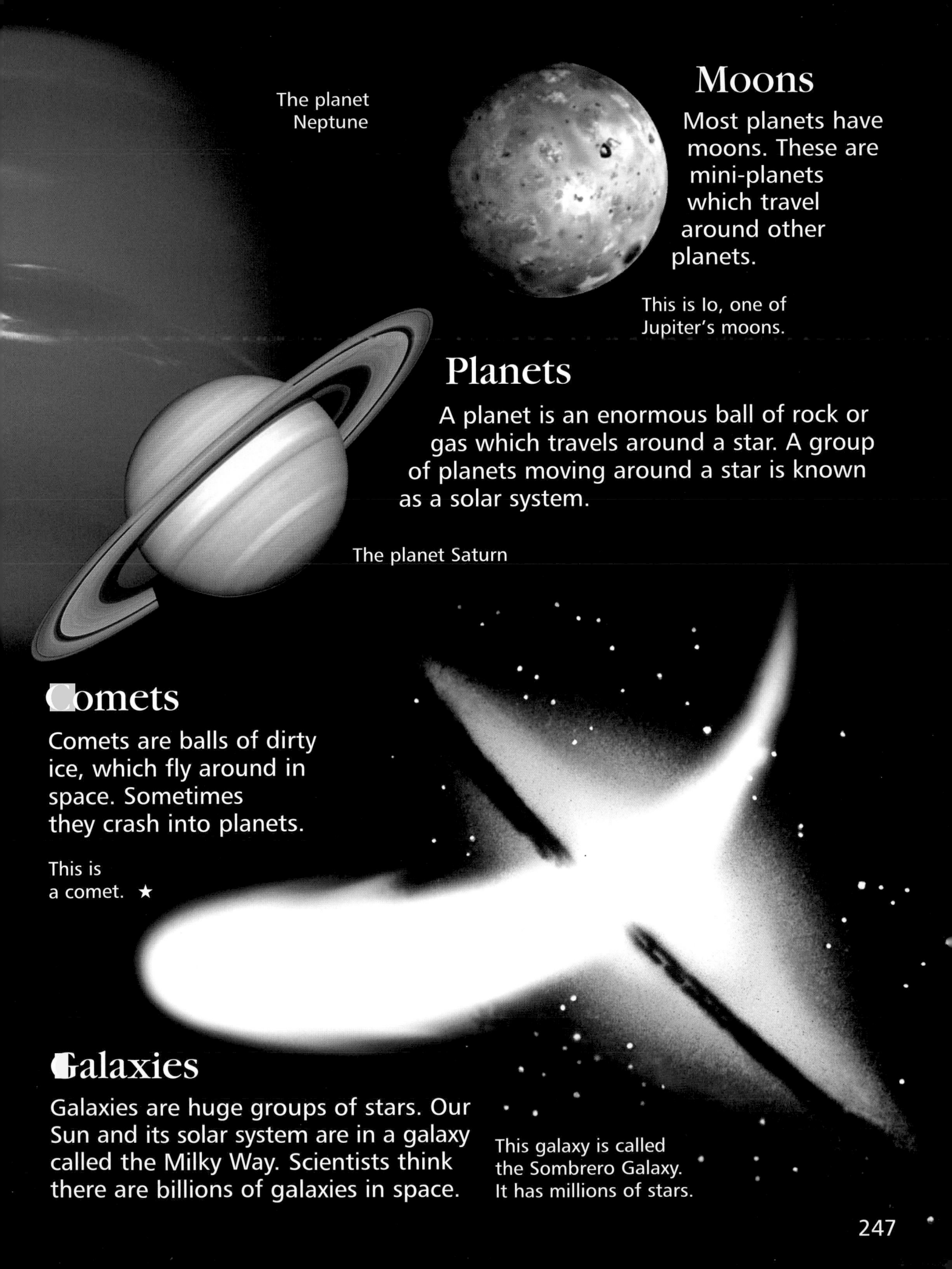

The planet Neptune

Moons

Most planets have moons. These are mini-planets which travel around other planets.

This is Io, one of Jupiter's moons.

Planets

A planet is an enormous ball of rock or gas which travels around a star. A group of planets moving around a star is known as a solar system.

The planet Saturn

Comets

Comets are balls of dirty ice, which fly around in space. Sometimes they crash into planets.

This is a comet. ★

Galaxies

Galaxies are huge groups of stars. Our Sun and its solar system are in a galaxy called the Milky Way. Scientists think there are billions of galaxies in space.

This galaxy is called the Sombrero Galaxy. It has millions of stars.

Trips into space

People have only been sending rockets into space since 1957. Before then, rockets fell back to the ground before they could reach space. They were not powerful enough to go any farther.

The space shuttle

The first people went into space in 1961. Since then hundreds of men and women have followed them. Today, astronauts fly into space in a rocket called a space shuttle. This is how it works.

Life on the shuttle

Seven people can live and work on the shuttle and they can stay in space for up to 17 days. They live in the crew compartment which is at the front of the shuttle. Inside this compartment the astronauts don't have to wear spacesuits.

The top level of the crew compartment is the flight deck, where the pilot flies the craft. Below, there is space for the rest of the crew to do experiments and rest.

This robot arm is putting a space telescope into orbit.

The pilot sits here.

Cargo bay

Can you see a sleeping astronaut?

The big cargo bay can carry telescopes, satellites or parts of a space station.

Internet link

For a link to the NASA website where you can find out more about the space shuttle, go to **www.usborne-quicklinks.com**

4. On its return, the shuttle glides back though the Earth's atmosphere. Its underside gets very hot.

5. The shuttle touches down. It lands on wheels like a plane.

A walk in space

Space is deadly. There is no air to breathe, so outside a spacecraft, an astronaut must wear an outfit called a spacesuit to stay alive. Spacesuits are like body-size spaceships, with their own air and water supplies.

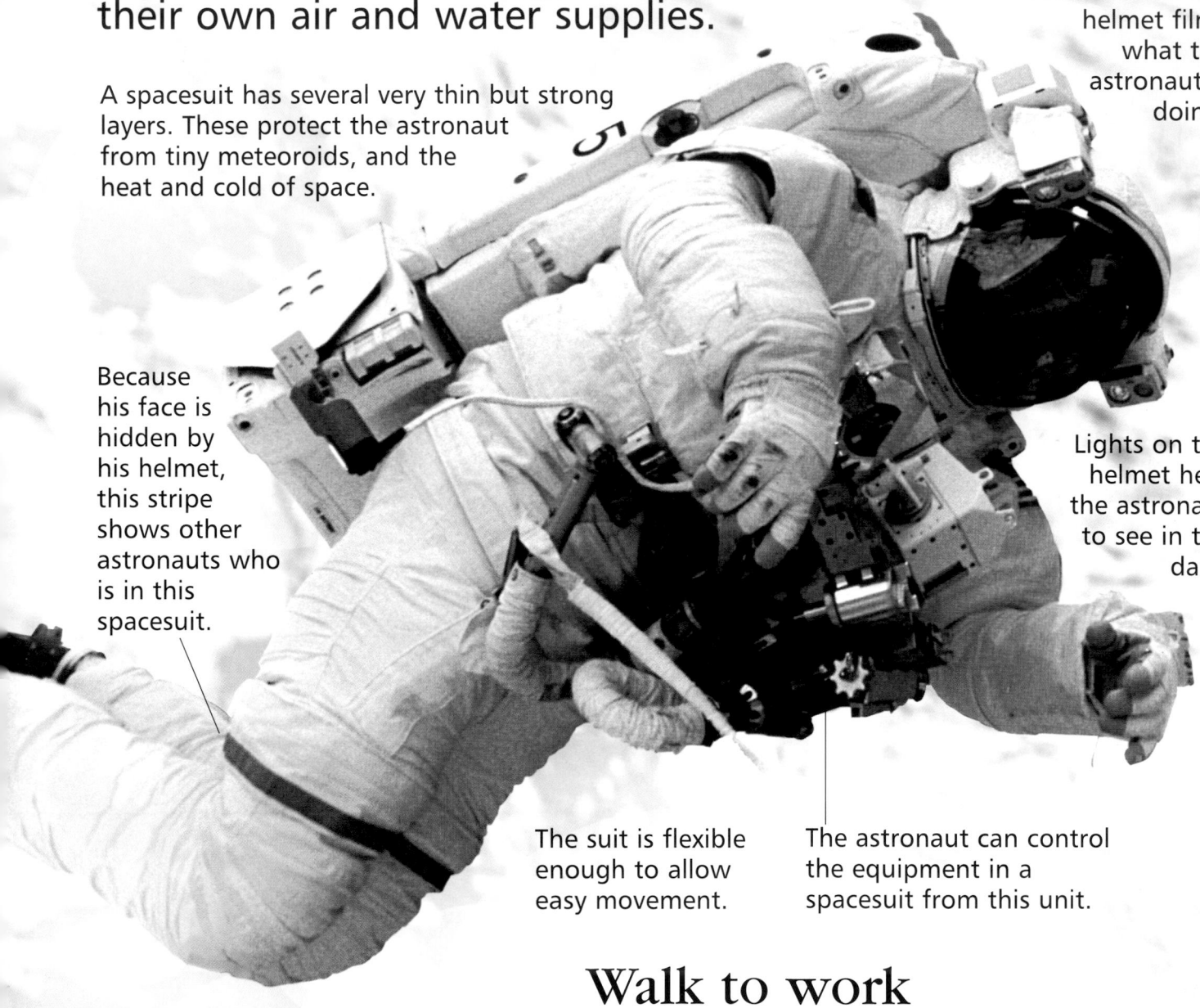

A spacesuit has several very thin but strong layers. These protect the astronaut from tiny meteoroids, and the heat and cold of space.

A camera on the helmet films what the astronaut is doing.

Because his face is hidden by his helmet, this stripe shows other astronauts who is in this spacesuit.

Lights on the helmet help the astronaut to see in the dark.

The suit is flexible enough to allow easy movement.

The astronaut can control the equipment in a spacesuit from this unit.

Walk to work

Astronauts make space walks to repair satellites, build space stations or check the outside of their spaceships. On these pages you can see two American astronauts making a space walk from their space shuttle in 1997.

Internet link

For a link to the NASA website where there is a history of human space flight, go to **www.usborne-quicklinks.com**

Survival equipment

Here is some of the equipment astronauts need to stay alive and comfortable outside their spaceships. Sometimes space walks can last for five hours or more.

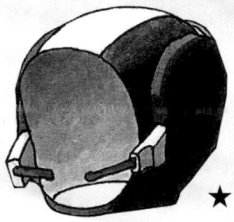

This cap holds a radio microphone and ear piece in place.

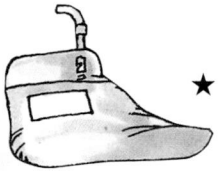

A drink bag has a tube which goes straight to the astronaut's mouth.

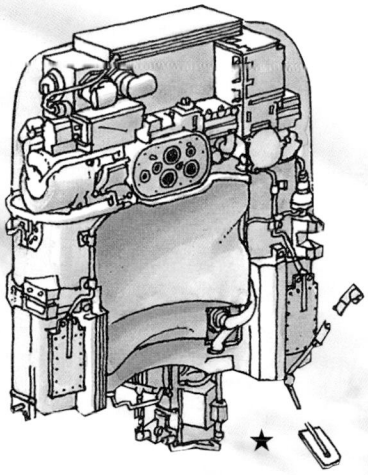

This is the "Primary Life Support System". It contains air for the astronaut to breathe.

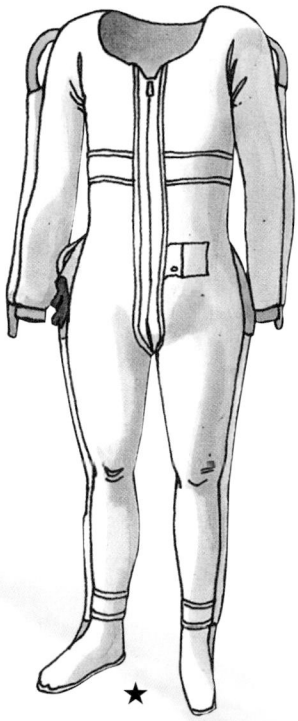

This outfit is worn next to the body. It has tubes of water which the astronaut can make hot or cold, to warm up or cool down.

The shiny visor of the helmet protects against blinding, bright sunlight.

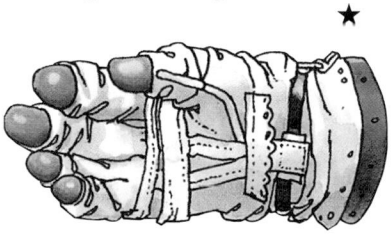

Padded gloves have rubber fingertips so the astronaut can feel things more easily.

Boiling and freezing

When astronauts on a space walk face the Sun, its rays are hotter than boiling water. But when their spaceships travel around the dark side of the Earth, temperatures drop way below freezing.

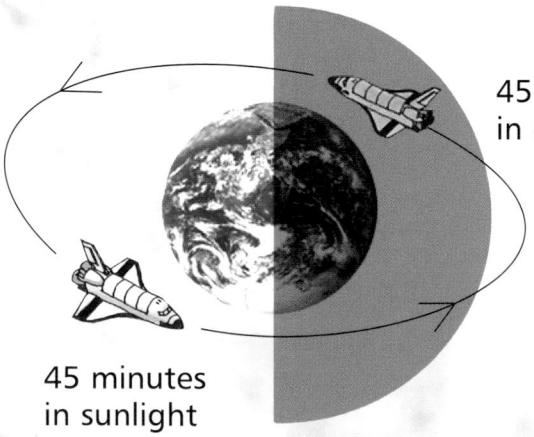

Living in space

Space stations are homes in space where astronauts can look at the Earth and do experiments. People can live in them for many months at a time. The first space station was set up over 30 years ago.

The ISS

This is the International Space Station (ISS). It floats 230 miles above the Earth with three people on board. The first crew arrived in 2000. A space shuttle takes them up and back to Earth. The station is still being built, but when it is finished, seven or more people could live here.

This is the inside of a laboratory where scientists can do tests to see how things behave in space.

Internet link

For a link to the NASA website, where you can take a great tour of the International Space Station, go to **www.usborne-quicklinks.com**

Radio antennae and dishes send signals to and from the Earth.

Criss-cross steel tubes hold the station together.

These are solar panels. They make energy by collecting heat from the Sun, and turning it into electricity.

There are 16 different layers in the walls. They keep heat or cold out, and stop meteorites from getting in.

Crew members live here and carry out experiments.

This tiny spacecraft could take the crew back to Earth if anything went wrong.

Living area

The living area is where the crew will go when they are not working. Below is one idea of what this might look like when the station is finished. Because there is no gravity in space, the crew will float around inside it, and will not need chairs or beds.

Space toilet

This is what a space toilet looks like. It is quite tricky to use.

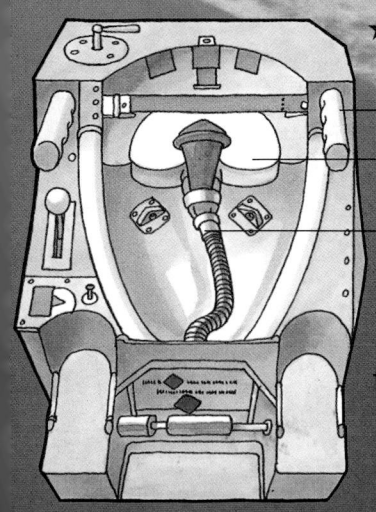

★ Handles for the astronaut to hold onto

Seat

Air sucks waste through this tube.

Urine is cleaned and turned back into water. Solid waste is frozen and returned to Earth.

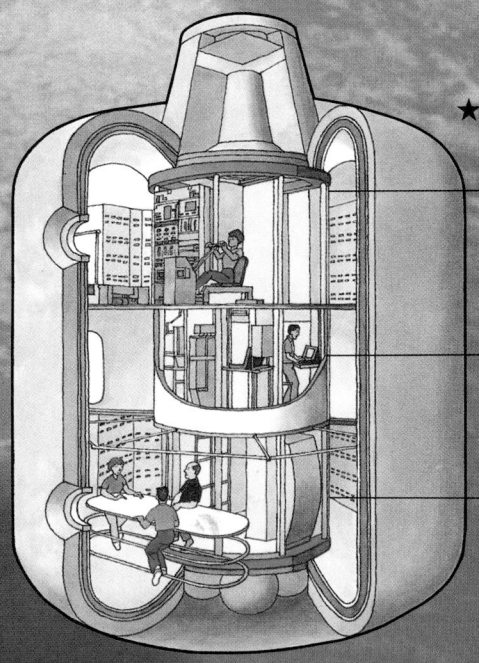

★ Level three
The crew can exercise here.

Level two
Sleeping area. Each person has a small, private space.

Level one
The crew can eat together around this big table.

Satellites and space probes

Satellites and space probes are spaceships with no people in them. Instead, scientists control them from Earth. Most satellites and probes have cameras or other kinds of viewing equipment.

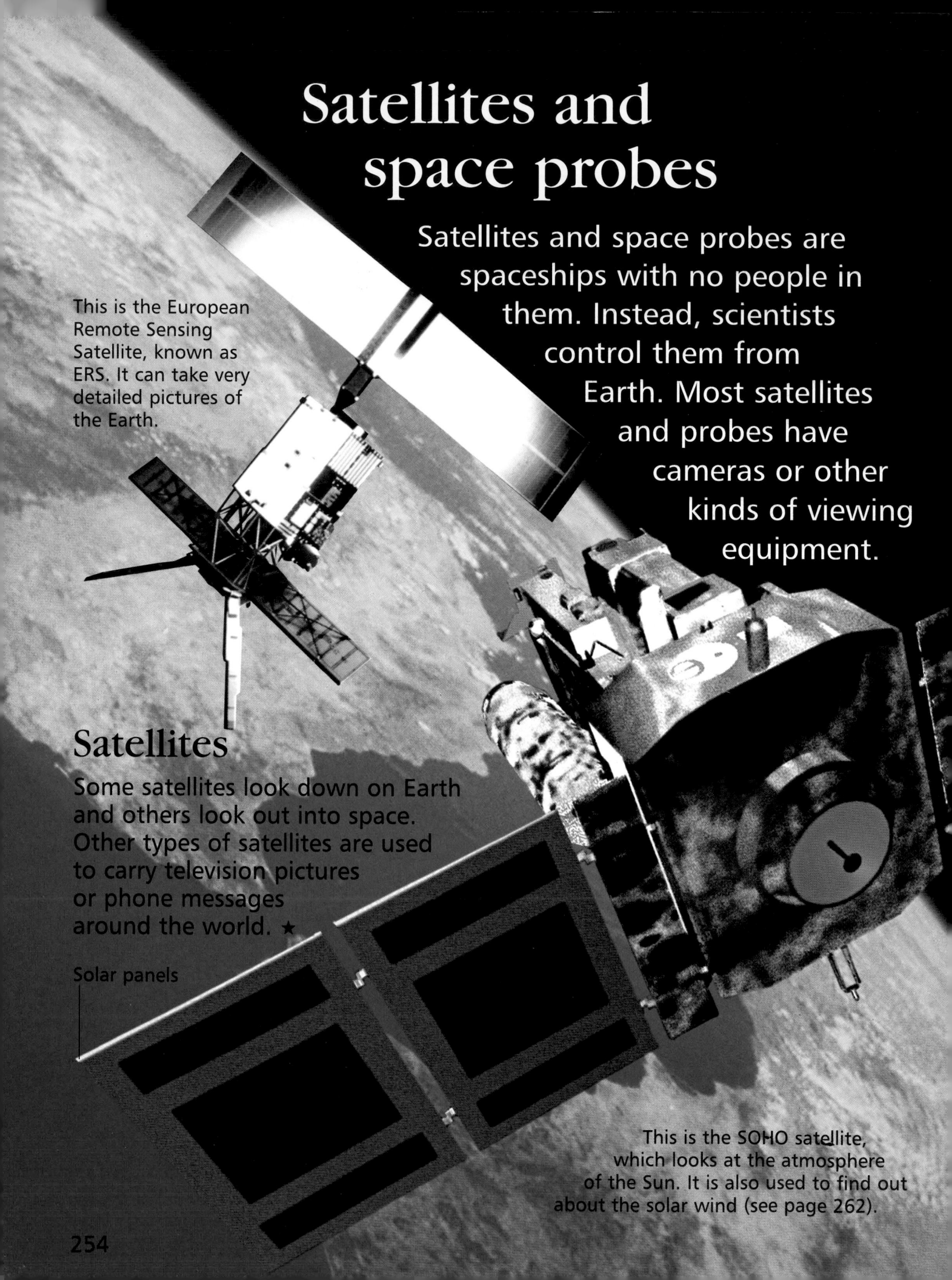

This is the European Remote Sensing Satellite, known as ERS. It can take very detailed pictures of the Earth.

Satellites

Some satellites look down on Earth and others look out into space. Other types of satellites are used to carry television pictures or phone messages around the world. ★

Solar panels

This is the SOHO satellite, which looks at the atmosphere of the Sun. It is also used to find out about the solar wind (see page 262).

Space probes

Space probes do similar jobs to satellites, but instead of orbiting the Earth, they visit other planets. All the planets have been visited, apart from Pluto. Sometimes space probes even land on other planets.

The painting on the right shows the Voyager space probe heading toward Neptune in 1989.

Internet link

For a link to a website where you can learn more about satellites, go to **www.usborne-quicklinks.com**

Space views

Here are two pictures taken by satellites. Special cameras are used to show particular details, which can also be made clearer with computers.

This ERS picture shows a hole in Antarctica's atmosphere.

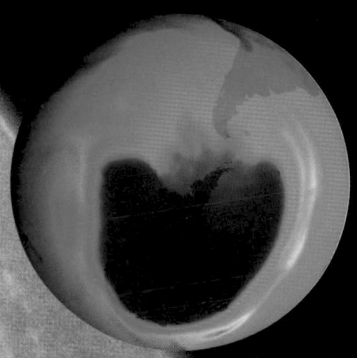

This SOHO picture shows the outer edge of the Sun's surface.

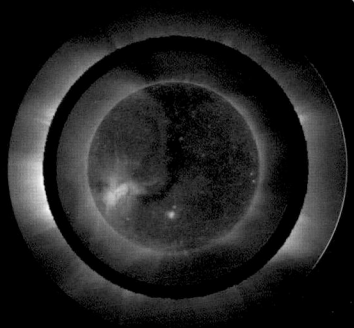

A big picture

A satellite named COBE took the picture below. It is a temperature map of the entire universe.

Some parts of space are hotter than others. The red and blue areas show different temperatures.

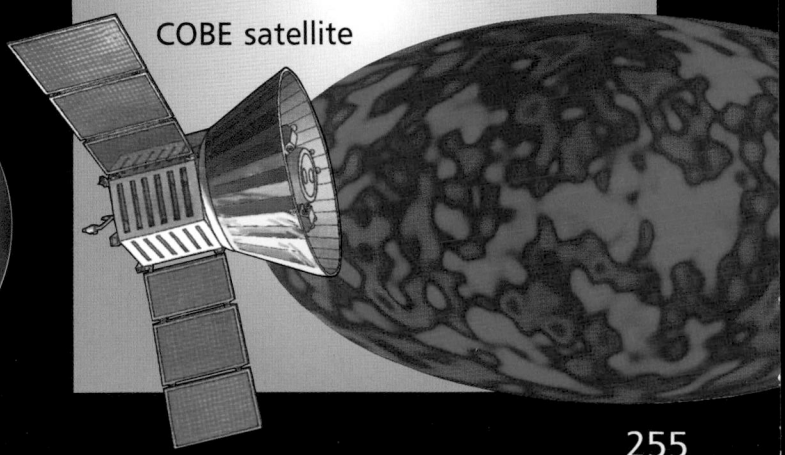

Is anyone out there?

Ever since people first began to study the stars, they have wondered whether there is life in space. At the moment we don't know. Some astronomers think we will find evidence of alien life before the end of the century.

Reaching out

Two kinds of space probes are heading out of our Solar System. Pioneer probes carry a picture of people and a map that shows where Earth is. Voyagers carry a disc with sounds and pictures of Earth. These are to show any alien who may find them what we look like.

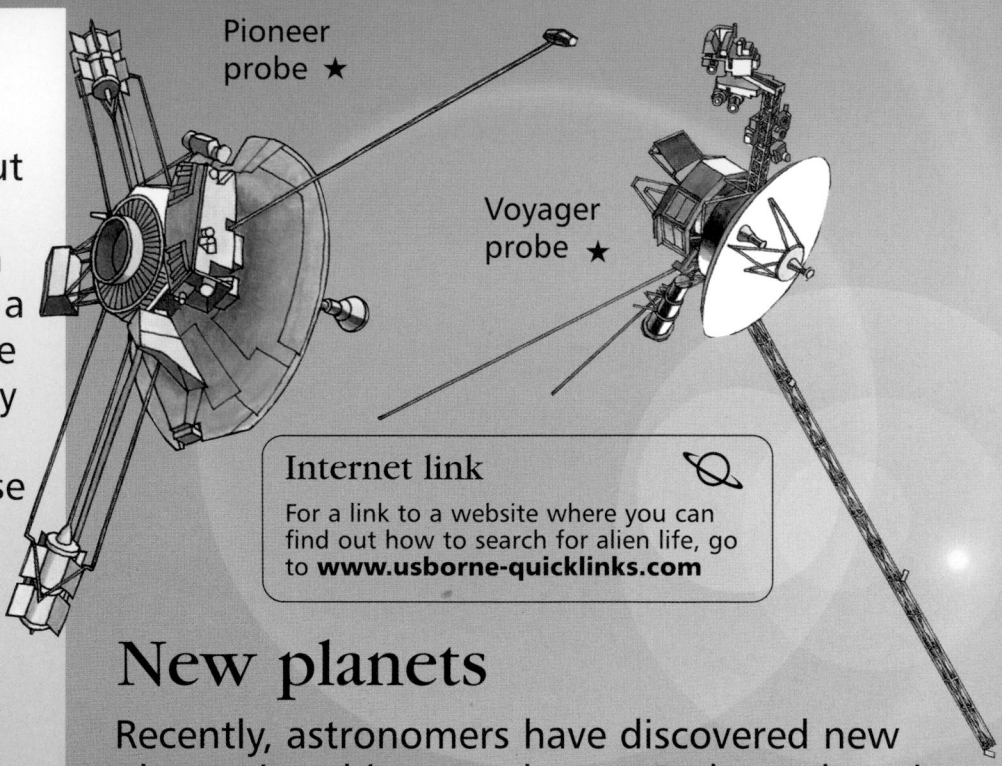

Internet link

For a link to a website where you can find out how to search for alien life, go to **www.usborne-quicklinks.com**

The Voyager disc

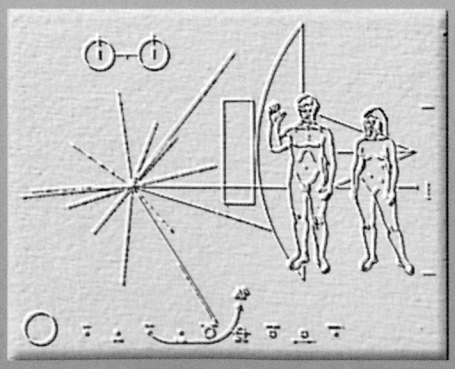

The Pioneer map and picture

New planets

Recently, astronomers have discovered new planets in orbit around stars. Perhaps there is life there. Radio telescopes, such as the one in Puerto Rico shown below, search the skies near these planets, looking for alien signals.

Arecibo radio telescope is the largest in the world.

Life on Europa?

Europa, one of Jupiter's moons, has an icy surface. Under it there may be a cold, dark sea. Scientists think they may find creatures there, perhaps like those that live deep underwater on Earth. A space probe may go to visit Europa in the future to try to find out more.

Europa

In the future submarine probes from Earth may explore under the ice of Europa.

What might aliens look like ?

If we do find life in space, it may not look very interesting. It could be slime or moss, rather than intelligent creatures with arms, legs and heads, like us.

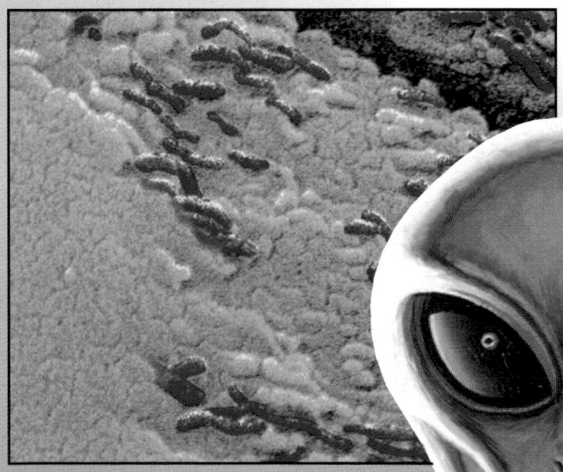

Some scientists think germ-like blobs found in a rock from Mars show life existed there.

Aliens may look like this in films, but we don't really know what they might look like.

★

What's in our Solar System?

Our Solar System is the Sun and everything that revolves around it. It includes all the planets and their moons, and space objects such as comets. There are also two vast bands of drifting rocks called the Asteroid Belt and the Kuiper Belt.

In this picture of the Solar System the planets are not shown to scale.

Comets fly around the Solar System.

Days and years

A day is the time it takes for a planet to spin around once. Earth's day lasts 24 hours. A year is the time it takes for a planet to go all the way around the Sun. Earth's year lasts for 365 days.

A day

A year

Asteroid Belt

Saturn is the second biggest planet.

Neptune is a gas planet, like Jupiter, Saturn, and Uranus. The gas planets are all much bigger than the rocky planets in our Solar System.

Internet link
For a link to a website where you can take an incredible tour of the Solar System, go to www.usborne-quicklinks.com
Jupiter is the biggest planet.
Venus
Mercury
The Sun
Mars
Earth
Uranus spins on its side. It has rings like Saturn.
Pluto is a tiny, rocky planet.
Beyond Pluto lies a band of icy rocks named the Kuiper Belt.
Atmosphere
Most planets have an atmosphere – a layer of gas that covers the surface. The Earth's atmosphere is made of air. It stretches 250 miles above us. It provides air to breathe, and helps protect us from the Sun's heat.
Earth's atmosphere

The Moon

The Moon travels around the Earth, just like the Earth travels around the Sun. So far, the Moon is the only part of the Solar System that people have been able to visit.

Sea of Crises

The Moon's "seas" are actually dark patches of melted rock.

Sea of Tranquility

Craters were made by rocks from space, crashing into the Moon.

Sea of Serenity

Apollo 15 landed here in 1971.

Sea of Rain

Earth

If you were orbiting the Moon in a spaceship, this is how far away Earth would look.

When people went to the Moon between 1969 and 1972, it took their spaceships three days to get there.

What is the Moon like?

The Moon is very different from Earth. There is no air, no weather, and no life. It is a dreary, dusty place that is boiling hot by day and freezing at night. The surface is covered with saucer-shaped holes called craters. You can see some if you look at the Moon on a clear night. Some are so huge, a city the size of London could fit inside them.

Where did the Moon come from?

The Moon is about the same age as the Earth. Here is one idea about where it came from.

1. Soon after the Earth formed, a planet hit it. ★

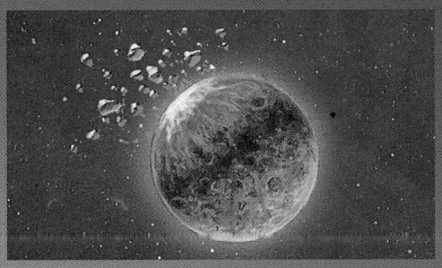

2. Rocks broke off and shot into space. ★

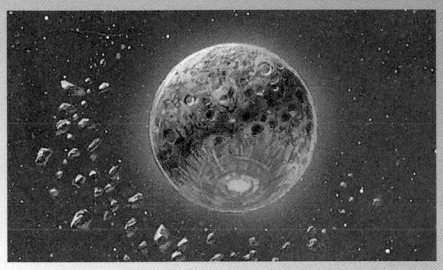

3. The rocks were held in orbit by Earth's gravity. ★

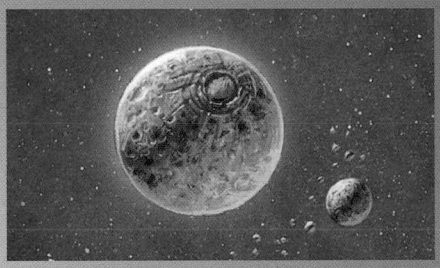

4. These rocks slowly formed into the Moon. ★

Did you know?

- The Moon does not give out any of its own light. We can only see it because the Sun shines on it.
- The Moon takes 27 days to spin around once, and 27 days to go all the way around the Earth too.
- We never see one side of the Moon, because it is always facing away from us.
- The Moon was known as "Luna" by the Romans. The first unmanned spacecraft to visit the Moon was Luna 2 in 1959.

Moon landings

People have visited the Moon six times, but not since 1972. Each spaceship that landed there carried two astronauts. They stayed up to three days before returning.

Internet link

For a link to a website where you can find out more about Moon landings, go to **www.usborne-quicklinks.com**

The astronaut is saluting the American flag.

This spaceship is called a lunar module.

This is the Apollo 15 Moon landing. See where they are on the Moon, on the facing page.

Car powered by electricity

The Sun

The size of the Earth, compared to the Sun

The Sun is a star. It is a huge ball of blazing gas that makes vast amounts of light and heat which we call sunshine. It is so big it could hold a million planets the size of Earth. It looks like it's burning, but it's actually exploding like a massive bomb.

The Sun's surface is called the photosphere. The temperature there is 10,000°F. The dark areas are sunspots. The temperature is lower there.

Internet link

For a link to the NASA website where you can find out more about the Sun, go to **www.usborne-quicklinks.com**

The solar wind

As well as light and heat, the Sun also sends out a stream of invisible specks, called particles, into space. This is called the solar wind. When the particles pass by the North and South Poles of Earth they can make the air glow beautiful reds, blues, greens and purples.

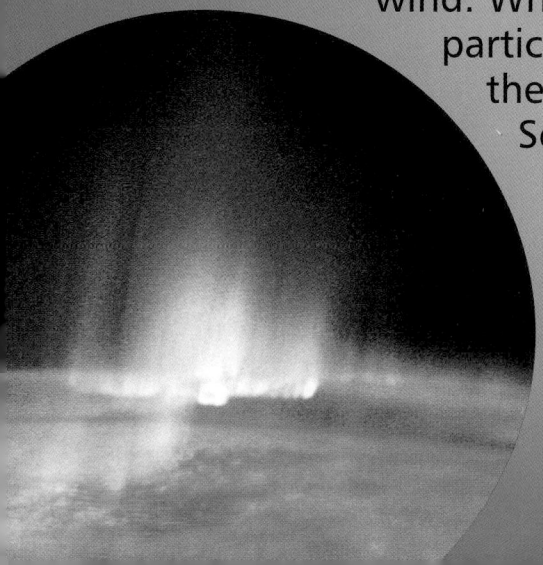

This is the solar wind lighting up the sky near the North Pole.

This is a solar prominence. It is a massive arch of hot gas, which reaches out into space like a huge, flaming tongue.

Solar surface

The Sun makes sunlight by burning four million tons of fuel every second. You can see in this picture that the Sun's surface is a churning mass of explosions. Solar flares and fiery loops of gas leap out into space.

The photo on the right shows a close-up of the Sun's surface. You can see jets of gas called plasma loops.

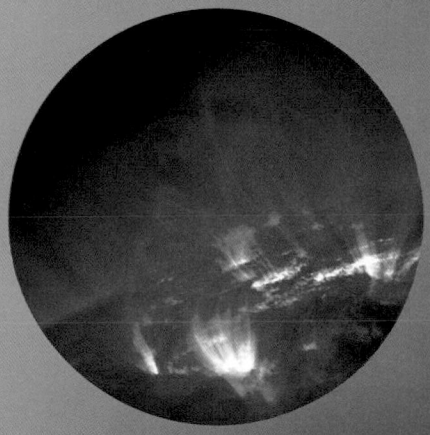

Sometimes, white areas appear on the surface of the Sun. These are called faculae. The temperature here is even higher than that of the rest of the Sun.

Liquid, ice or gas?

Life exists on Earth because our planet is just the right distance from the Sun for water to be a liquid, rather than ice or a gas.

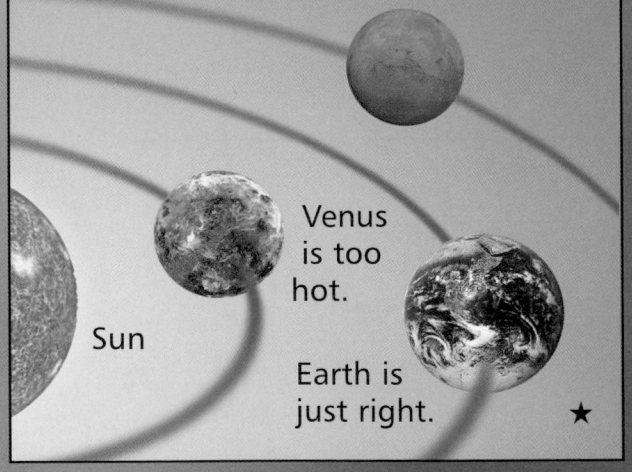

Mercury and Venus

Mercury and Venus are the two planets closest to the Sun. Both are small and very hot. Mercury has almost no atmosphere, but Venus is covered with a thick layer of gas.

Tiny Mercury

Mercury is a tiny planet. Billions of years ago many rocks crashed into it, so its surface is covered with lots of craters. Because it is so close to the Sun, it has the shortest year of any planet. Mercury takes just 88 Earth days to travel around the Sun.

Mercury is a third the size of Earth, but is almost as heavy. It has a core of dense metal. This makes up nearly three-quarters of its inside.

Four billion years ago an enormous meteorite crashed into Mercury. It made a massive crater called the Caloris Basin. This is more than 800 miles across.

Meteorite hitting Mercury

Internet links

For links to the NASA website where you can see more pictures of Mercury and Venus, go to **www.usborne-quicklinks.com**

Beneath its clouds, Venus is a world of volcanoes, mountains and canyons. The pink and white areas on this computer picture show high, rough areas. Low, flat ground is shown in green.

Sweltering Venus

Venus is the nearest planet to us. Although it is farther away from the Sun than Mercury, its surface is actually hotter. This is because it has a thick atmosphere of the gas carbon dioxide. This atmosphere traps the Sun's heat and stops it from escaping back into space.

Magellan probe

The picture below shows the surface of Venus. It was taken by the Magellan probe which visited Venus between 1990 and 1994.

Mars

If you were standing on Mars, being there would be a little like being on Earth. There is a bright sky during the day, and you could see thin clouds, morning mists and light frosts. But Mars is a lot colder than our planet.

Mars in detail

Mars is half the size of Earth. It is mainly covered with rocks and dust. Most of it looks like a great big desert. It has a thin atmosphere of poisonous gas.

Internet link

For a link to the NASA website, where there is more detailed information about Mars, go to **www.usborne-quicklinks.com**

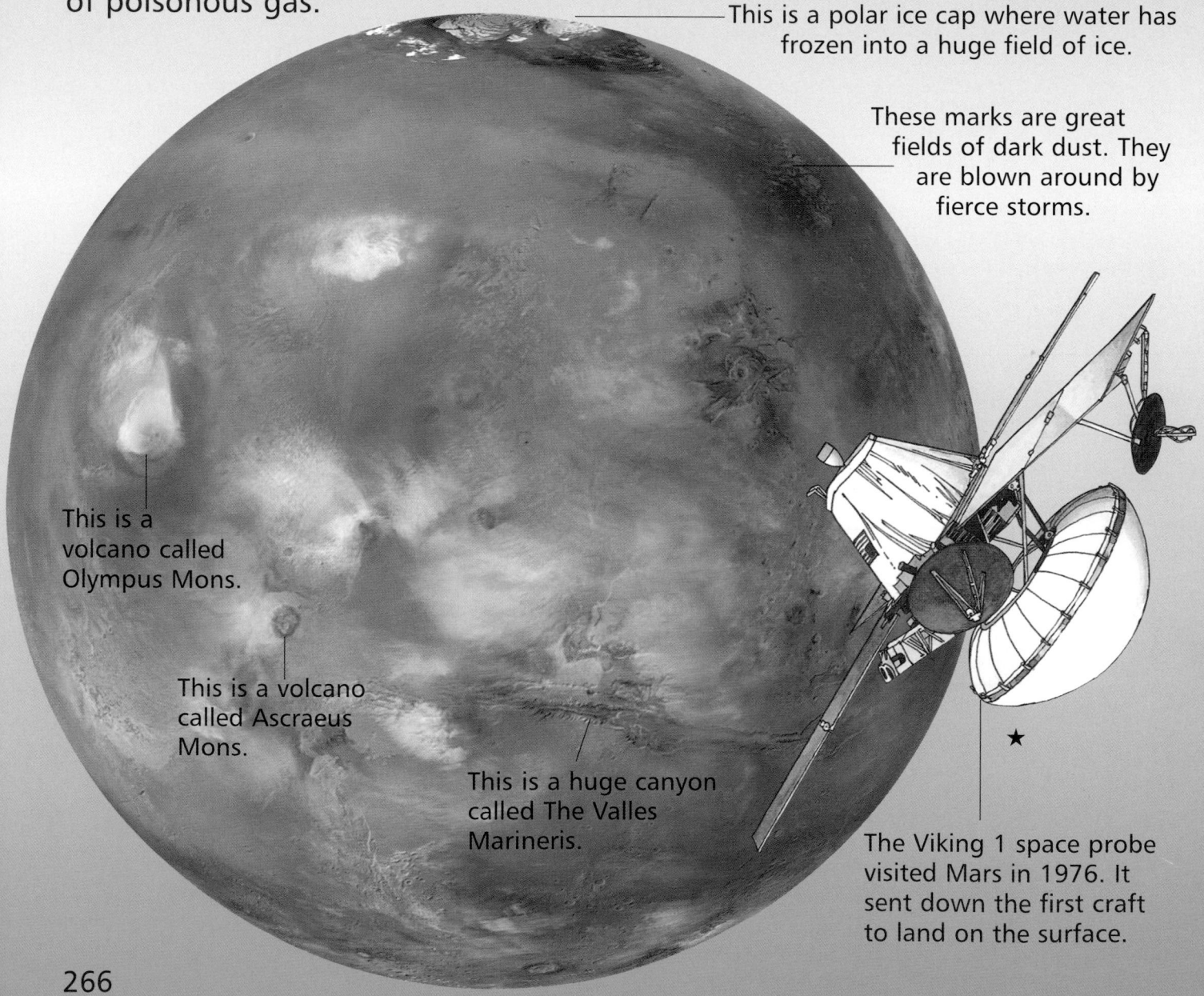

Volcanoes and canyons

Mars has some very interesting features. There are several volcanoes. The biggest one is called Olympus Mons. It is the largest in the Solar System. It rises 15 miles above the surface of Mars. There are also huge canyons and dried-up water channels.

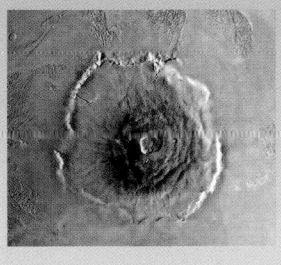

The Olympus Mons volcano seen by a visiting space probe.

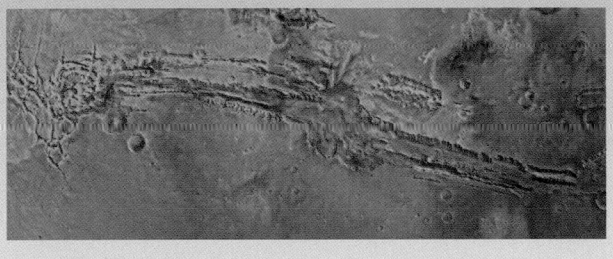

The Valles Marineris canyon is a huge crack along one side of the planet. It is so long it would stretch across the entire USA.

Astronomers think that channels like this were made by running water, which has now frozen or leaked away.

Visitors to Mars

The photograph below shows the surface of Mars. It was taken by the Pathfinder space probe, which landed there in 1997. On board was a little mobile robot called Sojourner. It carried TV cameras and could be moved around by scientists on Earth.

Scientists think that the rocks you can see in this picture were left here by a big flood, billions of years ago.

The Sojourner robot is the size of a microwave oven. This picture shows some of its more important features:
Ⓐ Solar panels make power from sunlight.
Ⓑ Small wheels with studded rims grip the surface.
Ⓒ Radio antenna keeps the robot in contact with Earth.
Ⓓ A camera and laser are used to help steer the robot.

Jupiter and Saturn

Beyond the Asteroid Belt lie four huge planets that are mainly made up of gas.

The largest of these four are the bright, stormy planets Jupiter and Saturn.

Swirly world

Jupiter is the biggest planet in the Solar System and has at least 61 moons. It also has the shortest day. It takes only 9 hours and 50 minutes to spin around once. Jupiter is a stormy planet. Swirling clouds of gas race around it, in dark and light bands.

The Great Red Spot is a storm three times the size of Earth.

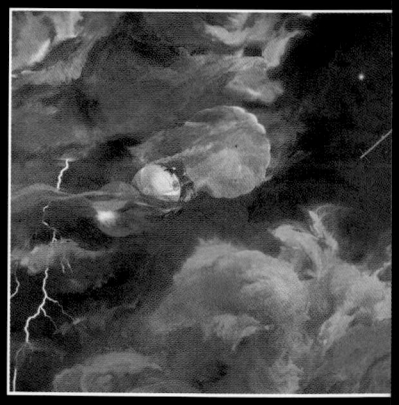

A pod from the Galileo space probe parachuted into Jupiter's gassy atmosphere in 1995.

Internet links

For links to a website where you can find out more about Jupiter and Saturn, go to **www.usborne-quicklinks.com**

This space probe photo shows thick, hot gas erupting from volcanoes on the surface of Io, one of Jupiter's many moons.

Ring world

Saturn is the second biggest planet in the Solar System. Many broad rings of rock and ice orbit around it. Saturn is very light. If you could put it in a huge swimming pool, it would float there.

All shapes and sizes

The rocks in Saturn's rings may have come from one of its moons. You can see what might have happened below. Some rocks in the rings are as big as a house, others are smaller than a pebble.

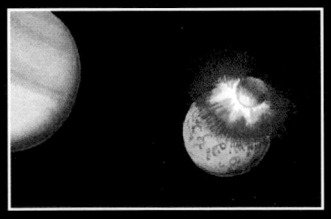

A moon collided with a planet.

It broke into billions of pieces.

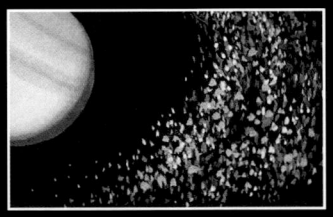

The pieces stayed in Saturn's orbit.

Eventually, they formed Saturn's rings.

Saturn's moons

Saturn has 31 moons, and there may be more. Titan is the largest. It has a thick atmosphere.

Earth's Moon

The planet Mercury

Here you can see how big Titan is compared to the planet Mercury and our Moon.

Titan

This picture shows what Titan's atmosphere may look like, close up.

Uranus and Neptune

Uranus and Neptune are huge gas planets. Both are around four times bigger than Earth. They are hard to spot in the night sky, but you can see them with a telescope.

Uranus

Neptune

Earth

This is how big Uranus and Neptune are compared to the Earth.

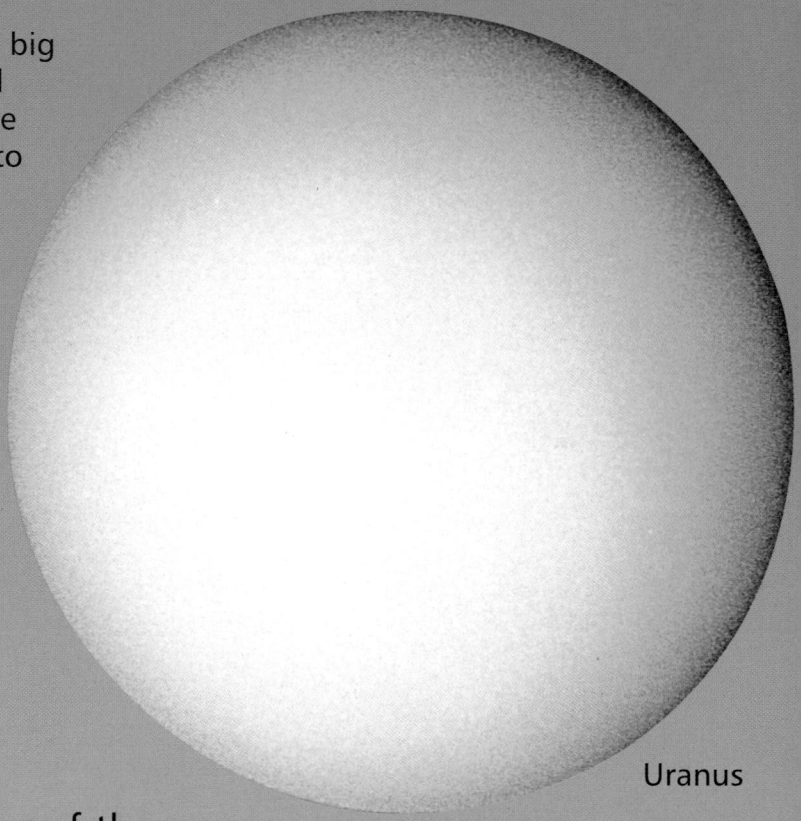
Uranus

Uranus

This world spins on its side. Its outer surface is cloaked by a thin mist, which wraps around a thick gassy surface. Further inside, Uranus has a core of solid rock.

Here are some of Uranus's moons.

Umbriel

Ariel

Titania

Oberon

Miranda

Puzzle moon

Uranus has 21 moons. One of them, Miranda, looks like a huge jigsaw puzzle. Perhaps, millions of years ago, it broke into pieces. Gradually time and gravity put it back together.

★ 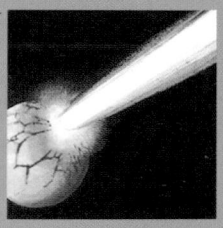
A comet may have crashed into Miranda.

★ 
Miranda's pieces drifted together.

★ 
Miranda slowly put itself back in one piece.

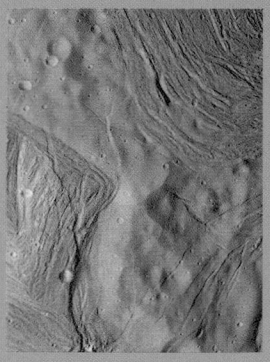
This is what Miranda's surface looks like now.

Neptune

Neptune has the worst storms in the Solar System. Winds of 1,250mph whip clouds of methane around the planet.

Neptune has eight moons. One, named Triton, is a frozen world. Ice on its surface acts like a greenhouse, magnifying the Sun's feeble rays, and heating gas that lies beneath. This causes hot jets of gas and slush to spout out through the ice and into space.

Internet links

For links to a website where you can find out more about Uranus and Neptune, go to **www.usborne-quicklinks.com**

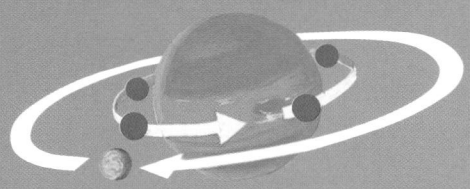

Triton orbits in the opposite direction from all of Neptune's other moons.

Visitor from Earth

The Voyager 2 space probe visited Uranus and Neptune in 1986 and 1989. The probe took 12 years to get to Neptune from Earth.

Voyager 2

This picture shows what the surface of Triton might look like. A jet of gas and slush is spouting out.

Pluto and beyond

Pluto lies at the very edge of the Solar System, nearly 4 billion miles away from the Sun. Pluto is so far away it was only discovered in 1930. Unlike the gassy planets Uranus and Neptune, Pluto is a solid ball of rock and ice.

Moon-sized

Pluto is a tiny planet. It is smaller than our Moon. Both Pluto, and its moon Charon, could fit into the borders of the USA. Some astronomers think Pluto is an asteroid, and not a planet. ★

Odd orbit

Pluto takes 248 Earth years to go around the Sun. For 20 of these years it is closer to the Sun than Neptune. While all the other planets orbit on roughly the same level, Pluto spins around on a different path. ★

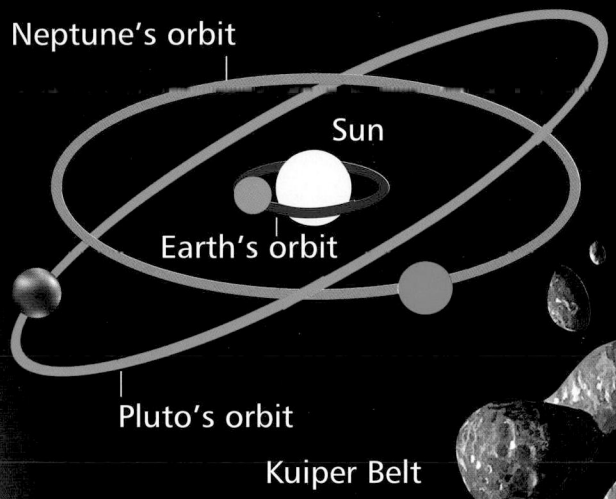

The Kuiper Belt

Beyond Pluto lies a huge ring of frozen rocks known as the Kuiper Belt. These drifting rocks did not merge into one of the planets when the Solar System was formed. Some astronomers think a few of them are bigger than Pluto.

Internet links

For links to websites where you can find out more about Pluto, go to **www.usborne-quicklinks.com**

Oort Cloud

Even farther away sits a huge, misty cloud, which may be made up of trillions of comets. This is called the Oort Cloud.

The Oort Cloud surrounds the outer edge of the Solar System like a vast, dusty ball.

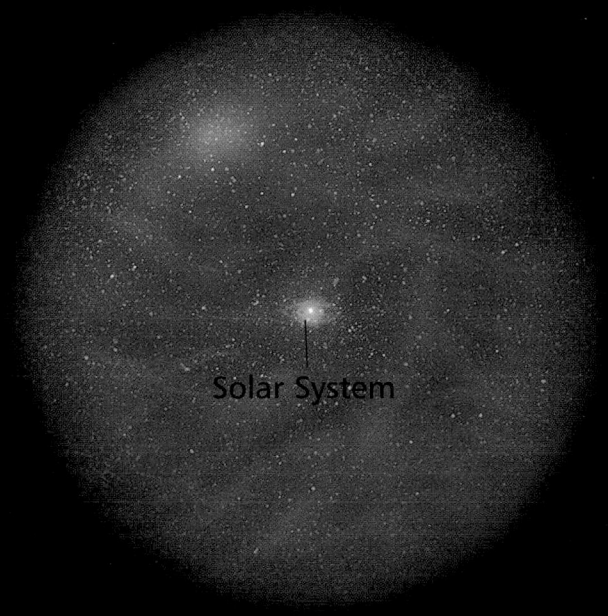

Bits and pieces

Our Solar System isn't just the Sun, the nine planets, and their moons. There are countless asteroids, meteoroids and comets flying around in it too.

The Asteroid Belt. Some asteroids are barely bigger than boulders.

Asteroids

Asteroids are lumps of rocks and metal. Between Mars and Jupiter lies a large band of them, called the Asteroid Belt. The biggest one, named Ceres, and is about 605 miles across. Some asteroids even have their own little moons.

Meteoroids

Meteoroids are smaller pieces of rock from space. Most are no bigger than a grain of instant coffee, but some are the size of large rocks. Most burn up in the atmosphere as they fall to Earth, but some are too big to burn, and cause damage when they reach Earth.

Meteoroids that burn up in the sky are called meteors or shooting stars.

This crater in Arizona, USA, was caused by a meteoroid.

Comets

Comets are large balls of ice and dust. They come in from the outer edge of the Solar System to circle the Sun. Once past Jupiter, the heat from the Sun begins to melt the outer layer of the comet, and the solar wind blows a trail of gas and dust behind it.

Part of the Bayeux Tapestry shows people looking at a comet in 1066.

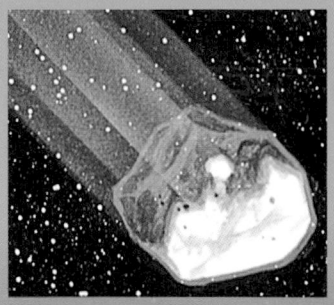

A comet far away from the Sun has no tail. It is just a solid block of dirty ice.

Deep Impact

Scientists are working on a space probe named Deep Impact that will visit a comet called Tempel 1. It will blast a hole in the comet to try to find out more about it.

Closer to the Sun, the outside begins to melt, and forms a trail of gas and dust.

By the time it flies by Earth the comet's tail is glowing. This makes it easy to spot.

This picture shows the comet Hale-Bopp when it passed by the Earth in 1997.

Internet link

For a link to the NASA website, where you can find out more about comets, asteroids and meteorites, go to **www.usborne-quicklinks.com**

Galaxies

Galaxies are collections of billions of stars, held together by gravity in one vast group. Most galaxies have a spiral shape, but some have a more scattered pattern. There are billions of galaxies in the Universe.

The Milky Way

The Sun is part of a galaxy called the Milky Way. It has over 100 billion stars, and is about 100,000 light years across. The Milky Way is not the biggest galaxy in the Universe, but it is much larger than many others. Like most galaxies it is spinning around a central hub. ★

Astronomers think the Sun and our Solar System are here.

A long trip

It takes 225 million years for the Milky Way to go all the way around. The last time our Solar System was in the same place in space that it is now, dinosaurs roamed the Earth.

If you could see the Milky Way from the side, it would look like a flat plate with a bulge in the middle.

The middle of the Milky Way is hidden by great clouds of dust.

Internet link

For a link to a website where you can find out more about the Milky Way and other galaxies, go to **www.usborne-quicklinks.com**

Galaxy shapes

Not all galaxies look like the Milky Way. There are several other galaxy shapes. You can see three of them on the right.

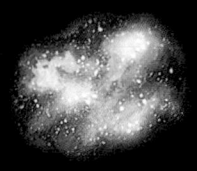

★ This type is known as an irregular galaxy. It doesn't have any real shape at all.

★ This round type is called an elliptical galaxy.

★ This type is a barred spiral galaxy.

Radio view

A kind of telescope called a radio telescope can "see" the Milky Way much more clearly than other kinds. The picture below shows the big bulge in the middle of our galaxy.

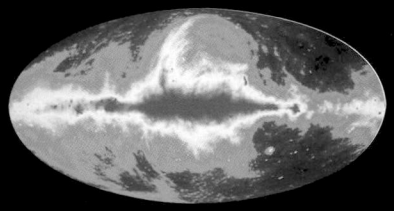

The red patch in this picture shows where most of the stars are in the Milky Way.

How many galaxies?

A hundred years ago astronomers thought the Milky Way was the only galaxy in the Universe. But over the last century, telescopes and radio telescopes have detected many millions of other galaxies.

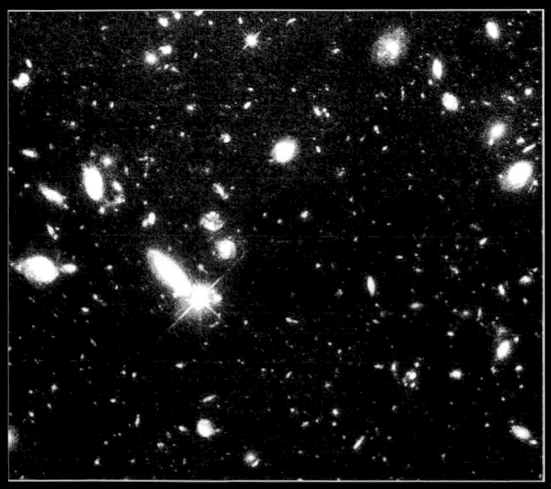

This photograph shows some newly discovered galaxies. Before this picture was taken, astronomers thought there was nothing in this part of space.

Looking at the night sky

Although many of the pictures in this part of the book were taken using very powerful telescopes, you can still see many amazing things in the night sky just with your eyes.

Spiral galaxy

Milky Way

The Moon

Star cluster. This one is called the Hyades.

Old star. This one is called Betelgeuse.

This group of stars is called Orion.

This star is called Sirius. It is the brightest star in the sky.

These are some of the things you may be able to see without a telescope.

The Moon

The clearest sight in the night sky is the Moon. You can see it glowing brightly in the darkness because it is lit up by light from the Sun. As the Moon orbits the Earth it seems to change shape.

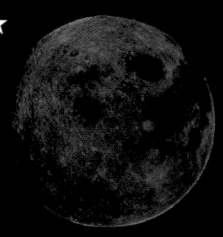

New Moon
When no light shines on the Moon, it is impossible to see it.

Waxing Moon
Gradually a sliver of light returns. The Moon appears to grow.

Full Moon
Once every 28 days all of one side of the Moon is lit by the Sun's light.

Waning Moon
As the Moon moves in its orbit less light falls on it. It seems to shrink.

What you can see

There is a lot to see in the night sky, if you know what to look for. Using just your eyes, you can see the Moon, stars, planets, shooting stars, comets and sometimes even spacecraft.

Stars

A clear night sky is full of stars. There are certain patterns you can look for. These patterns are called constellations, and there are 88 altogether.

This is a star pattern called Orion, which you can also see on the left-hand page. Ancient people thought this shape looked like a hunter.

This is a photograph of the constellation of Orion.

The Milky Way

This is what the Milky Way looks like on a very clear night. You can see it at certain times of the year if you are away from city lights.

Internet link

For a link to a website that has a good introduction to astronomy, go to **www.usborne-quicklinks.com**

Space words

alien a living thing from another world.

asteroid a rock orbiting the Sun. There are thousands of them in a part of the Solar System called the Asteroid Belt.

astronaut someone who goes into space.

atmosphere layers of gas that surround a planet or a star.

cluster a group of space objects gathered together, such as stars or galaxies.

comet a chunk of dirty ice orbiting the Sun which can form a long tail as it melts.

core the middle of a planet, moon, star or other space object.

crater a hollow on the surface of a planet, moon or asteroid, caused by something hitting it, such as a meteorite.

day the time it takes a planet or moon to spin all the way around.

galaxy a group of hundreds of millions of stars all held together by gravity.

gravity a force that pulls objects toward other objects. (Usually smaller objects to larger objects.)

meteor a meteoroid that burns up in a planet's atmosphere. Also called a shooting star.

meteorite a piece of rock or metal from space that is found on the Earth.

meteoroid dust, or small chunks of rock, in orbit around the Sun.

moon a mini-planet in orbit around another planet.

orbit the path of an object in space, as it travels around another object.

planet a huge ball of rock or gas, which travels around a star.

rocket a type of engine in a spacecraft which uses exploding fuel to make it move.

satellite 1) something in space which orbits something else. **2)** an unmanned spacecraft which orbits the Earth.

solar system a group of planets, and other objects, all in orbit around a sun.

spacecraft (also called spaceship) a vehicle that is used for space travel. If it has no people in it, it is unmanned.

space probe an unmanned spacecraft which collects information about objects in space.

space station a large spacecraft orbiting the Earth, where astronauts learn about living and working in space.

spacewalk when an astronaut in a spacesuit leaves a spacecraft and floats in space.

star a huge ball of exploding gas.

Universe everything that exists in space.

year the length of time it takes a planet to travel around the Sun. Earth's year lasts 365 days.

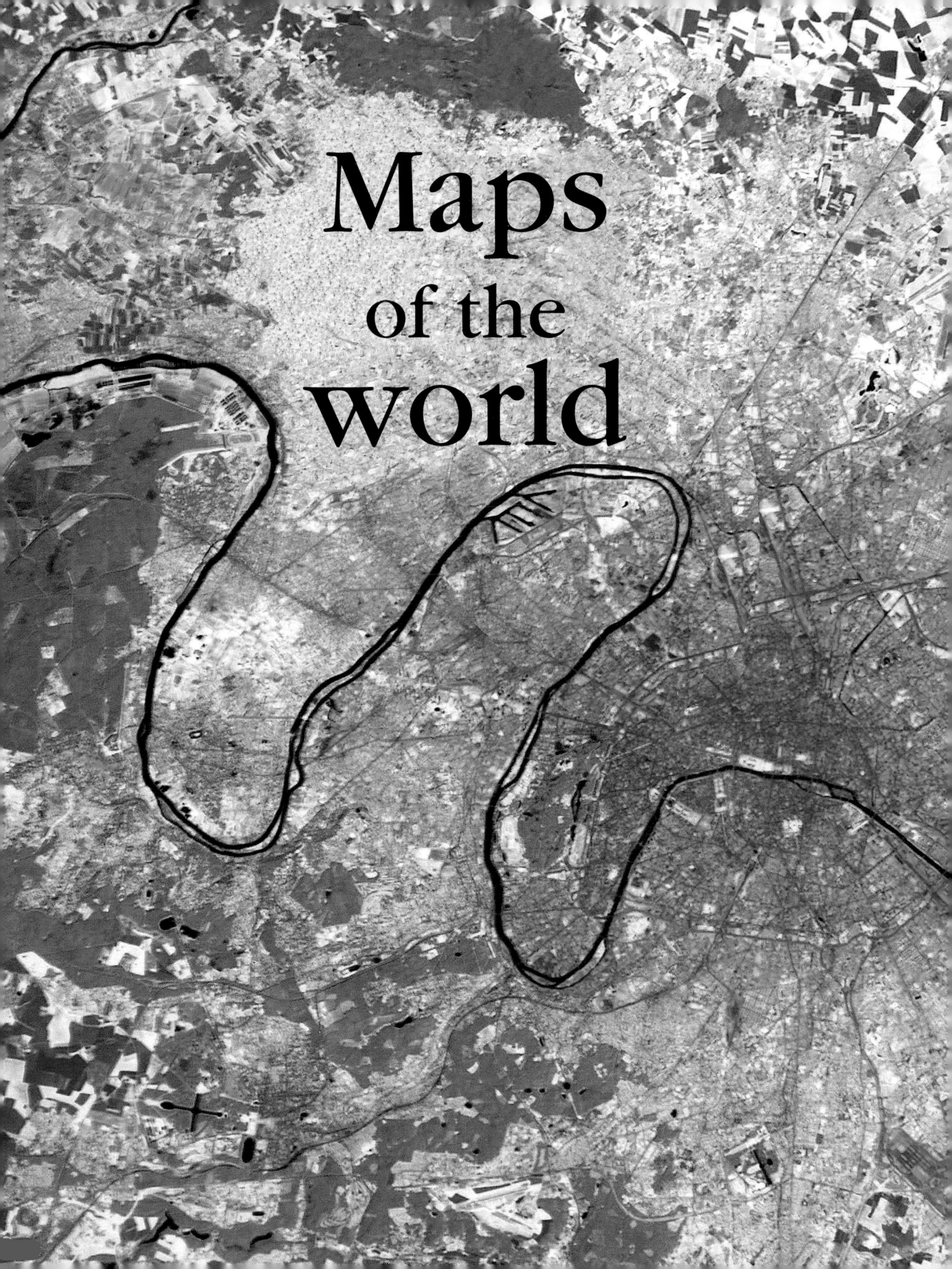

Maps of the world

About maps

A map is a picture that shows a particular area of the world. Places are usually shown as you would see them from above and much smaller than in real life. A map can show the whole world or just one street.

This map shows what the land in South and Central America is covered with.

Rio Grande
Mississippi
Gulf of Mexico
Central America
Cuba
Caribbean Sea
Guiana Highlands
Amazon
Amazon Rainforest
SOUTH AMERICA
Andes
Atacama Desert
Pampas
Patagonia
Cape Horn

Key to map of South and Central America

- Forest
- Desert
- Grassland
- Mountain
- Crops

Scale bar

Approximate scale

0km — 2,000km
0 miles — 1,240 miles

What will you see on a map?

Maps are designed to be easy to understand. Colors and symbols on a map all mean different things. A key tells you what they all stand for.

The size of a map compared with the area it shows is called its scale. Some maps show this with a scale bar. This is a line that tells you how many kilometers or miles are represented by a certain distance on the map.

Which way is up?

The Earth doesn't have a top and a bottom, but north is usually shown at the top of maps. Some maps have a symbol to show which way is north.

This compass symbol shows which way is north (N), south (S), east (E) and west (W).

N
W E
S

Kinds of maps

A map can show features of an area in a clear, simple way. There are lots of different kinds of maps. Here are three of them.

Political maps show countries or states. They often show the names of important cities and towns.

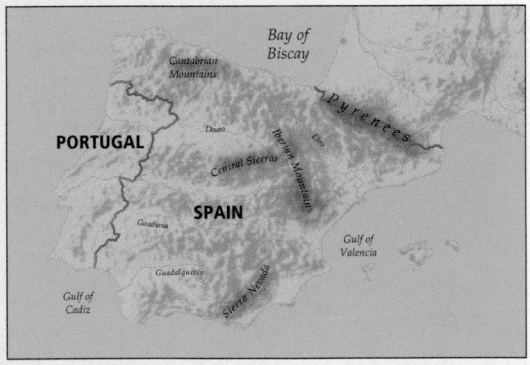

Physical maps show natural features such as mountains, rivers and lakes. They usually have a key.

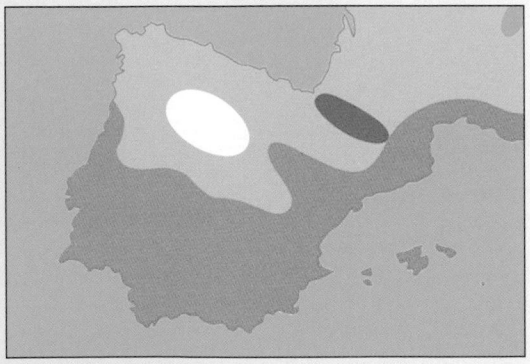

Thematic maps show various types of information, such as which types of plants grow in which regions.

Dividing lines

Map makers divide up the Earth with imaginary lines. These are numbered in degrees (°) and minutes (′) to help us measure distances and find places on a map. There are two sets of lines. They are called latitude and longitude.

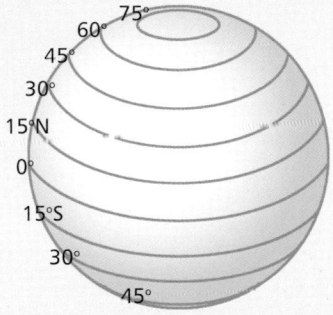

Lines of latitude run around the globe. They are the same distance apart.

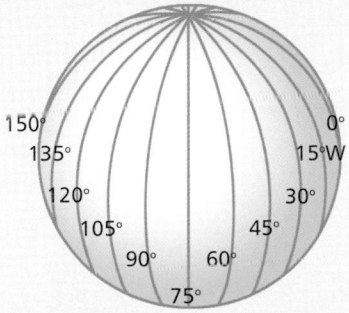

Lines of longitude run from the North Pole to the South Pole.

Here is a drawing of the Earth showing the North Pole and the main lines of latitude and longitude.

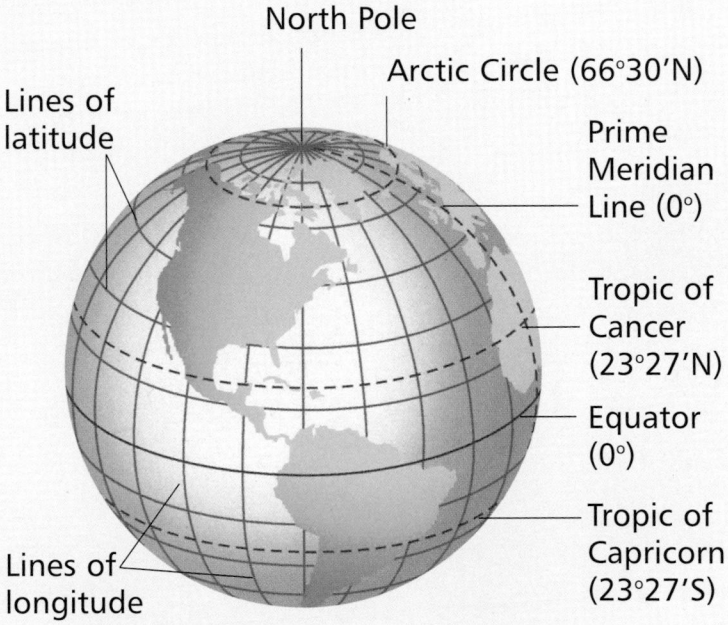

The South Pole is at the bottom of the globe, but you can't see it here.

Internet link

For a link to a website where you can get maps and facts for every country in the world, go to **www.usborne-quicklinks.com**

Countries of the world

This map shows the different countries that make up each continent.

Key to map of countries of the world

Boundary, where one country is joined to the next one

Coast

Lake

Some country names had to be shortened to fit on the map. This list has the names written in full.

ARM.	Armenia
AUST.	Austria
AZER.	Azerbaijan
BELG.	Belgium
B.H.	Bosnia and Herzegovina
CRO.	Croatia
CZECH REP.	Czech Republic
LEB.	Lebanon
LUX.	Luxembourg
MAC.	Macedonia
NETH.	Netherlands
SLOV.	Slovenia
S.M.	Serbia and Montenegro
SWITZ.	Switzerland
U.A.E.	United Arab Emirates

The world's environments

This map shows the different types of land, or environments, such as desert or mountain.

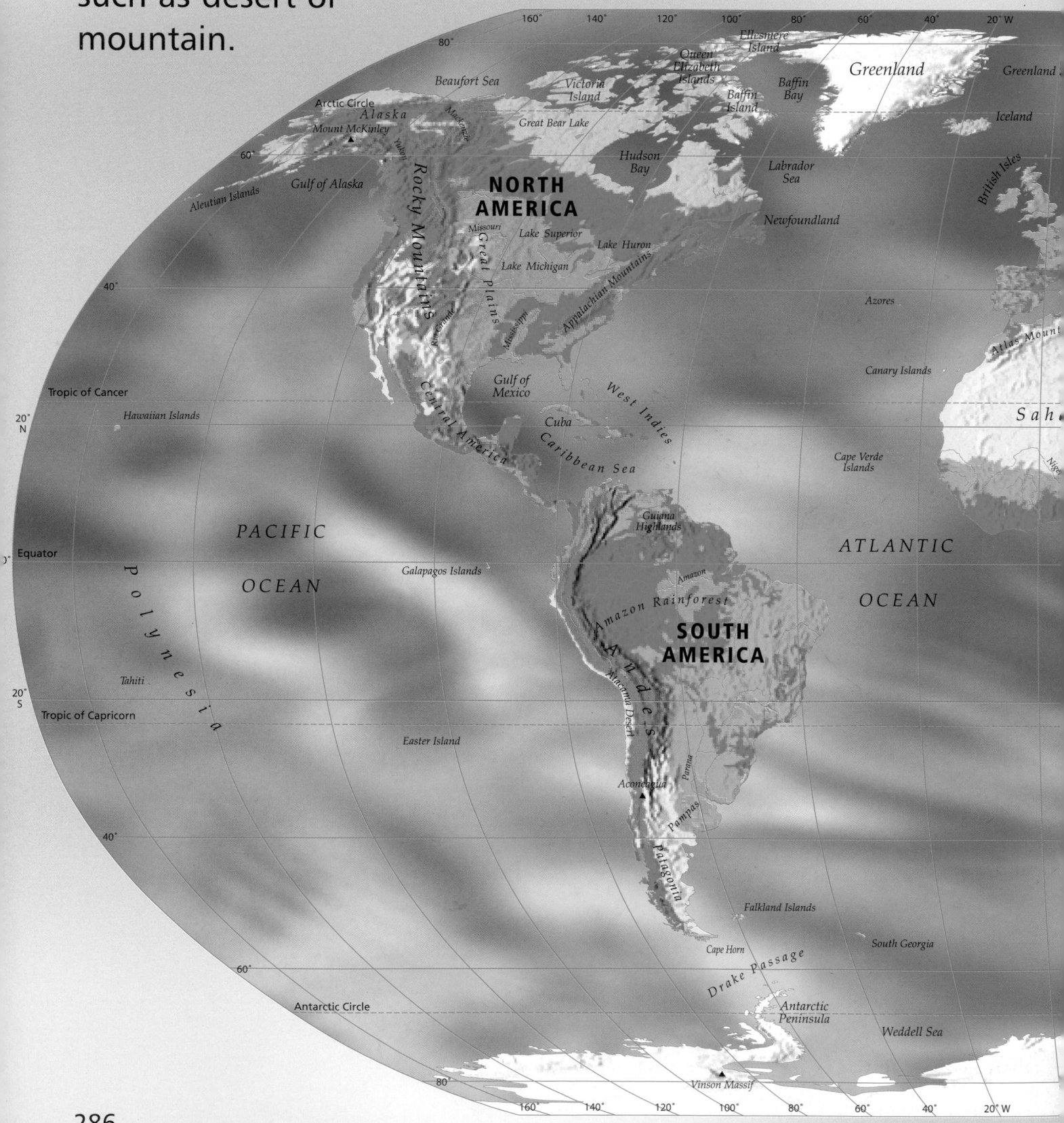

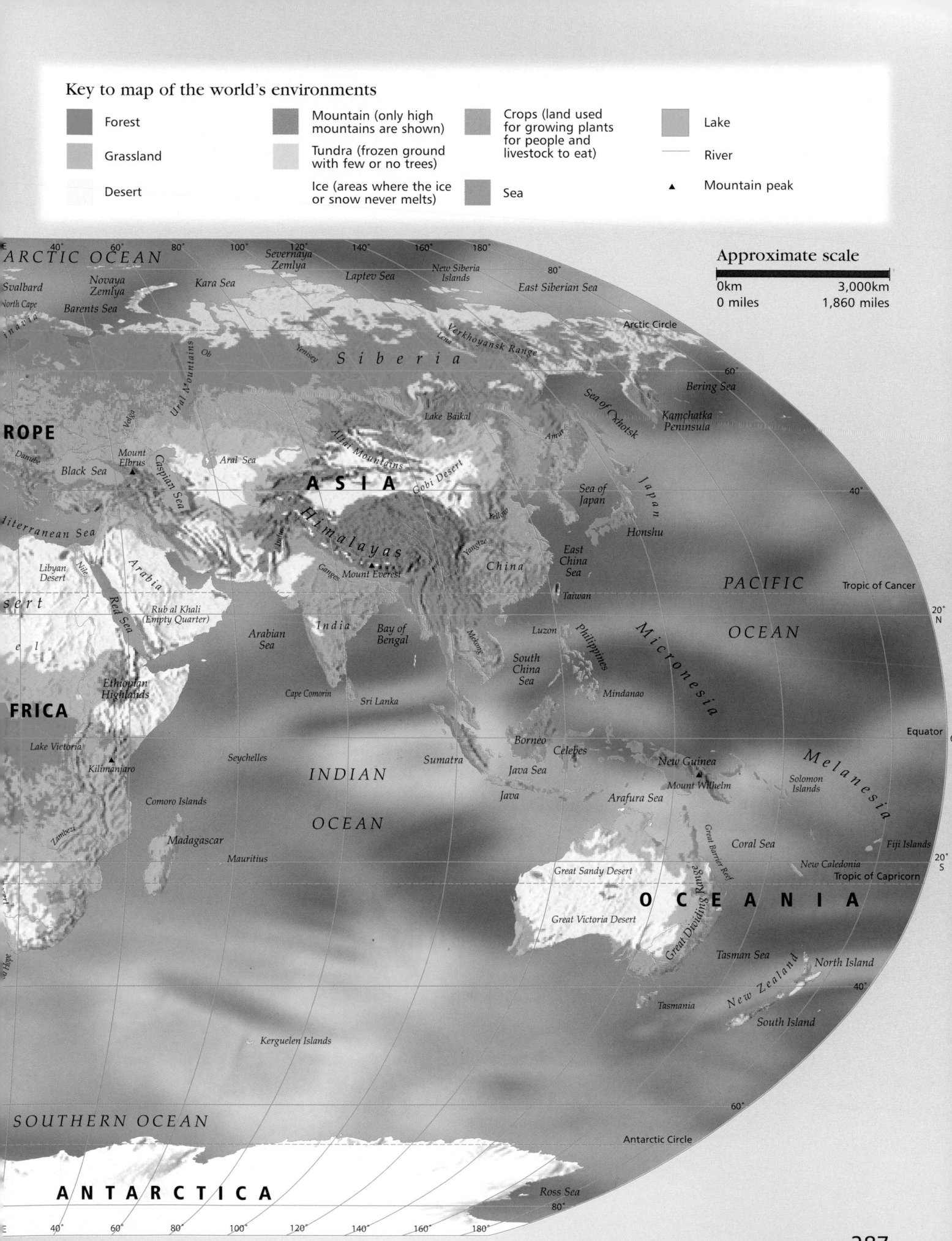
Key to map of the world's environments
Forest
Grassland
Desert
Mountain (only high mountains are shown)
Tundra (frozen ground with few or no trees)
Ice (areas where the ice or snow never melts)
Crops (land used for growing plants for people and livestock to eat)
Sea
Lake
River
Mountain peak
Approximate scale
0km
3,000km
0 miles
1,860 miles
ARCTIC OCEAN
Svalbard
Novaya Zemlya
Kara Sea
Barents Sea
Severnaya Zemlya
Laptev Sea
New Siberia Islands
East Siberian Sea
Arctic Circle
Verkhoyansk Range
Siberia
Ural Mountains
Ob
Yenisey
Lake Baikal
Altai Mountains
Gobi Desert
Bering Sea
Sea of Okhotsk
Kamchatka Peninsula
Amur
Volga
Danube
Black Sea
Mount Elbrus
Caspian Sea
Aral Sea
ASIA
Himalayas
Sea of Japan
Japan
Honshu
Yellow
Yangtze
Indus
Ganges
Mount Everest
China
East China Sea
Taiwan
Libyan Desert
Nile
Arabia
Red Sea
Rub al Khali (Empty Quarter)
Arabian Sea
India
Bay of Bengal
Mekong
Luzon
Philippines
South China Sea
Mindanao
Micronesia
PACIFIC
OCEAN
Tropic of Cancer
Ethiopian Highlands
Cape Comorin
Sri Lanka
Lake Victoria
Kilimanjaro
Seychelles
Borneo
Celebes
Sumatra
Java Sea
Java
New Guinea
Mount Wilhelm
Solomon Islands
Melanesia
Equator
INDIAN
OCEAN
Comoro Islands
Zambezi
Madagascar
Mauritius
Arafura Sea
Great Barrier Reef
Coral Sea
Fiji Islands
New Caledonia
Tropic of Capricorn
Great Sandy Desert
Great Victoria Desert
Great Dividing Range
OCEANIA
Tasman Sea
North Island
New Zealand
Tasmania
South Island
Kerguelen Islands
SOUTHERN OCEAN
Antarctic Circle
ANTARCTICA
Ross Sea
40°
60°
80°
100°
120°
140°
160°
180°
20° N
20° S
0°

North America

This continent includes three very large countries – Canada, the USA and Mexico. It also covers Greenland, the Caribbean, and the countries that join North and South America.

Key to map of North America

- Capital city
- Major city or town
- Boundary (where one country joins another one)
- River
- Coast

Approximate scale

0km 1,000km
0 miles 620 miles

Arctic Circle
ARCTIC OCEAN
Queen Elizabeth Islands
Bering Strait
Point Barrow
Beaufort Sea
Parry Islan
Bering Sea
Yukon
ALASKA (U.S.A.)
Mount McKinley
Anchorage
Victoria Island
Mackenzie
Great Bear Lake
Gulf of Alaska
ROCKY MOUNTAINS
Great Slave Lake
CANAD
Lake Athabasc
Reindeer Lake
Vancouver
Calgary
Winn
Seattle
Columbia
Great Plains
Missou
PACIFIC OCEAN
Great Salt Lake
UNITED STATE
San Francisco
California
Denver
Colorado
Hawaiian Islands (U.S.A.)
Los Angeles
Phoenix
Ciudad Juarez
Tex
Lower California
Hermosillo
Rio G
Tropic of Cancer
Monterrey
MEXICO
Guadalaj
Mexico City
Acapulco

Raccoons are found mainly in North and Central America. They usually sleep in trees during the day and come out at night to feed.

Internet link

For a link to a website where you can find information and stories about each of the states in the USA, go to **www.usborne-quicklinks.com**

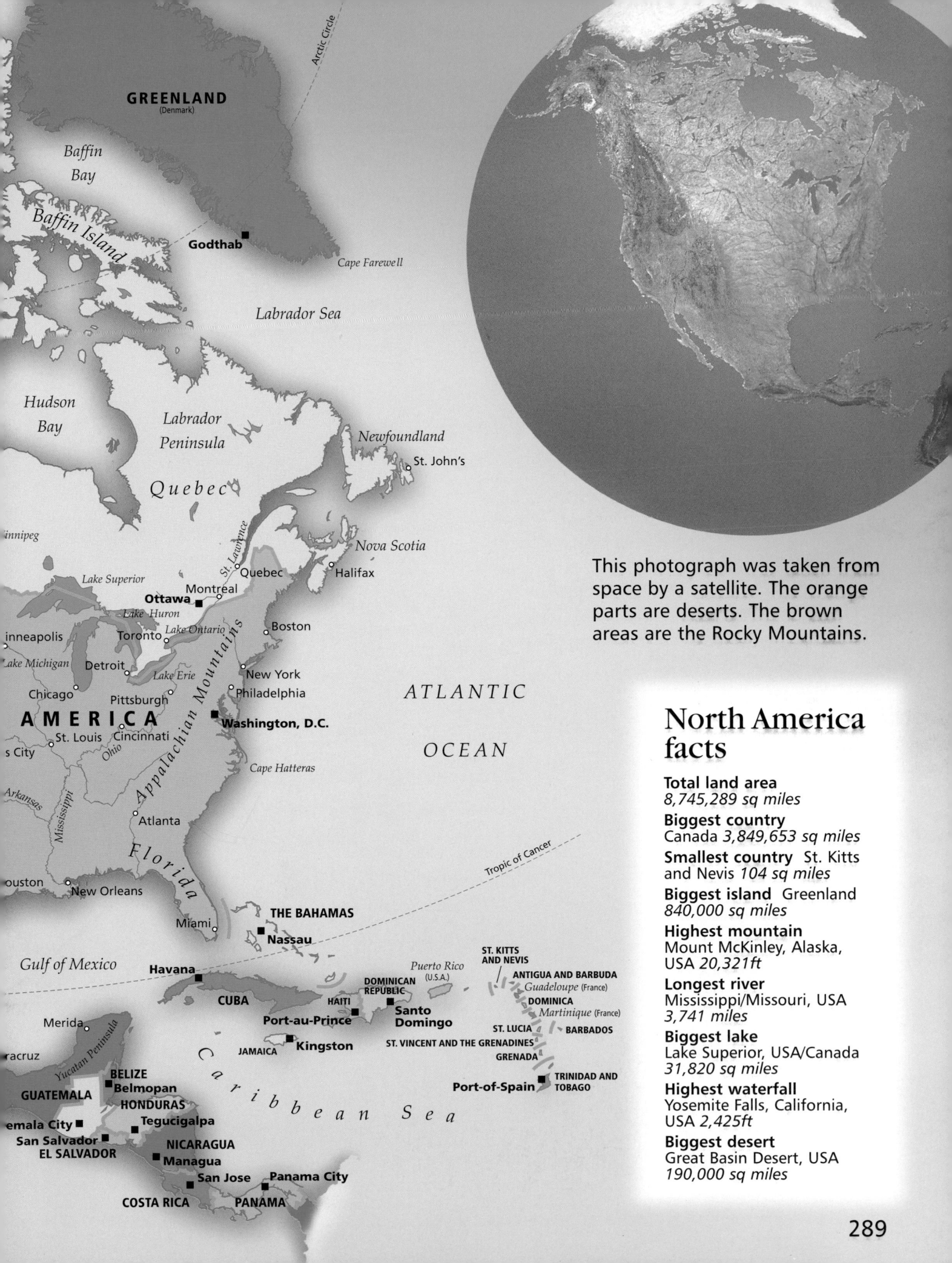

This photograph was taken from space by a satellite. The orange parts are deserts. The brown areas are the Rocky Mountains.

North America facts

Total land area
8,745,289 sq miles

Biggest country
Canada *3,849,653 sq miles*

Smallest country St. Kitts and Nevis *104 sq miles*

Biggest island Greenland *840,000 sq miles*

Highest mountain
Mount McKinley, Alaska, USA *20,321ft*

Longest river
Mississippi/Missouri, USA *3,741 miles*

Biggest lake
Lake Superior, USA/Canada *31,820 sq miles*

Highest waterfall
Yosemite Falls, California, USA *2,425ft*

Biggest desert
Great Basin Desert, USA *190,000 sq miles*

South America

South America stretches from just north of the equator almost to Antarctica in the south. Brazil is the biggest of the twelve countries in South America.

Key to map of South America

- ■ Capital city
- ○ Major city or town
- Boundary (where one country joins another one)
- River
- Coast

Approximate scale

0km — 1,000km
0 miles — 620 miles

Toucans live in the rainforests of South America. They use their long, jagged beaks to pick and eat fruit from the trees.

This is what South America looks like from space. The gray, mottled patch on the left-hand side is the Andes mountain range.

Internet links

Website 1 Go on an adventure in many different parts of South America.

Website 2 Find out about many different animals found in South America.

For links to these websites, go to **www.usborne-quicklinks.com**

South America facts

Total land area
6,898,113 sq miles

Biggest country
Brazil *3,300,151 sq miles*

Smallest country
Surinam *63,039 sq miles*

Biggest island
Tierra del Fuego *17,900 sq miles*

Highest mountain
Aconcagua, Argentina *22,831ft*

Longest river
Amazon, Brazil *4,000 miles*

Biggest lake
Lake Maracaibo, Venezuela
5,140 sq miles

Highest waterfall
Angel Falls, on the Churun River, Venezuela *3,212ft*

Biggest desert
Patagonian Desert, Argentina
260,000 sq miles

Asia

Asia is the world's biggest continent, covering thousands of miles. It stretches from the Arctic Circle to the equator, and from the Ural Mountains in western Russia to Japan in the east.

Key to map of Asia

- Capital city
- Major city or town
- Boundary (where one country joins another one)
- River
- Coast

Approximate scale

0km 1,000km
0 miles 620 miles

Giant pandas live in bamboo forests in the high mountains of western China. There are fewer than 1,000 giant pandas left in the wild.

Internet link

For a link to a website where you can share the travels in India and China of a group of children, go to **www.usborne-quicklinks.com**

The white streaks across the middle of this satellite photograph of Asia are the snowy peaks of mountain ranges.

Asia facts

Total land area
17,196,090 sq miles

Biggest country Russia
Total area: 6,592,735 sq miles Asiatic Russia: 4,934,667 sq miles

Smallest country
Maldives *116 sq miles*

Biggest island
Borneo *290,000 sq miles*

Highest mountain
Mount Everest, Nepal/China *29,035ft*

Longest river Yangtze, China *3,964 miles*

Biggest lake
Caspian Sea, western Asia *143,243 sq miles*

Highest waterfall
Jog Falls, India *830ft*

Biggest desert Arabian Desert, the name given to the deserts of Saudi Arabia *900,000 sq miles*

Africa

Africa is the second largest continent, and the hottest. It stretches from the Mediterranean Sea in the north, across the equator, and far into the southern hemisphere.

Mediterranean Se

ATLANTIC OCEAN

Atlas Mountains

Algiers
Oran
Tunis
Casablanca
Rabat
MOROCCO
Marrakech
TUNISIA
Tripoli
Bengha.
ALGERIA
LIBYA
Laayoune
SAHARA DESER
Tropic of Cancer
WESTERN SAHARA
(Morocco)
Ahaggar Mountains
Tibesti Mountains
MAURITANIA
Nouakchott
MALI
Tombouctou (Timbuktu)
NIGER
CAPE VERDE
Praia
Sahel
Senegal
Dakar
SENEGAL
Banjul
THE GAMBIA
CHAD
Lake Chad
Niger
Bamako
Niamey
Bissau
GUINEA-BISSAU
GUINEA
Ouagadougou
BURKINA FASO
Kano
Ndjamena
BENIN
NIGERIA
Freetown
Conakry
SIERRA LEONE
TOGO
Abuja
IVORY COAST
Lake Volta
GHANA
Porto-Novo
Monrovia
LIBERIA
Yamoussoukro
Lome
Lagos
Accra
CAMEROON
Bangui
Malabo
Yaounde
EQUATORIAL GUINEA
Ubangi
Equator
Libreville
CONGO
SAO TOME AND PRINCIPE
GABON
Brazzaville
Kinshasa
ATLANTIC OCEAN
Luanda
Benguela
ANGOLA
Namib Desert
NAMIBIA
Tropic of Capricorn
Walvis Bay
Windh
Orang
Cape Town
Cape of Good Hope

Key to map of Africa
- Capital city
- Major city or town
- Boundary (where one country joins another one)
- River
- Coast

Approximate scale
0km 1,000 km
0 miles 620 miles

Internet link

For a link to a website where you can join Femi, your guide, for an exciting tour of Africa, go to **www.usborne-quicklinks.com**

The pale brown areas on this satellite picture show how much of Africa is desert. The Sahara Desert is at the top of the continent.

Africa facts

Total land area
11,703,343 sq miles

Biggest country
Sudan *967,493 sq miles*

Smallest country
Seychelles *176 sq miles*

Biggest island
Madagascar *226,656 sq miles*

Highest mountain
Kilimanjaro, Tanzania *19,340ft*

Longest river
River Nile, (Burundi to Egypt) *4,145 miles*

Biggest lake
Lake Victoria, Tanzania *26,724 sq miles*

Highest waterfall
Tugela Falls, South Africa *2,000ft*

Biggest desert
Sahara, North Africa
3,500,000 sq miles

This lion's sandy brown coat helps it blend in with its surroundings in its dry African grassland home.

Europe

Europe stretches from the Arctic Circle to the Mediterranean Sea, and from the Atlantic Ocean in the west to the Ural Mountains in the east.

Europe is home to many types of birds, such as this common European kingfisher.

Arctic Circle
ARCTIC OCEAN
Reykjavik
ICELAND
Norwegian Sea
SWEDEN
Bergen
NORWAY
Oslo
Stockholm
Lake Vaner
Gothenburg
British Isles
Edinburgh
Belfast
North Sea
DENMARK
Copenhagen
Baltic Sea
IRELAND
Dublin
UNITED KINGDOM
Gdansk
Cardiff
London
Amsterdam
Hamburg
ATLANTIC
NETHERLANDS
The Hague
Berlin
POLAND
English Channel
Brussels
BELGIUM
Rhine
GERMANY
Elbe
Oder
OCEAN
Seine
LUXEMBOURG
Luxembourg
Prague
Paris
CZECH REPUBLIC
Nantes
Danube
Munich
Loire
Vienna
Bratislava
Bay of Biscay
FRANCE
Bern
LIECHTENSTEIN
Vaduz
AUSTRIA
SWITZERLAND
Budapest
Lyon
The Alps
Bordeaux
Milan
SLOVENIA
Ljubljana
Zagreb
CROATIA
Turin
Po
Bilbao
BOSNIA AND HERZEGOVINA
Oporto
Andorra la Vella
MONACO
SAN MARINO
Adriatic Sea
ANDORRA
Marseille
Sarajevo
PORTUGAL
ITALY
Madrid
Corsica (France)
Lisbon
Barcelona
Tagus
Rome
VATICAN CITY
SPAIN
ALBANIA
Tirana
Valencia
Naples
Cordoba
Sardinia (Italy)
Gibraltar (U.K.)
Mediterranean Sea
Sicily (Italy)
MALTA
Valletta

Key to map of Europe
- Capital city
- Major city or town
- Boundary (where one country joins another one)
- River
- Coast

Approximate scale
0km — 500km
0 miles — 310 miles

Europe facts

Total land area
3,940,428 sq miles

Biggest country
Russia *Total area: 6,492,735 sq miles Area of European Russia: 1,658,068 sq miles*

Smallest country
Vatican City *0.17 sq miles*

Biggest island Great Britain *88,417 sq miles*

Highest mountain
Mount Elbrus, Russia *18,510ft*

Longest river
Volga *2,298 miles*

Biggest lake
Lake Ladoga, Russia *6,834 sq miles*

Highest waterfall
Utigard, on the Jostedal Glacier, Norway *2,625ft*

Biggest desert There are no deserts in Europe.

Internet link

For a link to a website where you can learn about different festivals and traditions from all over Europe, go to **www.usborne-quicklinks.com**

This satellite photograph of Europe shows how the continent joins on to Asia at the right. The white patch at the top of the picture is the ice that covers the Arctic.

Oceania

Oceania is the smallest continent. It is made up of Australia, New Zealand and Papua New Guinea, as well as thousands of small islands scattered throughout the Pacific Ocean.

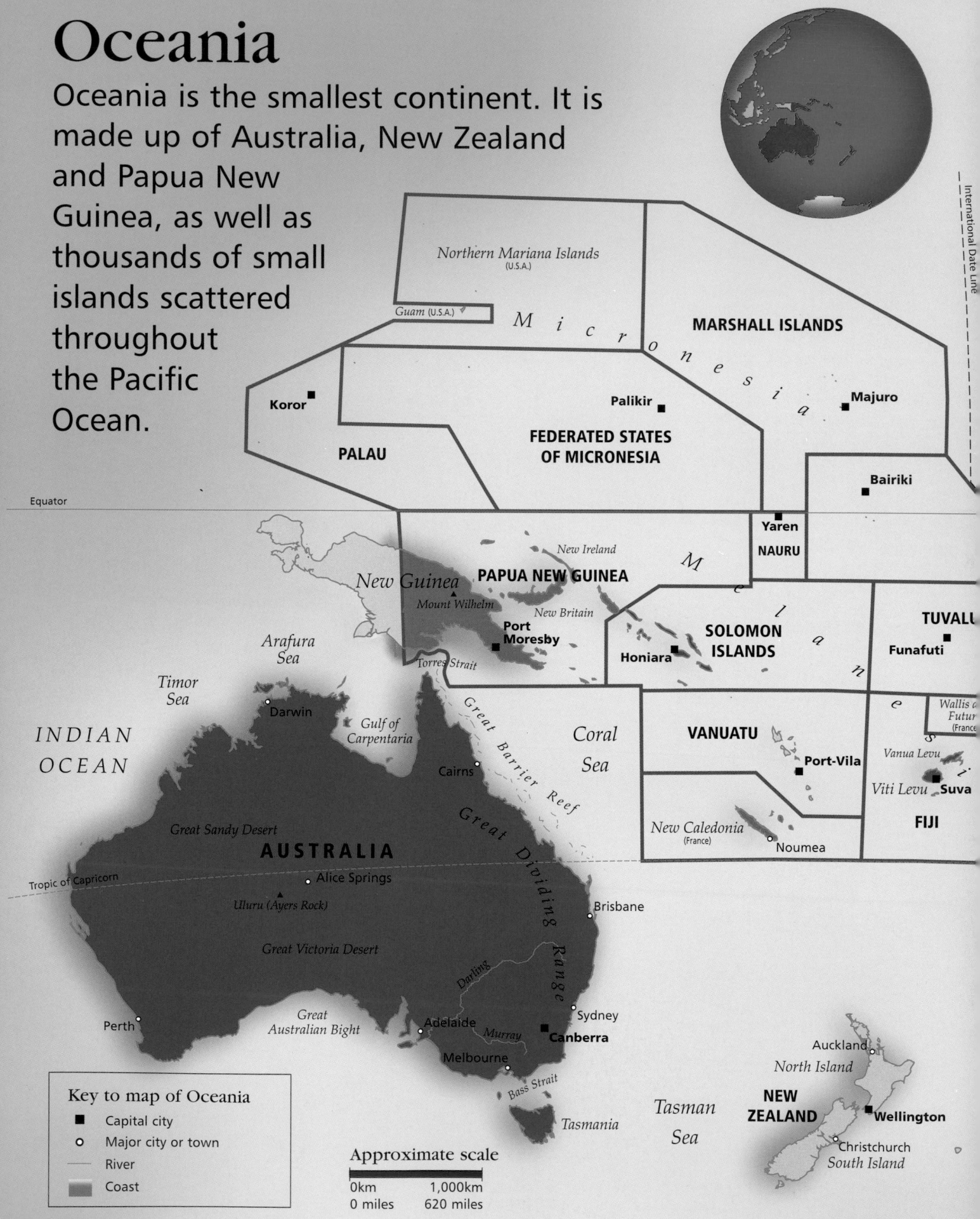

Oceania facts

Total land area
3,306,715 sq miles

Biggest country
Australia *2,988,885 sq miles*

Smallest country
Nauru *8 sq miles*

Biggest island
New Guinea *309,000 sq miles*

Highest mountain
Mount Wilhelm, Papua New Guinea *14,793ft*

Longest river
Murray/Darling River Australia *2,310 miles*

Biggest lake
Lake Eyre, Australia *3,470 sq miles*

Highest waterfall
Sutherland Falls on the Arthur River, New Zealand *1,904ft*

Biggest desert
Great Victoria Desert, Australia *150,000 sq miles*

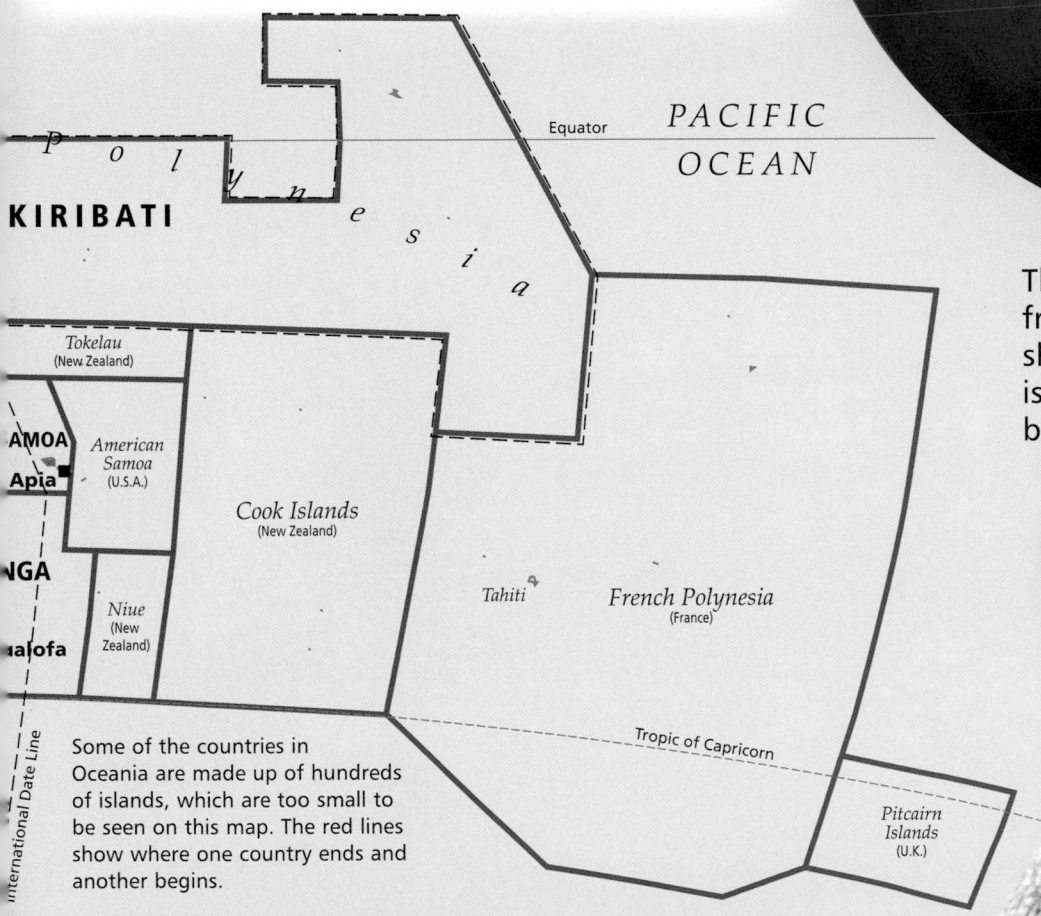

Some of the countries in Oceania are made up of hundreds of islands, which are too small to be seen on this map. The red lines show where one country ends and another begins.

This photograph was taken from space. The yellow areas show that much of Australia is desert. The large, white area below Australia is Antarctica.

Internet links

Website 1 Explore Australia, meet its animals and learn about its people and way of life.

Website 2 Games, stories and a quiz, all about Australia.

For links to these websites, go to **www.usborne-quicklinks.com**

Like this kangaroo, many mammals in Australia are marsupials. This means that they carry their babies in a pouch.

Flags of the world

North America

Antigua and Barbuda

Bahamas

Barbados

Belize

Canada

Costa Rica

Cuba

Dominica

Dominican Republic

El Salvador

Grenada

Guatemala

Haiti

Honduras

Jamaica

Mexico

Nicaragua

Panama

St. Kitts and Nevis

St. Lucia

St. Vincent and the Grenadines

Trinidad and Tobago

United States of America

South America

Argentina

Bolivia

Brazil

Chile

Colombia

Ecuador

Guyana

Paraguay

Peru

Surinam

Uruguay

Venezuela

Asia

Afghanistan

Armenia

Azerbaijan

Bahrain

Bangladesh

Bhutan

Brunei

Burma (Myanmar)

Cambodia

China

East Timor

Georgia

Asia (continued)

India

Indonesia

Iran

Iraq

Israel

Japan

Jordan

Kazakhstan

Kuwait

Kyrgyzstan

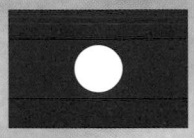
Laos

Lebanon

Malaysia

Maldives

Mongolia

Nepal

North Korea

Oman

Pakistan

Philippines

Qatar

Russian Federation

Saudi Arabia

Singapore

South Korea

Sri Lanka

Syria

Taiwan

Tajikistan

Thailand

Turkey

Turkmenistan

United Arab Emirates

Uzbekistan

Vietnam

Yemen

Africa

Algeria

Angola

Benin

Botswana

Burkina Faso

Burundi

Cameroon

Cape Verde

Central African Republic

Chad

Comoros

Congo

Congo (Democratic Republic)

Djibouti

Egypt

Equatorial Guinea

Eritrea

Ethiopia

Africa (continued)

Gabon

The Gambia

Ghana

Guinea

Guinea-Bissau

Ivory Coast

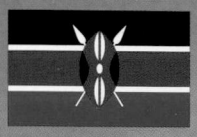
Kenya

Lesotho

Liberia

Libya

Madagascar

Malawi

Mali

Mauritania

Mauritius

Morocco

Mozambique

Namibia

Niger

Nigeria

Rwanda

Sao Tome and Principe

Senegal

Seychelles

Sierra Leone

Somalia

South Africa

Sudan

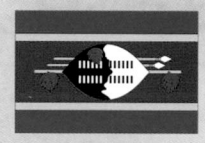
Swaziland

Tanzania

Togo

Tunisia

Uganda

Zambia

Zimbabwe

Europe

Albania

Andorra

Austria

Belarus

Belgium

Bosnia and Herzegovina

Bulgaria

Croatia

Cyprus

Czech Republic

Denmark

Estonia

Finland

France

Germany

Greece

Hungary

Iceland

Europe (continued)

Ireland

Italy

Latvia

Liechtenstein

Lithuania

Luxembourg

Macedonia

Malta

Moldova

Monaco

Netherlands

Norway

Poland

Portugal

Romania

Russian Federation

San Marino

Serbia and Montenegro

Slovakia

Slovenia

Spain

Sweden

Switzerland

Turkey

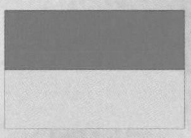
Ukraine

United Kingdom

Vatican City

Oceania

Australia

Federated States of Micronesia

Fiji

Kiribati

Marshall Islands

Nauru

New Zealand

Palau

Papau New Guinea

Samoa

Solomon Islands

Tonga

Tuvalu

Vanuatu

Changing flags

Flags of the world change frequently. New flags are invented as new countries are born, or their situation changes.

For example, in 1991, there were important changes to the way South Africa was run. All adults in the country were allowed to vote in free elections for the first time. To celebrate this, a new flag was designed.

New flag of South Africa

South African flag until 1994

Internet links

For links to websites with flag facts and a game, go to **www.usborne-quicklinks.com**

Earth facts and records

The continents

Continent	Area sq miles	Countries
Asia	17,196,090	48
Africa	11,703,343	52
North America	8,745,289	23
South America	6,898,113	12
Antarctica	5,150,603	–
Europe	3,940,428	46
Oceania	3,306,715	14

Internet link

For a link to a website where you can find out more about the Earth's features, go to **www.usborne-quicklinks.com**

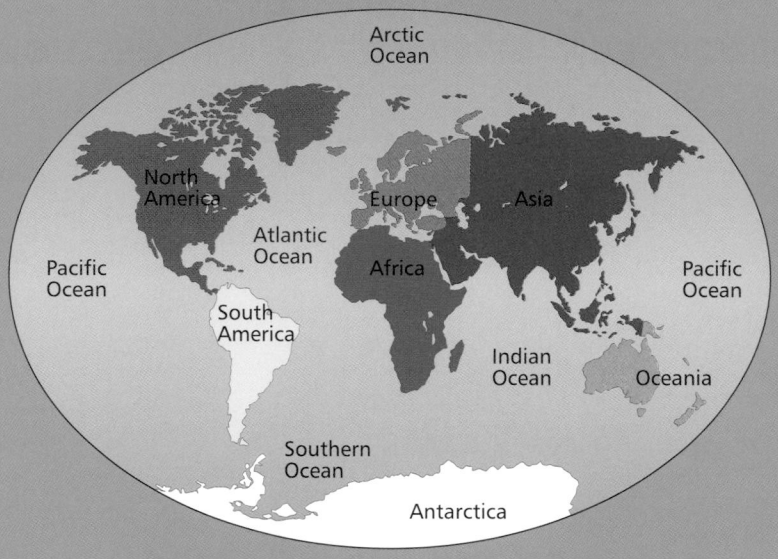

This map shows the Earth's continents and oceans.

Highest mountains in each continent

Continent	Mountain	Other name	Height ft	Location
Asia	Mount Everest	Chomolungma	29,035	Nepal/China
South America	Mount Aconcagua	Cerro Aconcagua	22,831	Argentina
North America	Mount McKinley	Denali	20,321	USA
Africa	Mount Kilimanjaro	Oldoinyo Oibor	19,340	Tanzania
Europe	Mount Elbrus	Gora El-brus	18,510	Russia
Antarctica	Vinson Massif	Mount Vinson	16,066	–
Oceania	Mount Wilhelm	Korel-Khu	14,793	Papua New Guinea

Largest oceans and seas

Body of water	Area sq miles	Deepest point ft
Pacific Ocean	60,060,893	36,161
Atlantic Ocean	29,637,974	28,373
Indian Ocean	26,469,620	25,344
Southern Ocean	7,848,300	23,737
Arctic Ocean	5,427,052	17,881
Mediterranean Sea	967,186	15,200
South China Sea	894,985	16,457
Bering Sea	876,066	15,660
Caribbean Sea	750,196	22,789
Gulf of Mexico	596,142	12,425

Climate records

Location	Notes
El Azizia, Libya	Hottest recorded temperature on Earth: 136°F (1922)
Vostok, Antarctica	Coldest recorded temperature on Earth: –128.6°F (1983)
Mawsynram, India	Wettest place on Earth: 467.5in of rain in a year
Atacama Desert, Chile	Driest place on Earth: less than 0.06in of rain in a year

Longest rivers

River	Length miles	Flows from	Flows to
Nile	4,145	Ruvyiranza River, Burundi	Mediterranean Sea (Egypt)
Amazon	4,000	Andes Mountains, Peru	Atlantic Ocean (Brazil)
Chang Jiang (Yangtze)	3,964	Kunlun Mountains, China	East China Sea (China)
Mississippi-Missouri-Red Rock	3,741	Montana, USA	Gulf of Mexico (USA)
Yenisei-Angara	3,442	Tannu-Ola Mountains, Russia	Kara Sea (Russia)
Huang He (Yellow River)	3,395	Kunlun Mountains, China	Gulf of Chihli (China)
Ob'-Irtysh	3,362	Altai Mountains, Russia	Gulf of Ob, Kara Sea (Russia)
Amur-Shilka-Onon	2,744	Altai Mountains, Mongolia	Tatar Strait (Russia)
Lena	2,734	Baikal Mountains, Russia	Laptev Sea (Russia)
Congo (Zaïre)	2,718	Democratic Republic of Congo	Atlantic Ocean (D.R. of Congo)

Greatest lakes

Lake	Area sq miles	Depth ft	Location
Caspian Sea	143,243	3,104	Europe/Asia
Lake Superior	31,820	1,332	USA/Canada
Lake Victoria	26,724	269	Tanzania/Uganda
Lake Huron	23,010	751	USA/Canada
Lake Michigan	22,400	922	USA
Lake Tanganyika	12,650	4,708	Tanzania/Congo
Lake Baikal	12,162	5,712	Russia
Great Bear Lake	12,096	269	Canada
Lake Nyasa	11,555	2,316	Mozambique/Tanzania
Aral Sea	11,043	223	Kazakhstan/Uzbekistan

Largest islands

Island	Area sq miles	Location
Greenland	840,000	Atlantic Ocean
New Guinea	309,000	Pacific Ocean
Borneo	290,000	Pacific Ocean
Madagascar	226,656	Indian Ocean
Baffin Island, Canada	195,928	Atlantic Ocean
Sumatra, Indonesia	168,961	Indian Ocean
Honshu, Japan	88,979	Pacific Ocean
Great Britain	88,417	Atlantic Ocean
Victoria Island, Canada	83,896	Atlantic Ocean
Ellesmere Island, Canada	75,767	Atlantic Ocean

Deepest cave

The deepest cave ever explored is Voronja Cave in the Caucasus Mountains in Georgia, Russia. It is just over a mile deep.

Waterfalls

The widest waterfall is Khône Falls on the Mekong river in Laos. It is 6.7 miles wide. So much water pours over it that it would take only 17 minutes to fill a lake the size of Lake Superior, in North America. The highest waterfall is Angel Falls in Venezuela. It is 3,212ft high.

Angel Falls is over three times as high as the Eiffel Tower in Paris, France.

Space facts

Solar System facts

Name of planet	Distance from the Sun (miles)	Time to travel around the Sun	Time it takes to spin once	Number of moons	Largest moon
Mercury	36 million	88 days	59 days	0	–
Venus	67 million	224.7 days	243 days	0	–
Earth	93 million	365.3 days	23 hours, 56 minutes	1	Moon
Mars	142 million	687 days	24 hours, 37 minutes	2	Phobos
Jupiter	483 million	11.9 years	9 hours, 50 minutes	At least 61	Ganymede
Saturn	887 million	29.5 years	10 hours, 14 minutes	At least 31	Titan
Uranus	1,784 million	84 years	17 hours, 54 minutes	21	Titania
Neptune	2,796 million	165 years	16 hours, 6 minutes	11	Triton
Pluto	3,674 million	248 years	6 days, 10 hours	1	Charon

Comparing planet sizes

Distances across planets are given in miles.

Moon map

This map shows the near side of the Moon, that is, the side which always faces the Earth. The Moon's "seas" are patches of dark rock. The triangles mark places where some important spacecraft landed:

1. Luna 9 (USSR, 1966). The first unmanned spacecraft to land safely on the Moon.

2. Apollo 11 (USA, 1969). The first manned spacecraft to land on the Moon. Two of its crew, Neil Armstrong and Edwin ("Buzz") Aldrin, were the first people to walk on the Moon. They collected rock samples and took photographs of the Moon's surface.

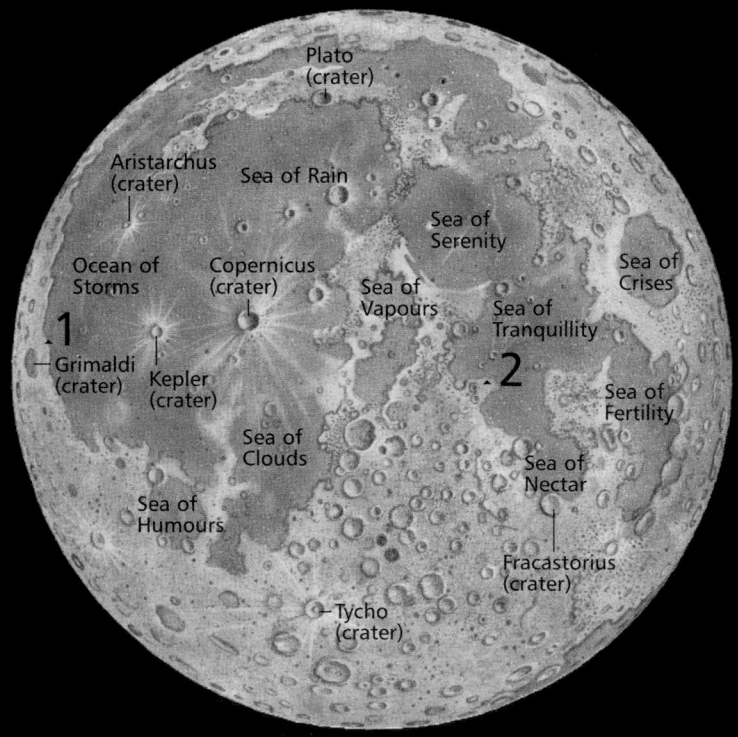

Star types

Our Sun is a star – one of billions in the Universe. Stars are huge balls of blazing gas. The Sun looks biggest because it is the closest. Stars vary in size, color, temperature and brightness.

The biggest known stars are called supergiants. Rigel is a blue supergiant over 100 times bigger than the Sun.

The hottest, brightest stars are blue.

Most stars are the size of the Sun, or smaller. They are called dwarfs. The Sun is a yellow dwarf.

Sun

Compared to other stars, red stars are cooler and dimmer.

Stars bigger than the Sun are called giants. Arcturus is an orange giant.

Sailing by the stars

In ancient times, sailors used the stars like a map to find their way at sea. The pictures below show the constellations (star patterns) they used to find the celestial poles – the points in the sky directly above the Earth's north and south poles.

Internet link

For a link to a website where you can find out more about stars, planets, moons and space exploration, go to **www.usborne-quicklinks.com**

Finding north

The star pattern called the Big Dipper has two stars which, if lined up, point to the Pole Star. This marks the north celestial pole.

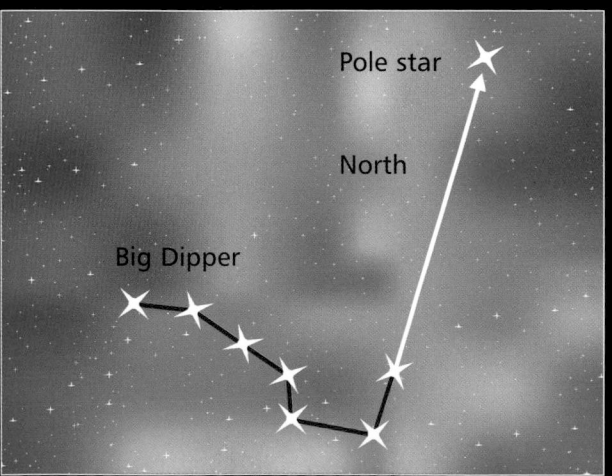

Finding south

The south celestial pole is not marked by a star. To find south, sailors started at the Southern Cross constellation and traced a line from its longest part.

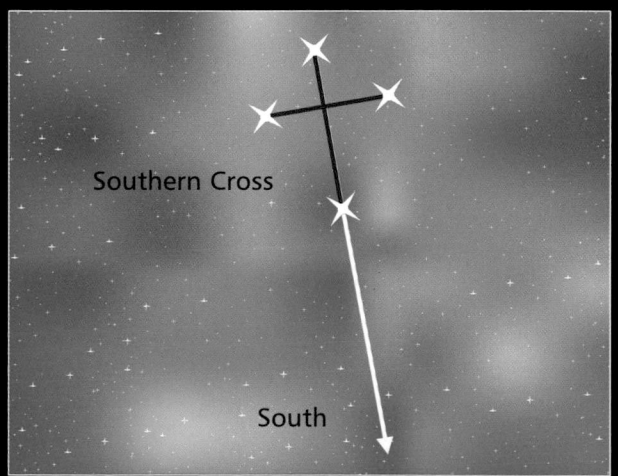

Animal and plant records

The biggest...

Living thing	"Pando", a grove of aspen trees	Area: 0.3 sq mile	These trees in Utah, USA, are all joined by the same roots.
Animal	Blue whale	Length: 108ft	Longer than a tennis court – the largest animal of all time
Land animal	African elephant	Height: 12ft	Even a newborn African elephant is almost 3ft tall.
Bird (flightless)	Ostrich	Height: 9ft	Lives in Africa
Bird (flying)	Wandering albatross	Wingspan: 12ft	Can fly over 600 miles in a day
Reptile	Saltwater crocodile	Length: 23ft	Lives in Australia
Spineless animal	Giant squid	Length: 60ft	Has the biggest eyes of any animal – the size of basketballs
Insect	Longhorn beetle	Length: 6.5in	Lives in South America
Tree (tallest)	The "Mendocino tree", a coast redwood	Height: 367ft	Grows in California, USA

Comparing animal sizes

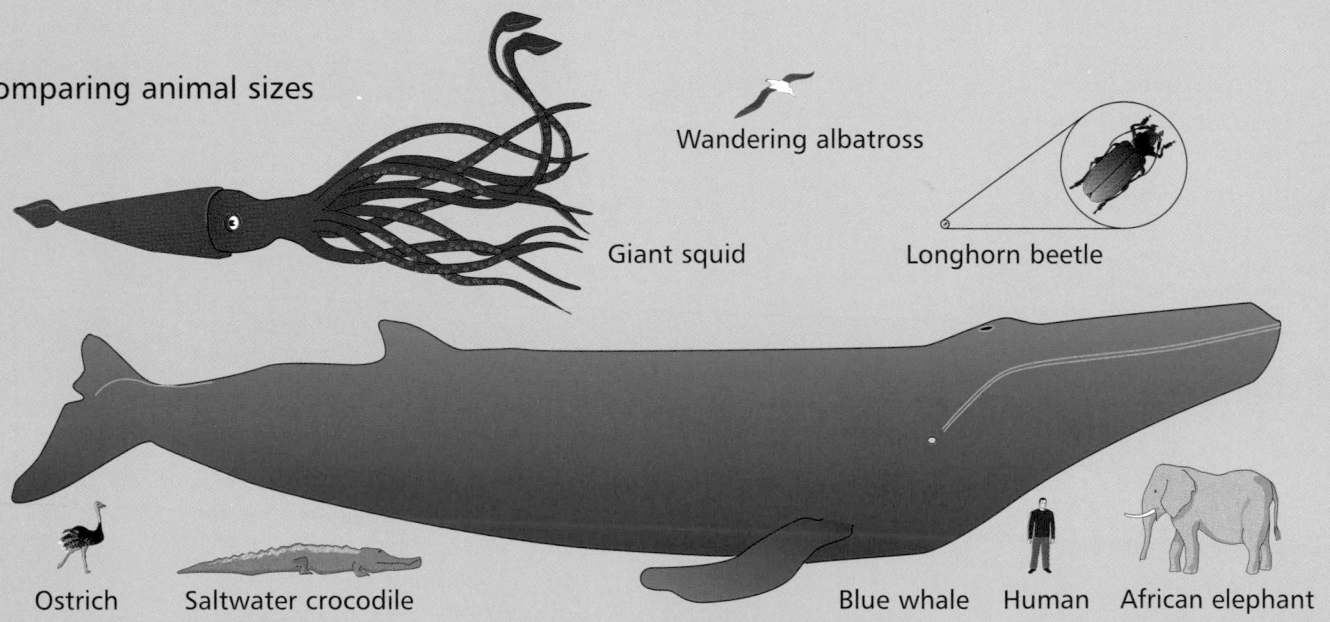

The smallest...

Living thing	Mycoplasma genitalium	Length: 0.00001in	A germ living in the human body
Insect	Fairyfly	Length: 0.006in	A tiny wasp from Costa Rica
Land mammal	Savi's pygmy shrew	Length: 3in	Lives in Africa and Arabia
Flying mammal	Bumblebee bat	Length: 1in	Lives in Thailand
Bird	Bee hummingbird	Length: 2.2in	Lives in Cuba
Reptile	Dwarf gecko	Length: 0.6in	Lives in the Dominican Republic

The oldest...

Living thing	Bacillus 2-9-3	Age: 250 million years	These ancient germs were found inside salt crystals in a mine in New Mexico, USA.
Tree	"Methuselah", a Bristlecone pine	Age: 4,767 years	Grows in California, USA
Sea creature	Ocean quahog	Age: 220 years	A type of large clam
Land animal	"Harriet", a Galapagos giant tortoise	Age: about 172 years	Harriet was born in the Galapagos Islands in about 1830. She now lives in an Australian zoo.

The rarest...

Living creature	Small blue macaw	Just one male remains in the wild.
Land mammal	Javan rhinoceros	Just 60 Javan rhinoceroses remain, in Indonesia and Vietnam.
Water mammal	Yangtze River dolphin (Baiji)	About 150 left in the Yangtze River (Chang Jiang), China
Reptile	St. Lucia racer	A snake living only on Maria Islet, St. Lucia. Few are ever seen.
Plant	Cooke's koki'o	A small Hawaiian tree with red flowers. Just one remains.

The fastest...

Animal (over a short distance)	Cheetah	65mph
Animal (over a long distance)	Pronghorn antelope	55mph
Swimmer	Sailfish	68mph
Bird	Peregrine falcon	112mph

Internet links

For links to websites where you can find out more about animal record breakers, and see pictures of them, go to **www.usborne-quicklinks.com**

Galapagos giant tortoises are some of the longest-living animals in the world. The Galapagos Islands are northwest of South America.

Map index

This is an index of the countries named on the maps and their capital cities. The names of countries are written in heavy type **like this**.

A

Abu Dhabi (United Arab Emirates, capital) 292
Abuja (Nigeria, capital) 294
Accra (Ghana, capital) 294
Addis Ababa (Ethiopia, capital) 295
Afghanistan 285, 292
Albania 285, 296
Algeria 284, 294
Algiers (Algeria, capital) 294
Amman (Jordan, capital) 292
Amsterdam (Netherlands, capital) 296
Andorra 296
Andorra la Vella (Andorra, capital) 296
Angola 285, 294
Ankara (Turkey, capital) 292
Antananarivo (Madagascar, capital) 295
Antigua and Barbuda 289
Apia (Samoa, capital) 299
Argentina 284, 290–291
Armenia 285, 292
Ashgabat (Turkmenistan, capital) 292
Asmara (Eritrea, capital) 295
Astana (Kazakhstan, capital) 292
Asuncion (Paraguay, capital) 291
Athens (Greece, capital) 297
Australia 285, 298
Austria 285, 296
Azerbaijan 285, 292

B

Baghdad (Iraq, capital) 292
Bahamas, The 284, 289
Bahrain 285, 292
Bairiki (Kiribati, capital) 298
Baku (Azerbaijan, capital) 292
Bamako (Mali, capital) 294
Bangkok (Thailand, capital) 293
Bangladesh 285, 292
Bangui (Central African Republic, capital) 294
Banjul (The Gambia, capital) 294
Barbados 289
Beijing (China, capital) 293
Beirut (Lebanon, capital) 292
Belarus 285, 297
Belgium 284, 296
Belgrade (Serbia and Montenegro, capital) 297
Belize 284, 289
Belmopan (Belize, capital) 289
Benin 284, 294
Berlin (Germany, capital) 296
Bern (Switzerland, capital) 296
Bhutan 285, 292
Bishkek (Kyrgyzstan, capital) 292
Bissau (Guinea-Bissau, capital) 294
Bloemfontein (South Africa, capital) 295
Bogota (Colombia, capital) 290
Bolivia 284, 290
Bosnia and Herzegovina 285, 296
Botswana 285, 295
Brasilia (Brazil, capital) 291
Bratislava (Slovakia, capital) 296
Brazil 284, 291
Brazzaville (Congo, capital) 294
Brunei 285, 293
Brussels (Belgium, capital) 296
Bucharest (Romania, capital) 297
Budapest (Hungary, capital) 296
Buenos Aires (Argentina, capital) 291
Bujumbura (Burundi, capital) 295
Bulgaria 285, 297
Burkina Faso 284, 294
Burma (Myanmar) 285, 293
Burundi 285, 295

C

Cairo (Egypt, capital) 295
Cambodia 285, 293
Cameroon 284–285, 294
Canada 284, 288–289
Canberra (Australia, capital) 298
Cape Town (South Africa, capital) 294
Cape Verde 284, 294
Caracas (Venezuela, capital) 290
Cayenne (French Guiana, capital) 291
Central African Republic 285, 294–295
Chad 285, 294
Chile 284, 290
China 285, 293
Chisinau (Moldova, capital) 297
Colombia 284, 290
Colombo (Sri Lanka, capital) 292
Comoros 285, 295
Conakry (Sierra Leone, capital) 294
Congo 285, 294
Congo (Democratic Republic) 284–285, 294–295
Copenhagen (Denmark, capital) 296
Costa Rica 284, 289
Croatia 285, 296
Cuba 284, 289
Cyprus 285, 292
Czech Republic 285, 296

D

Dakar (Senegal, capital) 294
Damascus (Syria, capital) 292
Denmark 284, 296
Dhaka (Bangladesh, capital) 292
Dili (East Timor, capital) 293
Djibouti 284, 295
Djibouti (Dijbouti, capital) 295
Dodoma (Tanzania, capital) 295
Dominica 284, 289
Dominican Republic 284, 289
Dublin (Ireland, capital) 296
Dushanbe (Tajikstan, capital) 292

E

East Timor 285, 293
Ecuador 284, 290
Egypt 285, 295
El Salvador 284, 289
Equatorial Guinea 284, 294
Eritrea 285, 295
Estonia 285, 297
Ethiopia 285, 295

F

Federated States of Micronesia 285, 298
Fiji 285, 298
Finland 285, 297
France 284, 296
Freetown (Guinea, capital) 294
French Guiana 284, 291
Funafuti (Tuvalu, capital) 298

G

Gabon 285, 294
Gaborone (Botswana, capital) 295
Gambia, The 284, 294
Georgetown (Guyana, capital) 291
Georgia 285, 292
Germany 285, 296
Ghana 284, 294
Godthab (Greenland, capital) 289
Greece 285, 297
Greenland 284, 289
Grenada 284, 289
Guatemala 284, 289
Guatemala City (Guatemala, capital) 289
Guinea 284, 294
Guinea-Bissau 284, 294
Guyana 284, 291

H

Haiti 284, 289
Hanoi (Vietnam, capital) 293
Harare (Zimbabwe, capital) 295
Havana (Cuba, capital) 289
Helsinki (Finland, capital) 297
Honduras 284, 289
Honiara (Solomon Islands, capital) 298
Hungary 285, 296–297

I

Iceland 284, 296
India 285, 292
Indonesia 285, 293
Iran 285, 292
Iraq 285, 292
Ireland 284, 296
Islamabad (Pakistan, capital) 292
Israel 285, 292
Italy 285, 296
Ivory Coast 284, 294

J

Jakarta (Indonesia, capital) 293
Jamaica 284, 289
Japan 285, 293
Jerusalem (Israel, capital) 292
Jordan 285, 292

K

Kabul (Afghanistan, capital) 292
Kampala (Uganda, capital) 295
Kathmandu (Nepal, capital) 292
Kazakhstan 285, 292
Kenya 285, 295
Khartoum (Sudan, capital) 295
Kiev (Ukraine, capital) 297
Kigali (Rwanda, capital) 295
Kingston (Jamaica, capital) 289
Kinshasa (Congo (Democratic Republic), capital) 294
Kiribati 285, 298–299
Koror (Palau, capital) 298
Kuala Lumpur (Malaysia, capital) 293
Kuwait 285, 292
Kyrgyzstan 285, 292

L
Laayoune (Western Sahara, capital) 294
Laos 285, 293
La Paz (Bolivia, capital) 290
Latvia 285, 297
Lebanon 285, 292
Lesotho 295
Liberia 284, 294
Libreville (Gabon, capital) 294
Libya 285, 294
Liechtenstein 296
Lilongwe (Malawi, capital) 295
Lima (Peru, capital) 290
Lisbon (Portugal, capital) 296
Lithuania 285, 297
Ljubljana (Slovenia, capital) 296
Lomé (Togo, capital) 294
London (United Kingdom, capital) 296
Luanda (Angola, capital) 294
Lusaka (Zambia, capital) 295
Luxembourg 296
Luxembourg (Luxembourg, capital) 284, 296

M
Macedonia 285, 297
Madagascar 285, 295
Madrid (Spain, capital) 296
Majuro (Marshall Islands, capital) 298
Malabo (Equatorial Guinea, capital) 294
Malawi 285, 295
Malaysia 285, 293
Maldives 285, 292
Male (Maldives, capital) 292
Mali 284, 294
Malta 296
Managua (Nicaragua, capital) 289
Manila (Philippines, capital) 293
Maputo (Mozambique, capital) 295
Marshall Islands 285, 298
Maseru (Lesotho, capital) 295
Mauritania 284, 294
Mauritius 285, 295
Mbabane (Swaziland, capital) 295
Mexico 284, 288–289
Mexico City (Mexico, capital) 288
Minsk (Belarus, capital) 297
Mogadishu (Somalia, capital) 295
Moldova 285, 297
Monaco 296
Mongolia 285, 293
Monrovia (Liberia, capital) 294
Montevideo (Uruguay, capital) 291
Morocco 284, 294
Moroni (Comoros, capital) 295
Moscow (Russia, capital) 292, 297
Mozambique 285, 295
Muscat (Oman, capital) 292

N
Nairobi (Kenya, capital) 295
Namibia 285, 294
Nassau (The Bahamas, capital) 289
Nauru 285, 298
Ndjamena (Chad, capital) 294
Nepal 285, 292
Netherlands 284, 296
New Delhi (India, capital) 292
New Zealand 285, 298
Niamey (Niger, capital) 294
Nicaragua 284, 289
Nicosia (Cyprus, capital) 292
Niger 284, 294
Nigeria 284, 294
North Korea 285, 293
Norway 284, 296–297
Nouakchott (Mauritania, capital) 294
Nukualofa (Tonga, capital) 299

O
Oman 285, 292
Oslo (Norway, capital) 296
Ottawa (Canada, capital) 289
Ouagadougou (Burkina Faso, capital) 294

P
Pakistan 285, 292
Palau 285, 298
Palikir (Federated States of Micronesia, capital) 298
Panama 284, 289
Panama City (Panama, capital) 289
Papua New Guinea 285, 298
Paraguay 284, 291
Paramaribo (Surinam, capital) 291
Paris (France, capital) 296
Peru 284, 290
Philippines 285, 293
Phnom Penh (Cambodia, capital) 293
Poland 285, 296–297
Port-au-Prince (Haiti, capital) 289
Port Louis (Mauritius, capital) 295
Port Moresby (Papua New Guinea, capital) 298
Port-of-Spain (Trinidad and Tobago, capital) 289
Porto-Novo (Benin, capital) 294
Portugal 284, 296
Port-Vila (Vanuatu, capital) 298
Prague (Czech Republic, capital) 296
Praia (Cape Verde, capital) 294
Pretoria (South Africa, capital) 295
Pyongyang (North Korea, capital) 293

Q
Qatar 285, 292
Quito (Ecuador, capital) 290

R
Rabat (Morocco, capital) 294
Rangoon (Burma/Myanmar, capital) 293
Reykjavik (Iceland, capital) 296
Riga (Latvia, capital) 297
Riyadh (Saudi Arabia, capital) 292
Romania 285, 297
Rome (Italy, capital) 296
Russia 285, 292–293, 297
Rwanda 285, 295

S
St. Kitts and Nevis 289
St. Lucia 289
St. Vincent and the Grenadines 289
Samoa 285, 299
Sana (Yemen, capital) 292
San Jose (Costa Rica, capital) 289
San Marino 296
San Salvador (El Salvador, capital) 289
Santiago (Chile, capital) 290
Santo Domingo (Dominican Republic, capital) 289
Sao Tome and Principe 284, 294
Sarajevo (Bosnia and Herzegovina, capital) 296
Saudi Arabia 285, 292
Senegal 284, 294
Seoul (South Korea, capital) 293
Serbia & Montenegro 285, 297
Seychelles 285, 295
Sierra Leone 284, 294
Singapore 285, 293
Skopje (Macedonia, capital) 297
Slovakia 285, 296–297
Slovenia 285, 296
Sofia (Bulgaria, capital) 297
Solomon Islands 285, 298
Somalia 285, 295
South Africa 285, 294–295
South Korea 285, 293
Spain 284, 296
Sri Jayewardenepura Kotte (Sri Lanka, capital) 292
Sri Lanka 285, 292
Stockholm (Sweden, capital) 296
Sudan 285, 295
Surinam 284, 291
Suva (Fiji, capital) 298
Swaziland 285, 295
Sweden 285, 296
Switzerland 284, 296
Syria 285, 292

T
Taipei (Taiwan, capital) 293
Taiwan 285, 293
Tajikistan 285, 292
Tallinn (Estonia, capital) 297
Tanzania 285, 295
Tashkent (Uzbekistan, capital) 292
Tbilisi (Georgia, capital) 292
Tegucigalpa (Honduras, capital) 289
Tehran (Iran, capital) 292
Thailand 285, 293
Tirana (Albania, capital) 296
Togo 284, 294
Tokyo (Japan, capital) 293
Tonga 285, 299
Trinidad and Tobago 284, 289
Tripoli (Libya, capital) 294
Tunis (Tunisia, capital) 294
Tunisia 284, 294
Turkey 285, 292
Turkmenistan 285, 292
Tuvalu 285, 298

U
Uganda 285, 295
Ukraine 285, 297
Ulan Bator (Mongolia, capital) 293
United Arab Emirates (U.A.E.) 285, 292
United Kingdom (U.K.) 284, 296
United States of America (U.S.A.) 284, 288–289
Uruguay 284, 291
Uzbekistan 285, 292

V
Vaduz (Liechtenstein, capital) 296
Valletta (Malta, capital) 296
Vanuatu 285, 298
Vatican City 296
Venezuela 284, 290
Victoria (Seychelles, capital) 295
Vienna (Austria, capital) 296
Vientiane (Laos, capital) 293
Vietnam 285, 293
Vilnius (Lithuania, capital) 297

W
Warsaw (Poland, capital) 297
Washington, DC (United States of America, capital) 289
Wellington (New Zealand, capital) 298
Western Sahara 284, 294
Windhoek (Namibia, capital) 294

Y
Yamoussoukro (Ivory Coast, capital) 294
Yaounde (Cameroon, capital) 294
Yaren (Nauru, capital) 298
Yemen 285, 292
Yerevan (Armenia, capital) 292

Z
Zagreb (Croatia, capital) 296
Zambia 285, 295
Zimbabwe 285, 295

Index

A

Aboriginals, 151, 173
acid, 105
acorns, 97
acting/actors, 123, 135, 174–175
adders, 29
addresses, website, 229
Africa, 13, 28, 30, 35, 38, 52, 58, 60, 124, 177, 294–295, 304, 308
aircraft, 15, 145
airfoils, 240
Aldrin, Edwin, 306
algae, 57, 92
aliens, 256, 257, 280
alligators, 70
ammonites, 18
amoebas, 57
amphibians, 59, 72–73
amplifiers, 222, 223
anacondas, 33
angelfish, 82
anglerfish, 91
animals *(see also individual names of animals)*, 8, 18, 19, 25, 27, 30, 31, 32, 34, 35, 43, 46, 47, 48, 49, 54, 55, 56, 57, 58–59, 60, 61, 62, 63, 64, 67, 70, 71, 74, 75, 78, 80, 81, 82, 83, 84, 85, 86, 88, 90, 91, 93, 94, 114, 116, 117, 118, 127, 137, 141, 148, 153, 164, 165, 182, 206, 207, 209, 227, 237, 308–309
  endangered, 49, 52
Antarctic, 42, 43
Antarctica, 51, 70, 255, 290, 299, 304
antelopes, 28, 31, 309
antennae
  on creep-crawlies, 75
  on mobile phones, 225
  on Sojouner robot, 267
  for TVs, 221
Apollo Moon landings, 260, 261, 306
apples, 97, 129, 193
arachnids, 75
arches, 41
Arctic, 42, 43, 51, 283, 292, 296, 297
armadillos, 33
armies, 124
Armstrong, Neil, 148, 306
arrows, 117, 166
art, 150, 172–173
Asia, 17, 35, 38, 153, 292–293, 297, 304, 305
Asteroid Belt, 258, 268, 274, 280
asteroids, 272, 274, 280
astronauts, 198, 246, 248, 249, 250, 251, 252, 253, 261, 280
astronomers, 185, 256, 267, 272, 273, 276, 277
Athens, Greece, 122
athletes/athletics, 123, 169
atmosphere, 9, 50, 51, 249, 254, 255, 259, 264, 265, 266, 268, 269, 272, 274, 280
atoms, 186–187, 191, 204, 212, 231
Australia, 35, 38, 75, 151, 166, 173, 298, 299, 308, 309
Austria, 144
axes, 117
axolotls, 72

B

babies
  animal, 54, 58, 60, 62–63, 65, 68, 69, 71, 73, 88
  dinosaur, 114
  human, 102, 108–109, 151
baboons, 30
bacteria, 57, 105
Bali, 175
ballet, 175
balloons, 200, 201
  hot-air, 196
bands (music), 167, 177
bark (of trees), 96, 173
barley, 118
barnacles, 79, 87
Barnard, Christiaan, 148
barramundi, 173
baseball, 167, 168
baths, 125, 153
bats, 45, 61, 308
batteries, 193, 225, 244
battles, 144
Bayeux Tapestry, 275
beaches, 39, 40, 41
beaks, 64, 65, 66–67, 83
beans, 95, 110, 131, 136, 137
bears
  black, 45
  brown, 45
  polar, 43, 58, 63
beef, 129
bees, 74, 93
beetles, 55, 308
Beijing, China, 132
Belgium, 144
Berlin, Germany, 147
berries, 94, 116
binoculars, 246
birds *(see also individual names of birds)*, 20, 25, 43, 52, 54, 58, 64–65, 66–67, 68–69, 70, 77, 94, 114, 116, 193, 308, 309
bison, 45, 116
blennies, 78
Blitz, 146
blood, 43, 100, 101, 105
blowholes, 86
boats, 47, 126, 201, 203, 242–243
bodies, 56, 59, 60, 64, 66–67, 70, 72, 74, 75, 77, 78, 86, 90, 91, 93, 193, 203
  human, 100–101, 102, 103, 104, 105, 106, 108, 109, 110, 111, 112, 121, 176, 183, 187, 211, 251, 308
boiling, 190, 251
bombs, 146, 147, 262
bone(s), 19, 39, 56, 61, 64, 102–103, 112, 119, 127, 183
books, 166, 171, 178, 179, 219
Botswana, 152
bow (of a ship), 243
Braille writing, 107
brains, 100, 106–107, 182
  computer, 226
brakes, 235
Brazil, 191, 290, 291, 305
breaching (in whales), 87
bread, 98, 110, 118, 137, 158
breathing, 59, 61, 72, 73, 81, 86, 87, 88, 100, 244, 250, 251, 259
bricks, 119, 132, 152, 163
bridges, 131, 197
Britain, 124, 126, 137, 142, 144, 145, 146, 148, 157, 297, 305
brittle stars, 82
broadcasting, 221
bromeliads, 33
bronze, 127, 169
brooches, 127
browsers, 229
Buddhism, 178
bullets, 144
buses, 30, 52
butter, 187
buttercups, 54
butterfish, 78
butterflies, 32, 76–77
buttons, 216, 223, 237, 239

C

cables, 210, 211, 224, 225, 228
cactuses, 29
caimans, 33
cakes, 129
Cambodia, 25
camels, 28, 29, 58
cameras, 174, 216–217, 250, 254, 255
  digital, 217
  infrared, 196
  TV, 267
  video, 193
Canada, 26, 65, 288, 289, 300, 305
canyons, 265, 266, 267
capybaras, 33
carbon, 187
carbon dioxide, 92, 189, 265
Caribbean, 288
cars, 48, 50, 52, 153, 155, 173, 193, 203, 227, 234–235, 261
cartilage, 102
carving, 126, 127
castles, 128–129
caterpillars, 77
cats, 62
cattle, 141
caves, 41, 44–45, 116, 117, 305
CDs/compact discs, 148, 222, 223, 226
cells, 56–57, 101, 105, 106, 107, 108, 109
cement, 191
centipedes, 59, 75
Central America, 282, 289
cereals, 110
chainmail, 129

Channel Tunnel, 148
chariot races, 125
cheese, 98, 110
cheetahs, 31, 55, 309
chemicals, 48, 93, 97, 104, 105, 165, 183, 191, 212, 217
chemistry, 187
children, 111, 134, 143, 146, 150, 159, 163, 166, 167, 193
chimneys, 142
chimpanzees, 52, 60
China, 44, 132–133, 150, 158, 159, 171, 180, 293, 304, 305, 309
chopsticks, 159
Christianity, 178
churches, 134

cisterns, 233
cities, 122, 124, 130, 131, 132, 146, 147, 154–155, 169, 172, 260, 279, 283
clams, 83, 309
claws, 66, 115
clay, 47, 118, 159, 172
cliffs, 40, 41, 65
climates, 161, 304
Clinton, Bill, 156
clocks, 214–215
clones, 148
cloth, 118, 127, 133, 140, 142
clothes, 15, 45, 46, 127, 135, 139, 160–161, 162, 174
clouds, 8, 11, 14, 15, 16, 189, 210, 265, 266
coaches, 133
coal, 46, 47, 50, 51, 142, 143, 210
coasts, 21, 34, 36, 40–41,
cobwebs, 68
cockpits, 241
coconuts, 38
code, 222
coffins, 121
coins, 134
cold-blooded, 70, 71
colleges, 167
Cologne, Germany, 146
color(s), 15, 46, 76, 93, 97, 150, 173, 186, 206–207, 220, 282, 307
combs, 127
comets, 185, 247, 258, 270, 273, 274, 275, 278, 280
communicating, 170–171, 174, 243
compasses, 204, 282
competitions, 123
computer games, 148
computers, 103, 148, 162, 167, 168, 171, 173, 210, 217, 224, 226–227, 228, 229, 255, 265
Concorde, 148, 240
concrete, 191
condensing, 190, 230
cones, 92
conifers, 27, 92
constellations, 279, 307
contests, 129
continents, 8, 284, 292, 294, 295, 297, 298, 304
control panels, 241
cooking, 46, 118, 153, 158–159, 162
copper, 119
coral reefs, 80, 82–83
corals, 82, 83
corn, 131, 136, 137, 158
corsets, 143
costumes, 123
cotton, 46
countries, 8, 13, 122, 137, 144, 146, 147, 151, 152, 156–157, 158, 161, 163, 166, 178, 180, 283, 284, 288, 289, 290, 291, 293, 295, 297, 299, 304
cowboys, 141
cows, 118, 119, 141, 165
CPU/central processing unit, 226, 227
crabs, 78, 79, 116
crafts, 127
craters
  in volcanoes, 22
  made by meteoroids, 274
  on planets, 264, 280
  on the Moon, 260, 280, 306
creepy-crawlies, 59, 74–75
crinoids, 91
crinolines, 143
crocodiles, 70, 173, 308
crops, 119, 164, 165, 175
currents, 38
cuttlefish, 39
Cuzco, Peru, 130

D

daggers, 124
dancing, 111, 123, 174–175, 177
day(time), 9, 10–11, 28
Dead Sea, 201
deciduous trees, 97
deer, 60, 116, 137
democracy, 156, 157
Denmark, 126
density, 200, 201, 212
dermis, 101
deserts, 28–29, 120, 140, 161, 266, 286, 289, 291, 293, 295, 297, 299
  Kalahari, 152
  Sahara, 28, 295
desserts, 129
developing (photos), 217
digestion, 100, 104, 105, 159
diggers, 195, 236
dinosaurs, 114–115, 276
disks, hard, 226, 227
diving, 34, 84, 87
doctors, 112, 148
dog whelks, 79
dogfish, 39
dogs, 209
dolphins, 59, 80, 85, 88–89, 203, 309
dragonflies, 74
dragons, 126, 180
drainpipes, 232
duck-billed platypuses, 61
dungeons, 128
DVDs, 174, 205

E

eagles, 27, 65, 66
ears, 107, 208
earthquakes, 17, 20–21, 180
echoes, 89
eclipse, 11
eels, 82, 90
eggs, 39, 47, 54, 58, 61, 68, 69, 70, 71, 72, 73, 76, 77, 110, 116, 132, 158, 165, 185, 187
  dinosaur, 114
  human, 108, 109
Egypt, 124, 295, 305
  Ancient, 120, 171
Egyptians (Ancient), 120–121
Eiffel Tower, 305
elections, 157
electricity, 16, 17, 47, 50, 52, 192, 193, 195, 206, 210–211, 212, 220, 223, 224, 238, 253, 261
elephants, 30, 63, 86, 115, 133, 209, 308
emails, 170, 217, 228
emoticons, 170
emperors, 157
  Inca, 130
  Ming, 132, 133
energy, 37, 51, 52, 54, 76, 84, 87, 92, 104, 105, 192–193, 195, 196, 203, 206, 208, 210, 211, 212, 253
engines, 46, 234, 235, 237, 238, 240, 242, 243, 244, 248, 280
England, 134–135, 136
environments, 286–287
epidermis, 101
Equator, 13, 32, 283, 290, 292, 294
Euphorbia, 28
Europe, 13, 35, 38, 126, 128, 134, 138, 139, 146, 147, 148, 296–297, 304, 305
Europeans, 137, 140
evaporation, 230
evergreen trees, 96, 97
exams, 167
exercise, 105, 111, 125, 253
experiments, 182, 184, 185, 212
explorers, 134, 140
eyes, 77, 85, 90, 91, 107, 141, 150, 207, 212, 246, 278, 308

F

factories, 48, 142, 143, 162, 227
falcons, 29, 309
fall, 12, 13, 97, 182
families, 69, 125, 128, 129, 132, 134, 138, 140, 141, 143, 153, 157, 162, 164, 166
farmers/farming, 48, 50, 118–119, 120, 130, 131, 141, 162, 164–165, 166, 209, 237
  organic, 165
farmland, 31, 140
farms, 48, 164
fashions, 139, 143, 160–161
fat, 105, 110
faucets, 233
feasts, 129, 136, 137, 159
feathers, 58, 64, 65, 68, 182
feather stars, 83
feelers, 75, 78
ferns, 33, 92
festivals, 123, 130, 159, 176
fields, magnetic, 204
film, 216, 217, 218
films (movies), 174, 257
fins, 78, 81, 85

fire, 127, 147, 159
fireworks, 132
First World War, 144–145
fish *(see also individual names of fish)*, 24, 43, 47, 49, 54, 59, 64, 66, 67, 72, 81, 82, 83, 84, 85, 86, 89, 90, 91, 110, 116, 136, 173
fishing, 24, 47, 116
flags, 135, 147, 193, 261, 300–301
flashlight fish, 91
fleas, 145
flies, 55
flight decks, 249
flint, 117
floating, 42, 56, 79, 94, 101, 185, 196, 198, 200–201, 205, 212, 242, 253, 269, 280
floods, 16–17, 51, 152, 267
flour, 118
flowers *(see also individual names of flowers)*, 27, 55, 76, 92, 93, 95, 97, 309
fluking (in whales), 87
flying, 58, 59, 61, 64, 65, 66, 76, 77, 115, 123, 148, 193, 226, 240, 241, 248, 308
food, 39, 43, 46, 52, 54, 60, 65, 66, 67, 69, 75, 79, 82, 91, 114, 115, 184
  for humans, 100, 101, 104–105, 108, 110, 116, 118, 120, 128, 129, 131, 134, 140, 146, 153, 158–159, 162, 164, 165, 166, 193, 196, 208, 230, 231
  for plants, 92, 93, 94, 95, 97, 98, 192
Forbidden City (in Beijing, China), 132
forces, 194–195, 198, 199, 202, 204, 212, 280
forests, 16, 50, 60, 67, 70
  of seaweed, 34
fossils, 18–19
fountains, 138
foxes, 29
foxgloves, 95
frames (in movies), 218, 219
France, 124, 126, 138–139, 144, 145, 148, 151, 172, 238, 305
freezing, 15, 42, 43, 190, 251, 260
French Revolution, 139
friction, 202–203, 212
frogs, 32, 59, 72, 73
frosts, 266
fruit(s), 67, 94, 95, 97, 98, 105, 110, 131, 158, 165
fuel(s), 46, 50, 51, 210, 234, 235, 248, 263, 280
fungi, 98

G

Gagarin, Yuri, 148
Galapagos Islands, 309
galaxies, 185, 247, 276–277, 280
Gambia, 177
games, 89, 168–169
  computer, 148, 226
  Olympic, 123
gardens, 125, 132, 137
gas(es) *(see also individual names of gases)*, 9, 14, 22, 46, 47, 50, 54, 92, 100, 142, 145, 187, 188–189, 190, 201, 210, 230, 246, 247, 258, 259, 262, 263, 264, 265, 266, 268, 270, 271, 272, 275, 280, 307
  greenhouse, 50
Gauguin, Paul, 172
geese, 64, 65
generators, 210
genes, 109
Germany, 144, 145, 146, 147, 171
germs, 101, 110, 159, 308, 309
gills, 72, 81
giraffes, 31, 62, 227
Giza, Egypt, 120
glaciers, 27, 42, 297
gladiators, 125
glands, 60
glass, 46, 52, 128, 187, 207, 212, 218
global warming, 50
Globe playhouse, 135
glow worms, 206
goats, 29, 139, 165
goddesses, 118, 122, 180
gods, 122, 123, 175, 178, 179, 180
gold, 120, 127, 141, 169, 186, 188
Gold Rush, 141
governments, 52, 156, 157
grain(s), 110, 118
Grand Canyon, 18, 19
grass, 30, 31, 141, 152, 237
grasslands, 30–31
gravity, 182, 194, 198–199, 212, 253, 261, 270, 276, 280
Greece (Ancient), 122–123, 169
Greeks (Ancient), 123
Greenland, 126, 288, 289, 305
grinding, 118, 137
guinea pigs, 33, 131
gunpowder, 132
guns, 145
Gutenberg, Johannes, 171

H

hair, 58, 68, 86, 101, 139, 150, 160, 162, 165
hammers, 130, 193
hares, 27
harvest, 136, 164
hatchetfish, 90, 91
hatching, 68, 69, 72, 73, 77, 114
hats, 161, 162
hay, 237
headlands, 41
heart, 100, 101, 103, 111, 148
heat(ing), 9, 14, 18, 22, 29, 46, 47, 50, 55, 70, 76, 77, 107, 125, 187, 190, 192, 193, 196–197, 203, 210, 212, 230, 231, 232, 250, 253, 259, 262, 265, 275
helmets, 124, 250, 251
hens, 165
herons, 65, 67
hieroglyphs, 121
Hinduism, 179
Hitler, Adolf, 147
holly, 97
Holocaust, 147
honey cakes, 129
Hong Kong, China, 158
hoopoes, 69
horn, 127
horses, 116, 129, 139, 218
hospitals, 154
houses, 8, 20, 22, 37, 96, 119, 125, 127, 136, 142, 152–153, 154, 163, 224, 225, 232, 269
hull (of a ship), 243
human(s), 56, 60, 63, 84, 101, 102, 103, 139, 150, 183, 308
hummingbirds, 32, 93, 308
hunting, 49, 52, 62, 63, 64, 66, 67, 70, 79, 80, 81, 84, 90, 91, 114, 116, 117, 166, 279
hurricanes, 15, 16
hydrogen, 186, 187
hyenas, 30

I

ibises, 33, 67
ice, 15, 17, 27, 42, 43, 51, 185, 189, 190, 247, 257, 259, 263, 266, 269, 271, 272, 275, 297
ice hockey, 168
icebergs, 42
icefish, 43
Iceland, 23, 126
ICT, 167
iguanas, 71
Incas, 130–131
India, 70, 151, 159, 161, 176, 178, 293, 304
insects *(see also individual names of insects)*, 59, 69, 70, 74, 75, 76, 93, 308
instruments (musical), 129, 167, 176, 177, 209
Internet, 148, 166, 170, 228–229
inventions, 148, 182, 183, 212
iron, 124, 186, 191, 200, 201, 204, 205
Islam, 179
islands, 23, 35, 51, 147, 289, 291, 293, 297, 298, 299, 305, 309
Israel, 201
Italy, 124, 126

J

jaguars, 32
Japan, 146, 147, 148, 160, 161, 239, 292, 293, 305
jars, 121, 133, 189
jazz, 177
jellyfish, 59
jerboas, 28
jesters, 129
Jews, 147, 179
joints, 102, 197
jokes, 129
jousts, 129
Judaism, 179
jumbo jets, 148

K

kangaroos, 28, 63, 299
keel (of a ship), 243
Kenya, 170
keyboards, 226, 227
kimonos, 161
kingfishers, 64, 296
kings, 120, 128, 134, 138, 139, 157
  Henry VIII, 134
  Louis XIV, 138
knights, 129
knives, 117, 159
Kpelle tribe, 166
Kuiper Belt, 258, 259, 273

L

laboratories, 167, 186, 252
lacquer, 133
lakes, 14, 155, 191, 201, 232, 283, 289, 291, 293, 295, 297, 299, 305
lamps, 142, 206
lances, 129
languages, 151, 170
lanternfish, 91
Lascaux, France, 117
lasers, 222, 267
latitude, 283
lava, 22, 23, 35
laws, 52, 156, 179
leather, 47, 141, 165
leaves, 12, 15, 27, 55, 68, 75, 77, 92, 93, 95, 96–97, 173, 182, 207, 208
  dandelion, 116
  laurel, 169
  tea, 133
leopards, 49
levers, 215, 236, 239
lianas, 33
Liberia, 166
libraries, 171
lice, 145
lichen, 32, 68
life cycles, 95
lifeboats, 242
light(s), 9, 11, 33, 52, 55, 76, 79, 91, 107, 170, 173, 174, 192, 206–207, 210, 212, 216, 217, 218, 219, 222, 230, 244, 250, 261, 262, 278, 279
lightning, 16, 17, 210
limpets, 79
lions, 30, 58, 62, 295
liquids, 23, 76, 93, 101, 105, 108, 188–189, 190, 208, 230, 235, 263
lizards, 58, 70, 73, 116
llamas, 131
lobsters, 59
logs, 127
London, UK, 135, 172, 260
longitude, 283
looms, 127
lords, 128, 129
lunar modules, 261
lungs, 100, 111

M

macaws, 33, 182, 309
machines, 46, 47, 164, 165, 171, 183, 192, 195, 210, 212, 216, 226, 228, 229, 236, 237, 244
Machu Picchu, Peru, 130
mackerel, 129
magic, 117
magnets, 194, 204–205, 212, 239
maize, 158
makeup, 174
Malaysia, 35
mammals, 58, 59, 60–61, 86, 308, 309
  baby, 62–63, 88
Mandela, Nelson, 157
maps, 282–298, 307
marble, 122
markets, 131, 158, 165
marsupials, 63, 299
Masai, 161, 170
masks, 120, 123, 145, 174
materials, 187, 188, 189, 190–191, 196, 205, 212
Mayflower, 136
meanders, 25
meat, 47, 67, 70, 110, 115, 116, 117, 119, 131, 159, 165
medals, 169
medicine(s), 46, 98, 112, 133, 183
melting, 17, 24, 27, 35, 42, 51, 187, 190, 275, 280
messages, 131, 174, 227, 228, 254
  text, 170
metal, 9, 47, 52, 119, 129, 159, 172, 187, 203, 204, 205, 211, 212, 214, 231, 236, 237, 238, 242, 264, 274, 280
meteorites, 253, 264, 280
meteoroids, 250, 274, 280
meteors, 274, 280
Mexico, 65, 288
Mexico City, Mexico, 155
mice, 62
microchips, 148
microphones, 251
microscopes, 56, 57, 98
microwaves, 231
Middle Ages, 128, 129
Middle East, 118
migration, 65
Milan, Italy, 160
milk, 47, 58, 60, 63, 107, 110, 119, 165
Milky Way, 247, 276, 277, 278, 279
millipedes, 75
minerals, 92, 93
mines, 47, 143, 309
Ming times (in China), 132–133
minstrels, 129
mirrors, 138, 206, 222
mists, 266, 270, 273
moats, 132
modems, 229
mold, 98
molecules, 186–187, 188, 191, 196, 208, 210, 212
money, 156, 162
monitors, 226, 227
monkeys, 32, 33, 67
monks, 178
monsoon, 17
Moon/moons, 11, 148, 198, 199, 207, 246, 247, 257, 258, 260–261, 268, 269, 270, 271, 272, 274, 278, 280, 306
Moore, Henry, 172
moorhens, 69
Morocco, 161
mosaics, 125
mosses, 68, 92, 98, 257
motorcycles, 162, 234–235
motors, 205
mountains, 14, 24, 26–27, 42, 131, 140, 166, 180, 283, 286, 289, 291, 292, 293, 295, 297, 299, 304
  Andes, 130, 291, 305
  Caucasus, 305
  Himalayas, 293
  on Venus, 265
  Rocky, 26, 289
  under sea, 34, 35
  Urals, 296
mouse (computer), 226
mouth (of a river), 25
movies, 173, 174, 218–219
mummies, 121
muscles, 56, 64, 81, 102–103, 104, 105, 111
museums, 154
mushrooms, 98, 116
music, 167, 174, 175, 176–177, 184, 209, 222
musicians, 123, 129, 177
Muslims, 159, 179
mussels, 78
myths, 180

N

Native Americans, 136, 137, 140, 141
necklaces, 161
nectar, 76, 93
negatives, 217
Nepal, 166, 293, 304
nerves, 107
nests, 27, 61, 62, 65, 66, 68–69
nets (fishing), 49, 67
networks, 228
neurons, 106, 107
New Guinea, 299, 305
New Orleans, USA, 177
New York, USA, 154, 160
New Zealand, 298, 299
night, 9, 10–11, 28, 71, 185, 260, 270, 278–279
nitrogen, 272
nomads, 153
North America, 31, 35, 38, 126, 134, 136–137, 140, 288–289, 304, 305
North Pole, 13, 42, 204, 262, 283, 307
northern hemisphere, 13
Norway, 126, 297
noses, 107
numbers, 167, 214, 224, 225, 283
nuts, 94, 110, 116, 158

O

oars, 243
oases, 28
observatories, 130
Oceania, 298–299, 304
oceans, 17, 21, 34–35, 36, 38, 51, 59, 80, 84, 86, 88, 91, 180, 244, 304
  Arctic, 35, 304
  Atlantic, 35, 296, 304, 305
  Indian, 35, 304, 305
  Pacific, 35, 147, 298, 304, 305
  Southern, 35, 304
offerings, 118

offices, 162
oil, 34, 46, 47, 48, 50, 51, 236
Olympia, Greece, 123, 169
Olympic Games, 123, 169
Oort Cloud, 273
orbits/orbiting, 199, 249, 255, 256, 260, 261, 269, 271, 273, 278, 280
orchestras, 167, 177
orchids, 32
organic farming, 165
organs (of body), 100, 102, 106
ostriches, 30, 308
ovens, microwave, 231
overfishing, 49
owls, 62
oxen, 140
oxygen, 54, 81, 92, 95, 100, 101, 108, 186, 191

P

paella, 159
paintings, 121, 123, 134, 138, 172–173, 255
  cave, 45, 117
palaces, 130, 132, 138
pandas, 292
Papua New Guinea, 298, 299, 304
Paralympics, 169
Paris, France, 138, 160, 305
parks, 154
parrotfish, 83
Pearl Harbor, 147
pelicans, 67
penguins, 54, 184
peppers, 131
pests, 81, 165
pharaohs, 120
photos, 173, 183, 216, 217, 218, 306
photosynthesis, 92
pictures, 121, 125, 129, 133, 170, 171, 216, 217, 218, 219, 220, 221, 226, 227, 254, 255, 256
pies, 129, 137
pigs, 116
Pilgrims, 136
pillars, 122
pilots, 241, 244, 249
Pioneer (space probe), 256
pioneers, 140
pirates, 134
pistons, 234, 235, 236
pitch, 209, 212
pixels, 217
plains, 30, 141
planes, 145, 147, 148, 203, 208, 240–241, 249
planets, 8, 28, 34, 50, 52, 54, 182, 185, 198, 199, 204, 206, 246, 247, 255, 256, 258, 259, 261, 262, 263, 264, 265, 266, 267, 268, 269, 270, 271, 272, 273, 274, 278, 280, 306
  Earth, 8, 9, 10, 11, 12, 13, 16, 18, 22, 26, 30, 34, 35, 42, 46–47, 50, 54, 70, 86, 114, 150, 198, 199, 203, 204, 206, 221, 248, 249, 251, 252, 253, 254, 255, 256, 257, 258, 259, 260, 261, 262, 263, 264, 266, 267, 268, 269, 270, 271, 274, 275, 276, 280, 282, 283, 304–305, 306, 307
  Jupiter, 198, 247, 257, 258, 259, 268, 274, 275, 306
  Mars, 198, 257, 259, 263, 266–267, 274, 306
  Mercury, 198, 264–265, 269, 306
  Neptune, 246, 247, 255, 258, 270–271, 272, 273, 306
  Pluto, 255, 259, 272–273, 306
  Saturn, 247, 258, 259, 268, 269, 306
  Uranus, 246, 258, 259, 270–271, 272, 306
  Venus, 199, 259, 263, 264–265, 306
plants *(see also individual names of plants)*, 8, 12, 18, 27, 28, 29, 32, 33, 38, 43, 46, 48, 54, 55, 56, 57, 68, 69, 76, 77, 78, 82, 90, 92–93, 94–95, 96, 114, 115, 116, 118, 133, 183, 184, 192, 283, 308–309
plasma, 101
plastic, 46, 52, 187, 190, 211, 212, 216
platelets, 101
playhouses, 135
plays, 122, 123, 135, 174
playwrights, 174
plugs, 224, 234
poison, 77, 80, 82, 98, 145, 266
Poland, 146
polar regions, 42, 43, 51
  on Mars, 266
poles, magnetic, 204, 212
police, 142, 162
pollen, 93
pollution, 48, 52
polyps, 82
Pope, 134
poppies, 144
porcelain, 133
potatoes, 131, 134, 158
pots, 118
pottery, 133
pouches, 63, 299
power, 47, 192, 212, 214, 224, 225, 237, 238, 243, 244, 267
power stations, 50, 210
  nuclear, 148
prairies, 31
presidents, 137, 156, 157
printing, 171
prisms, 207
prisoners, 128
programs
  computer, 227, 229
  radio, 223
  TV, 220, 221
projectors, 218, 219
propellers, 242, 243, 244
pterosaurs, 115
Puerto Rico, 256
puffins, 66
pulse, 101
pumpkins, 136, 137
pupae, 77
pylons, 210
pyramids of Egypt, 120
pythons, 70

Q

quarries, 47
queens, 134, 139, 157
  Elizabeth I, 135
  Victoria, 142

R

raccoons, 288
radar, 243
radio(s), 221, 222, 223, 225, 239, 253, 277
raids, 126
rain, 14, 15, 16, 17, 24, 28, 29, 31, 32, 44, 125, 135, 153, 189, 190, 191, 207, 304
rainbows, 15, 207
rainforests, 32–33, 48, 49, 72, 75, 161
  Amazon, 32
Ramadan, 159
rats, 145
rattlesnakes, 208
reactions, 191, 212
reading, 166, 167, 171, 179
recycling, 52
reflection, 206, 207, 216
refrigerators, 205, 230
religions, 151, 159, 177, 178–179
reptiles, 58, 70–71, 72, 114, 115, 308, 309
reservoirs, 232
restaurants, 154
rhinos, 30, 49, 309
rice, 110, 132, 158, 164
riverbanks, 24, 61, 70
rivers, 14, 17, 24–25, 38, 67, 120, 126, 131, 140, 189, 283, 289, 291, 293, 295, 297, 299, 305
  Amazon, 32, 291, 305
  Colorado, 19
  Nile, 120, 295, 305
  of ice, 27
  of liquid rock, 23
  Thames, 172
roads, 124, 131, 155, 156
robots, 183, 212, 227, 249, 267
rock(s), 9, 18–19, 20, 22, 23, 24, 25, 26, 27, 34, 35, 40, 41, 44, 45, 78, 79, 173, 187, 191, 238, 247, 257, 258, 259, 260, 261, 264, 266, 267, 269, 270, 272, 273, 274, 280, 306
  igneous, 18
  sedimentary, 18, 19
rockets, 148, 208, 226, 246, 248, 280
rocklings, 78
rollercoasters, 193
Roman Empire, 124
Romans (Ancient), 124, 125, 180, 261
Rome (Ancient), 124–125
roofs, 122, 127, 135, 136, 152, 153, 163
roots, 29, 33, 38, 92, 93, 95, 96, 101, 308
ruins, 122, 130, 146
running, 64, 169, 193
Russia, 31, 144, 147, 292, 293, 297, 304, 305

S

sailors, 126, 307
sails, 243
salamanders, 73
saliva, 104
salt, 185, 187, 201, 309
sand, 18, 25, 28, 29, 40, 46, 187, 191
sand dollars, 19

sand dunes, 29
sandgrouse, 28
saris, 161
satellites, 221, 228, 249, 250, 254–255, 280
saxifrage, 27
schools, 21, 143, 154, 155, 156, 162, 163, 166–167
of dolphins, 88
science, 180, 182–212
scientists, 43, 50, 56, 57, 84, 150, 182, 183, 184–185, 186, 187, 194, 207, 209, 239, 247, 252, 254, 257, 267, 275
scissors, 195
screens, 219, 220, 227
scribes, 171
sculptures, 172, 173
sea(s), 10, 14, 16, 18, 19, 21, 23, 24, 25, 34–35, 36, 37, 38, 39, 40, 41, 42, 46, 47, 48, 51, 61, 66, 71, 80, 82, 85, 88, 89, 90–91, 115, 126, 180, 189, 201, 228, 242, 257, 304, 307, 309
of the Moon, 260, 306
Mediterranean, 124, 294, 296, 304, 305
sea anemones, 59, 79, 83
sea fans, 82
sea lemons, 79
sea scorpions, 79
sea slugs, 80
sea urchins, 79, 82
seabed, 21, 34, 35, 36, 46, 49
seagulls, 37, 39
seals, 43, 59
seashore, 36, 38, 67, 78–79
seasons, 12–13, 116
seaweed, 34, 39, 78, 79
Second World War, 146–147, 148
sediment, 18, 19
seedlings, 95
seeds, 38, 92, 93, 94, 95, 97, 98, 118
senses/sensitivity, 55, 106–107, 207
servants, 128, 132, 138
servers, 228, 229
settlers, 136, 137
shadows, 11, 76, 206
Shakespeare, William, 135, 174
sharks, 80, 84–85
sheep, 29, 118, 148, 165
shellfish, 116
shells, 19, 40, 71, 75, 78, 79, 83
shields, 124, 129
ships, 21, 37, 48, 126, 134, 135, 136, 145, 147, 201, 242–243
cruise, 201, 242–243
shoots, 95, 164
shrimp, 67, 78
shrubs, 52
sickles, 119
Sikhism, 179
silk, 133, 139
silver, 127, 169
SIM cards, 225
singing, 129, 176, 177
sinking, 18, 37, 155, 200, 242, 244
skeletons, 78, 82, 102, 103
skin(s), 43, 49, 56, 58, 59, 61, 70, 71, 72, 73, 77, 78, 81, 87, 101, 105, 107, 114, 116, 119, 150, 151, 179, 230
skulls, 102, 106
sky, 9, 11, 14, 16, 22, 185, 241, 256, 262, 266, 270, 274, 278–279, 307
sleeping, 111, 127, 152, 153, 249, 253
sloths, 33
smileys, 170
smoke, 127, 142
snails, 54, 59, 75, 116
snakes *(see also individual names of snakes)*, 33, 70, 180, 309
snapdragons, 95
snow, 14, 16, 17, 24, 26, 27, 42, 43, 152, 180, 194, 202, 293
snowboarding, 202
snowflakes, 15
snowline, 26
soccer, 132, 168
soil, 17, 48, 92, 96, 164, 195
solar panels, 47, 253, 254, 267
solar systems, 247, 256, 258–259, 260, 267, 268, 269, 271, 272, 273, 274, 275, 276, 280, 306
soldiers, 124, 128, 129, 131, 144, 145, 147
solids, 186, 188–189, 190, 208
sonar, 89
songs, 123
sound, 89, 107, 148, 171, 176, 192, 208–209, 222, 223, 256
sound systems, 222–223
source (of a river), 24
South Africa, 156, 157, 295
South America, 13, 32, 35, 38, 130, 134, 282, 288, 290–291, 304, 308, 309
South Pole, 13, 42, 204, 262, 283, 307
southern hemisphere, 13
space, 9, 34, 50, 148, 185, 198, 199, 212, 221, 228, 246–280, 291, 306–307
space probes, 254–255, 256, 257, 265, 266, 267, 268, 271, 272, 275, 280
space shuttles, 148, 203, 248–249, 250, 251, 252
space stations, 249, 250, 252–253, 280
spacecraft, 8, 246, 250, 253, 261, 266, 278, 280, 306
spaceships, 250, 251, 254, 260, 261, 280
spacesuits, 246, 248, 249, 250, 280
Spain, 124, 126, 134, 135, 159
Spanish Armada, 135
spawn, 73
speakers
on sound systems, 222, 223
on telephones, 224
spears, 117, 124, 129
sperm, 108, 109
spiders, 59, 75
spinning, 118
sponges, 82
spoons, 127
spores, 98
sports, 167, 168–169
spouting (in whales), 86
spring (season), 12, 13, 45, 136, 176
springs, 214, 215,
spy hopping, 89
squash (food), 131, 137
squid, 87, 90, 308
squirrels, 94, 129
stacks, 41
stalactites, 45
stalagmites, 45
starfish, 79, 91
stars, 130, 185, 198, 246, 247, 256, 262, 276, 277, 278, 279, 280, 307
shooting, 274, 278, 280
static, 211
stations
radio, 223
sewage, 232
TV, 221
statues, 118, 138
steam, 23
stems, 29, 33, 92, 93, 96
steppes, 31
stern (of a ship), 242
stockings, 139
stomachs, 82, 100, 104, 105
stores, 154, 155, 160, 164
stories, 171, 173, 174, 175, 180
storms, 16–17, 37, 210, 266, 268, 271
straw, 119, 127, 135
streamlining, 203
streams, 24, 27, 119, 141
submarines, 145, 244
submersibles, 244
sugar, 92, 110
summer, 12, 13, 17, 42, 116
sun/Sun, 8, 9, 10, 11, 13, 14, 15, 28, 47, 50, 54, 55, 71, 76, 92, 152, 153, 161, 192, 197, 199, 206, 207, 246, 247, 251, 253, 254, 255, 258, 259, 260, 261, 262–263, 264, 265, 271, 272, 273, 274, 275, 276, 278, 280, 306, 307
sunflowers, 55, 165
sunlight, 10, 11, 13, 15, 54, 97, 207, 251, 263, 267
sunrise, 10
sunset, 10
Surtsey, Iceland, 23
swallows, 68
swans, 69
Sweden, 126
swimming, 64, 66, 71, 72, 73, 81, 84, 85, 88, 89, 90, 91, 103, 108, 111, 115, 309
swords, 124

T

tadpoles, 73
Tahiti, 172
tailor birds, 68
tamarins, golden lion, 49
tanks, 145
tea, 133
teapots, 133
technology, 183, 212
teeth, 80, 83, 84, 85, 104, 110, 115
inside clocks, 215
on diggers, 236

telephones, 170, 224–225, 228, 229, 254
mobile, 148, 170, 182, 225
telescopes, 185, 246, 249, 256, 270, 278
Hubble Space, 148
radio, 277
televisions, 148, 170, 210, 220–221, 254
satellite, 221
temperatures, 50, 60, 71, 190, 197, 212, 251, 255, 262, 263, 304, 307
temples, 122, 130, 132
tentacles, 82, 90
tents, 116, 152, 153
termites, 30
terns, Arctic, 58
terraces, 131
tests, 167, 184, 199, 212
Texas, USA, 173
Thailand, 164, 308
Thanksgiving, 136
theatres, 174
thermometers, 190, 197
thrushes, 54
thunder, 16, 208
Tibet, 160
tide pools, 78
tides, 39, 78
tits, 68
toads, 72, 73
toadstools, 98
toilets, 105, 110, 125, 127, 142, 232–233, 253
tomatoes, 131
tombs, 120
tongues, 79, 107
tools, 67, 117, 119, 140, 185, 237
tornadoes, 16
tortoises, 71
Galapagos giant, 309
toucans, 33, 67, 290
tourists, 30, 31, 43
towns, 8, 16, 23, 51, 124, 142, 154–155, 283
tracks, train, 238, 239
tractors, 164, 237
traders, 126, 131
trains, 52, 141, 142, 205, 238–239
Bullet, 239
maglev, 205, 239
TGV, 238, 239
transformers, 210, 211
transmitters, 184, 221, 225
treasure, 134
treeline, 26
trees, 12, 20, 26, 30, 32, 33, 46, 47, 48, 72, 93, 94, 96–97, 173, 308, 309
baobab, 30
beech, 96
cedar, Atlas, 97
conifer, 27
cypress, 96
horse chestnut, 97
oak, 96, 97
palm, 28
sycamore, 94
trenches, 35, 144, 145
Mariana Trench, 35
tributaries, 24
trilobites, 19
Tropic of Cancer, 283
Tropic of Capricorn, 283
trunks
of elephants, 63
of trees, 30, 96
tsunami, 21
Tudor times (in England), 134–135
turbines, 47
Turkey, 118, 124
turkeys, 137
turnips, 137
turtles, 33, 70, 71
Tutankhamun, 120
twins, 150

U

UK, 151, 303
uniforms, 162
Universe, 192, 207, 212, 255, 276, 277, 280, 307
universities, 167
USA, 10, 17, 18, 20, 137, 140, 145, 146, 147, 148, 154, 156, 157, 166, 173, 177, 191, 197, 267, 272, 274, 288, 289, 300, 304, 305, 308, 309

V

valleys, 24, 131
under sea, 34
vegetables, 110, 158, 165
Venezuela, 291, 305
Venus flytrap, 55
Versailles, France, 138, 139
vibrations, 208, 209
Victorian times, 142–143
videos, 174
Vietnam, 17, 309
Vikings, 126–127
villages, 118, 126, 137, 166
viperfish, 91
volcanoes, 18, 22–23, 268
in sea, 17, 23, 35
on Mars, 266, 267
on Venus, 265
volume, 208, 223
voting, 156, 157
Voyager (space probe), 255, 256
vultures, 31, 67

W

wagons, 140
walls, 122, 127, 128, 129, 132, 138, 163, 166, 224, 231, 253
walruses, 43
warm-blooded, 60, 71
warriors, 126
wars, 137, 144, 145, 146, 147
warthogs, 31
Washington, DC, USA, 157
Washington, George, 137
wasps, 59, 308
waste, 50, 55, 105, 232, 233, 253
watches, 205
water, 14, 15, 16, 17, 21, 24, 25, 28, 29, 30, 34, 35, 36, 37, 39, 41, 42, 44, 45, 46, 47, 48, 51, 54, 59, 64, 66, 71, 72, 73, 75, 78, 79, 80–81, 85, 86, 87, 89, 92, 93, 95, 96, 105, 119, 120, 125, 138, 142, 153, 155, 163, 185, 186, 187, 189, 190, 191, 200, 201, 203, 210, 212, 230, 231, 232, 233, 242, 243, 244, 250, 251, 253, 257, 263, 266, 267, 305, 309
water lilies, 33
water vapor, 14, 189, 190
waterfalls, 24, 25, 289, 291, 293, 295, 297, 299, 305
waterproof, 81, 101
waves, 16, 17, 21, 23, 36–37, 38, 40, 41, 180, 231
radio, 221, 223, 225, 231
wax, 190
weapons, 128, 132, 145, 147
weather, 12, 14–15, 43, 60, 152, 160, 164, 197, 260
weaving, 118, 127
Web sites, 228, 229
webs, 75
weddings, 177
weight, 199, 200, 242
West (American), 140–141
whales, 58, 61, 85, 86–87
blue, 86, 209, 308
humpback, 86, 87
killer, 85
minke, 86
right, 86
sperm, 86, 87
wheat, 31, 118, 158, 164
wheelchairs, 169
wheels, 214, 215, 218, 234, 235, 237, 238, 249, 267
White House, 157
wigs, 139, 160
wildebeest, 30
wind, 14, 15, 16, 17, 27, 29, 36, 37, 40, 47, 93, 94, 95, 98, 153, 243, 254, 271
solar, 262, 275
windows, 127, 128, 163
wine, 98
wings, 58, 59, 61, 64, 65, 66, 74, 75, 76, 77, 115
of plane, 240, 241
of space shuttle, 248
of submersible, 244
winter, 12, 13, 17, 27, 42, 45, 64, 65, 116, 127
woks, 159
wood(en), 47, 48, 96, 119, 121, 124, 127, 132, 133, 136, 140, 144, 152, 153, 159, 163, 172, 187, 212, 238
wool, 47, 118, 165
work, 142, 143, 153, 154, 161, 162–163, 166, 249, 250, 253, 280
workhouses, 143
World Wide Web, 148, 228, 229
worms, 67, 70
wrestling, 169
writing, 121, 166, 167, 170, 171, 174, 179, 184, 226, 227

X

X-rays, 102, 112, 183

Y

yachts, 243
yeast, 98
yeti, 180

Z

zebras, 31

Acknowledgements

Every effort has been made to trace and acknowledge ownership of copyright. If any rights have been omitted, the publishers offer to rectify this in any subsequent editions following notification. The publishers are grateful to the following organizations and individuals for their contributions and permission to reproduce copyright material
(t = top, m = middle, b = bottom, l = left, r = right, SPL = Science Photo Library):

Cover: globe, astronaut, volcano, water drop, sunflower, tiger, owl, Digital Vision; chick, starfish, Stockbyte; rainbow, tree, Digital Stock; Tutankhamun funeral mask, Sandro Vannini/CORBIS; snowflake, Mehau Kulyk/SPL; p1, leopards in tree, Digital Vision; p2-3, school of fish R.W. Jones/CORBIS; p7 Digital Vision; p8b, Digital Vision; p9tr, Digital Vision; p10ml, Digital Vision; p10bl, Digital Vision; p11r, Digital Vision; p11b, Digital Vision; p12, Digital Vision; p12, Richard Hamilton Smith/CORBIS; p14r, Digital Vision; p14m, Douglas Peebles/CORBIS; p14l, Digital Vision; p16ml, Digital Vision; p16m, CORBIS; p16mr, Digital Vision; p16bl, Digital Vision; p16-17, CORBIS; p17mr, Michael S. Yamishita/CORBIS; p20, Joseph Sohm, ChromoSohm/CORBIS; p22t, Digital Vision; p22b, Digital Vision; p22-23b, Digital Vision; p23t, GeoScience Picture Library; p25t, Kevin R. Morris/CORBIS; p26-27b, Digital Vision; p27t, Ian Walker, Eye Ubiquitous/CORBIS; p31br, Ron Watts/CORBIS; p35bm, Steve Raymer/CORBIS; p36ml, Gary Braasch/CORBIS; p36-37, Digital Vision; p42-43, Digital Vision; p44-45, Arne Hodalic/CORBIS; p47bm, Chinch Gryniewicz, Ecoscene/CORBIS; p47bl, Digital Vision; p47br, Digital Vision; p48ml, Digital Vision; p48b, Digital Vision; p49b, Digital Vision; p51, National Oceanic and Atmospheric Administration (NOAA)/Dept. of Commerce; p52, Digital Vision; p53, Digital Vision; p54t, Stockbyte; p54b, Digital Vision; p54-55 (background), Digital Vision; p55b, Kim Taylor/Bruce Coleman Collection; p56t, Prof. P. Motta/Dept. of Anatomy/University, "La Sapienza", Rome/SPL; p57 (main), Dr Linda Stannard, Uct/SPL; p57br, Colin Cuthbert/SPL; p58tr, Digital Vision; p58m, Digital Vision; p58bl, Digital Vision; p59tr, Digital Vision; p59br, Digital Vision; p60l, K & K Ammann; p61tr, Jack Fields/CORBIS; p62, Karl Ammann/CORBIS; p63b, Jean Hosking, Frank Lane Picture Agency/Corbis; p64, George Lepp/CORBIS; p65, Wolfgang Kaehler/CORBIS; p67, Michael Sewell/Still Pictures; p68, Uwe Walz/CORBIS; p69t, Digital Vision; p69b, Jonathan Smith, Cordaiy Photo Library/CORBIS; p70tl, Brian Kenney; p70br, K Jayram/Planet Earth Pictures; p71, S. J. Vincent/Planet Earth Pictures; p72bl, Jane Burton/Warren Photographic; p72-73, Digital Vision; p73r, Linda Richardson/CORBIS; p74l, Geoff du Feu; p75br, Mick Martin/Planet Earth Pictures; p80t, Bruce Coleman Collection; p80mr, Francois Gohier/Ardea London; p80bl, Sergio Hanquet/Still Pictures; p80br, Secret Sea Vision/Still Pictures; p82tr, Alain Compost/Still Pictures; p84bl, Stuart Westmorland/CORBIS; p84-85, Jeffrey L. Rottmann/CORBIS; p85tr, Phillip Colla; p85br, Brandon D. Cole/CORBIS; p86-87t, Francois Gohier/Ardea London; p87br, Johnny Johnson/Bruce Coleman Collection; p88, Digital Vision; p89tl, Digital Vision; p89mr, Digital Vision; p89(main), Horst Schaffer/Still Pictures; p92t, Paul A. Souders/CORBIS; p93b, Gary W. Carter/CORBIS; p95bl, Kim Taylor/Bruce Coleman Collection; p96-97b, Bob Krist/corbisstockmarket.com; p97ml, Digital Vision; p98, Pat O'Hara/CORBIS; p99, Mehau Kulyk/SPL; p101tr, National Cancer Institute/SPL; p101b, Lester V. Bergman/CORBIS; p102bl, Dave Roberts/SPL; p105br, Juergen Berger, Max-Planck Institute/SPL; p106, Mehau Kulyk/SPL; p107br, Garry Gay/Alamy; p108tr, Dr G. Moscoso/SPL; p109, Laura Dwight/CORBIS; p111, Rick Gomez/corbisstockmarket.com; p112, Dept. of Clinical Radiology, Salisbury District Hospital/SPL; p113, Archivo Iconographico S.A./CORBIS; p114b, The Natural History Museum, London; p115b, The Natural History Museum, London; p117t, Gianni Dagli Orti/CORBIS; p117b, George Roos, Peter Arnold Inc./SPL; p118bl, Johnathan Smith/Cordaiy Photo Library Ltd./CORBIS; p118tr, Copyright The British Museum; p120b, Charles & Josette Lenars/CORBIS; p120tr, Archivo Iconografico, S.A./CORBIS; p121tl, Copyright The British Museum; p121bl, Gianni Dagli Orti/CORBIS; p121r, Royal Albert Memorial Museum, Exeter, Devon/Bridgeman Art Library; p122b, Fergus O'Brien/Getty Images; p123bl, Michael Holford; p124l, National Museums & Galleries of Wales; p125mr, Roger Wood/CORBIS; p126tl, The Vikings, Britain's oldest Dark Age re-enactment society; p127br, Werner Forman Archive/Statens Historiska Museum, Stockholm; p129tr, The Art Archive/University Library Heidelberg/Dagli Orti; p130tl, Alan Levy; p130b, Getty Images/Kevin Schafer; p131tl, Wolfgang Kaehler/CORBIS; p132tl, L. Clarke/CORBIS; p133tl, The Art Archive/Topkapi Museum Istanbul/Dagli Orti; p133tr, Asian Art & Archaeology, Inc./CORBIS; p133mr, Asian Art & Archaeology, Inc./CORBIS; p134bl, Photo Scala, Florence; p134tr, Adam Woolfitt/CORBIS; p135t, Detail of portrait by courtesy of the National Portrait Gallery, London; p136tl, Kevin Fleming/CORBIS; p137b, Philadelphia Museum of Art/CORBIS; p138tr, Archivo Iconografico, S.A./CORBIS; p139tr, V & A Picture Library; p141br, Bettmann/CORBIS; p143br, Mary Evans Picture Library; p144tl, Neil Beer/CORBIS; p145tr, George Hall/CORBIS; p146tl, The Imperial War Museum, London; p146mr, Hulton-Deutsch Collection/CORBIS; p146b, Bettmann/CORBIS; p147tl, Bettmann/CORBIS; p147br, CORBIS; p148, Digital Vision; p149, Galen Rowell/CORBIS; p150t, Bob Krist/CORBIS; p150bl, Digital Visions; p150-151b, Penny Tweedle/CORBIS; p151tr, Laura Dwight/CORBIS; p152, Britstock-IFA/HAGA; p153br, Janet Wishnetsky/CORBIS; p154t, Jeremy Horner/CORBIS; p154-155, Britstock-IFA; p156t, Wally McNamee/CORBIS, p156b, Peter Turnley/CORBIS; p157tr, Lee Snider/CORBIS; p157bl, Peter Turnley/CORBIS; p157br, Crown Copyright Historic Royal Palaces (Reproduced by permission of Historic Royal Palaces under licence from the controller of Her Majesty's Stationery Office); p158b, Reed Kaestner/CORBIS; p159b, Julia Waterlow, Eye Ubiquitous/CORBIS; p160tr, Keren Su/CORBIS; p160b, Getty Images/Alan Becker; p161r, Carl & Ann Purcell/CORBIS; p162t, Getty Images/Yellow Dog Productions; p164t, Kevin R. Morris/Bohemian Nomad Picturemakers/CORBIS; p165l, Annie Griffiths Belt/CORBIS; p165br, Peter Bowater/Alamy; p166t, StockConnection/Alamy; p166-167b, John Henley Photography/ CORBIS; p168-169, Wally McNamee/CORBIS; p169tr, JFPI Studios, Inc./CORBIS; p169bl, Wally McNamee/CORBIS; p170b, Getty Images/Joseph Van Os; p171r, O'Brien Productions/CORBIS; p172r, Rudolph Staechelin Foundation, Chateau de Malmaison, Paris, France/Lauros-Giraudon, Paris/Superstock; p172l, Angelo Hornak/CORBIS, reproduced by kind permission of the Henry Moore Foundation; p173m, Charles & Josette Lenars/CORBIS; p173b, Steve Vidler/SuperStock; p174tr, Jeffrey L. Rotman/CORBIS;

p174b, Elliott Franks/PAL; p175b, Paul A. Souders/CORBIS; p176b, Lindsay Hebberd/CORBIS; p177l, Robert Harding World Imagery/Alamy; p177br, Getty Images/Scott Morgan; p178, Getty Images; p179tr, David Reed/CORBIS; p179bl, Trip/H. Rogers; p180bl, Adam Woolfitt/CORBIS; p181, Gary Bartholomew/CORBIS; p182tr, Digital Vision; p182m, Samsung Electronics UK: The Samsung SG-A400 is another example of an innovative product from Samsung Electronics UK; p182bl, Jorg & Petra Wegner/Bruce Coleman The Natural World; p183tr, Mehau Kulyk/SPL; p183br, Sam Ogden/SPL; p184, William Curtsinger/SPL; p185tr, RobertHarding.com; p185br, Roger Ressmeyer/CORBIS; p186b, Digital Vision; p187tr, BSIP, Barthelemy/SPL; p187br, Digital Vision; p188tl, Michael Freeman/CORBIS; p188lm, Adrienne Hart-Davis/SPL; p188bl, Larry Lee Photography/ CORBIS; p189r, Digital Vision; p190tr, foodfolio/Alamy; p190bl, Adrienne Hart-Davis/SPL; p191tl, Oscar Niemeyer/www.arcaid.co.uk; p191br, Phil Schermeister/CORBIS; p195b, Lowell Georgia/CORBIS; p196tr, Digital Vision; p196b, Alfred Pasieka/SPL; p197t, Dave G. Houser/CORBIS; p198, Courtesy of NASA/JPL/Caltech; p198tr, NASA/JPL/Malin Space Science Systems, USGS; p198br, Courtesy of NASA/JPL/Caltech; p199, Courtesy of NASA/JPL/Caltech; p199tl, NASA; p199ml, Digital Vision, Courtesy of NASA/JPL/Caltech; p201, Hugh Sitton/Getty Images; p202m, Brian Bailey/CORBIS; p203tr, Digital Vision; p203br, George D. Lepp/CORBIS; p204tr, TEK IMAGE/SPL; p205tr, Alex Bartel/SPL; p205b, Transrapid International; p206ml, Bruce Coleman The Natural World; p206br, NASA; Digital Vision; p207tl, Digital Vision; p207rm, Phototake/Robert Harding Picture Library; p207br, Digital Vision; p208tl, Digital Vision; p208mr, D. Robert & Lorri Franz/CORBIS; p209br, Howard Allman; p212 (background), Digital Vision; p213, Digital Vision; p217br, HP Omnibook 6100; p217bl, Nikon Coolpix digital camera. Image courtesy of Nikon UK Ltd; p217br, Digital Vision; p217tr, Digital Vision; p218-219b, CORBIS; p219tr, Disney Enterprises, Inc./Pixar Animation Studios; p220m, Digital Vision; p221b, Digital Vision; p227bl, MARSHALL EDITIONS LTD and Clear Channel Entertainment-Exhibits, Inc.; p228l, www.TryScience.org TryScience/New York Hall of Science; p228r, Use of screenshot from www.roalddahl (© RDNL) by kind permission of Dahl&Dahl; p228m, Digital Vision; p228-229m, Digital Vision; p229l, BrainPOP 2002 www.BrainPOP.com; p232ml, WildCountry/CORBIS; p232br, London Aerial Photo Library/CORBIS; p235br, Jean-Yves Ruszniewski, TempSport/CORBIS; p241b, www.aviationpictures.com; 244tr Norbert Wu, Natural History Photographic Agency; p245, Digital Vision; p246-247t, Digital Vision; p247tr, NASA/NSSDC; p247br, NOAO/SPL; p248bl, Digital Vision; p248-249, Digital Vision; p249br, NASA; p251bl, Digital Vision; p251br, NASA/SPL; p252-253 (background), Digital Vision; p252-253 (foreground), NASA; p254l, Digital Vision; p254tl, Genesis Space Photo Library; p254-255, NASA/SOHO/ESA; p255tr, Julian Baum/SPL; p255bl, NASA; p255bm, NASA/SOHO/ESA; p255br, Digital Vision; p256bl, NASA/SPL; p256br, Stephanie Maze/CORBIS; p257tl, Victor Habbick Visions/SPL; p257ml, NASA/JPL; p257bl, NASA/SPL; p258m, Digital Vision; p258br, Digital Vision; p259l, Digital Vision; p259tl, NASA/SOHO/ESA; p259tl, NASA/NSSDC; p259mt, Digital Vision; p259m, NASA/NSSDC; p259ml, Kenneth Seidelman, U.S. Naval Observatory; p259bl, NASA; p259tr, NASA/NSSDC; p259br, Digital Vision; p260l, NASA/U.S. Geological Survey; p260mr, Digital Vision; p261b, Digital Vision; p262bl, NASA/SPL; p NASA/SOHO/ESA; p263mr, NASA/SPL; p263brl, Digital Vision; p263brm, NASA/NSSDC/Viking; p263brr, Digital Vision; p265t, NASA/U.S. Geological Survey; p265b, NASA/JPL; p266l, NASA/JPL/MSSS; p267, NASA/JPL/Caltech; p267m, NASA/JPL/Caltech; p267r, NASA/JPL/MSSS; p267b, NASA/JPL/MPF; p268ml, NASA/SPL; p268mr, CORBIS; p268br, NASA; p269tm, SPL; p269mr, NASA; p269bm, Astro-geology Team/USGS; p269br, Digital Vision; p270mr, NASA; p270m, JPL/CALTECH/NASA/Calvin J. Hamilton; p270ml, JPL/CALTECH/NASA/Calvin J. Hamilton; p270l, JPL/CALTECH/NASA/Calvin J. Hamilton; p270bl, JPL/CALTECH/NASA/Calvin J. Hamilton; p270bl, JPL/CALTECH/NASA/Calvin J. Hamilton; p270br, NASA; p270-271b, David Hardy/SPL; p271mr, NASA; p274b, John Sanford/SPL; p274l, NASA; p275m, J.Finch/SPL; p277bl, Space Telescope Science Institute/NASA/SPL; p277m, Max Planck Institut für Radioastronomie/SPL; p279bl, Gerry Schad/SPL; p279tr, John Sandford/SPL; p281, Digital Vision; p288bl, Digital Vision; p289tr, Julian Baum & David Angus/SPL; p290bl, Digital Vision; p291tr, Julian Baum & David Angus/SPL; p292bl, Digital Vision; p293tr, Julian Baum & David Angus/SPL; p294tr, Tom Van Sant/Geosphere project, Santa Monica/SPL; p294br, Digital Vision; p296bl, Digital Vision; p297br, Julian Baum & David Angus/SPL; p299tr, Planetary Visions Ltd/SPL; p299br, Digital Vision; p300, Craig Lovell/CORBIS; p305br, James Marshall/CORBIS; p309br, Joe McDonald/CORBIS.

With thanks to Louise Baxter and Paul l'Anson at MINI UK (Cars and motorbikes), Vincent Deloménie, Centre audiovisuel SNCF (Trains), CR Frost (Clocks), Kester Sims (Clocks), Christopher Denne (Cameras), Tim Milbourne (Computers, The Internet), Balfour Knox (Toilets and taps), Albert Milbourne (Cars and motorbikes), Tony Furse (Tractors), Andy Hart, UK SNCF society (Trains), Shipmate Flags, Vlaardingen, The Netherlands, Hawkes Ocean Technologies (H.O.T.) for their permission to feature the Deep Flight submersible in this book. Special thanks to Bob Whiteaker for help with Deep Flight diagram on page 244.

Additional consultancy (Science): Dr. Tom Weston
Additional design and editorial: Verinder Bhachu, Kate Fearn, Georgina Hooper, Vici Leyhane, Laura Parker, Andrea Slane, Jane Rigby, Leonard Le Rolland and Nicky Wainwright
Additional illustrations: Sophie Allington, John Barber, Verinder Bhachu, Gary Bines, Isabel Bowring, Trevor Boyer, Andy Burton, Michèle Busby, Nicola Butler, Kuo Kang Chen, Adam Constantine, Pam Cornfield, Richard Cox, Gary Cross, David Cuzik, Tony Gibson, Robert Gilmore, Rebecca Hardy, Nicholas Hewetson, Inklink Firenze, Ian Jackson, Colin King, Steven Kirk, Rachel Lockwood, Chris Lyon, Philip Nicholson, Alex Pang, Justine Peek, Maurice Pledger, Leonard Le Rolland, Chris Shields, Guy Smith, Treve Tamblin, Mike Wheatley, Graham White, John Woodcock and David Wright

Answer to question on page 117: The cave painting shows a horse, some deer and a bull.